4/18

- 6 FEB 2018

1 0 APR 2018

0 1 DEC 2020
3 0 AUG 2022

Suffolk Libraries

Please return/renew this item
by the last date shown.

Suffolk Libraries
01473 351249

www.suffolklibraries.co.uk

30127080643237

Duress

Duress

The Life and Death of a Ton-Up

Clive F Sorrell

AuthorHouse™ UK Ltd.
1663 Liberty Drive
Bloomington, IN 47403 USA
www.authorhouse.co.uk
Phone: 0800.197.4150

Suffolk Libraries		
DON		12/17

© 2013 by Clive F Sorrell. All rights reserved.

No part of this book may be reproduced, stored in a retrieval system, or transmitted by any means without the written permission of the author.

Clive Frederick Sorrell has asserted his right under the Copyright, Designs and Patents Act, 1988 to be identified as the author of this work

This novel is a work of fiction. Names and characters are the product of the author's imagination and any resemblance to actual persons, living or dead, is entirely coincidental.

Published by AuthorHouse 12/03/2013

ISBN: 978-1-4918-8488-1 (sc)
ISBN: 978-1-4918-8489-8 (hc)
ISBN: 978-1-4918-8490-4 (e)

Any people depicted in stock imagery provided by Thinkstock are models, and such images are being used for illustrative purposes only. Certain stock imagery © Thinkstock.

This book is printed on acid-free paper.

Because of the dynamic nature of the Internet, any web addresses or links contained in this book may have changed since publication and may no longer be valid. The views expressed in this work are solely those of the author and do not necessarily reflect the views of the publisher, and the publisher hereby disclaims any responsibility for them.

Original Cover Photograph by Alex Markwick

For Sophia

BOOKS BY THIS AUTHOR - PUBLISHED BY AUTHORHOUSE

SIDDIQUI
KAWTHAR
JUMANA
Stories for Dark and Stormy Nights

1

1964

THE FACTORY SIREN WAILED, welcoming the start of yet another weekend in the lives of three hundred and sixty-two workers. The sound had barely faded before John Tucker was running to his locker and replacing his grease-stained coveralls with faded jeans and a black leather jacket. With his thoughts on the coming evening he routinely grabbed his helmet and goggles, slammed the locker shut and dashed from the factory into the heavy rain to where he had left his motorcycle. The engine unfailingly roared into life and he was soon ahead of the torrent of workers that had begun streaming towards the tall wrought-iron gates.

Arriving at his home in Bromley John found that his mother had already taken phone messages from two of his friends. The serried ranks of storm clouds marching across the sky complemented the dark anger he felt after reading Brian and Albert's lame excuses for not going out with him that night. It would seem that their bikes had developed similar mechanical symptoms that prevented them from riding to the coast.

John knew that they were telling porkies for he had seen them cruising through the town centre during his short lunch break. Squealing teenage girls were riding pillion and holding on to bouffant hairstyles with one hand while gripping the lads' leather jackets with the other. Their dresses and sugar-starched petticoats billowed, exposing stocking-clad thighs and suspenders to create a frisson of excitement amongst all the shoppers they passed. John's initial anger faded a little for he had to admit that if he had been given the opportunity to date one of those girls he most probably would have made a similar excuse.

The torrential rain continued as he stood in the open doorway of the garage and stared through the translucent pane of water that overflowed the leaf-clogged gutter. With blue eyes fixed on the pea-sized drops that peppered the driveway he wondered if Alan and Ted, his two other friends, would also forgo their habitual Friday-night trek to the seaside.

The four boys had been his closest friends all through their school days and although Alan, being three years older than John, had left school before him the bond had remained unbroken. This was despite Alan's occasional bullying that became more evident as the boys aged beyond puberty and approached manhood.

The incessant thrumming on the corrugated roof competing with his transistor radio and The Shadows' rendering of 'Apache' were beginning to grate heavily on John's nerves, causing the creases in his youthful forehead to deepen.

The storm clouds had prematurely darkened the day and sodium streetlights were now bathing Hawthorn Avenue in an amber light that glowed eerily through the rain.

Tonight will be a wash-out if this keeps up for another hour, he thought despondently while half-heartedly rubbing the lacquered fuel tank with the small scrap of chamois leather he had appropriated from the factory workshop.

For the last year it had been an unbroken ritual on Friday nights for the five friends to race to the coast, stopping only at their favourite café for a few minutes to down a cup of milky coffee and chat up any of the unattached girls who tended to congregate there. Their slicked-back ducktails, black leather jackets and powerful machines were irresistible and sexually potent.

If one of them got 'lucky' he would whisk his new-found date away to Hastings before any of the rival bikers in the café could cut in on the action.

After a high-speed run down to the coast the girls, still giggling and flushed with excitement, would be taken to the Red Lion. There they would invariably head straight to the ladies' restroom to primp their hair and excitedly discuss the new mini skirt by Mary Quant. On returning to their dates nervous excitement would take hold as they wondered on how far they might be expected or tempted to go.

While the girls were absent the young men would surreptitiously unseal their manila pay packets with the tiny glassine windows and transfer the crisp banknotes, florins and pennies to their pockets. Only then could the heavy drinking of Watneys Red Barrel and Babychams begin and the girls be made more amenable to any rapacious advances by their partners.

When the publican called *time* couples would down their drinks and make a beeline for the dark privacy that lay beneath the long pier. Those without a date were resigned to smearing mud on their registration plates to obscure the numbers while they raced home, daring each other to exceed the *ton*, one hundred miles per hour, as they outran any patrolling police car that futilely chased them. Few would remain in the town for fear that rockers on Harley Davidsons or mods on Vespas were spoiling for a night of fighting.

This was the first Friday that anyone had chosen not to go since Alan had suffered a bout of flu four months ago. John switched the radio off and lashed out with a grubby plimsoll to send an empty oil can clattering across the oil-streaked concrete floor. He then mentally chastised himself for his childish behaviour and re-entered the house through the connecting door to check whether Alan or Ted had bothered to call.

As John walked through the utility room the twin-tub began to pummel the week's wash and Mrs Tucker looked up to smile briefly at her son. Seeing the scowl on his face she tactfully remained silent and carried on with the laundry. It had been a long hard day of house cleaning and shopping and lines of weariness had begun to form on her normally smooth, jovial features.

'Will you be wanting your tea before you go out, dear?' she asked as she brushed a wayward grey lock from her eyes before continuing with the folding of one of his shirts.

John paused midstep and his expression changed to one of concern. Despite the empty feeling in his stomach his love for his mother took precedence and he shook his head. 'I'll get something to eat on the way, Mum. Don't you trouble yourself.'

'It's a foul night, John, so make sure you get something hot inside you at that nice café you're always talking about.'

John grunted his agreement and went on through to the kitchen and picked up the phone. 'Has anyone called me?' he asked loudly.

'No, son,' his mother shouted back from the other room and he quickly dialled Alan's number.

'Are you still on for tonight, you old bastard?' he asked grumpily, imitating his friend's father the moment the phone was picked up.

Mr Williams himself had answered the call and he exploded when he heard John's cheeky greeting. John mumbled an awkward apology and immediately regretted his actions. He knew that Mr Williams occasionally hit Alan, especially after one of his regular visits to the King's Arms. Despite being 22 years old and bigger than his father Alan never retaliated or tried to defend himself for fear that he would release his father's true capacity for violence.

Alan, being older and taller than his friends had automatically assumed leadership of the group since primary school. Quite often he enforced this with fits of bullying that were usually in response to his father's latest bouts of aggression. He also had a more powerful motorbike which, coupled with his longer riding experience, asserted his authority over the small band of friends. Kowing what Alan had to endure at home they accepted his reactionary bullying and secretly thanked God for the gentler, more apathetic attitude of their own parents.

'Sorry, Alan. I didn't mean to piss your dad off but are you on for tonight?' John asked as his friend picked up the receiver.

'Wouldn't miss it, mate,' Alan replied coldly. 'A spot of rain and a heavy clip on the ear because my friend couldn't keep his bloody mouth shut will never put me off a bit of 'bird' watching.'

'Sorry about that, mate, and what about Ted?'

'He's right here beside me; he came round earlier to give me some back issues of *Motor Cycling* and right now he's nodding his head and stupidly waving a packet of johnnies at me.' There was a muffled laugh and John heard Alan snarl, 'Put them away, moron, before my dad sees 'em.'

John heard Ted grumble in the background, 'For Christ's sake, Alan, you're twenty-two.'

'Brian and Albert say they're not joining us tonight. I reckon they've already got their bits of totty lined up for the night and they don't want to spoil their chance of scoring by joining us.'

'I don't think that's the reason, mate, they're just bloody chicken,' Alan growled. 'Those two could never understand that going on the run every Friday is to get our rocks off with a bloody good road race, not with some bloody tarts.'

'They've probably lost their bottle,' John replied forlornly in an attempt to change the subject.

Alan stormed on. 'Well, good! It means there'll be emptier roads for us and more birds to choose from at the café. I'll be coming round in ten minutes so be bloody ready this time.'

John glanced down at his watch. 'I've a couple of things to do; make it twenty minutes and I'll be outside waiting for you. We should still be able to make it to the seafront by nine-thirty which will give us a good hour of drinking before time is called.'

'I should have pulled something by then, if only three or four pints and you-know-what.' Alan did a crude imitation of heavy breathing before sniggering coarsely and hanging up abruptly.

John hurried upstairs just as his father was descending. Mr Douglas Tucker had slowly progressed to being a senior auditor with a major banking group and had commuted to the City from Bromley North station every day for thirty-three years. His jowls drooped slightly, not unlike a bloodhound's and his chain-smoking had resulted in a constant shortness of breath.

'You'll take it easy, son, won't you?' Douglas wheezed, pointing a nicotine-stained forefinger skyward. 'It's pretty nasty weather out there and the roads will be really greasy.'

The 19-year-old paused to watch with concern as his father huffed and puffed while descending before he hurried on up. 'I always take it easy, Dad,' he called over his shoulder before entering his bedroom and closing the door. He put the latest single by Bill Haley and the Comets on the turntable and began changing his clothes to the heavy beat of 'Rock Around the Clock'. It took only a matter of seconds to slip on some hand-bleached jeans and zip himself into his favourite Lewis leather jacket before pulling on a pair of second-hand flying boots that had cost him more than a week's wages. The metal cleats on the soles had been worn wafer thin by various road surfaces and the right-hand toecap was badly scuffed from constant gear changing. He never polished the marks away or replaced the cleats for he thought of them as his badges of honour. He rolled the long woollen socks over the top of the boots before tying a white silk scarf around his neck. Glancing in the full-length mirror he imagined himself as one of the heroic figures in the *Biggles* books he used to read late at night by torchlight beneath the blankets.

John had bought his mother a long warm scarf for her birthday and knowing that he was skint she thoughtfully reciprocated by giving him a pair of war-surplus aviator goggles. He grabbed the goggles and his black Jet helmet before hurrying downstairs. His father was in the living room and John could hear the faint sound of laughter. A quick glance at his wristwatch confirmed that he was watching Alf Garnett in *Till Death Us Do Part*. Although it was his father's favourite television programme John knew that he would be fast asleep long before the credits started rolling.

'Do take care, dear, and make sure you eat something,' his mother fussed as he rushed past her. She was still hard at work in the utility room and John blew her a kiss which she didn't see for she was busily folding pillowcases.

He placed his helmet on the narrow racing seat of his Norton Dominator 99 and primed the carburettor. Opening the garage doors he stood looking out into the rain, listening for the specific sound that never failed to exhilarate.

Within seconds the burbling exhausts of Alan's powerful Triumph and Ted's BSA penetrated the hiss of the rain and John quickly rolled the Dominator out into the fading light. Helmeted and with goggles down, he kick-started the bike into life. With a snap of the wrist he throttled back to reduce the first deafening snarl that always raised the small hairs at the base of his neck. He toed into first gear and released the brake to glide down the drive and into the avenue just as Alan and Ted came round the corner and raced towards him. Net curtains along the avenue twitched irritably as they made their thunderous approach.

John accelerated to match their speed and they sped away to be rapidly concealed by the curtain of rain. Mr Tucker, pipe clenched between teeth, watched from the sitting-room window with an unhappy expression. He could never quite understand his son's passion for motorcycles and his constant craving for high speed. For the middle-aged auditor the expression ton-up only meant a ton of trouble. So far there had been four police cautions and two hefty fines which had further strengthened his intense dislike of the machine.

Although he was quite fond of the other three, Mr Tucker had grown to dislike Alan from the very first day he came round to play with his son. John was highly impressionable and was easily led by those he considered to be more knowledgeable than himself. Mr Tucker sensed, rather than knew, that the 'rough kid from the housing estate', as he described the boy to his wife, had been at the root of all John's misdemeanours but no matter how many times he had tried to dissuade his son from associating with the older boy the bond had remained. Now they were fully grown and John was still in awe of his friend.

Oddly enough, his wife had never seen things his way and Gloria thought it was all harmless fun. She saw Alan as a pleasant friend and John as the perfect son. John was still her little boy in short trousers who was incapable of doing any wrong.

The three friends turned out of Hawthorn Avenue and were soon racing into and then out of Sevenoaks before bypassing the elegant spa town of Royal Tunbridge Wells. Closely following each other they swept on, a stirring sight in the rain, until they were on the main road and racing south.

It was an accepted rule that after a few minutes the leading bike would fall back to be replaced by the next in line. This allowed everyone the opportunity to throttle back and be pulled along in the slipstream of the leader. However, Alan constantly held his alpha position which meant his mates had, by default, fallen into the habit of changing their order from time to time while following Alan for the whole run.

They weaved in rhythmic unity to overtake or avoid oncoming traffic, their front tyres rarely deviating from the white centre line on the road. Fine spray fanned from their rear wheels and glowed brightly when caught in the headlights of the traffic.

Moving up to take his turn in Alan's slipstream John recalled his father's words and suddenly felt he should have told his friend to limit their top speed to 70 mph but then he mentally shrugged for he knew that Alan enjoyed riding in bad weather. He deliberately forced them to push their bikes hard in order to gain the advantage of each other's slipstream. Their goggles streamed from the spray that blurred their vision but the constant adrenalin rush prohibited any throttling back.

As they raced past outraged drivers at 80 mph car horns blared, soon to be muffled by the rain that had thankfully begun to fall more lightly. With his senses sharpened John pressed his body down on the petrol tank and saw that the vibrating needle was now hovering over the 100 mark and a shiver ran the length of his prone body.

The trio raced past Lamberhurst with exhausts snarling and then reluctantly began slowing as they approached the roadside café that they habitually used. Alice's Café was the bikers' customary meeting place and had built its reputation on excellent coffee and, more importantly, the prettiest girls seeking Friday night thrills and the chance of a dangerous ride on the pillion of a powerful 'café racer'.

With bursts of staccato backfiring all three rapidly decelerated and then stopped in front of the main door. There were already a dozen café racers parked, their wet chromework glinting under the two floodlights that illuminated the concrete forecourt of the low building. Some prankster with an air pistol had taken pot shots at the neon sign over the door and reduced it to 'lice' Café.

Alan led the way and swaggered through the door and into the chaotic confusion of teenagers and twenty-somethings wearing leather jackets and flaring cotton-print dresses. They were all talking at once at the top of their voices and blue cigarette fug swirled as young bikers swaggered to and from the counter. Aunt Alice, as she was fondly known to all of her regular customers, was dispensing shots of black, bitter coffee from a massive Gaggia machine that constantly hissed and gurgled.

Ted immediately made a direct path through the crowd to where two girls with gyrating hips were dancing to 'The Twist' by Chubby Checker in front of the jukebox. He inserted the coins, selected his favourite track and after watching the gyrating hips and teasing glimpses of stocking tops for a few seconds he rejoined his friends. While waiting to be served by Alice John scoured the room until he spotted Doris Trencher. He had successfully chatted up the 17-year-old girl the previous week and her pretty face and outstanding figure had readily prompted a promise that she could ride his pillion next time they met. The Woolworths counter assistant was seated on a small pine settle in the corner of the room and she was in a four-way conversation with her girlfriends who sat around the table on tubular-framed chairs. She was offering a five-pack of Weights to her friends and they all began lighting up, giggling and stealing sidelong glances at the young bikers crowding the café.

'Isn't that the girl you met last week, John?' Alan shouted over the music as he nodded towards the group of tittering girls. He slipped a hand into the side pocket of John's jacket and took out a half-crown coin. He placed it on the counter and grinned. 'Coffee's on you tonight.'

'Yeah, that's her,' John said, putting another coin on the counter to cover the cost of all three coffees; taking the steaming mug that Alice had placed before him he weaved through the various groups of leather-clad riders and their girls to stop at the table where Doris was waiting with a smile and a halo of smoke about her head.

Alan had been following close behind and without being invited he pulled an extra chair from the next table and squeezed in amongst the girls before stretching out his long legs and putting his boots on the coffee-ringed oil cloth covering the table. He placed a gold-tipped Sobranie between his lips and lit it with a Zippo in a calculated manner to impress. Ted simply shrugged at John and took another spare chair which he placed at the end of the table.

John caught Alan's eye, looked down at the Cuban-heeled boots and gave a small shake of his head which was ignored and then he turned to smile at Doris who had been following Alan's callow manners.

'Hi, Doris, sorry about my mate but he's feeling a little Neanderthal tonight.'

'Not like you, John,' Alan snapped back. 'You're always feeling yourself.' He said this with a leering look at Doris who drew back with a puzzled expression. A sudden understanding of the lewd innuendo made her grin and laugh out loud. The other three girls who had been studying the new arrivals also gave shrill laughs that penetrated the conversation level in the room and turned many a curious head in their direction.

John squeezed in to sit on the pine settle beside Doris who quickly pressed the layers of petticoats beneath the cotton dress close against her thigh in order to make space for the slender young man. Sitting so close to the teenager John was immediately overcome by her recently applied perfume that masked the ever-present smell of coffee, perspiration and the toxic smog of countless cigarettes.

'Do you fancy Hastings tonight, Doris?' John asked, his pulse racing and his eyes pleading for her to give the right answer.

She turned her head and looked at him for a full three seconds that he found himself consciously counting in his head before she slowly nodded her head. 'I said so last week and that's why I'm here tonight, innit? And you've got to go really fast, yeah?' she said in a throaty way that seemed to bypass his brain and head straight for his groin.

John's hand shook slightly as he sipped his coffee. 'Oh, we'll go fast, if that's what you want, Doris,' he replied with a slight tremor in his voice as he placed his hand over her long, tapering fingers that rested lightly on the oilcloth.

'You should come with me, darling,' Alan said loudly as he put his legs down and leant across the table. He held a hand out towards Doris. 'John's underpowered scooter ain't as much fun as mine. Know what I mean?' He slapped the other hand around his bicep and thrust a fist upward to complete the vulgar gesture. 'My Triumph Bonneville will show you what fast is all about.' The girls giggled and Ted boldly put his arm around the shoulders of the tall brunette beside him. She didn't object to his familiarity and slyly edged her chair closer to the burly teenager.

'Touch Doris and you'll answer to me,' John muttered. Then he smiled, clenched a fist and shook it at Alan in a show of mock bravado. He then flipped his leather jacket open with the other hand to reveal a straight razor in the top pocket of his denim shirt. The girls stopped giggling, eagerly anticipating a fight as they stared at the half-hidden ivory handle before realising that John had only been acting.

'You'd better watch who you're threatening, mate,' Alan said in a harsh, menacing voice. 'We may have been friends for many years but if you threaten me again, whether joking or not, I'll put an extra hole in your head.'

John had always harboured a suspicion that Alan had a pistol or some form of firearm hidden somewhere at home and his friend's words confirmed it. His smile vanished and he looked at Alan with new insight, realising that his habitual bullying hinted at something more sinister.

'For God's sake, John, calm down,' Doris muttered nervously close to his ear and John closed his jacket, unclenched his fist and laughed.

'You should try to keep a rein on your temper. It can only lead to a lot of trouble,' Doris whispered as she squeezed his hand.

'Just a joke, sweetie,' John murmured as he leant close and tried to kiss her. She twisted her face away at the last second and he frowned. Her friends began talking all at once in a vain attempt to defuse the new tension and Alan took advantage of the situation by offering his gold-tipped cocktail cigarettes to the girls. John offered everyone another coffee but when all but Ted declined he remained where he was and just stared across the table at Alan.

A light touch startled John and he looked down to see that Doris had placed her hand on his thigh. 'I think we should get going if we want to have a bit of fun tonight,' she said smiling nervously and turning her head to include all at the table.

The tall blonde called Penny and Toni, a freckle-faced girl that Alan had possessively been holding around the waist, squealed with delight in expectation of the bike-riding thrills to come.

The blonde suddenly pouted and stared accusingly at John. 'Where's your other two friends, then,' she complained as she ran varnish-tipped fingers through her hair. 'How are we *all* supposed to get to Hastings?'

'I'm sorry, Penny. I didn't realise there would only be three bikes tonight,' Doris said, her eyes accusing John of letting her down. 'Maybe next week we can all do it together.'

'If you're not going, Penny, then I can't go either,' Toni said. 'It's not fair for you to be all alone on a Friday night.' She unwound Alan's arm from her waist and she continued, 'Anyway, it would be no bloody fun without you.'

Penny shrugged with mock indifference and stood up. 'I'll get Jake to run us home then,' she said and stalked away to the red telephone box that stood outside the main door.

'Who's Jake?' Ted asked just as the Shangri-Las began singing their latest hit about rockers and their bikes and the room erupted to cheers from all the young men present.

'It's her older brother,' Doris shouted above the bedlam. 'He's married with two kids. He's six foot three and a professional rugby player; plays for Croydon y'know.'

Ted winced. 'Wouldn't want to get into her bad books then.' He stood up and waited for the tall brunette he fancied to join him. Penny and Toni sat down again with eyes already covertly looking round the café as they assessed their options.

After the girls had said their goodbyes the five left the café with the latest release and bikers' shouts ringing in their ears.

It was a still, crystal-clear night.

John looked up and saw that all the rain clouds had vanished leaving a glorious swathe of stars in their wake. The rank of wet café racers gleamed invitingly and the three ton-ups hurried to their respective bikes with the two girls trailing behind. The brunette, whom Doris had introduced as Louise, climbed up behind Ted and felt for the high footrests with her kitten-heeled pumps.

Doris was about to get onto the Dominator when Alan beckoned to her. If he couldn't have Toni he would make sure that John wouldn't score either: 'I meant what I said,' he shouted over the sound of the engines. 'You need a Bonneville throbbing between your legs. It goes a lot faster and is a lot more fun as well.'

Doris hesitated briefly and with a brief apologetic glance at John she skipped across to Alan with barely disguised eagerness and climbed onto the bike. Alan gave a wicked grin as he felt her arms encircle his waist and her knees press against his upper thighs. With a brief derisive wave to John he accelerated across the forecourt and sped out onto the main road. Ted followed with Louise trying to hold on tightly whilst controlling her unruly petticoats at the same time. John fumed and twisted the grip angrily, causing the bike to rear and rubber to burn before he brought it down and raced after the others.

Alan's 650 cc engine, combined with the superior handling of the duplex frame, carried the extra weight with ease and he was soon centre-lining at 75 miles per hour. The more cautious Ted lagged a half-mile behind and was overtaken by the Dominator as John made every effort to catch up with Alan.

As they approached the outer limits of Hastings he was forced to reduce his speed as an abnormally high number of police patrols were preparing for the hordes of rockers who had hinted that on the Bank Holiday weekend they would be using the seafront as a battleground; they had a score to settle with the gangs of scooter-riding mods.

John slowly cruised into town and headed for the Red Lion where they had all agreed to meet for the first drink of the evening. Pushing his way through the throng of people he made his way to the bar and looked around, half-expecting to see Alan and Doris. He ordered a pint and prepared to wait, naturally assuming that he had been the first to arrive.

This means Alan owes me a pint, he thought as he took a deep draught. Approximately five minutes later Ted entered the pub with his arm possessively draped over Louise's shoulders.

'Hi, Ted, where's Alan?' John said as the couple joined him at the bar. 'He should have got here long before you.'

'I saw him, John. He's up at the pier. He said he would join us in thirty minutes but that we should go ahead and start getting Brahms and Liszt without him.'

'Was Doris with him?'

'Yeah! And she looked really cool,' Louise said. She looked into John's eyes with undisguised amusement as she waited for his reaction. 'She'd already let her hair down and I thought she had a lot more colour in her cheeks than usual.'

John winced inwardly. 'What did they stop at the pier for? Could you see why they had bothered to go there first?'

Louise sniggered. 'Why does anyone go under the pier.'

'They weren't under the pier, John, they were simply sitting on the bike, talking,' Ted said quickly and he dug Louise in the ribs to stop her going on.

She squealed in surprise. 'Sitting on the bike *and* kissing was more like it,' she said, giving Ted a dirty look. 'I wouldn't be at all surprised if they weren't getting set for a quickie under the pier before they joined us for a drink.' She didn't bother to conceal the smirk on her face when she saw jealousy clouding John's face.

'Leave it, mate. She's not worth the aggro,' Ted said while glaring at Louise who leant back against the bar in triumph.

John slammed his glass down and stormed out of the bar with Ted trailing and pleading with him to stay and have another drink. John ignored his friend, leapt astride his bike and quickly sped away. Ted ran to his bike and then remembered the attractive girl with the very long legs waiting for him inside the pub. His shoulders dropped and he went back inside to see what he could salvage from the evening.

Aware of the growing police presence John rode along the seafront well within the speed limit while his anger raced within.

Alan became his first friend when he was only 7 and buried under three bullies who were pummelling his body with their fists. The trio had made a habit of extorting dinner money from a number of his class mates who were smaller than them. When they accosted John by the swings in the recreation park and made their demand he refused to pay them.

Suddenly a taller, older boy had appeared on the scene and started pulling the bullies off John one by one. He gave each a number of resounding kicks that had them doubled over and writhing in pain for a good five minutes before they were able to slink away.

This rescue and the subsequent feeling of safety John felt when he was with Alan instilled new confidence in him and as the years passed the friendship strengthened until the two young men were inseparable and going everywhere together.

Now he had been betrayed by the one person he thought he could always trust. The girl he thought was attracted to him had been lured by the mere promise of a twenty-minute ride on a café racer. He thought bitterly about the blood oath he and Alan had made years ago to be friends forever.

John was tempted to race to the pier to confront Alan as soon as possible but he resisted the urge when a police motorbike whipped past him on its way to a new scuffle that had broken out on the beach.

It only took him three minutes to reach the spot close to the pier entrance. He immediately began searching for the Triumph and soon spotted Alan's bike lined up with four other café racers and he parked alongside. After heaving his bike up onto its stand John scoured the immediate area in front of the pier but could see no sign of the couple.

Posters announcing the forthcoming concert by The Rolling Stones were being posted by a lone man in a paste-stained duffel coat and the few couples strolling on the boardwalk were mainly elderly and taking post-dinner constitutionals.

John trotted to the concrete steps leading down to the pebble beach and slowly walked towards the incoming tide that shimmered in the moonlight. His leather boots slipped and dug into the smooth stones as they shifted beneath his weight. After twenty yards he abruptly turned left and walked under the massive steel structure. Like a surreal regimented forest of steel the pillars, sprouting branches at the top to support the pier, faded into the darkness and John had to slow his pace until his eyes became accustomed to the dim light. Against the pale grey of the sea he could make out moving silhouettes amidst the vertical geometry of the barnacle-encrusted steelwork.

A number of couples were leaning against the pier legs as they embraced and kissed while awkwardly fumbling with the fastenings of each other's clothing. A few squeals of protests from girls who'd changed their minds were swallowed by the sound of the sea. Other hardier souls had spread waterproof ground sheets on the cold pebbles and were openly engaged in making love.

John had dismissed the panting faces briefly turned towards him as he passed until he was within fifty yards of the water. It was there that he spotted a couple leaning against one of the steel uprights. He could see that it was Alan and that he was kissing Doris. With one hand he was busily raising her petticoats to expose the whiteness of her naked thighs while the other tugged at the waistband of her underwear. John could clearly see that Doris wasn't a reluctant or passive participant and he gave out a loud bellow of rage.

'Damn you, Alan,' he shouted as he grabbed his friend's shoulder and spun him round. Doris was thrown off balance and was unable to prevent herself from falling backwards. The back of her head struck the stanchion and she slowly slid down the cold steel to end up sitting on the wet pebbles with a dazed expression.

'Crikey, is that you, John?' Alan croaked in surprise, hurriedly trying to adjust his gaping jeans. 'Where did you come from?'

'The bloody pub, that's where. And that's where you should have been half an hour ago, you bastard!'

'Look, mate, you know how things go. You may not like it but she fancied me and next thing we both wanted it. God, she had her arms around me and was already touching me up while we were doing eighty on the road. Then when we entered Hastings she suggested that we stop at the pier.'

'And that's your bloody excuse for taking my bird and having it away with her?'

Alan held his hand up in protest. 'Look here, mate—firstly, we hadn't got that far yet and secondly, she definitely came on to me.'

'Whether she took a fancy to your family jewels or not you should still have had the decency to back off. Doris was mine for the night and as my best friend you should have—' Alan clamped a hand over John's mouth to stop him talking.

'Shush! For God's sake, shut up John. I think something's wrong with Doris.' He dropped to his knees beside the seated figure and bent over to slap her lightly on the face. There was no reaction and the girl kept on staring into the distance. Alan lifted her hand and felt for her pulse.

John stood in silence with a puzzled expression for a few seconds before whispering, 'What's wrong with her?'

'She's bloody dead. That's what's wrong with her,' Alan croaked, letting the hand fall limply onto the hard pebbles. 'She must have hit herself really hard when she fell. There's a lot of blood on the back of her head.'

'Christ, what do we do now?' John said with a rising feeling of panic. 'They'll have us for murder. We could hang!' he shouted and Alan had to clamp his hand over John's mouth to prevent any further outburst.

'Shut up, you fool,' he hissed. 'We don't want everyone to know we were here. We've got to leave as quickly as possible without attracting any attention to ourselves. It has to look as if she had an accident while walking along the pier.' Alan pointed and John began walking as though in a daze. He still had the sense to circle round the sexually pre-occupied couples to avoid being recognised.

John was halfway back to the steps when Alan caught up and, putting an arm around his shoulders, steered him away from where the lovers were more thickly gathered. They emerged from under the pier furthest from any other walkers on the beach and into starkly revealing moonlight.

'Keep your head down and turned away from the pier,' Alan hissed and John did as he was told until they were climbing the steps to the promenade.

Both men then hurried to their bikes where John broke the silence between them. 'What now?' he asked as they mounted their machines and started the engines.

Alan leant towards John to be heard above the sound of the bike engines. 'We do nothing, John. We simply go and join Ted and his girl at the Red Lion and then we tell them that Doris had met a rocker on the pier and buggered off with him. Then we'll all have a good time and go home.'

'You must go to the police, Alan, and tell them because I don't think I've got the nerve.'

'Believe me, John, when I say the slut's dead and we'll only get into a lot of trouble with the police if I report it.' John was rendered speechless by Alan's cool attitude, yet too dazed to argue.

'Keep well below the speed limit so that we don't get stopped,' Alan warned. 'The last thing we need is for our names and addresses to be taken by the coppers,' he added before pulling away along the seafront to the pub.

As they parked at the Red Lion Alan gripped John by the arm and pulled him close. 'Just remember, John Tucker, you owe me big time and you'll have to come across sooner or later, or else. Okay?' Alan's voice was cold and dispassionate and another shiver ran through John. He wanted to argue that he didn't push Doris but he couldn't. He realized that Alan was no longer his best friend and that he was probably under his control.

From now on Alan could ensure that John did exactly as he was told and he smiled secretly to himself. They both entered the pub and Alan cheerily waved to Ted and Louise as though the horror of the past fifteen minutes had never taken place. John trudged behind, unable to follow his friend's example.

'Hi, John, you look as though you've lost ten bob and found sixpence. Where's Doris, or is it her you've lost?' Ted asked with a broad grin as he raised his hand to the harassed bartender to indicate two extra pints were required.

John could only shake his head while stuffing his hands in his pockets to prevent them from shaking.

'The stupid girl met a greasy rocker she fancied more than our mate,' Alan said and burst into laughter.

John turned towards the man he thought he could always count on, his face drained of all colour. 'Damn you, Alan, you're really going to go too far one of these days.'

Ted held his hands up. 'Steady guys. It's nobody's fault. Some girls can be pretty fickle and quite often a bloody pain in the neck,' he said soothingly as he passed the beers to his friends. 'One minute they want to go to the pier for a snog and the next they're all hoity-toity and want to stay in a pub drinking Babycham.' Ted's laughter was cut short by the girl's bony elbow digging into his side.

'Doris isn't like that,' Louise said with a sullen look. 'Like me she hates rockers 'cos all they want to do is pick fights with mods at one café or the other.' She was warming to the subject. 'She's a real junkie for speed which is why she chose you guys. That's all you buggers are interested in apart from getting into some poor girl's knickers.'

'No matter what you say, darling, she was chatted up by a long-haired git with enough metal studs in his jacket to make himself another bike,' Alan said in an offhand manner as he turned away from Louise and took a long drink from his glass. 'Boy, this Double Diamond is silky smooth. It really does work wonders,' he murmured, making a point of holding John's look as though to say, 'cool it or else'.

'It's bloody beer, Alan, not a magic potion to raise the dead,' John muttered and he broke the deadlock by looking down at his glass that was still standing untouched on the bar. Alan raised an eyebrow in warning and John turned away to face Ted. 'What's your opinion, Ted. Can a really good beer raise Lazarus from the dead?'

'Did for me, mate,' Ted answered with a loud guffaw. 'Last time I came off the old Lightning it was four excellent pints of the best in the Crown that helped me to get back on straightaway and I didn't fall off again until I was virtually in my own street.'

'Yeah, I remember that, Ted,' Alan enthused and John could see that the girl's death still hadn't touched him and wasn't likely to. 'It was that vicious S-bend on Hosey Common Road that threw you, mate. You are a bit of a tosser when it comes to those reverse cambers.'

Before Ted could compose a suitable retort John interrupted. 'I want to go home now,' he said and drained the contents of his glass in one go.

'What about Doris?' Louise asked sharply. 'We can't leave her in Hastings. How will she get home?'

'The lucky rocker who's now well into her knickers can take her home. He's got a bike, hasn't he?' Alan jeered derisively.

'You're disgusting,' she spat out and turned to John. 'Well?'

'I don't know where she's got to or with whom. It'll be impossible to find her on a night like this. The mods and rockers are starting to congregate along the seafront and I want to get out of this bloody town before the drunken brawls begin and the police climb in with their truncheons.'

It was clear that Louise was dissatisfied with John's answer and she squeezed Ted's arm. 'What about you? Are you going to abandon my friend, too?

'Like John said, love, it will be pretty difficult to find her but I'll give it a try for a little while at least.' Picking up his helmet and blowing a kiss to Louise he strode across the floor. Since his friends had returned without Doris he had felt that any luck he may have had in scoring with Louise had drained away as fast as John's pint. 'You guys can take Louise back to Alice's Café while I look for Doris,' he called back gloomily before going through the door.

'I'm not going to horn in on your bird, Ted. It's not what mates do. John can take her back,' Alan said haughtily.

John spun round and was about to hit the bigger man when the look on Alan's face stopped him dead. He slumped back against the mahogany bar and nodded resignedly to Louise. 'Okay, when do you want to leave?'

The girl drained her Babycham and started walking towards the door. 'Since the night isn't going to get any more exciting than this I'd like to go now,' she said over her shoulder. John picked up his helmet and followed her out.

'I'm sure you could give her a bit of action on the way home, John,' Alan called after him and received a quick look of pure hatred in response.

Alan shrugged uncaringly while assessing how he could use his vastly increased control over John to his advantage. It needed testing and an idea had already begun to form as he slowly sipped his beer.

Despite the urging of Louise who was gripping him tightly around the waist, John cruised slowly on the main road, keeping well below the speed limit. He could sense the girl's frustration in the way she moved about on the saddle behind him. It was as though she was encouraging him to go faster. Every time a jeering group of rockers passed them at high speed she turned her face away to hide her embarrassment.

Although John, with his dark ducktail, long sideburns, and high cheekbones was quite handsome, Louise had already set her mind on Ted and his good-humoured nature and she held on to John's jacket in a modest fashion during the journey.

They had just bypassed the dimly lit village of Flimwell when Louise, mortified by her need, was forced to shout in his ear that she had to relieve herself. He nodded and slowed the bike as they neared Chingley Wood until the headlight briefly illuminated a road sign. He quickly braked and turned into a small avenue that was overhung by dense branches that created a dark claustrophobic tunnel.

John stopped the bike and switched off the engine. 'You can go somewhere amongst the trees,' he said waving into the blackness that lined both sides of the narrow road.

'You must be joking. I need a proper convenience,' Louise protested and she adamantly remained seated on the back of the machine. John dismounted awkwardly with the girl refusing to budge an inch and waited patiently.

'For goodness sake, Louise, nobody can see you in there,' he said as he pointed into the darkness with an impatiently stabbing forefinger.

'Then keep talking to me so I know where *you* are,' she said as she climbed off the bike and crossed the road to enter the wood. There were a few choice words as her heels sank into the spongy leaf mould and John watched her as she wrapped her petticoats about her to avoid the brambles. She gingerly walked into the gloom and disappeared amongst the black tree trunks. He reached into a top pocket to retrieve a packet of Woodbines and lit a cigarette.

'Are you there,' a faint voice asked as he puffed out a blue cloud that hung above him in the windstill night.

'Yes, of course I am.'

'What really happened at the pier. Did Doris go off with a rocker as Alan said she did?'

'Yes,' he answered half-heartedly with a slight catch in his throat. There was a moment of silence and John strained his ears but could hear nothing. 'I don't believe you, John,' Louise finally said, her voice growing louder as she approached with shoes squelching in the thick leaf mould.

The girl suddenly emerged from the foliage and strode onto the road to confront the ton-up. She brushed her dress down and then tried to pick off the dozens of burrs she had picked up in the undergrowth. 'She wasn't like that at all,' she said defiantly.

'What do you mean?' John was now on the defensive for he knew that one wrong word would increase her suspicions and possibly give her the idea that all was not well with her friend.

'Once she's chosen a guy for the night she stays with him. She's never changed horses midstream, if that's the right expression,' she said as she waited for John to mount the bike before climbing back on herself.

'Well, she did tonight. We were under the pier and this guy came up to her and said that he knew her from when they were at school. She took him by the arm, intimate like, and pulled him away so that I couldn't hear what they were saying and Doris chatted to him for quite a while. Then she came back to me and said that she preferred to spend the rest of the evening with Tom—that was the name she gave—because he was an old friend she hadn't seen for a very long time.'

'You're lying. I've been her closest friend since primary school and Doris has never known anybody named Tom.'

'Call me a bloody liar one more time and you can spend the night right here in the wood,' John bluffed as he started the engine. Her hands grabbed at his jacket and tightened their grip as he released the clutch. The bike slowly burbled along the road in low gear to rejoin the main highway.

John was still in a state of extreme shock following the terrifying accident beneath the pier but he instinctively knew that he had to keep his mouth firmly shut about what had happened otherwise there was a very good chance that he would be caught. The thought of a cold rope tightening about his throat sent an icy shiver through him that even Louise could feel through the thick leather.

'Are you all right?'

'Perfectly,' he shouted over his shoulder as he considered his next move. John had been convinced by Alan and now didn't believe that the police, or anyone else, would accept the simple truth that it was a tragic accident. After all, in their eyes he was just another leather-jacketed irresponsible ton-up who carried a straight razor in his pocket in order to make him feel like a man who couldn't be trifled with.

The Norton slithered to a halt in a cloud of dust as he braked hard. Louise gave a small yelp as she was slammed hard into his back. John partially unzipped his jacket and took out the bone-handled barber's razor which he threw as hard as he could into the trees.

'What did you stop so quickly for? Was it a squirrel?' Louise squealed. She had been peering over his left shoulder and hadn't seen John dispose of the blade with his right arm.

'Yeah,' he muttered. 'It was some sort of animal.' The bike jerked forward and Louise lurched backwards forcing her to reach out and grab his shoulders in order to remain on the bike. John rejoined the main road and raced towards Lamberhurst, all thoughts of speed restrictions forgotten. All he could think of was that he had to dispose of the girl as soon as possible and then get back to the safety of his home.

He dropped Louise off at the telephone box outside Alice's Café. She called her friend Penny and pleaded with her to ask her brother Jake to come and collect her. Louise had made up a quick excuse that Ted had been unable to run her home due to a breakdown. Once John was satisfied that she would be okay for the rest of the evening he mounted his bike, waved a brief goodbye and headed for Hawthorne Avenue.

Alan's brain was racing, juggling every cold fact, and by the time he had finished his beer and stumbled out into the cool reviving night air he had a clear picture of the many difficulties that lay ahead.

It was a sure bet that the girl's body would be found very soon, undoubtedly that night, and 'Murdered Girl Under Hastings Pier' would make nationwide headlines the following morning.

Due to the circumstances of the accident John was now in his power; however, Ted's loyalty was with John, no matter what he had done. Louise presented the major threat as she could easily put two and two together to make both John *and* Alan equally culpable of manslaughter or even murder—a crime that carried the death penalty.

He had thought that he might be able to say to the police that he had witnessed John killing Doris. But the dead girl's best friend, Louise, would no doubt prove to be a very credible witness. She would swear that she had seen Alan kissing Doris in front of the pier.

'Oh Christ, she was the one who told John,' he said aloud. 'That's how he knew where Doris and I would be.'

He started the Bonneville and as he pulled away into the night he came to the conclusion that something had to be done about Louise and that he would have to make sure that it was John who did it. He smiled at the thought for this would give him even more leverage to manipulate John in any way he wished.

2

JOHN HAD JUST WOKEN FROM A FITFUL SLEEP when his father shouted up the stairs, calling him to the phone. He stumbled down in his pyjamas and heard Alan's voice at the other end; he sounded as though he hadn't had very much sleep either.

'We have a problem,' Alan said straightaway.

'What?' John mumbled, still befuddled with sleep.

'Louise is bound to tell the police that you were with Doris when she . . .'

'That's okay, we were both with her at the café long before we arrived in Hastings,' John replied. 'So what?'

'No, she'll say you were under the pier with Doris.'

'Don't forget we were both there, Alan. For Christ's sake, you were the one with his hand inside her knickers so don't keep saying it was only me under the pier.'

'Who else was there is irrelevant; what nobody must know is that *you* were under the pier because *you* were the one with the strongest motive for killing her—jealousy. Remember, you told me that both Ted and Louise saw you storm out of the pub in a foul mood,' Alan said and emphasised the word 'you' to clarify his point. John fell silent and there was only a light hiss on the line for a few seconds before Alan continued:

'You've got to talk to Louise and convince her that Doris went off with that unknown rocker. The police had a lot of trouble with the mods and rockers last night and will simply think that Doris was a casualty of one of the many battles that took place on the promenade and the beach.'

'I tried that story on the way home last night,' John said miserably. 'I said he was called Tom and that he was an old friend from primary school. I can tell you right now that Louise didn't believe a word of what I said. I wouldn't be at all surprised if she hasn't already contacted Doris's parents and told them about you and me,' John murmured while keeping an eye on the kitchen door.

'You'll have to try again, mate. Remember, it was you who hit her head against the pier support.'

'I didn't hit her!' John shouted. 'She slipped and fell against it. And stop calling me mate. You're no longer a friend of mine,' he added in a lowered whisper as the kitchen door opened. Mrs Tucker stepped into the hallway with a concerned look on her face.

'Is everything all right, dear,' she asked in a mock whisper, not wishing to interrupt her son's conversation.

John smiled and nodded his head and his mother put a finger to her lips and returned to the kitchen and her breakfast, closing the door behind her.

'I haven't got her telephone number or her address, how can I arrange to meet her?' John asked in a much lower voice, calmed by his mother's interruption and concern for him.

The line went dead for a while with both men deep in thought until Alan suddenly said, 'Ted'll have it, he was quite lovey-dovey with her last night. Give him a call now and get the number. Then arrange a meeting with Louise somewhere away from her home.'

'Okay Alan, as soon as I've had my breakfast I'll –'

'Do it right now, mate. There's nothing on the news yet but it will soon be and I'm sure you don't want Louise to hear about it before you've met with her. Right?'

'All right, I'll do it,' John said, his surly response noted with some satisfaction by Alan. John hung up and began dialling his friend's number. Ted's mother answered and soon the familiar cheery voice came on the line.

'Morning, me old china, how are you feeling today?'

'A bit woozy, Ted, too much bitter last night,' John said trying to sound casual despite the painful knotting of his stomach. 'Look, mate, I loaned Louise my favourite comb last night,' he lied. 'I haven't got her address and I need to ask her to post it back to me. Did she give you a telephone number?'

'Sure, she gave it to me last night. I think she's a bit keen on me and I was planning to call her today to turn the flame up a little. Why don't I ask her to post it to you?'

'No, that's okay,' John said hurriedly.

'Hey, you trying to make a bid for my bird?' Ted said with a slight edge to his voice.

'Good God, no. Not my type, Ted,' John exclaimed hurriedly in an attempt to placate his pal. 'No, I just want to apologise in person for being rude to her when I dropped her off at Alice's last night.'

Mollified, Ted gave John the number and the family name Walton, which he hastily scrawled on the telephone pad.

'Will I see you tonight at the Odeon?' Ted asked. 'They're showing that new film *Zulu*. It's got Jack Hawkins and Michael Caine in it and I heard that it's got some great battles in it. Our guys being stuck with assegais. I think I'll ask Louise to come as well so you'd better hurry up and get Doris lined up so that we can make it a foursome.'

'Doris won't be able to make it today but I'll play gooseberry and join you,' John said hurriedly. They agreed to meet outside the theatre and Ted hung up.

John read the scribbled number and with a shaking forefinger began dialling. After spinning the last number he waited with bated breath until a deep baritone voice answered. John assumed that it was Louise's father and he asked to speak to her without giving his name.

'Yes, who is it?' Louise asked and John took a deep breath to stop his hand from shaking.

'It's John, from last night,' he said and there was a surprised silence at the other end. 'I gave you a lift home. Well, to the phone box outside Alice's actually.'

'I know who you are, John, but why are you calling me at nine o'clock on a Saturday morning?'

'I need to see you about something very important,' he said as he turned his back on the kitchen door from behind which he could faintly hear *Housewive's Choice*, his mother's favourite programme on the BBC.

'Why don't you tell me what you want to say now?' Louise was puzzled by John's request and he could hear this in her voice.

'Not over the phone. What I want to tell you concerns your friend Doris and it's something I have to explain to you, face to face. Can I meet you in Westerham in half an hour?'

'Yes, but is it that important? Do you know where Doris went last night?' she asked, her voice heavy with curiosity.

'I'll tell you when we meet but please promise not to call her until after I've had a chance to tell you my side of things. If it's convenient for you let's make it the bus stop on the green. It's the one opposite the statue of Churchill.' John hung up without waiting for an answer and quickly dialled Alan's number.

He answered immediately. 'Is she going to meet us?'

'Westerham Green in half an hour,' John said. 'And what do you mean "us"? You didn't tell me that you wanted to see her too.'

'You'll need some moral support, my friend. She may need a lot of convincing that what happened was a genuine accident.' The line went dead and John ran upstairs to change into his riding gear. He had only just pushed the Dominator out of the garage when Alan turned into the driveway.

He braked next to John and raising the visor on his helmet he said slowly, as though addressing a child: 'Just explain to her that Doris tripped on the pebbles and fell against the pier. We rushed to help her but it was too late. We were too scared to call for an ambulance. No more than that, okay? And we must take her somewhere quiet to tell her,' he said as he scanned the net curtains at the front of the house for any movement. John nodded grimly as he studied Alan's face and then he released the clutch and pulled out into the avenue. Alan awkwardly carried out a three-point turn in the narrow drive and ignoring Mr Tucker who had just emerged from the front door and was standing on the porch with a concerned look on his face he raced after his friend.

The two young men sped through Biggin Hill and were soon descending Westerham Hill on their final approach to the small historic town. Riding into the large square at the heart of the town John immediately spotted the brunette standing at the bus stop. She was casually dressed in figure-hugging jeans and a fancy white blouse with a ruffled front that successfully concealed her small bosom. John braked and stopped beside her, indicating that she should climb aboard. Then he glanced to his right as Alan slowly cruised past to lead the way. As soon as Louise had a safe grip on his jacket he pulled away quickly to catch up with Alan.

Louise tried asking where they were going a number of times but the helmet and wind noise muffled her questions and she finally gave up and just leant forward and held on tight, her dark brown hair streaming behind her. It only took a few minutes before Alan braked to take an unexpected turn into Hosey Common Road and John followed, wondering why Alan felt it so necessary to go so far from the town to explain to Louise what had happened to her friend.

They had ridden half a mile along the road when Alan took a small side street that took them deep into Long Wood. Alan kept going until he spotted an overgrown bridle path and without hesitation turned his bike onto the rough track. John followed and overgrown nettles whipped their leather- and jean-clad legs until they finally reached a small clearing. Both bikes came to a stop and as the engines were switched off they were aware of the all-pervading silence punctuated fitfully by the harsh cawing of rooks circling high overhead.

'Why did we have to come here?' Louise asked, looking around in astonishment at the natural wilderness. They all dismounted and the two men removed their helmets. 'For goodness sake, this is really stupid.'

Louise looked at John with anxious eyes. 'Just say what you couldn't tell me on the phone and let's get back to town. I have some shopping to do for my mum.'

'John has something very important to tell you, Louise, and we needed maximum privacy because we didn't know what your response would be,' Alan said quietly, his dark eyes watching every nervous reaction to his words. 'Tell her, John.'

'What? Tell me what?' Louise shouted at the top of her voice and the rooks fell silent.

'Doris is dead, Louise, she's dead and I'm sorry, really sorry, cos she fell on the beach and hit her head—it was an accident,' John said in a breathless rush of words, wanting to say it all before the girl could react.

'Dead?' she whispered. 'You killed her?'

'No, I didn't kill her. I swear I never touched her,' John said in panic. 'It was an accident. She fell and hit her head on one of the steel supports under the pier.'

'You made her fall, that's why you brought me all the way out here. To tell me you killed her,' she sobbed. 'Oh my God, you've got to go and tell the police right now.'

'No! No bloody police,' Alan said forcefully. 'It was an unfortunate accident but people might believe the worst and John could go to the gallows.'

'You've got to turn yourself in, John. If it was an accident you've got to tell them. Oh my God, poor Doris,' she cried hysterically as the tears started to stream down her cheeks and caused the thick mascara to do the same.

'John can't do that, you stupid bitch,' Alan snarled. 'I've told you what will happen. All you have to do is keep your bloody mouth shut. That's all.' He made a slash across his mouth with his thumb and forefinger as though closing a zip.

John's head was beginning to hurt. He could see that Louise wasn't listening to any of their explanations and that she was dead set on telling someone everything they had just confessed to her. His hands began to clench, nails painfully biting into his palms, while his headache continued to increase.

'You'll have to keep quiet, Louise. It would destroy my mother if she knew what had happened.'

'I can't do that,' the girl screamed and turning on her heels she began to sprint back down the bridle path, unmindful of the nettles that brushed her hands and bare arms. John was frozen to the spot while he watched her slowly disappear down the winding path.

His mind wandered aimlessly as he stared at the plump red berries that dotted the woodland bushes bordering the path before Alan's harsh voice brought him back to reality.

'Go and get her, you've got to stop her, you fool,' Alan snarled, thrusting the Jet helmet into John's hands. 'Make sure you do it right,' he barked. John started his bike and accelerated back along the path, his rear wheel spewing rich leaf litter high into the air.

He soon saw the running girl up ahead. The overgrown path wasn't wide enough for him to pass her and she refused to stop despite his shouts. He slowed and then stopped, feeling completely inadequate, unable to do anything to prevent the teenager from running. He could see the end of his life rushing towards him as the girl ran away. He was suddenly jolted forward as Alan's front wheel struck his rear tyre.

'You stupid fool, don't let her get away!' he shouted at John repeatedly to make himself heard above the sound of their engines.

'How? I can't get past to cut her off and she'll soon be back on the main road,' John said weakly, holding his hands out in a gesture of helplessness.

'Stop her! Do it now before it's too late!'

John cringed under Alan's steely look and then flinched as his friend tossed a short length of reinforcing rod to him. He caught it and gave Alan a bewildered look.

'She can't be allowed to talk. It's your neck if she does,' Alan said with finality.

Totally confused, John unconsciously slipped the rod inside his boot and closing his mind to what Alan had just said he released the clutch and quickly rode along the path until he saw the breathless figure before him. She was stumbling along slowly now, gasping for air with every step she took. Louise glanced over her shoulder at the rapidly approaching machine and he could clearly see the fear in her eyes.

John's mind was still running over Alan's last instructions when, with glazed eyes, he twisted the grip, launching the bike like a missile to pass the running girl. At the last second his front wheel struck a rabbit hole and the bike was thrown to the left and struck Louise in the lower back. She was thrust forward and he ran over her. The jolt of the heavy motorcycle passing over the girl nearly unseated John but his grip on the jerking handlebars was firm and he was able to keep the bike under control. He brought the Dominator to a skidding stop before looking back at the pitiful figure lying face down in the mud. Still in a daze he pulled the bike up on its stand and stumbled back to where the stricken girl lay without moving.

Alan arrived within seconds and looked down at the mud-splattered girl. There was a moan and a slight movement of her shoulders and both men recoiled. Alan from obvious disappointment that she still lived and John from the horror at what lay before him.

'What have I done? Oh my God, what have I done?' he cried before clamping a hand over his mouth.

'The right thing, John,' Alan muttered harshly as he poked the girl in the ribs with the toe of his boot. 'Now you've got to finish her off otherwise they'll have you for murder and attempted murder too.' He bent over and removed the short rusty rod from John's boot and placed it in the shocked man's hand. 'Do it or die at the end of a rope, you fool.'

The girl was lying face down and now moaning louder. She began to writhe in pain, not unlike a reptile that had suffered a broken back, and John knelt in the mud and tried to see her face hidden by the clods of churned-up path.

'I can't do it, Alan,' he sobbed. 'It's wrong. Doris was an accident and we should have told the police but what you want me to do now would be sheer bloody murder.'

Alan walked over to stand beside the kneeling teenager and gripped his shoulder. 'Save yourself, mate, it's your future I'm thinking about and you won't have one if she survives to talk to the police.'

Louise turned her head a little and Alan could see her profile. It was obvious that she had broken her nose and he assumed that the copious amount of blood on the leaves was from her nose. Then he saw that a broken hawthorn twig had pierced the eye that was turned towards him.

John gasped and recoiled from the sight. 'I can't, Alan,' he pleaded, dropping the rod and looking up into the cold, calculating face looming over him.

'You must hit her or hang! Hit or hang! Hit or hang!' Alan chanted as he shook the shocked man by the shoulders. John finally jerked away from his grip and picked up the rusty rod. As his fingers closed around the flaking steel Alan's chanting throbbed in his head until he began moving as if in a trance.

He slowly bent over the girl and raised his arm as 'hit or hang, hit or hang' kept running through his mind and he brought the rod down half-heartedly on the back of her head. She screamed, half raising herself on thin arms and then fell forward onto her face to remain absolutely still. Alan's restraining hand on his raised wrist prevented any further blows to the girl's head.

'One was enough, John,' he said in a satisfied tone of voice as he felt for a pulse on the side of her neck. 'Now you've got to hide her and hide her well,' Alan said dispassionately as he studied John's ashen face for any signs of rebellion.

John threw the rod down and knelt beside the dead girl with his mind slowly clearing and tears began to pour down his cheeks. 'My God, Alan, what have you made me do?' he whispered hoarsely. He then stood and ran into the undergrowth where he threw up until all he could do was dry retch.

'I didn't make you do anything, moron,' Alan called after him. 'You were the one who ran the bitch down and beat her head to a pulp with an iron rod.' Alan looked down at the pathetic figure with total indifference. 'You killed her, mate, not me.'

'You said stop her, she musn't be allowed to talk,' John said as he returned to stand beside the body, wiping his mouth with the back of his sleeve. 'Hit or hang. You told me to hit her or hang.'

'But I didn't use the word kill, did I, John?' The suspicion of a smile flickered briefly across Alan's handsome face. 'Now you'll have to bury her body and do it quickly before any of the horsey set decide to come cantering along this path and find you at it.'

'You gave me this iron rod,' John said weakly as he picked the offending item up and threw it into the undergrowth, his eyes fixed upon the bloody wound on the back of the girl's head.

'To threaten her, not to smash her head in,' Alan lied. 'Now get her off the path and pull her into the undergrowth. Quick!' he barked, startling John out of his self-pitying apathy. He warily took hold of Louise by the wrists as if she might suddenly come back to life and dragged her dead weight into the trees. Alan followed more slowly, trying to disguise the drag marks in the undergrowth.

'Fifty feet in from the bridle path should be enough,' he called out to John who had stopped and, dropping the lifeless arms with a lost look on his face, waited for further instructions.

'Dig a hole you stupid bastard. You can't leave her out in the open. In a few days the smell would reach the path and then you'll be in big trouble,' Alan snapped.

'Why is it always me who'll get into trouble and not us?' John asked although he was past caring and already knew what the answer would be.

'Because you did all the killing, my friend.'

The words made no sense to John as he began scraping at the leaf mould and the loamy soil with his bare hands with a small piece of wood. After thirty minutes he had dug a shallow grave, tearing two fingernails and drawing blood in the process. Alan kept a lookout for any walkers and remained standing ten feet from where John was labouring. When he judged the hole deep enough he instructed John to stop.

'Now put her in and cover her up. Make sure that you put a final layer of moss and dead leaves on top to conceal the freshly turned soil.'

John took hold of the girl's shoulders and rolled her into the grave. She stared up at him with the mutilated eye and he drew back in alarm as if she was accusing him personally for the accident.

'Get a bloody move on. She can't hurt you now and we haven't got all day,' Alan said and then added, 'and make sure you bury the rod with her.'

'Where is it?' John asked dully, his frightened gaze fixed upon the girl's face.

'Where you threw it. Just go and get it as quickly as possible.' Alan picked up John's helmet and deliberately tucked the gauntlets inside and out of John's sight.

It took John five minutes to locate the spot where in a moment of self-disgust he had thrown the rod into the bracken. He looked both ways along the path but nothing stirred and he hurried back to the make-shift grave and placed the rod next to the girl. Her undamaged eye stared sightlessly up at him and he tentatively reached out to close the lid.

Alan removed a rolled up copy of the newly launched *Sun* newspaper from inside his jacket and spread it over the girl's head. A picture of Britt Ekland, vibrant and alive, was in sharp contrast to the body in the shallow grave and John snatched it up and angrily crumpled it into a ball before throwing it into the bushes. He then began to fill in the grave and tears gathered once more as he slowly covered the features that were beautiful despite having been dragged through the undergrowth. John thought of Ted, wondering how he would take the news of her death when the body was eventually found. He couldn't hazard a guess at what his mother would say if she learnt what he had been up to over the last two days.

Five minutes later the grave site was virtually invisible. The slight mound of fresh soil had been disguised by the small pieces of moss and twigs found amongst the trees.

They hurried back to their bikes and as John put his leg over the Norton's seat Alan tapped him on the shoulder. 'This was no accident, John. You deliberately murdered that girl and I'm a witness to what you did.'

John spun round on the seat to stare at Alan with wide open eyes. 'You're going to tell the police? You'll tell them about me?' he stuttered with panic rising and his head throbbing once again.

'Would I do that to my best friend? Of course not, John,' Alan said with a sly look. 'However, make sure you always remember that I know what you did in Hastings and Long Wood.' He started his engine and lifting his arm he gave John a contemptuous wave as he accelerated away on the bridle path.

John sat with his arms wrapped around his upper body, trying to still the shivering that racked his body. He knew that deep inside he wasn't bad and yet by cleverly manipulating his weakness and indecision Alan had turned him into a multiple murderer. Once again he wept.

Mr Tucker was reading his Sunday paper at the breakfast table when he came upon the report and read aloud to no one in particular the finding of a young girl's body beneath Hastings pier. The story was almost a repeat of the Saturday's when 72-point front-page headlines had blazoned the news of the riots between mods and rockers on the beach front. The story of the girl's death had lost importance and been devalued to page five, relying more on the columnist's conjecture than on the facts. In another day or two it would fade completely, overwhelmed by the latest poll results and in-depth coverages of Harold Wilson's campaign to win voters over to the Labour Party in the forthcoming General Election.

'The official statement is that the cause of death is still to be determined and that the police are seeking witnesses who had seen anyone with the girl after the public houses had closed on Friday night,' Mr Tucker said with the occasional 'tut-tut' from his wife. There was a full-face photograph of Doris Trencher that had been taken three years earlier. Without any make-up and her hair pulled back severely into long pigtails she looked vulnerable and innocent.

Mrs Tucker placed the plate of bacon and eggs in front of her husband and sat at the table to continue tut-tutting about young girls who didn't know any better than to stay out so late at night.

'They're just asking for trouble,' she said and then went on to blame the decline of moral standards on the blatant sexual content of modern music.

'I blame the whole thing on depraved lyrics and books like *Lady Chatterley's Lover*. The Lord Chancellor should never have lifted censorship and allowed it to be read by impressionable young people. Small wonder so many unmarried girls are getting themselves in the family way.'

Mr Tucker was tempted to interrupt his wife to say that it took two and that it was impossible for a girl to get pregnant on her own unless she was the mother of Christ but on seeing the mood his wife was in he chose to remain silent, hiding from her ceaseless chattering by raising his newspaper and sipping his tea noisily.

John had left the table earlier and long before his father had come down for his traditional belt-testing breakfast and was now in his room sitting on the bed, head in hands, thinking about the previous day.

The phone rang and he could hear the quiet murmuring of his father as he answered the call and then a sudden shout to inform him that Ted was on the line and also that his tea was getting cold.

Ted's first words to John struck a nerve. 'So, did you manage to meet up with Louise?'

Alan had warned him to expect this call and John passed on exactly what he was told to say. 'No, I called her and made arrangements to meet but for some reason she didn't turn up.'

'She didn't turn up last night either,' Ted said in a puzzled tone. 'And neither did you, mate!'

'What do you mean?'

'Savages and bloody battles won by the heroic Jack Hawkins and Michael Caine—now do you remember?'

'Damn!' John slapped his forehead. '*Zulu!* I was supposed to meet you last night at the cinema, wasn't I?'

'Now you remember, so what happened?'

'I was a little concerned about Louise not turning up and so I went back at ten o'clock last night to make sure she hadn't got the morning time mixed up with the evening. It would have been a bit embarrassing and I would then have owed her two apologies.'

'That's strange, because I called and her dad said that she had to meet a guy called John on Westerham Green yesterday morning—that was you, wasn't it?'

'That's right, but as I just told you she didn't pitch up. Lord knows where she got to unless she confused my instructions about where to meet with other arrangements she had made.' John tried to keep his voice calm and under control. 'She was most probably waiting in the coffee shop on Bromley High Street.'

'Well, Mr Walton is terribly worried because he checked her bed and found that she hadn't slept in it at all. She'd been out all night which she's never done before and he knows she hadn't been with any of her girlfriends as he had already rung them all.'

'She's most probably slept over with a friend that her father doesn't know about,' John said quickly as he tried to change the subject.

'Hmmm—I wonder if her disappearance has got anything to do with poor Doris,' Ted said thoughtfully. 'Have you seen the picture of Doris in all the newspapers? She was found dead in Hastings early Saturday morning. Talk about coincidence! It's the same girl you talked to in Alice's. You know, the little beauty Alan was snogging when Louise and I rode past the pier—the girl I said you should take to the pictures.' His voice had become more and more excited while talking as though his mind was leap-frogging towards a yet to be identified conclusion. He paused, the hissing of the open line being the only sound as John waited, the instrument pressed firmly against his ear.

Ted then continued more slowly as though considering each word carefully before speaking. 'Which brings me to why I rang. When you dashed out of the Red Lion did you manage to find Doris on the pier?' he asked. 'Or, under it?'

The second part of his question put John instantly on alert for he mistakenly thought that Ted had managed to arrive at the truth.

'Look, Ted, I think we should get together and talk about this in a quiet place where we can't be disturbed. Then I can give you the facts on what happened last night,' John said quietly.

'That sounds very ominous, mate. Do these so-called facts also include the disappearance of Louise?' Ted asked softly.

John began shaking and had to steel himself to reply. 'No, I know nothing about where Louise could be.' It was the first time he had purposefully deceived his mate and John suddenly felt unclean.

'Okay, I believe you. How about outside the gates of the old recreation ground at eight tonight?'

'See you there,' John said and before Ted could ask any more awkward questions he hung up. He was on the point of calling Alan to tell him of Ted's suspicions when his hand froze on the dial. He was inordinately fond of Ted, a friendship that had lasted since their early days at school; this loyalty prevented him from even imagining what Alan would do or might tell him to do so he returned to his bedroom to work out how he could possibly begin explaining what had happened on Friday night to his friend.

It was twilight and a blackbird was still singing his beautiful song and laying claim to his personal space before roosting for the night. The Dominator burbled up to the locked gates of the recreation ground and John switched off and parked the bike by the entrance. He removed a full pack of cigarettes from his pocket and lit one to await Ted. He switched off the lights so as not to attract unwanted attention and let his mind wander back to the night Doris had died. Although it was a balmy summer evening he shivered when he recalled how she had fallen and how the blood had appeared so black on the pebbles in the moonlight.

John was able to recall the events of the last two days but no matter how hard he tried, he couldn't recollect exact details about killing Louise. He could remember burying her corpse but otherwise if asked where she lay he would be unable to recall the location of the grave.

He heard the distant sound of a powerful bike approaching and swivelled round on his seat to watch Ted sweep in at the end of the street and come towards him. His friend stopped beside him and cut his engine. Removing his helmet he gave John a quizzical look. 'So, what's it all about, John? What did you want to tell me that's so mysterious that we have to meet like secret agents?'

'Whatever I tell you stays between us, is that agreed, Ted?' John asked softly and silently waited until Ted, after studying his friend's face in the evening light for a moment, nodded slowly.

'I think I know you well enough, John, to know that you would never knowingly do anything really bad and I would always stand by you, no matter what. I trust you.'

'Thanks, Ted. Now I can tell you what really happened to Doris,' John said and he quietly related the whole evening in Hastings including how Alan had insisted that they should cut and run.

'He said I could be blamed for her death and be hung for it,' John finished and the words remained hanging in the air like his vividly imagined noose, awaiting his friend's decision to either release the trapdoor or keep it shut.

The burly young man sat perfectly still, his mouth slightly open as though wanting to say something but unable to get the words past his teeth. Eventually he moved to seek a more comfortable position on the bike before speaking.

'Bloody hell, John, if you'd just thought about it at the time you'd have realised that it would have been far better to have called for an ambulance just in case she could still have been saved, and you should definitely have told the police as well. They could have conducted an immediate investigation that would have proved it to be an accident and you wouldn't be facing a more serious charge now.'

He paused for breath while looking at John with sympathetic eyes. 'By running, you silly bugger, you've given 'em just cause to believe that it may have been a deliberate act. Possibly that you bashed her head against the pier in a fit of jealousy when you saw Alan with his hand up her dress.'

'I know, but what can I do, Ted?' John pleaded.

'Well, you could still try to tell 'em the truth but it will be a lot more difficult to get them to believe you now that it's two days later and you ran from the scene. Alternatively, you can keep a really low profile for a number of years. You've got to get rid of the bike and then think of emigrating to Australia or Canada. At least get as far away from Alan as possible because it sounds like he has your balls in a nutcracker. To think he was our best friend all these bloody years.'

'Christ, get rid of the Norton, that sounds bloody extreme,' John said whilst thinking that putting some distance between himself and Alan made a lot more sense than putting a distance between himself and his beloved machine. He unconsciously began to stroke the fuel tank as he tried to calm his fears.

'Selling your bike ain't extreme, mate—hanging by the neck until dead is,' Ted whispered and put his hand on his friend's shoulder.

'Will you go to the police, Ted?'

'Only if you ask me to. I leave that kind of decision up to you entirely. I'm satisfied that you didn't kill her on purpose and that it was an accident. Now all I want to do is to see you right.'

'Jeez, you're a great mate, Ted,' John said thankfully and taking a deep breath he prepared to open up fully and tell him what had happened to Louise. 'There's something else I have to tell you—' He suddenly stopped mid-word when he recalled how Ted had looked at Louise the first time they had met. The way he had put his arm around her waist when they were in Alice's Café and how he had held her hand when walking along the seafront. He knew Ted had fallen for the brunette in a big way and that he would never forgive John for what had happened to her, even though John's mindless actions had been induced by Alan.

'What's that, John?'

'It's nothing, mate. I'll tell you another time. However, you're absolutely right. You always talk sense so, do you know of anyone wanting a damned good Dominator?'

'I'll put the word out,' Ted said sorrowfully and patted John's shoulder. 'I'll drop round tomorrow morning and then we'll talk about this a lot more—there has to be a way you can disappear as soon as possible and still be able to make a living. Don't worry yourself, we'll find a solution together.' He started his bike and with a wave of his gloved hand he rode into the dusk.

As his engine noise faded the street became silent except for the faint cawing from the rookery high above his head. John sighed and spoilt the quiet peace with the harsh roar of his own engine before riding to the nearest telephone box on the main road.

After three rings Alan answered and John told him everything he had said to Ted and the advice given which he said he intended to follow.

There was a long hissing silence before Alan spoke. 'You stupid fool, why did you have to tell that tub of lard? He'll go and blab it all over town,' he snarled in a low, menacing tone. 'Now you'll have to do something about him, too.'

John jerked his head away from the phone as if stung by a wasp that had been nesting in the instrument. 'Like hell I will, Alan. I've done your dirty work once and I'll not do it again, especially not to my best friend just because you think it would be best for you. Besides, he'll never tell on me, he said so tonight and I trust his word.'

'And like an idiot you believed him? Do I need to remind you, John, that I can very easily go to the police myself and you'll be immediately arrested for two murders. I can be very convincing when I tell tall tales. You should ask Doris, except you can't now, can you?'

John froze. He knew what Alan wanted him to do and the hand holding the bakelite instrument began to shake violently. He slammed it down and stood immobile in the brightly lit telephone box until he had calmed down a little. He then hurried home and without eating any supper or even saying a word to his parents he locked himself in his bedroom to think about his next move.

The next morning Mr Tucker called John down to breakfast as usual but when there was no answer he laboriously climbed the stairs calling all the way up. Still getting no response he pounded on the door. 'Have it your own way you lazy beggar,' he finally muttered to himself when there was still no answer and stomped downstairs to finish his own breakfast before dashing to the station for his normal commute to the City.

At 10 am John had still not made an appearance and worried that he might not be well Mrs Tucker went up the stairs and tapped lightly on his door.

'John, darling, you're terribly late for work. Are you coming down for something to eat? I've been keeping some bacon and sausages warm for you and it won't take a minute to make some toast.' There was no sound from within and she turned the handle and pushed the door open: her son's room was empty. The wardrobe was wide open revealing bare wire-frame coat hangers; most of the dressing-table drawers were half open and half empty.

Gloria Tucker instinctively knew that her son who represented nineteen years of her life had left home for good and the sudden onset of a new kind of loneliness, an emptiness that her husband was incapable of filling, made the woman feel physically ill. She threw up on the recently laid pale-blue Axminster carpet and then she began to weep silently.

3

DETECTIVE INSPECTOR WESLEY CRAMER was working late, writing a report on a burglary when in the middle of a sentence fatigue took its toll and he fell asleep, slumped across his desk. The remains of his fish-and-chip supper were in the out-tray and the upended yoghurt pot was leaking fruits of the forest which trickled across the desk and steadily dripped onto the front of his trousers.

Cramer was suddenly roused by the strident ring of the telephone and he jerked upright causing the half full carton of flat cola to topple over and soak his handwritten report.

The phone rang twice more before he was able to react. 'Yes?' he bellowed into the mouthpiece as he reached for the box of tissues.

'Cramer?' a voice inquired silkily. 'I trust that the hours you've worked tonight will not appear on any overtime sheets.'

'No, sir, just clearing up a couple of things,' Cramer replied while dabbing ineffectually at the white mess on his trousers.

The Chief Superintendent gave a satisfied grunt before continuing, 'I'm glad you're still in the office, Cramer, because I'm in my bed trying to sleep.' His voice rose in pitch: 'A bungling sergeant, yours I believe, didn't bother to check your office and tried to contact you at home and when you didn't answer the imbecile decided to report directly to me.'

The Superintendent's voice was now spitting out words like a gatling gun. 'You will now go and check on this report immediately. A young woman's body has just been found under Hastings pier—sort it out!'

'Under the pier you say, sir?'

'You have a problem with your hearing, Cramer?' The heavy sarcasm didn't go unnoticed and Cramer reluctantly agreed to investigate the matter despite having been on shift for more than twenty hours. The desk clock showed three in the morning when he hung up and redialled.

'Angstrom here, who's that calling at this God-forsaken hour?' the young woman demanded to know and Cramer was subjected to the loudest of yawns. He flinched and with a slight grin requested that Angstrom joined him at the entrance to the pier in fifteen minutes and not a minute later. There was a long shocked silence at the other end when Cramer's voice was recognised before the young detective constable replied.

'Do you know what time it is, sir?' she asked politely, flinging the blanket to one side and instantly regretting it as the draught from the partially open window chilled her nude body.

'I'm fully aware of the time, Angstrom, but do *you* know what time it is?'

'Yes, sir, time to get up and meet you at the pier,' she replied as she began dressing while holding the receiver to her ear.

'Correct! And what else?'

'Immediately, sir,' Angstrom said as she futilely attempted to fasten her bra whilst trying to clamp the handset between head and shoulder.

'I'm not that unfeeling, Angstrom, make it fourteen minutes from now. That should give you time to dress and drink some coffee to bring you up to speed.' Cramer hung up before Angstrom could reply and resting his interlaced hands on the suspicion of a growing stomach he cleared his mind for five minutes before wearily heaving himself out of the chair and leaving the police station.

All the officers in the station had fondly given Wesley Cramer the acronym WC that was used strictly behind his back. It was explained to DC Angstrom when she first arrived at the station that it didn't derive from his initials but from the simple fact that Cramer was always called upon to handle the really shit cases.

At precisely three-thirty in the morning Cramer parked between two patrol cars that were illuminating the unlit pier with blue and red light bars and met Jennifer Angstrom who had arrived two minutes before him. She was an attractive woman in her late twenties and this morning she had slipped into a dove-grey worsted suit with an elegance that never failed to turn heads in or out of the police station.

'Good morning, sir, I think we've got a bad one here,' she said by way of a greeting and then yawned to emphasise the inconvenience of the call-out. He ignored her unsubtle action and simply nodded his head in reply while secretly grinning. She fell in beside him as he strode to the steps that led down to the pebble beach.

A cheery-faced, 50-year-old man with shoulder-length grey hair was waiting at the foot of the steps. 'Ah, Cramer, I thought they'd get you out of bed for this one,' he said with a light laugh as he removed a monocle and began polishing it with his handkerchief. 'Mind you, I'm surprised they were able to wake you.'

'For your information, Patrick, I was still working in the office, unlike some lazy sods who always get a good night's sleep,' Cramer said grumpily as he stared down pointedly at the carpet slippers the police medical examiner was absentmindedly still wearing.

'Okay, Wesley, point taken,' Patrick Warren said, still grinning broadly as he walked towards the distant arc lights that had been set up under the pier. 'Now can we get on and get this done with quickly so that I can get back to my cosy bed?' Cramer made a rude gesture and followed with a grinning Angstrom trailing close behind.

There were six officers evenly spaced in a ring around the centre of the pool of light and as the newcomers approached they could see the crumpled figure at the foot of one of the steel supports.

'Looks like a sex crime, sir,' Angstrom murmured as they stopped to look down at the dead girl. 'Her blouse is undone and it looks like someone has interfered with her underclothing.'

'Rape?' Cramer asked as Warren knelt beside the body and began his initial examination. 'Or simply a curious pervert who found the body?' He cast his eyes over the brightly lit area. 'She may also have been here by herself, slipped on the pebbles and struck her head.'

'All are strong possibilities and I can't tell which is which until I get her back to the mortuary,' Warren said while pinching the waxen features and roughly estimating the girl's time of death in his head. 'However, not many people are capable of hitting their head twice when falling against something hard. I think she was a young girl, out for some fun on a Friday night with a bloke and finally bit off more than she could chew,' he added sadly.

'If it's murder after a rape it's a pity she didn't bite it off before it could be used,' Angstrom muttered heatedly as she took notes and then began exploring the crime scene with a small pocket torch.

'Blood and bits of skin here, Patrick,' Cramer said as he directed his torch at a dark stain on the support.

The medical examiner stood to take a closer look and nodded slowly. 'That could have been the point of first impact. There are indentations in the skull that roughly match the profile of the steel support and the crustaceans. I'll get the forensic chaps to take samples and a cast so that I can do a proper comparison back at the morgue.'

'Would you check if the officers were able to find any witnesses in the vicinity who may have seen what had happened?' Cramer said to Angstrom and she nodded and began walking around the crime scene perimeter, talking to each of the officers in turn.

She returned after a short time. 'Nothing, sir. Someone had anonymously phoned in to report the dead girl and the first officer on the scene found that the couples who normally gather here after the pubs have closed had all vanished.'

'There appears to be some disturbances of the pebbles that haven't been caused by the tide. This could mean that she wasn't alone when she hit the support. The girl must have been drinking somewhere with somebody before coming down here.'

'Which means there's a barman somewhere on the seafront who may remember seeing her last night,' Angstrom added.

'Looks like you have to organise a very tedious pub crawl tomorrow, Angstrom,' Cramer said as he fought to stifle a yawn.

'You mean I have to organise a pub crawl *today*, sir,' Angstrom corrected carelessly while pointing to her wristwatch and instantly bit her tongue when she got a sharp look from her sleep-deprived boss.

'I'll leave it up to you, Patrick, to finalise this end and arrange for the body to be taken away. Jennifer, you can brief the constables on keeping this area closed to the public, fingerprinting the stanchions and arranging relief shifts until the forensic boys are finished and have left the scene. You can then arrange for headshots to be printed to help with the identification in the bars. I'm off to get some sleep in a place more comfortable than my office.' Cramer nodded curtly to them both and strode off with his shoes sinking noisily into the pebbles that were arranged in regular tidal ridges.

After the arrival of the forensic team and having briefed the small group of police officers Angstrom took her leave from the medical examiner and drove back to the office. She had resigned herself to losing all hope of sleep and decided to start working on the case immediately.

Feeling a little more refreshed after three hours in his own bed Cramer arrived at the station to find Angstrom at her desk with her head resting on her folded arms. She had fallen asleep and none of the other officers had bothered to wake her. He tapped the leg of her desk with his shoe until she stirred and then when she lifted her eyes and stared blearily around her he beckoned her to follow him.

'Did you have a pleasant night?'

The tired woman stared at Cramer's back with her full lips tightly pressed together before replying. 'I spent the early hours doing precisely what you ordered, sir.'

Cramer turned his head and couldn't help but laugh at her expression. 'Sorry, Jennifer, I didn't mean to offend you,' he said as he entered his office and went to his desk. 'The photographs?' he asked in a more kindly tone when she closed the door behind her. 'Have they arrived yet?'

Angstrom looked puzzled at first and then recalled his instructions at the crime scene. 'I'll check with Patrick Warren immediately, sir,' she said and started to move towards the door.

'Wait, did you manage to get round to compiling a list of pubs and clubs in the vicinity of the pier. Places that the girl could have visited?'

'Yes, sir,' she said sharply, slightly peeved that he should doubt her thoroughness and placed a folder on his blotter. 'Twenty-five at the last count.'

'Then we can start as soon as the photographs arrive, can't we Jennifer?' Cramer tilted his head to one side and looked up at her with a quizzical expression. 'I saw that you'd managed to get some sleep so you should be up to it.'

Angstrom's cheeks began to glow. 'Right away, sir,' she said and hurried from the room. When she reached her desk she saw a lidded box with her name scrawled across the top in large felt-tip capital letters. Angstrom recognised Patrick Warren's terrible handwriting and silently thanked him for remembering her so early in the day. Removing the lid confirmed that he had sent her a tidy stack of headshots. The shots were good enough to help them check the girl's identity and her movements on the fateful night.

'Good, let's go!' a voice whispered close to her left ear and she jumped, startled by the sudden appearance of her boss. 'Distribute those to the team and we'll take a couple and go back to the pier and start asking questions of our own.'

They stepped out into a light drizzle and Cramer drove them to the pier in his own car, wipers slapping rhythmically on the windscreen. Once at the scene they began by stopping young people outside the main entrance and showing them the picture of the unknown girl. They asked the same question over and over again: 'Did you see this girl last night between the hours of eight and midnight?'

Later that morning when the rain stopped and the gulls rose on the light breeze with teeth-setting screeches Angstrom's new court shoes started to pinch. As she walked gingerly along the promenade she saw a stocky rocker in a heavily studded leather jacket kissing a tall, slender girl. They were in the bus shelter that stood outside the entrance to the pier.

Out of curiosity the couple had occasionally come up for air to peep out at the officers questioning passersby before losing interest and resuming their necking. Angstrom had noticed the couple earlier but politely left them alone until she saw them walking arm in arm towards the collection of bikes that were parked nearby. She hurried with feet throbbing to intercept them. After presenting her identification she showed them the post mortem photograph of Doris and asked if they had seen the girl.

The long-haired rocker shook his head, impatient to get his girlfriend to a more private location but the girl held the picture longer, shocked by the mask-like image until she began nodding very slowly, her tower of back-combed hair swaying back and forth.

'Yeah, I seen 'er with a bloke, a ton-up I think, at about nine thirty,' she said with a distinct Essex accent.

'Where was that, where did you see them?' Angstrom probed.

'Right 'ere, outside the pier. They was sitting on a bike snogging like there's no tomorrow.'

'S'right, Elsie,' her boyfriend suddenly exclaimed as he snatched the picture from his girl's hand and looked at it closely with eyes squinting in concentration. 'It was a 650 Bonni TR7 with a duplex frame,' he added.

'Trust you to spot the bloody bike first, Andy,' the girl said nudging him in the side with her elbow.

'And what's a Bonni?' Angstrom asked patiently.

'Triumph Bonneville, darling,' the girl said smugly. 'Every girl should know what a Bonni is,' and then added proudly, 'my Andy's got a Matchless G45.' She would have rattled off the entire list of G45 features, with the usual technical corrections from her boyfriend, if Angstrom hadn't interrupted their double-act.

'This was at nine-thirty? Did you see them again? Did they ride off in that direction, towards the pub?' She pointed along the seafront towards the Red Lion which was only four hundred yards distant.

'Naw, not that way, Andy and I were pretty busy but I think I saw 'em again under the pier. They was 'eading down the beach towards the sea,' the girl said with her arm stretched out and pointing towards the grey, uninviting waters that hissed over the pebbles.

'Did you note the registration of the Bonni?'

'No way, I was too busy keeping Andy's 'ands off my tits.'

The rocker laughed and snaked his arm around her waist. 'It was something like HT and there was a 2,' he said as his girl, now giggling, tried to pull away the hand that had started moving upwards.

'Could you identify the man again if you saw him?'

The couple shrugged their shoulders. 'The bloke was facing away from us all the time . . . we only saw the girl's face,' the girl said. 'I did get a quick look at the geezer when they passed under that light,' the young man said and pointed to the Victorian lamp-post by the steps that descended to the beach.

Angstrom took the couple's names and addresses and noted where they were staying in Hastings before thanking them. With heels starting to blister painfully she started looking round for Cramer. Ten minutes later she found him standing in the strong wind that whipped across the extreme end of the pier. He was questioning an elderly couple who kept insisting that they had seen the girl standing on the promenade at seven o'clock that very morning.

'She was with a man who was old enough to be her grandfather,' the elderly woman affirmed as she clutched the straw hat to her head in a manner that defied the wind. 'I don't know what the country's coming to, I really don't.'

As Angstrom approached she caught Cramer's eye and held up her notebook to indicate success. He politely stopped the pensioner's tirade and thanked them both profusely before hurrying to receive her latest report.

'This unknown man must have been the last person to see her alive,' she concluded but as Cramer didn't respond immediately she continued, 'Although the lad was more interested in his girlfriend he believes he might be able to recognise the man if he saw him again. He also said he was sure that he was a ton-up and not a rocker because he had no studs or ID on his jacket. He also said that the Bonni . . . the bike, sir, was stripped down for speed and had a race fairing.'

Cramer nodded. 'Good, that'll be very helpful later in identifying the bike,' he said as they ducked out of the wind and into the glass-panelled shelter where a middle-aged couple had been cuddling up close to escape from the cold wind. Angstrom gave an apologetic shrug for their intrusion as Cramer, unaware that he had spoilt a moment of intimacy, continued: 'In the meantime, the forensic report has just been delivered to me by hand. They believe that the victim could have been accompanied by two other people. Possibly men, judging by the size and depth of the boot imprints in the pebbles. Blood had also been smeared on the rocks which means that one or more people had walked around her after she had been killed.'

Angstrom waited for her boss to go on but he simply sank into a meditative silence while he lit a cigarette, shielding his lighter from the wind with cupped hands. The couple, romance forgotten and completely fascinated by the conversation, moved even closer together as they eavesdropped on the two officers.

'Anything from the medical examiner?' she asked.

'Yes, his report was included and it states that the girl hadn't been raped. There was no sign of violence, no bruising on the lower parts of the torso or anywhere else for that matter. In fact, the girl was still a virgin.' He fell silent again and drew deeply on his cigarette. Tendrils of blue smoke issued from the corners of his mouth and rose to be whipped away by the wind into a sky that was getting lighter as the clouds began dispersing.

'She was a young fool to go under a pier in the dead of night. No matter who she was with and how safe she thought the man or men to be,' Angstrom muttered angrily. 'One thing's for sure.'

Cramer looked at her, raising a questioning eyebrow.

'If she hadn't died she would undoubtedly have lost her virginity.' He nodded and stepped out of the shelter and back into the stiff wind. Angstrom turned the collar of her jacket up and followed him.

The couple gaped as they watched the two officers walk away and began whispering urgently to each other about what they had overheard. All thoughts of romance had long evaporated.

Cramer and Angstrom drove back to the police station as quickly as possible. Fresh news awaited both detectives in the operations room. A telephone message from the forensic department stated that the girl had been identified from her dental records as Doris Trencher and that she lived quite close to the village of Lamberhurst. The returning team of officers had also taken statements from three other couples who had seen the same couple kissing while sitting on a motorcycle by the pier. There had been no sightings of Doris in any of the public houses or nightclubs.

'We'll now go to Lamberhurst and give the parents the bad news before the next editions hit the street,' Cramer told Angstrom. The inspector drove his '56 Rover with the care that only a man who has bonded with his car can. They reached the pre-war semi-detached house in thirty minutes and Cramer turned into the brick-paved drive of No. 43. Low box-tree hedges lined a path that curved round the front lawn to a porch with multi-coloured leaded windows. A stout, motherly type with her black hair still in large red rollers answered the door.

'Sorry, whatever it is, I'm not buying it,' she said in a husky voice.

Cramer introduced himself by showing his warrant card and the woman's face paled. 'It's my Doris, isn't it? I knew something was wrong when she didn't call to say she was stopping out all night—she always did call, y'know.'

'Why didn't you report her missing?' Angstrom asked gently.

'Don't get me wrong. It was quite normal for 'er to be out cos she's always staying over at 'er girlfriends' homes.'

Angstrom took the woman lightly by the elbow and guided her back inside the house and into the living room where she sat her down before nodding to Cramer.

Cramer unzipped his document case and took out the photograph. 'Is this a photograph of your daughter, Mrs Trencher?' he asked softly, holding up the picture.

'Oh my God, yes. Why are her eyes closed? What's wrong with 'er?' she asked fearfully.

'There has been a terrible accident and your daughter has been killed, Mrs Trencher,' Cramer said in a low voice. The woman looked at him in disbelief before bowing her head and beginning to weep.

'We do not know the full circumstances of the accident and we'll let you know the details as soon as they become available. In the meantime we will require you or your husband to come to Hastings to make a formal identification. We'll contact you when and where this will take place before the end of the day,' Cramer said, hating every second spent in the company of the distressed mother. He had done this far too often during his career and he was getting tired of being the bearer of the worst possible news to parents—no mother, or father, could ever accept the fact that their children had died before them.

'My husband died three years ago,' the distraught mother sobbed. 'Now there's only me and 'erbert.'

'Herbert?' Angstrom asked as she took and held the woman's hand, rough-skinned from doing housework without the protection of gloves.

'Doris's cat.'

Cramer looked around the room but couldn't see any feline presence in the room. A number of photographs stood on the mantelpiece along with a couple of badly chipped porcelain figurines.

'He'll really miss 'er,' Mrs Trencher said as though in a daze.

'Do you know where your daughter went last night?' Cramer asked and then waited until the fresh bout of sobbing had ended. 'Is there somewhere she normally goes to on Friday nights?'

'She quite often goes to the roadside café on the A21 with her friends. It's just past Lamberhurst. Sorry, I don't know its name.'

'Who are her friends?' Angstrom asked.

'I only know them as Toni and Louise. I think there is a Penny too but I don't know their other names.' The middle-aged woman turned to gaze out of the window with red-rimmed eyes. Angstrom opened her notebook and was about to ask her some further questions when Cramer placed a hand lightly upon her arm and shook his head before standing up.

'Is there anyone we can contact who can come round to be with you?' the inspector asked.

'No, thank you, I'd rather be alone right now.'

Cramer offered his condolences again before quietly thanking Mrs Trencher for her time. The two officers then saw themselves out of the house and began driving back towards Hastings. They had only driven a couple of miles before Angstrom broke the melancholic silence between them.

'Just past Lamberhurst, Mrs Trencher said.' She gazed out at the dense woodland lining the road and then suddenly pointed through the windscreen at a small building set back from the highway up ahead. 'There! The one with the broken sign reading 'lice'. That looks like the sort of place bikers would stop at on their way to the coast.'

Cramer pulled off the main road and onto the forecourt where four immaculate café racers were ranked—all leaning at precisely the same angle like a dress parade of drunken soldiers.

The officers entered the smoky room to be hit by a wall of sound. The Dave Clark Five were telling the world at full volume that they were rather 'glad' about something. The chromed metal and Bakelite fittings of the Wurlitzer vibrated and buzzed to every bass note as the officers made their way to the high counter where a large middle-aged woman was putting clean cups on top of the steaming espresso machine.

Auntie Alice held up a cup and smiled broadly, expecting a request for coffees until Cramer showed his warrant card and then her face became dour and unwelcoming. 'What do you want, I don't want any trouble,' she mumbled putting the cup back.

'This is Doris Trencher. Has she ever been in your place?' Cramer asked as Angstrom passed the photograph to the woman. She took it reluctantly and glanced down at it briefly before handing it back again.

'No, don't think she was. If it was last Friday it would have been my busiest night and a full house,' she said handing the photograph back without giving it a second glance. 'I don't make it a habit of knowing every one of my customers, y'know.'

As Cramer looked into the woman's eyes she looked away and began wiping the counter with a damp cloth and the inspector knew she was lying.

'Madam, this isn't a photograph of the poor girl sleeping. She's dead. She was killed late last night in Hastings and I want to interview all the people who saw her last.' Cramer was irritated by the woman's obvious objection to their presence in her café.

Alice's head came up with an expression of shock and she held out her hand. 'You should have said she had been killed,' she said. 'Let me have another look at the unfortunate darling.'

Angstrom passed her the photograph and she immediately handed it back again. 'That's Doris,' she declared. 'Poor thing, she was in here every Friday looking for a ride. Y'know, a bit of a thrill on one of the boys' bikes. All the girls who come in here want to do it.'

'Did you see her leave with anyone yesterday?' Angstrom asked, indicating that she would like a coffee. Cramer frowned at her break in procedure but then shrugged and also raised a finger. Alice immediately began pulling on the large levers, cranking up the huge Gaggia which made conversation impossible for a few moments. Eventually the cacophony of sound began fading and she could be heard.

'She were here, with her friends,' she said, passing the officers their cups and taking the coins from Angstrom. 'Some nice young lads, ton-ups, not the rowdy rockers who only want a good punch-up to make a good night out. Doris and her friends were chatting to three lads, ton-ups by the look of them, at that table in the corner.' Alice pointed to where two leather-clad youngsters were waving their hands excitedly in the air to show off their latest high-speed manoeuvres, not unlike Battle of Britain pilots after a successful dogfight.

'I only recognised one of them. A taller chap called Alan who seemed to be a bit of a macho type. Can't say I ever knew his last name.'

'Williams,' a voice said and Angstrom turned to find one of the leathered youngsters standing behind her, holding up an empty cup for Alice. 'Another please, Aunty,' he requested jauntily and then looked at Angstrom with an infectious smile on his badly pimpled face. 'He's called Alan Williams, and Alice is right because he's a right randy sod. Never fails to pick up a bit of skirt on a Friday night. Then he always boasts that he has it away when he gets his bit of totty down to Hastings.'

'I assume by that you mean he has sex with every girl he gives a ride to?' Cramer asked casually, trying to clarify the point and the motorcyclist grinned and nodded his head. 'That's what I said, guv.'

'And where does he normally "have it away"?'

'Always under the pier. He gets into their pants with promises of a slap-up dinner and as many Babychams as they can drink and then once he's finished with them he sends them on their way.'

'You mean they have to find their own way home?' Angstrom said with disbelief written across her face.

'No, he'll drop them off at the bus station, give them the fare to Lamberhurst and then he'll say his thanks and leave 'em.' He took the steaming cup of coffee from Alice and wandered back to his mate.

'Didn't word get around amongst the girls that he was a bit of a creep?' Angstrom called after him.

'Yeah! But none of the girls really cared that much. They'd do anything to get on his bike cos he always rides flat-out which was a bigger thrill than what his old man could do,' he said with an expressive wink as he put his cup down and made a gesture to his friend that made them both burst into coarse laughter.

'By old man you mean his . . .'

'Where does this Alan Williams live?' Cramer interrupted and was replied with a casual shrug of the shoulders.

'I'll call Central and get the address. He must live fairly close to this place,' Angstrom murmured and she left to use the official police radio that Cramer had bent the rules to have installed in his own car.

The response was almost immediate and in thirty minutes they were parked outside a shabby-looking terraced house on a council estate near Tonbridge. Cramer pushed the wooden gate open and on their way to the front door they passed a rusting baby carriage and a heap of rubble in the middle of what passed for a small front garden.

The door opened as they stepped beneath the porch and they were confronted by a tall young man in his early twenties with long black hair that had been pulled back into a pony tail. His tight jeans were stained with motor oil as were his suede Cuban-heeled boots.

Angstrom couldn't help notice his perfectly symmetrical features but was instantly put off by the flinty cold light in his dark brown eyes.

'How can I help you?' Alan asked calmly without the hint of a welcome in his voice as he passed a critical eye over the physical qualities of the woman before him. He disregarded the middle-aged man in his tweed jacket and maroon waistcoat. The latter was stretched tightly over an obvious waistline, giving him the appearance of being either a kindly uncle or the youngish father of the woman.

'Detective Inspector Cramer and this is Detective Constable Angstrom.' The mandatory warrant card was held up and then swiftly pocketed. 'Are you Mr Alan Williams?'

Alan's eyes had narrowed slightly and he felt a light fluttering in his chest but stilled the rising panic before it started. 'That's right,' he replied, keeping as calm as possible. 'I'm Williams, how can I help you?'

'We'd like to ask you some questions regarding your movements last night. May we come in?' Cramer asked as he studied the body language of the young man through the eyes of an experienced police officer.

Alan stood to one side to permit both officers to enter before leading them into the front room. He nonchalantly threw himself onto a tired-looking settee and waited until Cramer and Angstrom were seated opposite him before he bothered to speak.

'Shoot, what do you want to know?'

'Did you meet up with a young girl called Doris Trencher in the A21 café called Alice's and then leave with her?' Angstrom asked with her pencil poised over the opened notebook.

'Yeah. Cool-looking bird. I gave her just what she wanted. An exciting ride to Hastings.' Alan drew his long legs up onto the settee and leant back against his arm.

'What time did you arrive?' Cramer asked, his eyes never moving from the young man's face.

'Can't really say but I think it was around nine thirty.'

'On your arrival at Hastings did you park your bike at the entrance to the pier and spend some time with Miss Trencher,' Angstrom asked.

'Kissing? Yeah, she was a fabulous snog,' Alan completed and he laughed while blatantly looking across the room at Angstrom's bared knees.

Cramer was tiring of the young man's smart responses and the way he eyed his junior officer and he suddenly spoke harshly. 'And did you take her under the pier and while there smash her head against a steel support?'

'Bloody hell, no!' Alan said, registering such genuine surprise at the suggestion that Cramer could only surmise that it was a truthful response.

'Be that as it may, did you go under the pier with her at any time during the evening?'

Alan realised he may have been seen and he admitted that he had gone down to the beach for a bit more snogging. He then deviated from the truth to say that they had bumped into a rocker who knew Doris. It appeared that she was extremely fond of the guy, someone she had gone to school with and this had resulted in a minor punch-up before the stranger had left taking the girl with him. The last time he had seen Doris she was walking into the dark shadows beneath the pier with the rocker's arm tightly wound around her waist.

'Good riddance, too,' Alan concluded waving a limp-wristed hand airily above his head. 'She didn't have that much up top and was more trouble than she was worth.'

Angstrom stared hard at the youth until he dropped his eyes. 'Can you give me a description of this rocker?' she demanded angrily as she turned to a new page in her notebook.

'Sorry, darling, but it was a bit dark. All I know is that he was a big beggar with hundreds of studs on his jacket that hurt like hell when I tried to hit him. However, after winding me with a sneaky punch they left me and moved down the beach in the direction of the sea—if that helps at all.'

'Detective Constable Angstrom is not your darling, Mr Williams, and I would advise you to show a little more respect. The girl you profess you couldn't care less about was killed either late Friday night or early Saturday morning and we are treating her death as highly suspicious.' Cramer held the photograph up in front of Alan's face.

The news that the police were classifying the death as murder came as a mild shock to Alan but despite this he remained outwardly calm and was able to present an expression of grave concern. 'That's awful, Inspector. I wish I could give you a better description of the man.'

'Would you please show me your hands, Mr Williams,' Angstrom said in a tone that would brook no argument.

Alan shrugged and then held them out for the officer to inspect. After carefully studying every inch of both hands Angstrom nodded, indicating that she was finished and Alan reached across the coffee table and picked up a booklet. Cramer immediately recognised the crest of the Metropolitan Police on the front cover.

'I should have seen a lot more because right now I'm trying to train myself to be more observant,' Alan said in a slightly apologetic tone. 'It's my dream to be a member of the Met as a motorcycle policeman,' he explained as he passed the booklet to Angstrom. 'I'm an excellent rider on 650 cc bikes and I have already sent in my application form.'

This rehearsed moment of enthusiasm distracted Cramer from his original line of questioning and he gave a half-smile of encouragement.

'We're always looking for top-class riders who take care when riding on the roads, Mr Williams. Remember, speed isn't everything. I wish you the best of luck with your application.' He rose to his feet. 'Thank you for your help and if you should remember anything please call me on this number.' Cramer handed the smug young man his card. 'However, should I catch you exceeding the speed limit I can assure you the only part of a police station you'll ever see will be the inside of a cell.'

Alan's smile disappeared but as he stood up Angstrom caught a momentary expression of triumph on the ton-up's face. She followed both men with her brow furrowed in puzzlement: why did Cramer decide to terminate the qustioning? Later, while they drove back to Hastings she raised her concern about the truth of the statement given by Alan Williams but Cramer shook his head.

'I'm sure he didn't kill the girl but I could see he had lied about hitting a brass-studded jacket. His knuckles were completely unharmed but whether he was involved in the actual death of Doris is another story. I have a feeling we have to look elsewhere for her actual killer or killers without losing sight of our smug Mr Williams.'

'I agree, his attitude told me that he had a lot to hide,' Angstrom nodded slowly. 'I don't know why it is but I am getting a bad feeling that this could end up as a cold case.'

They finished the rest of the journey in a deep, thoughtful silence.

4

AIDAN JONES LIT THE FIRE and climbed back into the bowtop to wake the womenfolk. It was 6 am and the songbirds in the hawthorn hedgerows were already in full voice as the first light of dawn spread across the clear sky. Aidan lightly rapped work-hardened knuckles on the decorative glass panel that separated the living section of the caravan from the raised double bed.

'Are you going to stay in there all day, woman?'

'I'll come out when I can smell the coffee,' Gwen replied, her sleepy voice muffled by the thick duvet.

Aidan grinned and turned his attention to the single bunk which he had earlier discovered was empty and he shook his head at his daughter's wayward behaviour.

'Looks like your daughter is tickling trout again,' he said loudly.

The frosted glass panel opened and his wife swung her bare legs over the edge of the bed and dropped lightly to the floor beside him. The unbrushed tangle of raven hair hung down to her waist and he instinctively swept his eyes over a voluptuous full figure that couldn't be concealed by the crumpled nightshirt.

'She's your daughter too, Aidan, so don't blame me for the delicious breakfasts you've been having since we camped beside this river.'

The big man grunted and slapped her shapely behind playfully. 'I have to admit she does know how to satisfy a man's hunger.'

'As long as it's just a man's stomach we're talking about.'

'C'mon woman, we're a long way from any village which means we're a long way from any form of masculine temptation.'

'It's the gamekeepers I'm worried about,' Gwen said as she started to dress for the day. 'They patrol rivers as well as the woods and if they catch her they may not treat her too kindly.'

'If you're that worried, Gwen, I'll take a walk down to the river and bring her back with fish or no fish.' Aidan gave his wife a reassuring hug and a kiss before he jumped down from the caravan and started to walk across the fields to where the river wound its way through the Welsh hills.

A gentle whinney in the shrubs drew his attention and he quickly detoured to where his horse was tethered with a number of others. He ran his hand over the gentle creature's flank and along to the powerful shoulders, feeling his much-loved Welsh cob shiver with pleasure at his touch.

'Morning, Eirwyn,' he murmured as he fondled the horse's ears. He had chosen the name, white as snow, when it was a little foal and despite the development of the traditional dark patches the name had stayed.

'I'm just off to find your little mistress and I'll tend to you when I get back,' Aidan murmured as he gave the beautiful cob a final pat and set off across the meadow.

He waved to the early risers of the other caravans that were placed in a large circle. They returned his greeting and went back to the task of starting their cooking fires.

Aidan strode faster with the long, dew-drenched grass caressing his ankles and calves. When he reached the lower hedge a number of creatures rustled in the thick foliage and a pair of startled blackbirds burst from the hedge with loud calls. He climbed over the primitive stile and hurried down to the last barrier between him and the river.

The water level had risen dramatically since the teenager had last lain down on the river bank. Violent rainstorms over the Beacons during the night had turned a quiet pastoral river into a raging torrent winding its way down to the sea. She had chosen her usual eddying pool since it always escapes the turbulence of the main torrent. Her breakfast, the delicious brown trout, used it to rest in their battle to travel upriver to spawn. She had been very successful for two consecutive mornings and was on the point of making it a hat trick.

Llinos had been named for the linnet bird by her father after her mother had remarked on the baby's melodious crying. 'She's just like a beautiful little linnet,' she had exclaimed to the admiring Romani midwife and other wives gathered about her bed in the caravan. However, after six months of sleepless nights Aidan was inclined to wish he hadn't been so hasty in his choice.

The 'beautiful little linnet' lay perfectly still with her bared arm submerged in the gently spriralling pool of icy water. Her long, tapering fingers had long turned deathly white and were beginning to feel numb but she persevered. The sleek, dark green body with dark speckling on its back and fins was hovering over her hand with its pectoral fins beating slowly to stay motionless in the light swirling current between the rocks.

Llinos very gently bent her fingers upward until it was within a fraction of an inch from the fish's underside. Its amber-ringed dark eyes flicked warily in all directions. She paused and waited until the eyes stopped moving and then, with breath tightly held, she slowly stroked the glassy surface of the creature from the tail towards the head. A tremor ran the length of the fish but unlike the last two trout it didn't suddenly beat its rear caudal fin and vanish. This particular beauty remained stationary and continued to permit Llinos to repeatedly stroke it lightly. The 18-year-old began to salivate mentally, knowing that they would be eating a hearty breakfast once more and without interrupting the rhythm of her finger she prepared herself to be ready for when the trout had fallen into a trance-like state.

Suddenly, without warning, the waterlogged bank collapsed and plunged Llinos into the river. The trout flickered and was gone as the water closed over her head and she struggled unsuccessfully to reach the surface. In her panic she had moved out into the fast-flowing current and her lungs began to feel as though they were on fire. She pinched her lips together to prevent any involuntary inhalation. As her body tumbled about in the depths there was a moment when she was forced upward and her head briefly broke the surface. She screamed before snatching a quick breath and then she was swirled around and back under the water.

Llinos spread her arms and legs to slow her tumble and once more she was able to get her head above the water and shout again. With rapid kicks of her strong legs she remained there, treading water and gasping for air between shouts for help. The river banks seemed to fly past as she was carried on the storm-fed river that had begun high in the wilds of Brecon Beacons.

It was only time before the river would become shallower, the water rougher and Llinos knew she would be battered to death on the rocks and boulders that littered the river bed. Suddenly, as she was turned around to face the east bank she glimpsed a figure racing along the bank. He was level with her when the current spun her around again and she lost sight of him. She choked as churning water filled her mouth and left her spluttering and gasping for air.

Aidan reached the river and began searching along the bank for his daughter. His decision to travel upstream was arbitrary and after a quarter of a mile of fruitless plodding through nettles and bindweed he gave up and began searching downstream. Barely one hundred yards past the original start of his search he heard a light squeal and a heavy splash above the roaring sound of the raging water. His heart gave a lurch when he heard a girl's voice screaming for help and he broke into a run and was just in time to see a small dark shape being rapidly carried away.

Terrified, he raced to catch up with his daughter but almost immediately encountered a barbed-wire fence that crossed his path and went down into the water itself. He frantically pulled the wires apart with his bare hands and blood began to stream from his palms. The barbs caught at his heavy sweater and it took precious seconds to free himself before he could resume the chase.

Two hundred yards further down the river bank Aidan was faced with a bigger obstacle. The man in the tweed suit couldn't have been much taller than five foot six inches but it was the 12-bore Purdey shotgun that stopped Aidan. The gun was being aimed at the traveller's head in no uncertain manner.

'Out for our morning constitution are we?' the gamekeeper asked sarcastically. 'Caught anything nice on your little walk?'

'My daughter, she's fallen in the river,' Aidan managed to gasp as he struggled to catch his breath. 'I must try to catch her.'

'Ah, you want to catch your daughter do you? Is she the one with a little white belly, spots all over her back and tastes nice with a little squeeze of lemon?' The man chuckled to himself and it was the last thing he heard for Aidan grabbed the barrel of the shotgun, twisted it out of his grasp and smacked the solid butt into his forehead.

Instantly rendered insensible the gamekeeper fell like a sack of potatoes and Aidan jumped over the man and resumed running. His eyes scoured the river as he raced through the prickly undergrowth, oblivious to the searing pain. Within seconds he saw a figure running along on the opposite bank. It was a young man with a ducktail hairstyle and wearing jeans and a black leather jacket. As he sprinted he began tearing off his jacket and it was at this point that Aidan again spotted a dark shape being carried along in the torrent—it was Llinos. He lengthened his stride, gasping for each tortured breath, and tried to catch up with his daughter.

The young man had gone beyond the helpless girl and as the river bent sharply to the right he launched himself into the air and disappeared beneath the foaming water. Without missing a stride Aidan kept staring at the water, holding his own breath in sympathy until the young man's head broke the surface close to Llinos. In three strokes he was beside her and he grabbed hold of her blouse and began towing her across the vicious current towards the opposite bank. The curving river helped to drive them into the reeds lining the bank and the young man grabbed the slender branch of a willow that was hanging in the water.

Aidan let out a sigh of relief when he saw that the man had saved Llinos. Gasping for breath he scrambled down the shallow bank to reach the couple who were holding on to a willow branch. He grasped Llinos's outstretched hand and gripping it tightly pulled her to safety. The powerful current was still trying to take the young man and he used his freed hand to get an extra grip on the branch. He looked up and saw that the man was wrapping the girl in his warm jacket. Even though she was in a state of shock and freezing she shouted something into her father's ear. Aidan turned immediately and began climbing down the bank; there was a sharp *crack* and the thin branch snapped off at the trunk. The exhausted young man was swiftly carried away.

Aidan and Llinos watched helplessly as he was whisked downriver, spinning around in the turbulent waters until his pale face disappeared from sight.

'We must do something, Da! He saved my life,' Llinos cried as Aidan climbed back up the bank and hugged his trembling daughter tightly to him.

'We first need to get you dry and into some warm clothes before you die from exposure, my girl,' he said and with his arm about her shoulders he began leading her back upstream.

'We can't just leave him,' Llinos exclaimed, roughly pulling away from Aidan and looking back at the raging river. 'He'll soon be in the shallows and—'

'And there's nothing we can do about it now,' Aidan interrupted. Once more he began walking back to the campsite and the girl reluctantly surrendered to the encircling protection of his arm.

They had hardly walked twenty steps when father and daughter were confronted by the outraged gamekeeper stumbling towards them. He had a trickle of blood running down the side of his face and was pointing the Purdey at Aidan, his finger on the trigger.

'Aidan!' There was a loud cry followed by other shouts as a group of men ran towards the trio. 'Aidan, are you all right?'

It was Owen who had the caravan next to their own and the man's round, cherubic features were a brighter pink than normal and he was sweating profusely. The gamekeeper swung round to face the new threat that was fast approaching.

'Stay back or I'll fire!' he shouted.

The group of travellers stopped and Owen raised a hand to the gamekeeper. 'I don't know what *you* think you're going to do with that popgun but I'll tell you what I will do with it if you don't stop pointing the bloody thing at me.'

The gamekeeper looked at the group of scowling faces and slowly lowered the barrels.

'Now what's the problem, Aidan?' Owen asked as he walked past the gamekeeper, ignoring him completely. 'We heard shouting and came as fast as we could.'

'Llinos fell into the river but luckily she was able to get to the bank just back there,' Aidan said with a jerk of his thumb over his shoulder.

'I was saved by a stranger but he was swept away when the branch broke,' Llinos interrupted. 'We must try to save him before he reaches the shallows.'

Three of the burly travellers behind Owen nodded vigorously and sprinted past the confused gamekeeper to follow the course of the river.

'They'll never get to him before he's cut to pieces by the rocks,' he smirked and Owen's piledriver of a fist broke his nose. He fell for the second time that day to join his Purdey in the long wet grass.

'I need to get Llinos dry as soon as possible,' Aidan said and Owen swiftly agreed; the bedraggled figure leaning against Aidan was showing her exhaustion.

'I'm still puffed out so you carry her on your back for a while until I get some wind and then I'll take over,' Owen instructed and he set off in the direction of the travellers' camp.

'On my back girl,' Aidan commanded and Llinos wrapped her arms around her father's chest as he grabbed her legs behind the knees and began trotting after Owen.

The stunned gamekeeper slowly recovered and sat up all alone in dawn's light wondering if it hadn't all been a dream. The pain in his nose reminded him that he hadn't been dreaming and he picked up the shotgun and set off in the direction of the village and the police station.

John had parked the Norton in a supermarket carpark and with a small camping pack on his back he had started walking into the foothills of the Brecon Beacons. His last lingering look back at his treasured bike had been blurred by tears for he knew he could no longer exist as John Tucker. Worse than that, he knew he could never return to the loving care of his mother and the rock-steady support of his father.

He had emptied his savings account in his local Halifax building society before taking the road to Wales. Still deep in shock he had travelled in that particular direction on instinct, not really knowing or caring where he went. John calculated that he could live rough, away from all habitation, for a number of months before being forced to seek casual work on farms.

After making a number of detours on bridal paths to avoid the main road his four-mile hike from Merthyr Tydfil to the Llwyn-on Reservoir had been doubled. It took him two and a half hours before he saw the silvery sheet of water that reflected the dull red sun sinking behind sheep-littered hills. John decided to camp in the thick woods two miles further upstream to avoid the heavy mist that would inevitably gather over the reservoir in the morning.

In his schooldays John had joined the scouts and had been taught a number of woodcrafts and could make fire in a number of ways. All were laborious and he made sure he would always keep warm by packing boxes of matches and wrapping them carefully to keep them dry. After erecting the ex-surplus US army pup tent in a dense thicket and spreading the groundsheet he began searching for dry wood and soon had a pleasant fire.

That night was the loneliest he had ever experienced. The realisation that he was no longer being sheltered by the security of the only home he had ever known and that his parents' comforting presence was lacking kept him awake. His self-pity was now being replaced by a deep concern for his parents who he knew would be worried sick. John tossed and turned in the sleeping bag until he decided he had to take a walk to clear his mind, and to attempt to forget the last few days.

After briefly warming his hands over the dying embers he walked through the trees, their canopies obscuring the clear starlit sky, until he heard a faint rushing sound. He walked in the direction of the noise and it grew in volume until he suddenly reached the bank of a river.

He sat down and watched the raging currents and the trapped leaves spiralling in the eddies until the mesmeric movements and sounds slowly forced his eyelids to droop. He leant back and as his eyes closed fully he slumped down onto the grassy bank and fell into a deep sleep.

John awoke to the bell-like sound of birds singing close by, their morning calls audible over the constant rush of the river. He blinked, sat up and shivered for he was covered from head to foot in early-morning dew. He leapt up and taking off his leather jacket he shook the drops from it before putting it on again and then wiping his jeans down with his hands to clear the shining droplets that covered his legs—rather like the 'suit of lights' of a matador. A large handkerchief in his pocket was used as a towel to dry his hair, face and hands.

John stuffed the damp cloth back into his pocket and was about to return to his tent when he detected movement on the opposite side of the river: a young woman was walking along the bank approximately sixty feet from where he stood and she seemed to be studying the water as though trying to find something important. Totally intrigued, John stealthily kept pace with her. Eventually she paused and fell to her knees where she remained motionless for a few seconds.

Completely mystified, he stopped and knelt down to avoid being seen as he watched her slowly lie down flat on her tummy. She pushed the sleeve of her blouse up as far as she could before putting her arm into the icy water. John shivered involuntarily and smiled as he realised what she was doing.

'She's trout tickling,' he said softly to himself and patiently watched the girl until she rapidly hooked her hand out of the water with a triumphant cry that soon died on her lips as the fish eluded capture.

This happened twice more and John was beginning to wonder if she would ever be successful. He was willing the fish to enter her trap and he became as absorbed as the girl.

His sense of time and place was lost while staring at the young girl until his reverie was shattered by her startled cry. His head came up and he watched in horror as the young woman toppled head first into the water: the soft, waterlogged bank had collapsed beneath her. He froze as he watched her being swept out into the centre of the river.

The shock passed and John jumped to his feet and began running along the bank in an attempt to keep pace with the struggling girl. He could see that the river swung sharply to the right fifty yards ahead and he knew he had to get to that bend before the current swept the girl beyond it. The prickly bushes whipped at his legs and hands as he ploughed on, regardless of the stinging sensation. His muscles were still stiff from all the walking he had done the previous day and his whole body was aching when he finally reached the river bend. Thrusting hard with both his legs against the edge of the bank he launched himself into the air.

The next few minutes seemed to take forever. He cleaved the frigid water and had to kick hard against the currents that seemed to tug him every which way but the right way. When he was finally able to reach out and grab the girl's blouse he immediately took advantage of those same currents to reach the nearest bank.

The pain in his calf muscles was beginning to feel like the onset of severe cramp as he kicked and pulled the girl along beside him. Suddenly he glimpsed a willow tree that trailed thin branches into the agitated water and as they were swept beneath it he reached up to take a firm hold on one of the branches. It felt as though his arm had been jerked out of its socket but his grip held and he stopped kicking. Using all his strength he swung the girl in towards the bank and she grabbed at a small shrub.

Half-submerged in the fast-flowing river John was vaguely aware of a figure on the river bank. The muscle-straining drag on the arm holding onto the girl stopped and he knew that the stranger had taken her from the water.

The willow branch snapped and he felt himself being whirled away into the raging waters. He tumbled over and over, slightly disorientated, before his tired limbs could begin functioning and with renewed kicks he was able to surface and gulp in a few breaths before checking his whereabouts.

Trees lining the river glowed yellow and gold as the first rays of the autumn sun illuminated the canopy but John had little time to admire their beauty for he was attempting to reach the bank again before his strength gave out.

Large boulders rose up from the river bed, severely bruising his calf and thigh muscles. An excruciating pain in his stomach doubled him up and in crying out he swallowed water. John choked as he tumbled head over heels in the turbulent river and vainly tried to raise his head above the surface. The agonising pain struck again and his reaction forced more water into his lungs. The pain in his chest was now overwhelming and blackness descended.

'What a way to die, Mum!' was his last thought before losing all consciousness.

5

THE FIRST THING HE SAW when he regained consciousness was a pair of dark eyes fringed with long curling lashes and only inches from his face. Realising that he was waking they fluttered briefly and pulled back enabling him to see the young woman's face. High cheekbones, a narrow nose and full rosy lips completed the stunning portrait.

'He's awake, Da!' the girl exclaimed as she sat back on the low stool she had drawn close to the bunk bed, her eyes fixed upon the stirring man.

'Good. Maybe we can find out who he is so that I can thank him properly,' a deeply-accented voice replied and John tried to lift his head to see the man who had spoken. A searing pain ran through his head and he dropped back onto the soft down-filled pillows.

'Easy, take it easy,' the girl whispered soothingly as she placed cool fingers upon his forehead and lightly pushed him down. 'You've taken quite a beating in the river and we've sent for a doctor to check you over properly before you even try to get up.'

The ache in John's head briefly blurred his vision and he had to wait a while before he was able to turn his head slightly and look properly at the young woman: straight black hair cascaded down to frame her face and complement a flawless olive complexion and sparkling eyes.

'You must rest and my mother will bring you something to eat later.' He could tell she was Welsh by the warm, musical lilt of her voice that seemed to rise on the last word of each sentence. As much as he wanted to keep looking at her lovely face he was unable to prevent his eyelids from becoming heavy and he sank back into a troubled sleep.

'He's resting again, Da,' Llinos said as she stood up and quietly crossed the caravan to where her father was sitting. He was reading a tattered copy of a first-aid book that the campsite women rarely referred to. They had their own ways for treating any illness, ways that stretched back many generations.

'You'd better go and help your mother prepare the lunch. Keep a lookout for Doctor Griffith while you're about it and and I'll keep an eye on our hero.'

Llinos nodded and she went across the clearing to where Gwen was holding court with three other women. She told her mother that the man had woken up and then dozed off again and Gwen smiled and nodded to the others.

'Looks like your boys managed to get to him in time,' she said and the women smiled with pleasure. They had all learned the story of how their husbands, Bryn, Dafydd and Gareth had linked hands at the river and waded out into the torrent of shallower water to grab the unconscious man before he could be dashed to death on the larger boulders downstream. Dafydd had a little knowledge of CPR and resuscitated the half-drowned man on the bank. John coughed up a great deal of water but remained unconscious and the three men swiftly fashioned a rough litter from the surrounding brush and carried him back to Aidan's caravan.

John was stripped and bathed by the older women who also tended to the many lacerations on his body with ancient herbal salves while Bryn's young son went running to the village to fetch the doctor.

Doctor Griffith was the son of a doctor who was also the son of a doctor and had lived in the village all his life except for the time spent at the London School of Medicine. He had set out by car within seconds of the boy giving him the news and eventually followed the scruffy lad on foot over two fields to the caravan site. The smell of roast pork drifted on the light breeze as he approached the camp and Gwen hurried to meet the man. Griffith had encountered many forms of intolerance during his long years in practice and he couldn't abide any village tittle tattle about the 'tinkers'.

Some locals claimed they were thieves and should be moved on by the police but Griffith had yet to see any signs that would back the malicious gossip and, on the contrary, he had experienced only kindness and good manners on his rare visits to their camp. Gwen Jones was a good example of the Romani Fokendi's good nature and all-round knowledge: she always warmed him with tots of brandy or a bowl of hot broth on the occasions when he'd had to make a visit in bad weather and on one occasion in the village, when young Mrs Thomas's water had broken in the Post Office, she had capably helped her until the doctor arrived.

Doctor Griffith climbed the bright red wooden steps and entered the bowtop. As always he couldn't help admiring the beautiful decorations that clearly represented years of hard work. Aidan stood up and greeted the man with a glass in his hand.

'It's not too cold today, Aidan, but I'll not insult you with a refusal.' Aidan nodded with a grin and the doctor downed the brandy in one swallow. He then turned to the narrow cot against the opposite wall. His patient appeared to be sleeping, his breathing steady, and the doctor carefully studied the bruising on the young man's face before turning down the sheet and blanket that covered his naked body. The old man winced at the number of cuts and bruises while at the same time admiring the professional bandaging and use of ointments and home-made creams on the uncovered grazes. He turned briefly to Gwen who had also entered the caravan and without any sign of embarrassment was watching the doctor as he methodically checked the naked body for breakages.

'You and the ladies have done a grand job in patching the poor fellow up, Gwen,' he remarked as he accepted another tot from Aidan. 'My thanks to you all.' The doctor raised his glass in a salute to the Romani women.

Gwen's plump cheeks reddened and she grinned at her husband as the doctor refocused his attention on the patient and continued checking each limb for breaks and fractures. John wimpered slightly as gently probing fingers found two fractured ribs and a badly bruised hip bone.

'I'll have to bind his ribs and let nature take its course. As far as the lacerations and bruising are concerned I'll leave those to the good ladies.' Griffith checked John's pulse once more before packing his instruments and bandages into the battered Gladstone bag. 'I am quite certain that there is no serious concussion but make sure you let me know if there's any dizziness or blurring of his vision when he wakes up,' the doctor said as he re-covered the sleeping man with the hand-embroidered blanket.

After strolling a few paces from the bowtop Aidan placed a hand on the doctor's sleeve: 'Doctor, I wish to thank you for coming out so far. I am well aware of the villagers' opinion of us but ever since we arrived you have shown us nothing but respect and for that I am very grateful. We're not people of wealth but I would still like to pay you.' He paused and looked into the doctor's kind eyes. 'Will you accept payment in kind?'

'I would consider that very generous, Aidan, and it would be an honour to accept whatever you can afford.'

Aidan waved to Owen who hurried across the clearing carrying a large brown paper parcel that was tied with coarse string. His smile almost split his round face in half as he handed the 'payment' to the doctor.

'Your wife will know what to do with it, Doctor Griffith,' Aidan said with a wink. 'I would suggest baking it with roasted almonds, coriander and orange slices.'

Griffith raised one eyebrow and looked at the gypsy with suspicion written across his face. He then glanced down at the heavy weight in his arms.

'My wife has her own recipe for a trout of this size, Aidan,' he said with the same mischievous twinkle as the Romani's. 'Provided I can get it past his lordship's gamekeepers.'

'There's at least one who'll not be troubling you today,' Aidan murmured.

'I think you must be referring to John Edwards. As I was leaving the village I saw him storming into the police station with a sticking plaster on his nose and a face as black as thunder.'

Owen chuckled having had a few rather heated words with the rather officious gamekeeper himself.

'I'd be very careful if I were you,' Griffith said, his voice ominously low. 'That man bears grudges like nobody I've ever met before. There's a very good chance that he'll insist on his pound of flesh.'

'Thanks for the warning, doctor, we'll be ready.'

The doctor smiled grimly and then strode away and across the field weighed down by his medical bag and the large parcel of a fishy nature.

I'll send my lad to help him with his bag, Owen thought and he whistled for his youngest to join him. After receiving some quick instructions the boy raced across the meadow to catch up with the doctor before he had reached the first hedgerow. The old man turned and waved his thanks to Owen before laboriously crossing the stile and disappearing into the next field.

Aidan re-entered the bowtop to watch over the sleeping man while Gwen continued with her preparations for the midday meal. Llinos left the communal campfire and followed her father into the warmth of the caravan with a number of questions already forming on her lips.

Her father leant over John for a moment and then returned to his seat and picked up a dog-eared copy of *Moby Dick* that, like all the other books he had read, had been passed from hand to hand in their community.

'Da, do you think he's an Englishman?' Llinos asked as she sat on the stool by the bunk bed. Aidan nodded.

'Why do you think so?'

'His hands are far too soft to be those of a hard-working Welshman.'

'We do have office workers too, Da!'

'The way he dresses shows that he's from London and you can see he is used to riding a motorbike.'

Llinos looked at her father with a puzzled expression. 'The boots he was wearing have steel plates that are burnished bright by contact with the road and his jeans are oil-stained. Bryn took a chance and bravely crossed the river further down where it widened and the current was less strong and he recovered a leather jacket that had been tossed aside before the young man dived into the water. He also discovered a very crude campsite.'

'You should have been a detective, Da,' Llinos said with a twinkle in her eyes and then she laughed. The two fell silent and Aidan returned to his book while Llinos clasped her arms about her knees and stared pensively at the profile of the sleeping man lying in her bed.

There was a sudden commotion outside and Aidan carefully noted his place before opening the top half of the stable door and leaning out.

'What's up, Dafydd,' he asked as his friend hurried past the bowtop.

'Looks like we have a posse of police coming down the top field and they're being led by His Lordship's lackey.'

'Tell the others to leave them to me.'

'What is it?' Llinos called out behind him.

'The police are coming—'

'PLEASE, no police.'

Aidan looked round to see the injured man was reaching out towards him as though beseeching him. Before Llinos could reach John he fell back in a dead faint.

'Da, please don't let them know he is here,' she said quietly and Aidan nodded.

'He is obviously in some sort of trouble which is nothing to do with us: we won't mention that he is in our home.'

The big man hurried out of the bowtop and quickly spread the word around the campsite that the injured lad should remain a secret. By the time he had received the last agreement the police officers, eagerly led by a needlessly bandaged John Edwards, were fast approaching the small group of travellers.

'Aidan Jones!' Edwards shouted, pointing to the tall man. 'You're under arrest for attempted murder.' He raised his shotgun threateningly.

'I'll be the one who says who's under arrest or not,' the police sergeant said strongly. 'And I'll thank you for that gun, Mr Edwards.' He held his hand out and the gamekeeper was reluctantly parted from his beloved Purdey.

'Sergeant Williams, I think I know why you are here and I readily admit that I did assault Mr Edwards.'

'You don't have to say anything without a solicitor present, Mr Jones,' the sergeant said as he handed the shotgun to one of the two constables standing behind him.

'It was a matter of life and death, Sergeant,' Aidan explained. 'My daughter had accidentally fallen into the river and was being swept downstream. I was trying to get to her when Mr Edwards confronted me with his shotgun and prevented me from going any further.'

'He was on private land and undoubtedly poaching,' Edwards interjected. 'He also hit me with a weapon.'

Williams held his hand up. 'I'll hear it from Aidan first,' the sergeant growled and the gamekeeper fell silent. The policeman turned back to Aidan. 'And then what happened?'

'I took his gun and gave him a smack on the nose before chasing after my daughter.'

'We saw the whole thing, Sergeant,' Gareth said while Bryn and Dafydd nodded vigorously behind him. 'We were a hundred yards behind Aidan when he showed that *twyllo* that his daughter was more valuable than his lordship's trout.'

'I'll judge who's the fool, Gareth,' the stocky sergeant said as he tried to suppress a grin. He turned to look pointedly at the gamekeeper: 'Although, if it's true that the *twyllo* tried to prevent Mr Jones from saving his daughter's life then he got what he deserved.'

Bryn and Gareth laughed when they saw the expression on Edwards's face and Owen shushed them to allow Williams to continue.

'From what I have heard from both parties I would like to state that we should all be grateful that a young life was saved today. My constables inspected the river earlier today after reports about the heavy rains and it is a miracle that anyone came out of that maelstrom alive.'

'That's right, Sarge,' one of the constables said. 'The river authority reported that it was at its highest for fifteen years and that the reservoir downstream could rise to a record level by the end of the week.'

'Mountain Rescue have been busy in the Beacons too,' the other constable added. 'They've already brought down six climbers.'

The sergeant held his hand up and the assembly fell silent. 'This matter is closed and I suggest, Mr Edwards, that you return to your own home and give a little thought to helping people before thinking of yourself first.' He gave the shotgun back to the disconsolate gamekeeper and they all watched him trudge away up the meadow.

'Aidan, I wish you to give my best wishes for a safe recovery to your daughter and I'll bid you *hwyl fawr am nawr!*'

'And a pleasant goodbye to you, Sergeant,' Aidan replied. As the three policemen walked back across the meadow in the balmy autumn sun the travellers turned to each other with broad grins.

'I suggest that when our visitor has recovered sufficiently that we hold a party in his honour,' Owen said earnestly. 'I'll bring the booze.'

'I agree and I'll make sure we have enough trout,' Aidan said, 'with the gamekeeper's blessing of course.'

The men roared with laughter and the women tending the food over the campfire looked round with curiosity.

After four days John felt able to sit up in bed. The bindings around his chest were replaced and clean dressings applied to the worst lacerations.

The women fussed like a clutch of hens over a chick until, red-faced and thoroughly embarrassed, John was permitted to slip down under the covers again.

The women had not been able to learn much more about the mystery youth other than that his name was John and that he was very nervous whenever mention of the police was made.

When John was once more modestly tucked up in bed Gwen permitted Llinos to sit by the wood burner to do some sewing. She occasionally glanced in his direction with lowered lashes but was disappointed to see that he had closed his eyes and fallen asleep again.

'Yes, he's a good-looking boy, Llinos,' Gwen whispered with the hint of a smile as she noticed her daughter's interest. 'Handsome, strong and brave. He also seems to have a very nice manner about himself. There's not much more a young girl could wish for.' She quietly lowered the large copper kettle onto the stove hotplate.

'Mummy!' Llinos exclaimed in embarrassment and then yelped as the needle she was using pricked her finger. 'You shouldn't say things like that. He probably has a girlfriend or possibly a wife at home.'

'Neither,' John murmured as he turned his face from the wall to look at them both.

Gwen laughed as Llinos hid her face behind the pillowcase she was decorating with the tiniest blue forget-me-nots.

'I'm sorry but I couldn't help overhearing your conversation,' John said as, wincing slightly, he pushed himself up against the headboard.

'Then you heard me say you are a very brave lad.'

'You flatter me, Mrs Jones, anyone else would have done exactly what I did,' John said.

'Not anyone, John,' Gwen said. 'And you're amongst friends so please call me Gwen.'

John smiled. 'I know I must be causing you a lot of trouble so I will try to get out of your lives as soon as the pain in my chest is a little more bearable.'

'I wouldn't hear of it. Our home is yours for as long as you wish.' As Gwen spoke the door opened and Aidan entered.

'I heard what you said, Gwen, and I support the sentiment wholeheartedly.' Turning to John he said, 'You saved the life of a Romani Fokendi, which means we owe you shelter, food and the protection of our camp for as long as you wish. No questions will be asked about your past for we all have our own secrets that nobody need know about.' John went to speak but Aidan stopped him again.

'As soon as you are able to move I have arranged for you to sleep in Dafydd's caravan. His wife died three years ago and not having any children he has two spare bunks that you are more than welcome to use.'

'I will thank Dafydd as soon as I have met him,' John said as his thoughts raced back to the loving parents and home he was forced to leave behind him and he felt his eyes moisten.

'You have already met, John. He was one of three who formed a human chain to pull you out of the river.'

Aidan poured a tot of amber spirit from a large porcelain jug and offered it to John. This led to a heated exchange of words between Aidan and Gwen in a language that John didn't understand.

'Mum's saying you shouldn't drink before you're better,' Llinos explained. 'They're speaking *kååle*—it's the ancient Welsh Romani language that is of Indo-Arayan origin.'

John nodded and rudely interrupted their angry words. 'Excuse me Gwen, but did Aidan say that three of your friends went into that terrible river because of me?'

The couple stopped talking and Aidan took the opportunity to offer John the glass once again. He accepted it with a broad grin, hoping his interruption had managed to calm the couple.

'They're tough lads. They made a stretcher and carried you back here,' Gwen said dully, her eyes fixed on the glass in John's hand.

'I owe them my life—when can I meet and give them my thanks?'

'You'll have plenty of time at the *abhinav* when you're able to get up and enjoy a good party,' Aidan said and Gwen seemed to brighten up at the thought.

John sipped the spirit while watching the couple over the rim of his glass and almost choked as the fiery liquid slipped down his throat.

'We make the *poitin* ourselves. It's made from barley and it's about 180° proof,' Aidan explained.

'Wow! I always knew that moonshine was believed to be strong but this blows your head off.'

Gwen visibly relaxed and walked over to the bunk bed. 'You can buy bottles of legally made poteen in the shops but they're not the real thing,' Gwen said proudly. 'They don't have the same kick as Aidan's or Bryn's *poitin*.'

Gwen grabbed a glass from a shelf and held it out to Aidan who raised one dark eyebrow.

'Well, if a man with two fractured ribs can get drunk so can I!' Gwen said. Aidan burst into laughter.

6

TWO DAYS LATER, aided by Aidan and Dafydd, John descended from the bowtop to step onto grass that was still damp from a light afternoon shower. He confidently walked to the group of people who turned to welcome him into the warmth of their communal campfire where a whole lamb was being roasted on a spit.

The fire was as high as the toddlers that ran around it and the acrid smell of wood smoke filled the air, prompting memories of the Guy Fawkes Nights when he was a youngster and at home.

Aidan held his hands up and everyone fell silent as he began talking to John in a loud, emotionally charged voice.

'This evening is to celebrate the good fortune that brought you into our community. It may have been sheer chance that you were in the vicinity but if you hadn't chosen to dive into that terrible river I would have lost my daughter forever.'

Everybody cheered and John blushed as he looked over the fire at Llinos who was shyly staring through the heat haze.

Aidan thrust a glass into John's hand and poured a generous tot of *poitin*. The rest of the evening began to blur for John as more and more was being drunk. He vaguely recalled a large plate of roast meat being put in his lap before Aidan came into focus with the familiar jug of spirit again. John attempted to see where Llinos had got to but he only caught glimpses as she rushed around helping the other women to serve the food.

After the plates had been cleared away fiddles were produced and Romani songs were sung in an exotic dialect. John was on the point of being lulled to sleep when the fiddlers stopped to be replaced by a harp and a clear soprano voice that floated across the meadow.

He looked up to see Llinos sitting with a small Welsh harp in her hands. She sang with her eyes closed and John was mesmerised by the beauty of her song. As Llinos sang his mind drifted back to the evenings he had spent reading while his mother quietly hummed along to the Palm Court Orchestra on the radio and he felt a sudden sense of longing.

'It a lovely ancient lullaby,' Dafydd murmured as he stood beside John. 'It's really a duet and it used to be sung by Llinos and my wife.'

John sighed and strove to rise from the chair and Dafydd stepped closer and quickly slipped a supporting arm about his waist.

'Aidan's *poitin* is about to strike you down, John,' Dafydd said and laughed loudly as they tottered towards his Welsh wagon with its delicately carved scarlet dragons sheltering on the crownboards of the front porch.

'I'd better get you into bed quick because there's no way I will be able to carry you without help.' The two men struggled up the six steps of the narrow ladder and entered the welcome warmth of Dafydd's lonely caravan. The walls were covered in photographs of a beautiful woman in the traditional dress of the Romani people.

'Meet Branwen, my wife,' Dafydd said waving a hand to encompass all the pictures. 'It means blessed raven and by God she was beautiful!'

'You were well blessed to have been her husband,' John said, his voice reduced to a whisper.

The following day John managed to dress and leave the wagon under his own steam and he greeted everyone he saw with a polite 'good morning'. They all responded with *bore da* and big grins for they knew what the *poitin* was doing to his head. Gareth's wife took pity and offered John a foul-tasting herbal remedy that he was assured would soon stop his head from splitting in half.

'Morning, John,' Llinos said and pointed to the kettle hanging over the small fire she had made near the bowtop. 'Do you fancy a cup of tea?'

Dafydd descended the wagon's steps and greeted Llinos in *kååle*. 'Will you be having your breakfast with the common Jones's or with a Wood?'

'He claims to be a direct descendant of Abram Wood who first arrived in England in the eighteenth century,' Llinos said. 'Now what about that breakfast?' she said quietly. John nodded and followed the girl who was tripping lightly up the steps.

The parlour was filled with the wonderful smells of bacon and fresh coffee and John made quick work of the plate that Llinos set before him. 'What do you plan to do today?' Llinos asked with curiosity in her voice.

'Dafydd said that he had some work for me.'

As the days turned into weeks John regained his strength, fuelled by the magnificent breakfasts with the Jones family and the heavy protein-rich evening meals that Dafydd cooked.

When the autumn rains turned to winter sleet and the first flurries of snow began to settle Dafydd started to grow restless. John thought it was due to his constant presence in the Welsh man's wagon but Dafydd reassured him that it was simply time to visit his cousin in the north.

'Your cousin is a Scot?' John asked one evening as the two men sat sipping *poitin* by the warmth of the cast-iron stove.

'No, he's a Romani but has lived in the Highlands all his life,' Dafydd replied. 'I try to visit him at least once every two years. He's now getting on in years and I'll have to be going soon which means we'll have to decide on who you can bed with.'

'Sounds like you want me to marry someone,' John said.

'Not a bad idea, lad.' Dafydd put his glass down. 'Y'know, there's someone who is very interested in you and you couldn't do any better.'

A puzzled look crossed John's face.

'I'm talking about Llinos *ffwl ddall*, you blind fool! She's fallen head over heels for you. Haven't you noticed how the other women look at you? At first they were measuring you for a coffin but now it's a wedding suit! And the single women, see how they avoid speaking to you—Llinos would tear their hair out by the roots if they did.'

John fell silent and he went to the door and looked through the etched-glass window at Aidan's bowtop. His mind was racing back to one night in Alice's café. He saw himself crossing the crowded room to where a pretty young woman was waiting with large eyes and an innocent smile. Then he shuddered as the picture in his mind switched to the darkness beneath the pier and the crumpled figure on the pebbles.

'Are you all right, John?' Dafydd asked when he noticed the change in John's expression. 'Have I frightened you with thoughts of marriage?'

'No, Dafydd. It's just that I never thought of Llinos in that light. She is a beautiful girl, one that I greatly respect and because of that I haven't been aware of her feelings for me.'

'It always strikes when you least expect it, my friend.'

John wrapped a scarf about his neck and left the wagon. He walked across the meadow towards the sound of the rushing river and only became aware that he was being followed when his name was called.

He turned to be faced by Llinos walking close behind him and his heart skipped a beat. The full moon was high in the sky and the landscape had taken on a ghostly white sheen.

'Can I walk with you, John?' she said, grasping his hand and falling in step beside him.

'Of course you can, Llinos, provided it's not too cold for you.' He eyed the light coat that was being loosely worn over her cotton dress.

'I'm a tough Romani, the weather can never affect me.'

'Quite a little ice maiden, are you?'

'I'm not that cold, John, which you would know if you would only give me half a chance.'

'What do you mean?' John asked naively. He was suddenly swung round until they were facing each other and Llinos was able to fling her arms around his neck and kiss him. The sudden warmth of her full lips pressing on his took him by complete surprise and he froze for a brief moment before instinctively putting his arms around her and kissing her back.

'Is that the kiss of an ice maiden?' she finally whispered. Her frozen breath hung between them.

'It was the kiss of a maiden but not one made of ice,' John said slowly, knowing full well that it wasn't the answer she expected. He dropped his arms to his side and pulled back. 'I don't think it's right for us to be out here so late at night.' He slowly began to walk away.

A puzzled expression crossed the young woman's face and her eyes reflected her disappointment. 'I don't think my parents would mind, John, they know how I feel about you.'

John stopped walking and turned to face her. 'And how do you really feel?' he foolishly asked even though he could read the answer in her eyes.

'I have loved you since that first day when you woke up in my bed,' Llinos said sombrely and then giggled when she realised what she had said.

The image of Llinos seemed to fracture and her face changed into one with a bloodied eye. Louise was standing before him and he recoiled a step. His reaction had been brief but before he could speak Llinos had turned away with a sob in her throat and was running back to the bowtop, his reaction taken as a sign of total rejection of her confessed feelings for him.

'Louise wait!' John cried and then quickly corrected himself. 'Llinos, wait, let me explain,' he cried futilely but she kept running.

John sat on the wet grass and putting his head in his hands began to cry silently. The moment those soft lips had pressed against his own and her warm body had clung to him John had known that he was hopelessly in love with Llinos. He also knew that his love would be tainted by his terrible past, the only reason for intuitively pulling away from the girl. His guilt would always be an impenetrable barrier between them. John dried his eyes and decided that he would have to leave the camp and the open-hearted people who had come to accept him as one of their own.

Aidan had watched his distraught daughter running towards the bowtop and looked back towards the river to seek the source of her distress. Nothing moved in the darkness and he gave Eirwyn a quick pat on the neck, received a soft whinney in response, and hurried across the campsite to find out what had upset his daughter.

John eventually stood up and began to trudge back to the wagon to tell Dafydd of his decision. He had almost reached the steps when a shout made him turn. Aidan was hurrying towards him with a face suffused with anger.

'What have you done, John?' he barked on getting closer to the young man and then he was towering over him. 'You've upset my girl!'

'I'm sorry, Aidan, but I can't stay any longer. I am forced to leave you and—'

'Go on, say it—and leave Llinos with a broken heart.'

The door to the wagon opened and Dafydd stepped out to look down on the two men with a puzzled expression. 'What's going on here?'

'This damned outsider has scorned the affections of my daughter and decided to leave without any excuse,' Aidan said loudly. Other caravan doors opened and the curious peered out.

'As much as I love Llinos, Aidan, I have to leave. I could never make her truly happy because of what has happened to me recently. It's something I will always be running away from and I could never inflict that kind of life on your daughter, no matter how much I feel for her.'

Aidan was slightly mollified by John's words and he studied the distress that was clearly showing on the young man's face. 'You have done something terrible?' he asked quietly.

'Something I am forced to live with but could never force on others,' John replied softly.

Dafydd placed a large hand on the young man's shoulder. 'Then you can travel with me until such time as you think you can share your frightful knowledge and relieve yourself of the burden,' he said and he turned to the Romani father. 'As you know, Aidan, I have to visit my cousin from time to time and I think this is as good a time as any; to ease any unnecessary pain we will leave before Llinos wakes in the morning.'

Aidan took his friend's hand in gratitude. 'Thank you, Dafydd, I look forward to the day when you return to us and if we're not here you'll know where we've gone.' Dafydd nodded as he shook hands.

'With a bit of luck my motorbike may still be in the car park where I left it, possibly a bit rusty now, but I want you to have it. Please buy Llinos something pretty with the money you get for it,' John said.

Aidan hesitated before speaking. 'Thank you, John, I'll do as you say.' The big man held his hand out. 'I believe you when you say you want to spare Llinos pain in the future. I pray she may soon find happiness and I wish you safe travelling.'

Their hands parted and Aidan swiftly turned and walked back to the bowtop. John saw one of the silk curtains twitch and knew that Llinos had been watching. He turned to Dafydd who was climbing the steps. 'I wish to thank you for your generous offer. When do you think we can get going?'

Dafydd looked in the direction of the bowtop. 'I also saw the curtain move, John, so I think it would be best to give the impression that we are staying.' The two men entered the wagon and Dafydd extinguished the three oil lanterns and they sat in the dark to await the early hours of the morning.

The wall clock was lightly chiming at three in the morning when Dafydd pulled a curtain to one side and studied the encampment. All the caravans were in darkness and he touched John on the shoulder; he had only been sleeping lightly and he sat upright with a start.

'Softly, softly,' Dafydd whispered. 'I think we can leave now.' He made a last inspection of the wagon to make sure all fragile items were stowed safely with the cupboard doors latched before he went outside. John shivered as the morning's frosty air sucked the warmth from the wagon.

The cob was soon harnessed and with a light movement of the reins and encouraging 'clucks' the big horse strained and then shifted the heavy wagon out of the ruts it had settled into and they moved up the field.

John kept looking back at the bowtop with indescribable sadness. He'd had a number of girlfriends who were both good-looking and amusing but none had the poetic inner beauty of Llinos. There were no lights or any sign of movement within the caravan and John sighed deeply.

Dafydd looked briefly at the young man and then pulled on the reins to turn the horse out of the field and onto the road to begin the long trek to the north.

They travelled to Scotland and then journeyed for three more years before John decided that he would have to return home if he was to find any kind of peace. After summoning up the courage to tell Dafydd of his decision he struggled to explain why until the kindly Romani stopped him.

'As far as I am concerned whatever is in the past will remain unspoken and stay in the past,' Dafydd said. 'However, whatever you do tomorrow will map out your future. Make it good, John.'

'You've always known the right words, Dafydd. Whether calming a horse or a stranger with a troubling secret,' John said as he stroked the cob before picking up the small case Dafydd had given him.

The big Romani smiled and held out his hand. 'From the moment I first saw you I knew there was goodness in you, John. *Hwyl fawr am nawr!*

'Goodbye for now, Dafydd,' John echoed and turned away before any tears betrayed his overwhelming sadness.

7

1980

THE TWO-WHEEL WOODEN TROLLEY was loaded with boxes of fresh skate and cod. It rattled noisily along behind him as he leaned into the chest-high crossbar and trundled the heavy load through the market. The sun had yet to rise as scores of fish porters with numbered badges on their white coats rushed past him carrying towering baskets and boxes of fish on their heads. These were skilfully balanced on wooden 'bobbin' hats that had for decades been the trademark of a licensed fish porter.

John Davies was a lowly casual worker who had managed to get work as a 'pusher upper' despite not having the legal licence to work in the market. Frank Saunders, his employer, used his position as a union representative to bend the rules in order to employ cheap itinerant workers. The recent threat that in two years' time the Billingsgate market would be moved due to overwhelming traffic congestion had somehow made the employment issue easier; rules went out of the window and John could work without any trouble from the legitimate porters. 'Watch where you're going!' was often hurled at him in the beginning but he soon learned to keep out of their way and out of trouble.

The slender man making his way through the crowd, listening to 'Whatever You Want' on his Walkman, was a lot younger than his appearance suggested. Most of those he knew thought of him as being in his late forties because of the full set of matted whiskers that covered most of his face. This untamed mass of dark brown hair constantly reeked of fish despite every effort to wash out the lingering smell and John had consequently been given the nickname 'Fish Face' by all the children in the street where he lived.

He had moved to his London address seven years ago and luckily it was conveniently close to the fish market. It was a culture shock after the peaceful years he and Dafydd had spent wandering the length and breadth of the country looking for Dafydd's cousin who it turned out no longer lived in Scotland.

Through those icy winters and broiling summers John had thought of nothing but the pure, free spirit of Llinos and the brutal demise of Doris and Louise until his mind rebelled and memories of the deaths were buried deep in his subconscious and he was left only with horrific nightmares and sleepless nights.

They had been camping in a farmer's field in Lincoldshire for two days when after a very bad night John finally decided to give up his life of wandering. As he had travelled to London all he kept remembering was Dafydd's fond farewell that held an intrinsic promise to meet again.

John had then used the last of his savings to travel to London and had been sleeping rough in the streets, begging for the price of a meal when simply by chance he encountered a woman called Jane.

Jane Carstairs was the daughter of Robert Carstairs, the rector of a small parish on the Isle of Wight. Her parents had prayed for a son and the arrival of a little girl was a great and enduring regret. It was a cold, authoritarian household and she grew up to become a rebellious teenager. She began to spend more time with the lads from the local grammar school and at the age of sixteen, despite her father's constant preaching, she lost her virginity to three sex-obsessed adolescents behind the war memorial in the overgrown graveyard.

'Where have you been, you little slut, you're such a disappointment,' was a regular greeting when she returned at night.

The enth time this was said she replied on sudden impulse, 'But I've been a disappointment from the day I was born.' This response led to a heated row with her parents until she could stand it no more and on her seventeenth birthday she packed a small case and left home in the dead of night.

Jane hitch-hiked to London and accepted the offer of a job from an older man she had encountered at Victoria Station. The man's tiny eyes had gleamed while studying the young girl eating a sausage roll in the public house and then, placing a pudgy damp hand over hers, he offered her a place to sleep too. Jane soon realised that Frank Saunders expected her to share his bed and she learnt to tolerate his uncouth groping at night.

At the market she discovered that he was short-weighting his customers and falsifying his tax returns. This knowledge became invaluable and after five years she was able to break Frank Saunders' hold over her. He was told to keep his hands to himself and sleep in his own bed until summoned to Jane's bedroom; she knew it was in her own interest to keep Saunders satisfied from time to time.

This arrangement suited the fish merchant for he found that anticipating those rare invitations was as exciting as the physical act itself. However, it wasn't long before Jane met someone who was much thinner and younger than Saunders.

Benjamin Weston was a 40-year-old merchant seaman who sailed on coastal freighters, shipping coal around the British Isles. Unlike the other seamen he always ignored the temptations offered in every port and saved his money wisely; he now owned his own house in the East End which was the only reason for Jane's interest in him.

After a brief engagement they were married in a registry office during a December snowstorm. Jane didn't bother to notifty her parents of her new married status.

Frank Saunders didn't like being cast aside but he nonetheless told Jane she could keep her job when she moved out of his house for he knew she was overly familiar with the way he conducted business. She was also invaluable in that she knew every customer by name and had become highly experienced in all matters concerning fresh fish trading.

As soon as Jane had moved into Weston's house she dropped her genteel act and became harsh and domineering. Benjamin failed to satisfy Jane and she sought pleasure beyond the marital bed. It wasn't long before she acquired a reputation for being available to any man who had an open wallet.

After a couple of years Weston fled back to sea to escape his wife's iniquitous behaviour. He was subsequently drowned after 'falling' overboard during a drunken brawl about a fifth ace that had been slipped into a game of draw poker. The policeman delivering the tragic news claimed later that Jane had simply shrugged, refused to take charge of his remains, and declared that Weston's body could be returned to the sea for all she cared. The door had then been slammed in the constable's face.

And so, twelve years later, this woman, hardened by circumstances, literally stumbled across a man calling himself John Davies. At that time he was living rough on the street but even so Jane had to use all her persuasive powers before she was able to convince him to move into her terraced house in the East End.

This charitable act was not out of pity but for a purely practical reason: money. Jane had started to provide lodging for down-and-outs immediately after her husband's demise at sea. Simply by batting her eyelashes and lifting her skirts she had found them all employment with corrupt fish-stall owners. This was on the understanding that all the lodgers repaid her with a substantial percentage of their weekly wage.

Jane, who was five years John's senior, cared for him until he had fully recovered his strength before inveigling Saunders to give him a porter's job at the fishmonger's where she was working as his bookkeeper. John was unaware of her sex-for-favours arrangement for if he had known he would have left her house immediately.

In the beginning John had merely felt grateful that Jane had given him a roof over his head but as the weeks passed he strangely began to grow fond of the hard matter-of-fact woman; this was in part because he enjoyed the safety of living incognito in her house. It seemed to give him the same sense of seclusion and security he had felt when living with Dafydd and the Romani Fokendi. John slowly began to believe, or hope, that he could begin the task of wiping his slate clean.

The memories of Llinos were still refusing to fade completely and often he dreamed that he was holding her hand and running through scarlet flowers in a meadow, her lustrous hair streaming in the wind, before her image dissolved and the flowers became streaks of blood on a dark road. He would then awake, bathed in perspiration.

Jane's occasional flirtations with John soon became more frequent and intimate, unlike her sweaty interludes with the dealers. Her nights spent with John satisfied her needs and often he would awake from his nightmares and find Jane beside him, her chest rising and falling with soothing regularity and he would soon be lulled back to sleep.

After a few months the gentle, loving image she had created solely for John began to harden and her true character started to surface once more. It frequently emerged after arguments about small domestic issues such as how much she was taking from his wages and her lack of hygiene around the house. These tiffs always ended when she demanded that he obeyed the rules and spent every night in her bed or she would get him fired from work.

'You do as you're told, or else' became a sour weekly refrain in his life and yet, the advantage of being able to sleep without the fear of a knock on the door made her demands tolerable. In many ways they needed each other and as a result Jane bore him a healthy little boy one year later.

John loved his son dearly and named him Timothy after his grandfather. The defenceless little baby soon grew into a skinny, hyperactive 5-year-old whom John vowed to raise as his own parents had cared for him. While Tim's parents worked at the fish market he spent most of his time playing in the streets with a gang of disreputable boys.

In spite of Jane's plan that when the boy was 12 they would lie about his age and get him a job in the market John harboured a deeper desire to see his son achieve a great deal more in life than he had.

The crossbar bit through the tough rubber apron, bruising his chest, and he was relieved when he was able to stop at Saunders's market stall. An Armenian known affectionately by all as Benny, helped John to unload the barrow and he smiled his thanks before sluicing it down with buckets of water that he filled from a standpipe. John then returned to the lorry park for his next load of herring.

The Status Quo had just started a new track on his Walkman and John was awkwardly turning the heavy barrow between the fish stalls when a porter with a bobbin piled high with dripping fish boxes collided with him. Despite all efforts to maintain his balance the man stumbled back. The tower swayed precariously before crashing down to spill fresh mackerel across the paving stained with fish gut.

'You stupid bastard,' the porter screamed as he surveyed the loss his boss would dock from his wages. 'You're gonna pay for this little lot, you unlicensed lump of shite,' he demanded, stepping up so close his spittle speckled John's face.

'It was your bloody fault,' John shouted back as he removed his earphones and glowered at the porter who had bent over to recover his bobbin. 'You weren't looking where you were going.'

The porter leapt at John and swung his bobbin wildly, catching the bearded man on the side of his face. The wooden headgear gashed John's cheek and a bright scarlet stream ran down his face and dripped onto the Walkman clipped to his belt. The sudden pain forced him to clamp a hand to the wound and stagger back in shock against his barrow.

The porter stared in surprise at the amount of blood that flowed from the facial wound and was completely unprepared when John ducked under the crossbar and launched himself at his assailant.

Clenched fists began pounding the immobile porter in the face and the man reeled back under the attack, tripping over one of the broken boxes, sliding on the spilt fish and falling awkwardly onto the stone paving. John looked down at the man as he struggled to rise from the scattered debris of broken boxes and slippery fish.

He kicked the man in his side and gave a satisfied grunt when the porter cried out with pain. With blood still dripping from his chin John proceeded to kick the man repeatedly until two burly porters rushed forward to grab both his arms and pull him away. The porter remained in a foetal position with his arms wrapped around his head. John tried to shrug himself free but the steely grip on his forearms couldn't be broken.

'For Christ's sake calm down, mate!' one of the men shouted in his ear. 'You'll kill the bastard if you go on kicking him like that.' John forced himself to relax and the two men released their grip.

'What's going on 'ere, then,' a strong voice boomed and the crowd parted swiftly to allow a police constable to stride into the scene of conflict. 'Break it up, go back to your work,' he added in a deep resonant voice and the crowd began to disperse rapidly, muttering about the riff-raff who could just come into the market and do the work of legally licensed men.

The constable went to the beaten man and helped him to rise to his feet. 'What happened?' he asked and the dazed man painfully extended an arm to point a trembling finger at John.

'He knocked me down, ruined me fish and then when I asked for recompense he started kicking the shite out of me,' he mumbled in a broad Irish accent, his face showing the first signs of swelling and bruising. 'He's a bloody madman.'

John protested angrily until the constable raised his hand. 'Please shut your mouth until I ask you to open it, sir,' he said firmly. Inspecting the gash on John's face he said, 'You'll need stitches to close that cut, sir. Now, I'd like you to tell me how it happened.'

John just stared back at the constable and remained silent.

'He was hit with that man's bobbin,' one of the burly onlookers said and thereby saving John the grim task of getting a fellow porter into trouble. 'Fair cut his head in half; then the silly beggar hit back and that's when you came along.'

'You'll both have to come with me. You, to get that stitched,' he said pointing at John's face. 'And you . . . ' he added, pointing to the porter, ' . . . to have a physical checkup before facing a charge of assault with a dangerous weapon.'

'It weren't no dangerous weapon being used, it was my bloody 'at,' the porter complained weakly.

'And it's evidence because it's made of wood, leather and nails,' the constable said as he picked up the offending article and weighed it in his hand. 'You can do a lot of damage with this hat; it's not just a woolly beret, sir.'

As the four men waited the constable used his radio to call for a van. Signing off he turned to the two burly men. 'You'll have to come as well. I will need you both to sign witness statements.' The two men looked at each other and shrugged.

'As long as we're compensated for our time,' one said.

'Or at least given a chit we can give our gaffer,' the other said quickly when he saw the constable glaring at his mate.

A police doctor attended to John's gash at the police station, inserting three stitches that he assured him would leave very little scarring and applying a liquid that hurt more than the original blow from the bobbin. His assailant and the two witnesses were taken to separate rooms to prepare and sign their statements. John dictated his account of what had happened as the doctor worked on his face.

All four were allowed to leave and John decided that he might as well have breakfast at home. The wall clock in the police station had just struck eight and the market would very soon be finishing for the day.

John travelled home the usual way and as he walked down his street he spotted Timothy playing football. I wonder when she's going to start him in the infant school, he thought as he watched the little boy chase after the ball that was being passed around. Tim was with three other boys who were a lot older and bigger than him. They had been hogging the ball, refusing to pass it to Timothy which had resulted in a flood of tears. The boys were making the most of this as John approached.

'Who's a cry baby then?'

'Does diddums want to play with the ball?'

'Hey, you!' John shouted at them. They turned their heads in surprise as they hadn't expected the boy's father to be home so early in the day. One quickly gathered up the ball and they ran and disappeared from sight round the corner.

'Hello, son,' John called out and the boy ran to be gathered up in his father's arms and then carried up the steps to the front door of their home.

'Are you hurt, Daddy?' the boy said in alarm as he lightly touched the gauze pad on John's cheek.

'Just a little accident at work, son, nothing to be worried about.'

The boy sensed there was something else and was about to ask a question when his father bent over to wipe a tear off his cheek. Timothy remained silent.

John inserted the key Jane had grudgingly given him on the day she had announced her pregnancy. He opened the door and as they entered the hallway John noticed how quiet the house was and he carried Timothy into the kitchen where he put him down.

'Have you had any breakfast yet?' he asked. Getting a shake of the head he pretended to tut-tut disapprovingly and began preparing a meal for them both. The house remained silent. John had half expected to hear the radio or the new record player that Jane had bought on one of her recent shopping trips to Oxford Street; it was normally blaring out the latest popular release to irritate the men who were on night shift and trying to sleep.

He had just put a plate of scrambled eggs on toast in front of his son when the kitchen door opened and one of the lodgers, an ex-vagrant like himself, entered the kitchen wearing nothing more than a pair of tight underpants.

He stopped dead in surprise and mumbled, 'Oh, hello, John, I didn't know you'd be home for breakfast. You normally have something to eat at the market, don't you? And what the blazes happened to your face?'

'Good morning, Reggie. None of your business and why aren't you out working? You should be driving the company truck back to the docks at this time. What happened to you, not feeling too well today?'

'I, err, no, well yes, I've got a bit of a gippy tummy and I thought it best to stay in bed.'

John was about to tell the man to cover up in front of his son when Jane sauntered into the kitchen. 'What's keeping you, Reggie?' she said in her usual bossy manner and then stopped dead when she saw John.

'I know you said it was best to stay in bed, Reggie, but whose bed were you planning on staying in?' John growled. Jane's favourite diaphanous nightdress barely concealed her nakedness and he stepped between her and Timothy.

'My God, Jane! What the hell is going on?' he asked in an unexpectedly quiet, controlled manner.

'Why are you here at this time of the day?' she countered, her face colouring with embarrassment. 'And let me tell you, what I do in my own home is none of your bloody business.'

'Timothy, go to your room,' John said gently and shepherded the white-faced boy from the room. As soon as he heard his son climbing the stairs he closed the door and spun round, his face colouring with anger.

'How long have you been sleeping with her, Reggie?' he asked in a low voice. 'How often has this been happening?'

'I'm sorry, John, but Jane said that if I didn't entertain her she'd have me fired, just like the other guys,' Reginald said, his voice quavering with fear as he stared into John's enraged eyes.

'Entertain her?' He turned and glared at the woman who was arrogantly standing her ground. 'Up to your old blackmailing tricks again?'

'That's right, John. You've been neglecting me, so what did you expect? I was forced to look elsewhere and Reggie was always obliging,' she said, pulling her shoulders back in a self-righteous manner.

'And the others?' John whispered.

'There were no oth—'

'Robert and Harold!' Reginald retaliated in a high voice. 'They have to perform for Jane on Tuesdays and Thursdays, or else—'

John drew his arm back and struck the man forcefully in the face. Reginald stumbled back, tripped on the edge of the threadbare rug and fell to the floor. On his downward journey his head struck against the edge of the table. There was a hollow 'crack', a loud expellation of air and Reggie fell silent as he collapsed onto the linoleum. A small amount of blood began to trickle from beneath his head.

'My God, you've killed him!' Jane screamed and she backed away towards the kitchen door while John went and knelt by the fallen man. He lifted up a limp wrist to feel for any signs of a pulse.

'Shut up, Jane, he's just knocked out,' he said. 'You'd better put some clothes on and then do something about the cut on his head.'

John stormed out of the kitchen and went up to the bedroom. He hastily packed his suitcase and then went into Timothy's room. His son was lying on the bed crying, his arm around the large teddy bear that John had bought for him when he was only 2 years old. Tim and Snuffle were inseparable and John didn't attempt to move the bear when he sat on the bed to stroke the tousled head.

'Don't worry, Tim,' he said softly. 'We'll go away together and do something really exciting.'

The tear-stained face slowly turned. 'I don't want to leave Mummy,' he cried. 'I want you to stay here with us.'

'I can't do that, son. I have to go away for a while.'

'Why?' the inevitable question burst from between the child's quivering lips.

'I can't answer that until you're a lot older. Just know that I love you and will be quite close and I'll be keeping my eyes open to make sure you're always okay,' John said with a catch in his voice, knowing that he would have to leave his son behind until he had enough money to loosen the hold Jane had on him. Only then would he be able to buy himself a new identity so that he could raise and educate his boy properly.

John stood up and without a backward glance for fear that he would weaken he left the one thing he loved most in the world and walked from the room and went down the stairs, his suitcase in his hand.

Jane was waiting at the bottom step, a new silk dressing gown tied tightly about her shivering body. 'Not taking the boy, then?' she snivelled. 'I do love him, y'know.'

'You've a fine way of showing it.'

'If you take him I'll get you fired and then what'll you do?'

'I'm not taking Tim because he wants to stay with you, God only knows why,' John said coldly as he studied the woman's face for any sign of remorse. He thought he could detect a glimmer of triumph in her eyes and he turned on his heel in disgust and strode down the hallway.

'Make sure you look after him. If anything happens I will come back and you really wouldn't want me to do that.' John slammed the door behind him and went down the steps with a heavy heart. He looked up over his shoulder at his son's upstairs room and he could vaguely make out a small tear-stained face beyond the grimy glass. John paused and waved. When he saw the little boy's hand hesitantly wave back he smiled grimly to himself and walked on, gathering more speed as he went until he reached the underground station and ran down the escalator.

8

SERGEANT ALAN WILLIAMS pulled on thick leather gauntlets and mounted the police bike. It had taken him eight years of pounding the beat as a lowly constable, followed by months of rigorous training, before his innate skills at riding a motorcycle were finally recognised and he was able to achieve his first goal. After his transfer to an elite group of highway patrol officers he spent a further six years before being promoted to ride one of the most coveted 'chasers'—the Kawasaki 1000 which he had personally proven capable of topping 132 mph.

He rode the powerful machine out of the parking area behind the police station to join the heavy traffic that on this particular Thursday morning was flowing smoothly along the Thames Embankment. Alan took sadistic pleasure in the way he could intimidate road users simply by his reflected image in their mirrors and as cars slowed or pulled over, allowing him to pass, he made a point of looking pointedly at the drivers who tried in vain to look nonchalant, hoping not to be noticed for any inadvertent motoring misdemeanor.

It was as he cruised past the underground station that Alan Williams noticed a thin heavily-bearded man carrying a battered suitcase and hurrying towards the station entrance. A faint warning bell sounded in his head and he pulled over to stop at the kerb. The dishevelled man had a large medical dressing taped to one side of his face and as he hurried past Alan his eyes remained fixed on some point far away as though preoccupied with an insurmountable problem. The sergeant stepped off the bike and began to follow the man on foot.

Alan had a distinct feeling that he had seen the man before and he decided to make sure that the man wasn't on any of the wanted lists back at the station.

He had almost caught up with the hurrying man when he disappeared into the station and was lost amidst the crowd that was streaming down the escalators. The policeman stopped at the top and briefly glimpsed the man as he was carried down. He felt a shock of recognition when the man turned his head to look sideways: it was the unmistakable profile of John Tucker, his former friend who, for a number of years, had been sought by the authorities for questioning about the mysterious death of a young girl in Hastings. John had vanished and the incident was eventually designated a cold case and filed. Alan knew this for a fact for he had made a point of checking the case records after he had graduated from Police Training College.

As he mounted his bike Alan thought back to the time when John had disappeared. An inspector called Cramer had questioned both him and Ted and had seemed quite satisfied with their answers. John's disappearance plus sufficient evidence that he had been the one who had picked the girl up in the café convinced the police that the missing teenager could give them all the information they needed.

Alan also remembered the subsequent intense questioning that he was subjected to when Louise's remains were found in Long Wood by a group of ramblers. The inspector insisted that he had been seen in Westerham at the same time as John Tucker; John had been identified by witnesses as the motorcyclist who gave a lift to the deceased at the bus stop.

Alan admitted that he had accompanied John to Westerham but when they saw the girl John had shouted at him to go on as he wanted a chance to talk to her alone. He had told the interviewing officer that John had wanted the opportunity to take the girl somewhere quiet so that he could screw her. He lied and said that he had never seen John again. Once more the young man's story was accepted by the police and as in the case of Doris, Louise's death was also primarily attributed to John—until apprehension of the fugitive and further questioning could prove this to the contrary.

Having joined the police force the year after John's vanishing trick Alan had covertly run through the case files to check on the inspector's comments; the general conclusion was that Louise had witnessed

John killing Doris in Hastings and that she had planned to blackmail him. This had forced John Tucker to silence her and it was on this unsubstantiated assumption that a nationwide manhunt for John Tucker was initiated.

The manhunt had lasted for six months but failed to track down the teenager who had vanished into thin air, leaving his distraught parents without any clue as to whether he was still in the country or had fled abroad. Despite the harassment they suffered from the press who had immediately laid siege to Hawthorn Avenue when the police revealed his identity, John's parents continued believing in their son's innocence. They soon found themselves ostracised from most social activities and women openly snubbed Gloria at every opportunity.

Alan decided to check the underground station at the same time every morning in an attempt to spot John again. A radio message to investigate congestion on Ludgate Hill forced him to pull out into the traffic and accelerate away from the busy station.

As Alan was leaving John was catching the train and very soon he arrived at the fish market. The familiar smells were still hanging in the air but the early-morning pandemonium had dwindled to the occasional clatter of a barrow being ranked ready for the next day. John walked through the market, stepping round the large pools of water where the cleaners had hosed down the pavements, until he reached the Saunders Fish Company stall. The door was locked but there was a light showing through a small chink in the heavy wooden roller blind. John rapped on the blind and after a moment of fumbling and cursing the blind rolled up a foot and the ruddy features of Frank Saunders appeared in the gap.

'What d'ya want, Davies?' he snapped. 'I'm still in the middle of counting this morning's takings and doing all the bloody paperwork.'

'Sorry to trouble you, Mr Saunders, but I find myself in the embarrassing situation of not having a place to kip today. Can I get my head down in the truck?'

'For gawd's sake, John, I'm a damned fishmonger trying to run a business not a bleedin' doss house for vagrants.'

'It means I'll be on the job nice and early, sir,' John said obsequiously and then fell silent, waiting for Saunders to say something.

The face disappeared and John heard the metal cash box being slammed shut and the jingle of keys and Frank re-appeared. 'Here, make sure you don't drive the bloody thing an inch or pee in the cab. I expect the keys back at two tomorrow morning. The driver has to have 'em to make a pick-up down at the docks.'

John took them with a mumbled 'thank you' and picking up his suitcase he walked back through the market to where the company lorry was parked. It was nine thirty in the morning when John tossed his battered suitcase onto the passenger seat. He locked the cab and strolled across to the Piscatorial Café at the rear of the market to join the small crowd of porters who were tucking into fish pie and mash potato, washed down with 'builders' tea.

As the clatter of cutlery and the rumble of conversation swirled about him he thought about Jane and his son. He had a feeling that Jane would soon have a word with Saunders and get him fired on one pretext or another. Without an official P45 or any official identification as John Davies it would be impossible to get work in London. Even though sixteen years had passed he could not risk using his real identity and the crumpled, fish-stained driver's licence and birth certificate would have to remain in his back pocket.

Lighting up a cigarette after a satisfying meal he came to the decision that he would have to return to the house in the morning and beg Jane not to have him fired. If she insisted on him moving back in he knew, for his son's sake, that he would be unable to say no. He stubbed out his Woodbine in the overflowing ashtray and left the café to return to the reeking Bedford lorry.

For the rest of the day he spent his time listening to an old transistor radio that belonged to the regular driver. After hearing for the tenth time how John Lennon had been shot to death outside his New York apartment he switched off and read an old copy of the *Daily Express* that he had picked up in the café. Soon he began to feel drowsy and moving his suitcase to the floor he lay across the bench seat and fell into a fitful sleep. This dream didn't start with the usual image of Llinos but began straightaway with a high-speed ride on a motorway that felt so realistic that he was bathed in perspiration. The motorcycle ride then became a rapid sequence of disturbing images. Steel pier supports became a forest of tree trunks in the surf with the faces of strangers rising out of the waves and flying towards him. He saw the face of a girl with empty eye sockets that were bleeding heavily. The girl reached out towards him and as she drew nearer her hands turned into claws . . .

John awoke with a start to the roar of engines and he jerked upright to see the flaring headlights of trucks leaving the parking area on their way to pick up the early-morning deliveries of fish at the docks. He checked his watch and cursed when he saw that it had already gone past two o'clock. Grabbing his suitcase he hurried back into the floodlit market and rapped on the roller blind. Despite the sounds of barrows being trundled around, ready for when the porters began unloading the returning lorries, nothing stirred within and he was forced to wait a full fifteen minutes before Saunders strolled up to him with his hand outstretched for the keys.

'You'll be back at five to start work?' he asked and John nodded before turning and walking back to the café for coffee and a bacon sandwich. As he was considered persona non grata by the other porters he preferred to sit in the furthest corner while he ate his breakfast. To help pass the time he browsed a copy of the *Titbits* magazine he had found in the Bedford lorry, hardly pausing to look at the Rubenesque pin-ups in skimpy bikinis. He then picked up a discarded copy of the *Daily Mail*. The 72-point headline shouted about a volcano killing 57 people in Washington. The science writer's contribution on what made Mount St. Helens explode kept him occupied until five o'clock.

After a gruelling shift of three hours and reeking of fish once more John collected his suitcase from the stall where he had put it for safekeeping; mentally rehearsing what he would say to Jane he made his way on foot to the underground station.

The daily rush into the city didn't affect John as he was travelling in the opposite direction. However, he soon felt like a spawning salmon fighting against a fast-running river when he arrived at his station. The jostling crowd trying to get into the station while he was trying to exit slowed his progress and when he finally stepped out into the light drizzle he was so tired that he wasn't aware of the police motorcycle parked at the kerb. John had begun walking along the pavement with his head bowed against the chilling rain when a large hand fell upon his shoulder.

'John Tucker! It's you isn't it?' a gruff voice inquired and John flinched and lifted his face to see a burly uniformed figure standing before him.

'I'm sorry, you have me mistaken for someone else,' he muttered and would have pushed past the officer but for the tight grip on his shoulder.

'Same high cheekbones, same eyes and still the same voice. For God's sake John, don't you recognise me?' Fear was now making John tremble and the policeman could feel it beneath his grip.

'Come on, mate, I won't turn you in,' Alan said, releasing the man's shoulder. 'Why don't we get out of this bloody weather and have a nice cup of coffee?' he added, pointing across the road to a large teashop.

John looked into Alan's face, nodded and carelessly crossed the road without bothering to check for traffic. Alan followed and an approaching car screeched to a halt when the driver noticed the uniform, forcing the following car to brake sharply. They entered the teashop together and John immediately went to a table and sat down to wait. Alan shrugged and ordered coffee for two at the counter.

'Where have you been all this time?'

'Here and there,' John growled and he sipped the scalding black coffee, occasionally using the back of his hand to wipe the odd drops that gathered on his moustache.

'What name are you using?'

'John Davies.'

'Very ordinary sounding name.'

'That's the whole point; it's fairly forgettable. Unlike Tucker.'

Alan didn't probe any further and quickly moved on to reassure John that the police in Hastings were now treating the two fatalities as unsolved cases and had sent them down to the filing department to be put into storage.

Although he was listening intently and felt a certain amount of relief at the news, John still gave a non-committal grunt and continued sipping.

'I think you now owe me, John,' Alan suddenly said, angered by the monosyllabic responses. 'Fifteen years ago, after your disappearance, I mislaid two important witness statements that hindered any further investigation and possibly stopped it from progressing any further, which resulted in the whole case being shelved.'

John looked up in surprise. 'What made them so important?' he asked, putting his cup down carefully as though not to make a noise and interrupt Alan's answer.

'Do you remember Penny? And Toni her friend?' Alan whispered conspiratorially as he leant over the table until his head was almost touching John's. 'They were the two who couldn't come with us to

Hastings on that night.' John still looked puzzled as he racked his brains. 'They were questioned and proved quite capable of describing you, me and Ted from the time they were with us when we were all in the café. Good enough to strengthen the link between us all.'

'So what?'

'I'll tell you what,' Alan hissed. 'When I passed the police exams and was made a constable I made a little sortie into the crypt, the old filing rooms, and took those statements so that, should the worst happen, they couldn't be used in any trial.'

John's head jerked away. 'Trial, what trial?' he barked and curious heads turned towards them.

Alan patted the air in a gesture intended to calm John. 'Yours, you bloody idiot. When they catch you there'll be a trial and statements will be reviewed to select the most reliable prosecution witnesses. Without the two pieces of paper I took nobody will recall the two girls and what they said. They won't be called as witnesses. Get it?' Alan whispered.

John slumped back in his seat. 'You said I owed you—what's that all about?' he murmured, knowing what the answer would be.

'I'm actually offering you a job.'

'I've got a job,' John snapped.

Alan's eyes narrowed. 'You don't understand, John, you will take this job or I will take you in, like the law-abiding policeman that I am. You don't have any other option.' John sighed and sat back with his eyes fixed on the man who was once his friend.

'Apart from keeping the law I also have a little business that requires people to travel about the country very quickly delivering and picking up small packets—it's just like a courier service,' Alan explained.

'And what's in those packets?' John asked, knowing that with Alan running things they couldn't contain anything legal.

'Not for you to know, mate, all you have to do is get back into the saddle and do as you're told.'

'I no longer have a bike,' John said with a twisted half-smile.

'But I do. It's a 750 cc Norton Commando. Can you handle a bike that powerful?' Alan asked with a sly look at the bearded man, knowing that he had extended a challenge that had to be taken up by anyone who had ever been remotely interested in bikes. Such as a dyed-in-the-wool ton-up.

'Of course I bloody can,' John exclaimed angrily.

'Okay, keep your cool, I was only joking. The bike's kept in a lock-up garage in Catford quite close to where I live.'

'But I don't have anywhere to live myself!' John said, pointing at the battered suitcase standing by his chair. Can you do anything about that?'

'There's a flat only a hundred yards from the lock-up, you can use that until you get properly organised.' Alan had been writing on a slip of paper while talking and when finished he folded it in half and slid it across the table.

'That's the address and the name of the young guy who's been living there for a few days. He'll let you in, Tucker.'

'I told you, my name is Davies.'

Alan stood up and extended his hand to John who stared at the proferred hand in disbelief.

'My God, you want me to shake the hand of my blackmailer? Someone who I once considered a pal for life but who now wants to destroy my bloody life for a second time,' he hissed.

The few heads in the teashop turned once more to stare at the two arguing men with anxiety on their faces. They visibly relaxed when they realised that it was a policeman who was standing and went back to murmuring over their tea and cakes.

'Suit yourself, mate,' Alan said with a shrug and picked up his helmet. 'Just be there in two hours, or else I'll be looking for you to make an arrest for murder.' He turned to walk away. 'I have an urgent job for you, don't disappoint me.'

Alan crossed the street to where he had parked the Kawasaki, leaving John staring down into his cup with conflicting feelings of hopelessness and rage.

'Want another coffee, dear?' the timid voice of the waitress said, cutting through his murderous thoughts about Alan.

'No thanks, love,' he mumbled and quickly left the teashop. Walking back to the underground station he bought a ticket to Victoria station. As Alan had said, he had no option but to do as he was told.

9

IT WAS A HOT JUNE IN 1981 and Superintendent Cramer was now rapidly approaching retirement. As each day passed he became more noticeably irritated by the constant banter of the younger members of the force. He slammed his office door shut and glared at the empty in-tray on his desk. Complicated cases that would take time to solve were now being sidelined to younger officers to handle.

'It's as though they expect me to die mid-case,' he thought as he hung the jacket over the back of his chair and picked up the single sheet of paper that had been left on his blotter. It was a note from his boss, Chief Superintendent Saunders, warning him that he had to find time to make an appointment with the police doctor for a full medical before he completed his pension claim form. Cramer screwed it up and tossed it into the waste-paper basket to join the other forms and messages that were constantly reminding him that he was now rapidly approaching that day when he would be superfluous to their needs.

A polite knock on the door elicited a brusque 'come' and Detective Inspector Angstrom entered the office.

'Good morning, sir, just dropped in to let you know that I've been given a rather interesting case to follow up.'

'And I'm the one senior officer who has very little on his plate. Is that what you're inferring, Jennifer?'

'No, sir, I'm not joking. Far from it. It's just that I have some information that may re-open the unsolved case that we were forced to close fifteen years ago.'

Cramer's ears pricked up and he waved a hand towards the chair. 'What case was that?' he asked, as if he didn't know, his interest increasing. In his whole career there had only been two cases he had been unable to clear—the death beneath Hastings pier and a woodland murder, both victims being young women. It piqued him that he would soon be retiring without a clean sheet and the detective's words had raised a spark of hope.

'If you recall, sir, in 1964 when you were an inspector and I was a constable we investigated a death in Hastings which involved a number of bikers.'

'Ton-ups actually, there is a big difference, Jennifer,' Cramer corrected with the stir of excitement beginning to animate his craggy features.

'Well, one of them was a teenager called Edward Barker. He would have been 35 now.'

'I remember him,' Cramer murmured as he leant back in his chair, steepled his fingers on his stomach and dredged up memories of the case with his eyes closed which suddenly snapped open.

'What do you mean by "would have been 35"?'

'I have been ordered to investigate an automobile accident that took place yesterday morning, in which both Barker and his wife were killed,' Angstrom said.

'What have their deaths got to do with an old unsolved crime?'

'It was the husband's dying words, sir. The constable riding in the ambulance with the victims and the male paramedic both claim that the man seemed to be making a confession.

'Confession? Surely Barker didn't kill one of the girls?' Cramer sat bolt upright and fixed the detective with a steely gaze.

'No, sir, he confessed that his sin was in being loyal to his friends.' Reading from a scrap of paper she said, 'His words were, "Alan did it . . . Alan made me ride . . . I was late . . . made me ride . . ." ' Angstrom paused to look up at her boss. 'He then repeated the same words, adding ". . . protect John, he'll be next". Then he sank into an unconscious state from which he never recovered.' Angstrom slid the paper across the highly polished desk.

Cramer picked it up and read the words a number of times in silence. 'If my memory serves me right, this Alan could be Alan Williams, the ton-up who claimed that he had left Doris Trencher under Hastings pier with an unidentified rocker, a mystery man called Tom.'

Angstrom nodded.

'Then Williams supposedly went home. Whereas he could have been the one that killed Doris Trencher and was the actual one being blackmailed by Louise Walton, the murdered girl in Long Wood.' Cramer doodled furiously on the ink blotter even though his ballpoint pen had long run out of ink.

Angstrom was greatly impressed by the superintendent's memory and simply nodded in agreement. 'And John may refer to John Tucker,' Angstrom said.

'Our man on the run, right, but whatever became of this man, Alan Williams?' Cramer asked.

'I'd like to check that out, sir,' Angstrom said getting to her feet. 'Unfortunately I have to organise a full investigation into this motoring accident.' She held up a slim file.

'Okay, while you do that I'll start having a nose around in records,' Cramer said with a conspiratorial tone of voice. 'I'll see if I can find out where this little bit of smoke leads.'

'Smoke, sir?'

'The old adage, Angstrom, where there's smoke . . . in this case this smoke may come from that dying man's death-bed, and that means there has to be a fire somewhere. Also, Edward Barker must have had a *very* guilty conscience about something and I want to know what and why.'

Angstrom left the office deep in thought and was closely followed by Cramer who took the lift to the sub-basement where all the old case files were stored.

Sergeant Anson had been in charge of records for longer than Cramer could remember, possibly since the days when he was still a probationary constable, and like his precious files Anson appeared to have acquired a thin layer of dust upon his head. Approaching the desk Cramer noticed in the dim light that Anson's head was actually peppered with grey and his shoulders with dandruff.

'Morning, Superintendent. It's been a long time since I last saw you down here. How can I help you?' Anson's uniform reeked of shag pipe tobacco and the worn teeth on the left-hand side of his mouth was a result of clamping hard on the pipe-stem the minute he was off duty.

'For goodness sake, Harry. We've known each other for twenty years, so surely it's time you called me Wesley.'

'That would be very disrespectful, Superintendant. Maybe sir would be more appropriate. Less formal?'

Cramer sighed, admitting defeat. 'Okay Harry, now would you fetch me the 1964 files on the Hastings pier death and the Long Wood murder? Both happened in the same month,' Cramer said. The stout man slid from his habitual perch on the wooden stool and with the aid of his malacca cane stumped down one of the long aisles of steel filing cabinets.

During an armed robbery in 1954 Anson had taken a bullet in the thigh which had left that leg one inch shorter than the other and awarded him with the King's Police Medal and a permanent desk job. Although he was no longer on active service he took great pride in being able to remember every case handled out of 'his' police station and he made his way unerringly to two battleship-grey cabinets at the very back of the room. Pulling the ceiling-light cord Anson suddenly appeared in a bright pool of light like a cabaret singer and Cramer grinned, imagining the veteran bursting into a medley of Cole Porter favourites.

The rasping of steel on steel echoed throughout the basement as drawers in the cabinets were dragged open and then slammed shut again. The light was suddenly extinguished, plunging Harry's 'stage' into inky darkness and all Cramer could hear was shuffling feet and a cane tapping as Anson returned to his front desk, his arms laden with three bulging manila folders.

'You're the only person requesting to see these since 1966, sir,' he said dropping them onto the counter. Cramer stepped back to avoid the dust cloud that erupted from the folders. 'Yes, it was November and bloody cold it was too. I think it dropped well below zero for quite a few days and—'

Cramer's curiosity was aroused and he arrested the older man's flow with a raised hand. 'Someone wanted sight of these files in '66?' he asked. 'Who was that?'

'Let me think, sir.' The man perched himself back on the stool and stroked his straggly moustache. 'A young constable. That's right, it was a young constable, wet behind the ears, by the name of . . . err . . . Damn it! I'm sorry, sir. It isn't coming back.'

'Did the constable say what he wanted the files for?'

'Research, sir. He said he was preparing a thesis on unsolved crimes for a chief inspector he worked for in London and was visiting a selection of police stations in Surrey and Kent to gather data.'

'Did he read the files here or take them away?'

'Here, sir. Nobody of his low rank, no matter who he works for, is permitted to remove anything from my Records department,' Anson said officiously. 'I take pride in my security measures, sir.'

'I know you do, Harry and I'll make damned sure that these three files are returned to Records before you leave tonight.' Cramer left with the files under his arm to return to his office and found Angstrom sitting in his chair.

'Trying it for size, Jennifer?' Cramer asked lightly. 'I haven't left yet, okay?'

'Sorry, sir, I was reading the latest report on Edward Barker's car accident. It's just come up from forensic and I thought you might be interested to know that the brake hydraulics had been deliberately tampered with. His inability to stop at the red light was not due to too much alcohol or simple carelessness, as was first thought, but an act of premeditated murder.'

'Any suspects in mind, Jennifer?'

'Yes, sir, Alan Williams. His was the last name on Barker's lips.'

'So was John Tucker.'

'He could only be a suspect if Barker was referring to our on-the-run John Tucker and that Barker was going to give him up to the police. However, if Tucker is still alive and in the country then it may be that he is the one who is in danger. When Barker said, " . . . protect John, he may be next", he could very well have been pointing an accusing finger at Alan Williams.'

'Did you find out where Williams can be found?'

'It didn't take long because I contacted his parents who are now quite elderly and I learned that he had joined the police as a probationary constable in 1965 in Long Wood. When his skill on a motorcycle was made apparent he was quite rapidly promoted to the rank of sergeant with the Metropolitan traffic division.'

'My God! Don't tell me an ex-ton-up is now legally speeding around the city on a powerful motorcycle supplied by the government.'

'Absolutely correct, sir, but how did you know he was riding a bike?'

'I recall him saying that he wanted to join the force when we interviewed him and at the time he was a speed-crazy ton-up. I thought it was a bit of a joke then and that the youngster had simply been winding us up.' Cramer reclaimed his chair and thumped the three heavy files on top of Angstrom's report.

'Do you think he's a rotten cop?' Angstrom asked slowly as she sat staring at the old files with the distinct feeling that she was about to be given a very onerous task.

'It also explains who it was who wanted to read these files back in 1966,' Cramer said quietly, tapping the cover of the top file with a forefinger. 'Old Harry said an unknown constable who asked to look at these in '66 never took the files out of Records but it's my guess that it was Williams and I bet my pension that he did take something. It may even be something vital that could have implicated him or Tucker in the death of the girls.'

'Shall I get him brought down from London for questioning, sir?'

Cramer thought for a moment before shaking his head. 'No, I want to find out why he really wanted to become a policeman first. Was it to do his bit for society which I find hard to believe judging by his attitude when we last interviewed him. Maybe he wanted to continue indulging his passion for speed or perhaps there is an ulterior motive that's more sinister and possibly linked to the death of Edward Barker and his wife.' The senior officer sat thinking for a long time and Angstrom began to shuffle her feet impatiently.

'If you want to get moving and do something, I suggest you take these files, study every page, and find flaws, anything at all, that could strengthen our suspicions.' The dusty files were pushed across the desk to the detective inspector who picked them up with a sigh of resignation and left Cramer's office for her own cramped quarters. It was going to be a very long night.

John left Catford station and holding the piece of paper in his hand asked the ticket clerk for directions. The man grudgingly pointed him in the right direction and John set off, weighed down by his suitcase that was threatening his balance.

After ten minutes in the light rain the cold and dampness began to creep through his outer clothing and he was relieved when he finally saw the road sign.

Chester Road was a shabby run-down terrace of two-up-two-down houses not unlike Jane's place in London. Heaps of bulging black bin-liners were strewn along the pavement as a result of the recent strike by the refuse collectors. Some bags had burst, scattering their contents across the footpath. Apart from the usual kitchen scraps and baked-bean cans he also found himself trudging round discarded mattresses and rusting cookers as he counted off the house numbers until he stood outside a purple-painted residence with a cracked concrete pad for a front garden. A wheelless Volvo 140 stood on bricks and dripped oil from a cracked crankcase, adding to the air of neglect.

John went to the front door and ignoring the doorbell used the tarnished reproduction brass lion to knock energetically. As the sound reverberated throughout the house a number of net curtains twitched across the way but he was unable to see any of the curious faces behind the darkened windows.

Light footsteps approached the door and then three heavy bolts were withdrawn. The door was opened a few inches before being restrained by a steel chain.

An extremely thin young man that John estimated to be no more than 17 looked through the small gap at him. He had a sallow complexion and sunken cheeks that exaggerated his skull-like features and his pupils were constricted, clearly advertising his addiction to hard drugs. He stared at John blankly as he gripped the edge of the door with nail-bitten fingers. 'What d'ya want?' he grunted through the narrow gap.

'Alan sent me,' John snapped. 'Let me in or lose your fingers.' John had no intention of harming the teenager but his aggressive tone of voice hit the wrong nerve and the door began closing. John pushed hard against the door and screws ripped from the wood-wormed frame. The chain gave way allowing the door to open wide enough for John to gain entry into the hallway. His nostrils were immediately bombarded by the smell of tobacco, cat urine and that special kind of mustiness that comes from a blend of mildewed carpets, dirty laundry, boiled cabbage and damp walls.

'Where's the room I have to use?' John demanded as he began ascending the staircase. The surly youth with the words BULL and SHIT tattooed respectively on the knuckles of each hand didn't immediately respond and just stood staring at him as he closed the door until John turned and began to descend again.

'Second on right,' he said hurriedly while backing away and John recommenced climbing to reach the door. The dark blue paint was peeling in strips and the hinges were stiff with corrosion, squeaking in protest as he turned the handle and pushed against the door.

Heavy jacquard drapes that had seen better days had been drawn and the room was in darkness until he managed to find the light switch. A single fly-blown ceiling bulb lit up a scene that could have doubled as a set for a Hitchcock thriller. The steel-framed double bed was covered by a faded paisley quilt that probably dated from the fifties. Bracketing the bed were cheap pine cabinets that bore glass ashtrays filled with cigarette butts and spent matches. One even contained a used condom that none of the previous occupants had bothered to dispose of.

As John moved further into the room a shadow flitting along the rotting skirting board hinted at the presence of rodents. He put his suitcase down as the young addict appeared at the open door and asked if he wanted something to eat in a sullen tone of voice.

'I'll eat out,' John answered as his eyes flicked around the room at the accumulated filth and decay. 'I have a keen desire to survive any time I am compelled to spend here.'

The youth shrugged, scratched at something under his Che Guevara T-shirt and went down to the living room with John following close behind.

The living room was in a similar condition apart from having the luxury of a 21-inch colour televison that was on and currently teaching children how to swim. The sound had been turned down and the youth had thrown himself carelessly into the corner of a badly stained settee to stare at the flickering screen.

'What's your name?' John asked as he stood by the door.

The youth started at the question and then slowly turned his head to look at John. 'Tristan,' he muttered. 'My parents had a weird idea that one day I would meet a girl called Isolde. They also had a sick sense of humour.'

'Sounds perfectly logical to me. What do you do here?'

'I look after the place for the Sergeant.'

'Sergeant Williams?'

'S'right. I have to keep the place tidy and make sure it's locked up day and night,' he said and then turned back to stare at the instructor supporting the back of a 10-year-old in the Olympic-sized pool. 'I musn't use the telly in case someone breaks in to steal it so I turn the sound off. They don't know it's here then, do they?' he added craftily and he bared his dull, yellowing teeth in a poor semblance of a smile which accentuated his skull-like appearance.

'You've got a bloody aerial on the roof. Bit of a dead give-away that you have television, don't you think? Where's the nearest café?' John asked with a wry expression.

The lad raised a needle-marked arm above his head and pointed roughly in a direction that could have been anywhere. 'Hundred yards down the road. It's a pretty scruffy burger joint but I don't think you'll get food-poisoning. Just make sure you ask for your meat well done.'

John didn't bother thanking the teenager who, after giving directions, had immediately slumped back to mindlessly watch the swimming lesson. Tristan had been told it would be an hour before his supplier arrived with his next fix and he could already feel the onset of muscle cramp.

John left the house, took a deep breath of relatively fresh air, and then strode down the road seeking the means to silence his rumbling stomach.

The 100 yards became 300 before he spotted a dilapidated establishment that seemed to crouch ashamedly between a laundromat and a large electricity sub-station. He read the faded sheet of typewritten paper taped to the steamed-up window and ignoring all the greasy offerings he wisely decided on the simple cottage pie.

It was two hours before he re-entered the house and found Alan waiting for him with an expression of extreme impatience on his face.

'Where the hell have you been, John?' he demanded the moment John walked past him and threw himself into an armchair that had lost most of its stuffing. Broken springs complained beneath the extra helping of meat and potatoes and John stretched his legs before replying.

'A man has to eat, mate,' he said, using as much sarcasm as he could for the last word. 'No uniform?' he added studying Alan's civilian outfit that consisted of dark blue jeans and a black sweatshirt under a plain leather jacket.

'Don't be stupid, Tucker. I can't wear a uniform in this area and I certainly can't be seen entering this house as a cop. That's the quick way to get petrol poured through the letter box.'

John gave a brief nod and then said, 'Please don't call me Tucker, especially not in front of others, my name is John Davies.'

'Okay, whatever! So enough time-wasting. You have to get ready for work,' and Alan tossed a keyring on a long thin chain across the room. John snatched it mid-air and the keys and disc were inspected closely.

'Nice, a Norton just as you said,' John said approvingly as he inspected the enamelled badge with the large yellow N and the word COMMANDO etched beneath it.

'Naturally, there's one key for the Commando and the other for the lock-up. You'll always keep the bike locked in the garage when it's not in use and the key around your neck. That's what the chain's for.' John looped it over his neck and found that the keys hung at waist level.

'That enables you to use the keys without having to remove the chain from your neck. This is strictly for bike security as it's an expensive bit of kit.' Alan jabbed a stiff finger into John's shoulder. 'Do you understand?'

John winced before nodding slowly. 'And what's so urgent that I have to do it today?'

Alan took a brown packet from a large pocket inside his leather jacket and laid it on the small rickety side table that was covered with numerous cigarette burns and coffee-cup rings. It lay within John's reach but he didn't lean across to pick it up. 'It's to be delivered to that address,' Alan said, pointing to the blue writing on the packet. 'And it has to be there within two hours.'

John relented, picked it up and weighed it in his hand as he read the crude labelling. 'You want me to deliver this to Birmingham in two hours?'

'Didn't I just say that?'

'You want me to exceed the speed limit big time,' John muttered as he continued to balance the packet that had been sealed with a large blob of red wax. 'What's in it?'

'You don't ask questions, John. You just take it and deliver it without breaking that bloody seal. The man you're delivering it to will have your balls fried in batter if you so much as touch the wax. Afterwards you'll get back here and return the bike to the lock-up by five o'clock. Those are your instructions and for that you'll get a hundred quid plus the cost of the petrol. If you're caught you'll be completely disowned. I don't know you and can't help you. The bike was registered in my name but I reported it stolen and since then it has been used by a friend of yours. Anyone caught on it will be charged with theft, do you understand?'

'A friend of mine . . . what friend?'

'Edward Barker, remember him?'

'Have you got Ted making deliveries for you? Have you blackmailed him into doing your dirty work too?' John shouted as he dropped the packet, jumped up and grabbed at Alan's lapels.

The tall man easily batted John's hands away and stepped back with a sneer on his face. 'He was weak like you. No, he didn't want to betray your trust so when I said I knew where you were and would turn you in if he didn't do a little courier work for me he did as he was bloody told.'

'I swear I'll kill you one day, Alan. That's a promise,' John whispered. 'If I'm using his bike how can Ted do any work for you?'

'He doesn't work for me any more. The moment I saw you outside the underground station I got rid of him. His conscience was beginning to affect his performance and anyway you're the better rider by far,' Alan said tonelessly. 'Incidentally, the longer you hang about here getting on your high horse the less time you'll have to make your first delivery by the deadline which, to remind you, is midday.'

John glanced at his watch and the youth giggled. Alan strode across and kicked him hard in the shins with the tip of his steel-tipped boot. 'You'll keep your mouth shut while I'm here or you won't get another hit,' he snarled at the yelping addict.

'Sorry, Sarge,' he whined and immediately received another painful kick.

'Never call me by my rank! I'm Mr Williams, understand?' The boy nodded frantically as he tucked his legs up under him on the settee and looked up at Alan with pleading eyes.

'He's just a bloody waste of space,' Alan said looking at the cowering lad. 'But he's handy for running errands for me from time to time.'

'As I recall, you were always a bit of a bully at school, Alan. However, I can see now that you're also a bloody sadist,' John shouted as he picked up the packet. 'He's only a child and you're already killing him with hard drugs. What kind of bastard are you?'

'I hope a wealthy bastard very soon and you'd better get going. The people you're giving that parcel to don't like to be kept waiting. Ted kept them waiting and my partner decided to terminate his employment.' Alan turned on his heel and left the room. 'They have an amusing habit of cutting brake lines and putting sugar in fuel tanks if they think they've been insulted.' He said this while walking down the hallway and his last word was punctuated by the front door slamming.

After one pitying glance at the lad curled up on the settee with his eyes fixed on the television screen, John left the house and soon found the row of garages set back from the road.

It only took him a moment to unlock the brand-new padlock and raise the up-and-over door to reveal the gleaming beauty of a pristine 750 cc Norton. Lying on the seat was a set of new registration plates and a screwdriver and John slipped them inside his jacket, one on each side of his chest like the breastplates of a medieval suit of armour. He dropped the tool into an inside pocket and then swung the stand up with his foot and rolled the bike out into the road. John locked the garage and returned to mount the machine.

At the first turn of the key the bike burst into life with a throaty roar that brought back stirring memories of his old days on the Kentish country lanes. The black helmet that hung by its strap on the handle bar fitted perfectly and he tucked the packet inside his jacket behind one of the plates before zipping up to the chin and putting the bike into gear. As he released the clutch and twisted the throttle lightly the hairs rose on the back of his neck and he raced off down the road feeling sixteen years younger.

The spirit of the ton-up had been released to race once more.

10

JOHN LOST TIME ON THE ROADS leading to London and cursed the traffic as he checked his watch while crossing the Thames at Battersea Bridge. He only had ninety minutes to reach Birmingham and he began to rack up the speed as he dangerously weaved between the cars whilst circling Marble Arch before peeling off and accelerating up Edgware Road. Within ten minutes he had passed through Cricklewood, leaving angry motorists in his wake, and was approaching the beginning of the M1 motorway at Staples Corner. He checked for patrol cars before pulling over into an overgrown lay-by and quickly changing the registration plates. Putting the old plates under his jacket he pulled out and then peeled off onto the on-ramp leading to the motorway.

The traffic lanes stretched into the distance and John grinned to himself as he began to wind the throttle until the red speedo needle had passed ninety and he was overtaking cars and trucks as though they were stationary.

In the old days John had rarely travelled north of the Thames on his old Dominator and as the miles ticked by so did unfamiliar towns. The roar of the 750 cc engine and the smell of hot oil made John long for those times when his working week at the factory ended and he was let loose from the boredom of his apprenticeship to race on narrow country lanes, his footrests trailing glorious sparks in the air as he leant first one way and then the other to negotiate the tight S-bends.

He could almost hear the faint shouts of his old mates as they rode in his slipstream or raced past to take the lead before his reverie ended and he returned to the present to realise that he was hearing a totally different kind of sound. It was the nerve-stretching wail of a siren and glancing into his mirror he saw a motorway patrol car only yards behind him, roof lights flashing furiously. It was a Ford Granada and John grinned and slowly twisted the throttle. He lowered his body as the air pressure increased until he was lying flat on the tank with his feet pressing back on the high backrests.

The Commando was in complete harmony with the slightest movements he made and he was soon streaking away from the struggling chase car with 120 showing on the clock. As the Granada dwindled in his rear-view mirror he prepared himself mentally for the evasive action he would be forced to take if the chase car radioed ahead for assistance.

It didn't take long before the race really started.

John had passed three more on-ramps when he saw the two vehicles with flashing lights a mile ahead. Within fifteen seconds he was forced to slow down, for the police cars had created a rolling-roadblock by weaving from side to side, obstructing all lanes. Traffic had backed up and John had to filter between the vehicles. This forced him to reduce his speed to 30 mph. He occasionally sat upright to check on what the patrol cars were doing before crouching down to creep past the cars and trucks surrounding him. He emerged from the vehicles into clear space and began moving slowly towards the two zigzagging police cars. John could see that the officers had spotted him and were already using their radios to plan their next move to apprehend the reckless rider.

John checked his watch and frowned when he saw that he only had forty-five minutes to reach the Walsall address. He began to weave the bike from side to side, matching the tactics of the police cars until he felt he had the rhythm judged about right and then twisted the throttle wide. The bike responded by rearing a little before the front tyre dropped and then John roared down the side of the swerving Granada, the startled face of the officer in the passenger seat only inches away.

The Commando raced ahead of the two cars and before the drivers could react and begin chasing John was a hundred yards ahead and rapidly increasing his lead. The chase cars tried to catch up but as the rolling roadblock had created a totally empty motorway ahead without a single obstacle to slow their quarry they were unable to close the distance between them and John. Once more he adopted the prone position and pushed the bike well over the ton. With the throttle fully twisted the needle crept up to touch 125 as the junction for the next motorway raced towards him. He swept round the gentle curve, leaving the M1 dwindling far behind, and then continued on the M6 motorway until he spotted the slip road marking his exit for the district of Walsall. John judged his distances perfectly and left braking until the last second before leaning over and filtering down the off-ramp at high speed.

As soon as he had left the motorway and entered the densely built-up area he looked for a quiet street to stop and change the number plates. He then took out a well-thumbed A-Z street map for Birmingham that Alan had left on the side table next to the packet and began searching for the address.

It eventually turned out to be a junkyard at the end of a cul-de-sac in a shabby district and John rode through the half-open gates into a clearing surrounded by untidy pillars of scrap metal. Refrigerators, hot-water boilers and grotesque pieces of rusting objects towered on every conceivable square inch of the yard. John stopped outside a clapboard office with a corrugated tin roof and a peeling sign advertising *Dan's Scrap* in bold white lettering. The proprietor had apparently been targeted by one or more unhappy clients for someone had daubed black paint to obliterate the *S*.

John chuckled as he briefly imagined it to be the work of the same comic who had broken Alice's neon sign so long ago.

A face appeared briefly at the small window before the door swung open swiftly and a swarthy-looking man with a large prominent belly emerged to stand and stare at John in silence.

'Don't be rude, Dimitri, invite our visitor in,' a voice said from within the shack and as John pulled the bike up onto its stand the broad-shouldered man waved him in. He disappeared inside and John stepped through the door, pausing on the threshold to let his eyes become adjusted to the dim light.

An old man with a craggy face and silver hair tied back tightly waved at him to take the three-legged stool that stood before his desk. John extended his hand but the man ignored it and just looked at him while patting the air with his hands to encourage John to sit down.

'You arrived on time, good,' the elderly man said in an accented voice that John could only assume was Greek. 'I believe you have something for me.'

'Only if your name is Constantine Karras and you have some form of identity to prove it,' John replied quietly.

'A cautious man, that I like,' the Greek said as he reached inside his tailored jacket and withdrew his wallet. 'Will this be sufficient?' He slid a driver's licence across the desk. John leant forward to read the name, glanced up briefly to compare the photograph and then flicked the card back with his forefinger.

'That'll do fine, Mr Karras,' he said as he unzipped the leather jacket. The big man who had been leaning against the wall behind John's chair took a quick step forward but stopped in an instant when the old man held up his hand.

'It's okay, Dimitri. I am sure that Mr err . . . '

'Davies,' John volunteered.

'Mr Davies is harmless. Please give me my packet.'

Dimitri leant back against the wall but despite his master's words his eyes never left John's hands. The packet was withdrawn from behind the number plates and placed on the desk in front of the old man. He greedily took it and after breaking the wax seal began cutting the tape and unwrapping the stiff brown paper. Within was a further layer of thick white tissue paper which Karras took greater care to unwrap until there was a glint of metal and he gave a deep sigh of contentment.

'They had better all be here,' Karras said in a low expectant tone as he slowly pulled the tissue paper apart until he had exposed a number of ancient coins.

'Christ!' John exclaimed. 'Do you mean I pushed the bike to its limits and risked my bloody life for the sake of a few measly old coins?'

'What did you think it was, drugs?' Karras said quietly as he reverently picked up each piece and placed it to one side until he had twelve neatly arranged in three stacks. 'These coins are exceptionally rare Ionia Phokaia.'

'And what the hell are they?'

'Greek coins from the sixth century BC. Each weighs exactly 2.5 grams and is made from solid electrum.'

John stared unbelievingly at the historic pieces. 'You mean they're not even gold?'

'Electrum, Mr Davies, is a unique alloy of both gold and silver. The brighter the yellow the greater the percentage of gold.'

'What are they worth?'

'If you wish to be so vulgar as to talk about money when referring to these ancient artefacts then I shall tell you that each coin has a value of £500 and that I shall be taking them back to Athens.'

'Athens?'

'To the National Archaeological Museum to be more precise, Mr Davies. They are being returned home which is where they belong.'

John had not been listening but silently doing the sums and realised that he had transported £6,000 worth of antique coins. He zipped up his jacket and stood up, aware that the man called Dimitri was standing between him and the only exit from the office.

'Is that all?' he asked Karras. 'I take it I can go now.'

'Yes, Mr Davies, you can go.' The white head was bent over the coins as the man carefully studied them with a jeweller's loupe. 'I look forward to your next delivery. Just make sure you are on time again as I detest being kept waiting. Mr Williams's last courier knows how I feel about punctuality. I believe he was asked to take a very long trip.'

'He went to Australia. That's all I know and I would appreciate it if you could give me a little more travelling time next time. I was nearly stopped by the cops on my way here,' John said as he turned away to be faced by Dimitri.

'You were chosen to replace the last courier, Mr Davies, because you were rated as the very best and on that assumption I expect the goods to arrive on time no matter how tight the deadline is. Do you understand what I am saying?' The old man's voice had changed. It now had a sharp menacing edge.

John unzipped his jacket partially and placed his right hand on one of the number plates on the basis that it would make a handy weapon. Dimitri took a step towards John but then moved away to his right when his master gave a dismissive wave.

'Have a good trip, Mr Davies. See you again very soon. *Andio.*'

John nodded and left the office. When he reached his bike he looked back and saw that Dimitri was standing in the doorway once more, his dark eyes fixed on him. He started the bike and accelerated away, derisively throwing dust and cinders into the air. He glanced at his watch and realised that he had plenty of time before he had to be back at the Catford lock-up.

He cruised slowly along the motorway until he came to the first service centre and pulled in to have a leisurely all-day breakfast. There was a police Granada in the parking area and the two officers were drinking coffee at the table next to John. He smiled to himself as he relived the chase in his mind. It reminded him of the numerous occasions he had managed to evade the local bobby who rode a water-cooled Velocette yet still imagined he could catch a reckless 19-year-old on a 600 cc Norton.

The officers took it in turns to study the motorcyclist but the anonymity of the unadorned leather jacket, jeans and plain black helmet were the uniform of every other biker. When John left the restaurant and mounted the Norton they both looked through the plate-glass window to check his registration. Disappointment showed on their faces when they saw that it wasn't the number given in the recent radio bulletin.

As it was raining John took his time on the return journey and rolled the bike into the lock-up at precisely five o'clock. He switched the plates back and left the spares behind some empty oil cans that stood on a high shelf on the back wall of the garage. Returning to the house he found that the young addict was out and he went into the kitchen to make himself a coffee. The front door slammed and a heavy tread in the hallway told him that Alan had returned.

'Did you deliver the packet?' were his first words when he entered the kitchen. John nodded and he sat down at the table and placed a slightly smaller packet on the pine surface. 'This has to be taken to Brighton. There's not the same rush as the Birmingham run; you can take it tomorrow morning.'

'What was so urgent about the last one, it was only a bunch of old coins,' John said as he picked up the packet.

'You weren't supposed to know what was in the parcel,' Alan said harshly. 'Did you break the seal to have a look?'

'No, the Greek opened it in front of me and even told me what they were worth,' John said defensively. 'Six grand he said. Were those coins stolen or did you get them cheap from the dodgy partner you mentioned?'

'I never said my partner was dodgy and how I got them is none of your business. All you have to do is deliver what I give you to the address written on each packet. You'll find you'll be well paid for doing as you're told.' He took an envelope from his inside pocket and slid it across the table to John who picked it up and started counting the banknotes.

'As I said, you'll get a hundred for each delivery—'

Sudden thumping on the stairs interrupted Alan and both men turned as the kitchen door swung open and Tristan leapt into the room. His pupils were like pin pricks and every part of his body seemed to be vibrating from nervous energy.

'Hi, guys, what's new?' he shouted and then burst into a bout of coughing as he danced around the kitchen to a silent music track.

'Damn, he's found the stash,' Alan said before hurrying from the room and pounding up the stairs. Tristan gave a yelp and hurried after him, slamming the kitchen door shut behind him.

John shrugged unconcernedly and went on making his coffee. As he sat down to drink it he fingered the small packet, squeezing it and shaking it, trying to recognise the object that was hidden within. Completely baffled he dropped it back onto the table and read the Brighton address. It was an antiques shop in The Lanes which had been his preferred place on the south coast when he was a teenager. He could almost taste the mussels that he, Alan and Ted used to share when they went to their favourite restaurant in the maze of small streets. They only went on very special occasions for the prices charged were a little beyond their reach.

Alan stomped down the stairs and when the door was thrown open John could see that the sergeant was in a foul mood.

'The stupid kid discovered where I hid the drugs and gave himself one hell of a high,' Alan muttered between clenched teeth. 'I ought to kill the little bastard.'

'Is he all right?' John asked.

'No, he bloody well isn't. He's just taken a double whammy of the purer shit that I keep for special customers and now the kid's running up the walls and across ceilings. Tristan is so high I'm not so sure when he'll come down again.'

'What do you mean by that,' John said.

'He could die on us, that's what,' Alan jeered.

'Where is he now?'

'I've locked him in his room until he runs out of steam and sleeps the rest of it off. A damned nuisance because I have to go back on duty now and I was hoping Tristan could pick up something I had left with a friend in town.' Alan kicked at the cat bowl angrily, sending dry biscuits skittering across the dirty linoleum.

'What is it? Drugs?' John asked.

Alan snorted. 'Would I be so stupid as to let a hard-lining addict pick up drugs for me and expect to see them again? You have to be joking Tucker.'

'Davies!'

Duress

'Whatever. No, it's a small Georgian snuffbox that I promised to the same person you are delivering that packet to.' He pointed at the envelope on the table. 'It's a gift he wants to give to the young man who is planning to marry his daughter.'

'I'll pick it up and take it with me in the morning,' John volunteered. 'Where do you want me to go?'

'It's a small jewellery shop on the high street called Carson & Son. You are to go round the back at ten o'clock precisely and there you'll see that the back door has been left open. A small man who calls himself Jock will meet you there and give you the snuffbox.'

'Are you asking me to participate in a robbery, Alan?' John said, his eyes opening wide at the thought.

'No, you'll just be receiving an item that the man owes me.'

'A snuffbox he has just stolen!'

'You're not stealing the bloody thing. You're just receiving it on my behalf. Now do it before I lose my temper and do something I regret,' Alan shouted as he stormed out of the kitchen. The front door slammed loudly and the house fell quiet. John couldn't hear any movement upstairs and assumed that Tristan had fallen asleep. He checked his watch and slipped his leather jacket on before leaving the house.

The mental coin he tossed came down tails and he decided against using the bike and walked on past the lock-up towards the high street that was only half a mile distant. The rain had stopped and the streets were glistening in the amber glow of the sodium lamps. There were a few people about who were making their way home after a night at their local pub, their collars turned up against the brisk night breeze that had started to blow a little harder.

Shopfronts were still brightly lit despite being closed and John walked the full length until he came upon the small premises carrying the legend Carson & Son—Jewellers in gold letters over the door. It was one of the few shops that had turned its lights off and the display windows were in darkness. The velvet-covered racks and shelves had been emptied at closing time as a precaution against smash-and-grab raiders.

John kept walking and spotted a dark narrow alleyway. He glanced around and seeing that nobody was near he quickly darted into the darkness and trotted to the very end where a small wooden gate in the high fence stood ajar. After looking back to check for any movement against the brightly lit oblong of the street he slipped into the backyard of the jewellers'.

John walked carefully along the cinder path between raised vegetable beds towards the rear of the building but the back door was shut. A tabby leapt suddenly from under his feet with a blood-chilling shriek and merged with the blackness of the backyard. John froze to wait patiently while counting to twenty before making any movement towards the door. He was just reaching out for the door handle when the door opened by itself.

'Shit!' a startled voice loudly whispered in the blackness. 'Who the hell are you?' John stumbled back as an extremely short man carrying two briefcases stepped from the shop to confront him.

'I'm from Alan, you have something for him,' John said softly.

'Where's Tristan?' the man whispered back as he circled John, his eyes darting as though preparing himself to make a dash for it should John make a false move.

'Sick,' John said noticing the man's intention and taking two quick paces to cut him off. 'You have a snuffbox for Alan, give it to me now and then we can go our separate ways.'

The man paused and stared intently at John's face in the dark. 'Okay!' he said. 'Here it is! One George III silver snuffbox worth £390 as promised. Tell him the debt has been repaid.'

John took it and gave the man a pitying look. 'If you're under Alan's thumb the way I am then you know that you'll never be able to pay off your debt.' He went back along the alley towards the bright street beyond. Peering round the corner he checked both ways before stepping out and striding along the damp paving stones.

The terraced house was in darkness when he returned and John went straight to his room and took out the snuffbox. The silver and agate shone brightly in the light of the single light bulb as John admired the craftsmanship of the piece. He placed it with the packet and prepared himself for bed. He sorely needed to sleep but he feared closing his eyes in case he dreamt again.

It was Monday and the sun filtered through the filthy window to illuminate John's face, beaded with perspiration. He woke up and before moving a muscle he listened intently but the house remained deathly quiet. He leapt up and doused his face in the grubby corner basin before plugging in his electric razor.

Half an hour later, dressed and partly refreshed, John went downstairs to the kitchen. It was deserted and he considered going up again to check on Tristan's condition but decided against it. He had no wish to get involved in the young drug addict's life and settled for eating a simple breakfast and leaving the house.

The Commando burst into life, waking half a dozen benefit cheats who had planned to enjoy a lazy day, and John was soon on the road travelling south on all the back roads that led to Brighton. After he had cleared the urban areas, busy with early morning commuters, he entered the country roads that were thankfully empty.

John restrained the powerful engine to a burbling idle, quite content to keep below the speed limits while meandering along the smaller lanes that in the past had always heightened his feeling of freedom. It had been a euphoric sensation that thanks to Alan's hold over him he could no longer fully enjoy.

Using the more scenic roads that he and Ted had ridden he slowed even more to look at the beautiful scenes unfolding before him as the sun rose higher. John's mind began to wander and he recalled the relaxed family holidays. With the small boot of the Morris Minor crammed with suitcases they had driven on the narrow lanes and byways, deliberately avoiding major roads and stopping only to picnic and wander in the richly scented woodland. While his mother spread a tablecloth on the grass and unpacked trifles, jellies and lemonade his father identified yellow pimpernels, foxgloves and fungi for his son. John recalled squeezing puffballs until the spores were released to drift away on the wind. Although his father's explanation of the sex life of fungi was beyond him his interest in flora and fauna never waned and even rubbed off on Ted. He often accompanied John on their outings and grew fond of the Tuckers.

John had a sudden longing to see his parents again. He felt the need to apologise to them both for leaving so suddenly and without a word. He knew it must have caused his mother a great deal of pain. As he approached a crossroads he felt a strong impulse to change direction; he braked, planning to turn left and make a clean break but Alan's threat surfaced, cutting through his guilt and he kept going straight on.

He wasn't sure at what time exactly the lemony smell of new-mown hay had been replaced by the sharp tang of brine but he knew he was drawing near to the coast and within fifteen minutes he was making his way along the seafront. The continuous warning of skylarks high above the fields had been replaced by the shrieks of herring gulls.

The antique shop was easy to find and John was soon handing the packet over to a rather distinguished-looking man. 'I'm John Davies and I was asked to deliver this to you.'

'Thank you, Mr Davies. I'm Mr Jackson, and this is my shop.' Mr Jackson was in his late fifties and a good two inches taller than John. He had a habit of stroking his bushy moustache that like his neatly trimmed sideburns was streaked with silver.

'I have been waiting for this for a long time, John,' he said while eagerly unwrapping the packet on an inlaid mahogany writing table. John watched with curiosity as the antiques dealer uncovered a jade figurine. It was carved so exquisitely that even John who had little knowledge of such matters was greatly impressed.

'Wow, those fish are really beautiful,' he exclaimed.

'These are not just fish but *nishikigo* or brocaded carp, young man,' he murmured as he held the piece up to the light. 'White and green jade that was carved in China at the beginning of the last century.' He turned and held the piece out to John. 'Just feel how smooth it is. That's the result of thousands of admiring fingers and there's no reason why yours cannot join them.'

John gingerly took the small figurine and placed it in the palm of his hand. The white carp appeared lifelike as they leapt out of the green waves that were breaking against a rustic fence. On impulse he ran the tip of his forefinger over the scales as if to get a reaction from the creatures.

'Beautiful, isn't it?' the dealer said softly as he took the piece from John's hand. 'Worth every penny of the £600 your boss is asking.' He handed a small envelope to John. 'Make sure he gets this, John, and tell him that I would like more pieces of the same quality.' He placed the figurine on the desk blotter.

John was tucking the envelope inside his jacket when a door opened at the back of the shop and a vision that far exceeded the beauty of all the assembled antiques swept into the showroom. At least, she appeared as a vision to John who stood perfectly still with his mouth hanging open.

Her light-auburn hair hung down to her shoulders where it curled up and bounced with every movement as she walked towards the two men. The floral summer dress belted at the waist and swirling around her knees enhanced her feminine shape.

Even white teeth were revealed when she smiled at the dealer and then surprisingly, at John. He closed his mouth and swallowed as she stopped in front of him and a breath of eau de cologne lightly perfumed the space between them.

A brief image of Llinos appeared in his mind and the difference between her and the girl standing before him could not be denied. Llinois had been olive-skinned with long black tresses and dark fathomless eyes whereas Anne was cream and gold with blue-green eyes as rare as topaz.

'Aren't you going to introduce me, Daddy?' she asked in a low, mellow voice that sent a shiver down John's spine.

'Certainly my dear,' Jackson said with a half-smile. 'John, this is my unruly daughter, Anne. And this gentleman with the boisterous beard and open mouth is Mr John Davies.' He guffawed deeply and held the jade piece for his daughter to see.

'That's beautiful, Daddy. Is it for me?' She took it from him and held it up to her face and John thought that her flawless skin was equal to the smooth sheen of the jade.

'Sorry, honey, but that little piece already has a customer on the other side of the planet. A very nice or, should I say, very wealthy Chinese gentleman who is willing to pay me a handsome sum for that little *Cyprinus carpio*.'

Anne gave it back with an exaggerated pout of disappointment.

John chuckled, guessing that this was a charade the father and daughter regularly played and then noticed the time on the walnut long-case clock in the corner of the showroom. 'Flipping heck, is that the time? I've got to get going,' he said, genuinely disappointed at having to leave the tranquillity of the shop and more so, the dealer's attractive daughter.

'I hope I can get down this way again, very soon,' John added as he shook Jackson's hand while looking into Anne's green eyes. Then John unwillingly left the shop and walked briskly to the parked Commando.

He had seated himself when the young woman burst from the shop and hurried towards him.

'Did my father say that your name was Davis or Davies?' she asked as she held her hand out to him. Her eyes studied his face intimately and he felt himself blush.

'Davies, John Davies,' he stuttered. He took the long-fingered hand lightly and smiled, knowing that she had known the answer before leaving the shop. He reached into his pocket for the ignition key and his fingers encountered the small silver snuffbox.

'I almost forgot, I have something else that your father is also waiting for,' he said as he showed her the snuffbox. He dismounted and started walking back to the shop.

Anne reached out and stopped him. 'I think that's an excellent excuse for you to come back again,' she said in a conspiratorial tone of voice and she winked.

He nodded his head vigorously and with a broad grin he remounted the Commando. He gave Anne a wave and rode out of Brighton in higher spirits than when he'd arrived.

Despite being late he avoided the main roads and his trip back along the country lanes seemed even more beautiful than before. Colourful butterflies flittering against a backdrop of pink dog roses took on a totally new significance and he throttled back to cruise more slowly with the engine burbling. He immersed himself in the beauty of the day whilst his mind conjured images of Anne.

It was midday and back to reality when he re-entered his harsh world, the dismal street in Catford, and parked the bike in the lock-up. He clicked the padlock into place and walked towards the house. An ambulance was parked outside with an empty police car behind; the siren had been switched off but its lights were still flashing.

Without further thought John turned on his heel and walked in the opposite direction until he reached the greasy spoon. He immediately spotted Alan sitting by himself, partially hidden behind the newspaper he was reading. John went to sit opposite Alan and he looked up as though he had been expecting him.

'You're back, good,' he said nonchalantly. 'I thought this would be the first place you'd hide as soon as you saw the flashing blue lights. Did you give Jackson the parcel and the snuffbox?'

'What's going on at the house?' John said, ignoring the question.

'Some anonymous good citizen, namely yours truly, tipped off the ambulance service that there was a very sick person in No. 42. They came and found the door unlatched and a lad who had overdosed. Naturally, the paramedics then called my mates.'

'You mean the cops. Was it Tristan? Is he dead?' John whispered.

'Yes. The stupid bastard had taken all I had stashed in the toilet cistern, a grand's worth of the finest, and jabbed it in his stomach. You saw him just before you left this morning,' Alan said in a low voice. 'He wasn't feeling too good then but he went ahead and gave himself another shot an hour later. Keeled over stone cold.'

'Poor kid, he didn't stand a chance while working for you, did he?' John whispered harshly.

'Fuck the kid, did you make the delivery?'

'Yes, and there's your blood money,' John snapped throwing the envelope onto the empty plate. Alan picked it up with a look of distaste and wiped off the dried egg yoke and bacon fat that was sticking to the pristine white paper. Running a nail along the flap he withdrew the wad of cash and quickly slipped it into a side pocket before reaching into the other and taking out a few notes that he slid across the table to John.

'No fancy high speeds were required for that delivery so it's only fifty quid,' he said while watching John's face carefully. 'Don't forget, you pay your own expenses like petrol and food so you'll have to get your own lunch.'

'What about my things in the house?' John asked as he stuffed the notes into a side pocket where the snuffbox was. 'And where the hell do I sleep tonight?'

Alan wrote quickly on the back of a paper serviette and gave it to John. 'Ask for Bill, he's the joker who is planning to be the son-in-law of old man Jackson, the dealer you've just been to see. He used to take things down to Brighton for me and that's how he got involved with the bit of skirt.'

'She's not a bit of skirt as you put it,' John said with anger.

'They're all the same to me. Use them and lose them, that's my motto when it comes to women.'

'That's because you're an animal,' John snapped loudly and heads turned.

'You'll find Bill is a bit of an animal too but he comes in handy and he'll fix you up with a room. I'll arrange for your things to be collected and sent to you.' Alan stood up and walked towards the door. 'I'll see you at ten tonight. Be there,' he said over his shoulder as he left the café and the other diners returned to digesting their meals whilst reading their newspapers.

John ordered sausage and mash and a mug of tea and then sat mulling over John's words while he waited for his meal. He had been deeply disappointed to learn that Anne was engaged to somebody who associated with Alan and judging by Alan's comments probably just as amoral. He gave himself a mental slap for prejudging the man and began eating the moment the plate was put before him.

As he left the café he saw his own reflection in the mottled green glass of the door and realised how neglectful he had become. His hair hung down to his shoulders, not unlike Anne's, but there all similarity ended: his hair was almost as greasy as the meal he had just consumed. The full beard was matted and totally concealed his normally attractive jawline. He looked down at his stained jeans and scuffed boots and thought that he had seen better-looking people sleeping rough beneath newspapers on park benches.

John made a detour on his way to the lock-up to pay a visit to a high-street pharmacy where he purchased some basic toiletries. He then trawled the high street to buy a shirt, jeans and some underwear before retrieving the bike and riding to the address scrawled on the café serviette.

As he drew near to his new lodgings a restored fighter plane roared over his head, making an approach to Biggin Hill airfield. Large banners on the wrought-iron gates of the RAF officers' training base announced the forthcoming air show and as if to emphasise this a second fighter, a World War II Hurricane, flew over the road a mere fifty feet above John's head.

The house he was looking for was in a narrow unadopted road that was more like an assault course for tanks than a normal suburban street. The ruts and potholes in the hard surface tested the Commando's suspension to the limit and John's rear was given a severe beating. He turned into the driveway and stopped by the paved footpath that led to the front door.

The detached mock-Tudor house was set amongst dense greenery and he knew that Alan had found the perfect hideaway. As he pulled the bike up onto its stand the door opened and a man in his late thirties came out onto the porch. He wore a dazzlingly white open-necked sports shirt and a pair of cream linen slacks. He scowled at John who was walking towards him and held a hand up.

'That's far enough. Who are you and what do you want?' he demanded aggressively.

John kept on walking until he was only two paces from the man and able to judge that he was two inches taller than the stranger. 'My name is John. Alan phoned to tell you I was coming, yes?'

The young man grudgingly nodded his head and waved John past him into the house. The door was slammed and William Tyler coldly introduced himself as 'Bill' without offering his hand before striding down the hall and up the stairs.

'I'll show you where you can sleep until Alan finds you somewhere else to kip down,' he called down. 'I don't want you here for any longer than is necessary.'

John shrugged and followed him up the stairs thinking it inconceivable that a pretty woman such as Anne could be attracted to this lounge lizard.

The bedroom and bathroom were a good deal more luxurious than his usual digs and he immediately shut himself in and began making use of his purchases.

It took him almost an hour but eventually he felt respectable enough to descend the stairs in a new pair of jeans. The new blue shirt still had the maker's creases and his face was covered with razor nicks that had been patched with small scraps of toilet paper. His face felt decidedly naked and the cool air on his skin was a strange sensation.

'Apart from the confetti you're looking a bit more human, I see,' Bill sneered as John entered the living room. He put his glass down on the coffee table. 'Not quite the Neanderthal now that the whiskers are gone. In fact, you look a helluva lot younger. How old are you?'

'It's of no interest to you,' John growled as he went to the drinks cabinet. After carefully choosing from one of the bottles standing on the top he poured himself a stiff shot of malt whisky in a crystal glass.

'Pretty free and easy with my booze, aren't you?' Bill spat out.

'Alan extended the invitation to stay here so, please, make sure any quarrel you have is with him.' John sank into one of the easy chairs and took a sip of the fifteen-year-old malt.

'What do you do for Alan?' Bill's small yet cunning eyes watched John as he picked up his own glass.

'I provide him with a courier service. I run things around the country for him.'

'Snap! We're in the same business and I can tell what kind of packages you carry too: recreational goodies for the youngsters,' Bill probed with one raised eyebrow.

'What the hell are you talking about?'

'Amps, brown sugar, angel dust, coke, big H, drugs, you moron, what else.'

'No way, I don't touch that sort of poison. I've just seen a teenager die from an overdose and I don't plan to see any more.'

'C'mon, that hardly ever happens these days and only to punters who can't handle the stuff.'

'No addict can handle the stuff, as you put it. That's why they're called addicts and why hundreds of children are dying long before their parents every year!'

'Look, mate, if some punters don't have the same will-power as me to control how they take the stuff then that's not my problem. All I know is a lot of money can be made from running the snow for some of the importers. Great guys that I know very well.'

'How old are you, Bill?' John interrupted. The penny had dropped and he realized that the young man was an addict himself and concern creased his forehead.

'I'm 32, what's it to you?'

'You'll be dead before you reach 33 if you keep taking drugs and playing with those kinds of thugs.'

'You don't know what you're talking about, mate. I've been making a packet running uppers, downers, coke and the big H for a guy in London for over a year now and never had any bother. In fact, after Alan told me how you out-smarted the cops on the motorway so easily . . . '

'How did he know about it?' John banged his glass down on the coffee table. 'I never told anyone what happened on the run, not even Sergeant Williams.' John made the name sound like an obscenity.

'Alan's a traffic cop and all cops talk amongst themselves. Anyway, I mentioned it to my guy and he's really interested in getting you to make a few trial runs for him.'

'You're a bloody idiot!' John snapped angrily. 'You had no right to mention my name to anyone without my permission.' John picked his glass up and took a sip before continuing. 'Get this, mate, I'll never run drugs for anyone, right?'

'Oh yes you will, my friend, because you're Alan's boy and I've got his permission to make use of you any way I like provided it gives him the right percentage,' Bill said smugly. 'And that's good enough for me.'

John stormed out of the room and ran up the stairs, two steps at a time. He entered his room and threw himself onto the bed. His worst fears were now being confirmed: Alan was in with drug smugglers as well as acting as a go-between for stolen antiques. He closed his eyes, deciding to wait and see what Alan had to say about it when next they met.

Downstairs, Bill switched on the television and opened another bag of crisps and considered sniffing a couple of 'lines' while watching Blue Peter. The presenter was talking non-stop about the capuchin monkeys of northern Argentina when his eyelids began to droop and he leant back in the settee and fell fast asleep. Bill was unaware of John descending the stairs, walking along the hallway and leaving the house.

The ride to Brighton cleared his mind and he eagerly looked forward to seeing Anne again. He estimated that he was quite a few years older than the young woman; besides, she might never be attracted to him. Putting that to one side, his determination to stop the girl from marrying the obnoxious William Tyler strengthened. Parking the bike on the seafront he hurried across the road and went down one of the streets that led in to the labyrinthine Lanes.

An OPEN sign was still hanging on the door of the antique shop and John entered, carrying his crash helmet under his arm. There was nobody about in the shop and he rang the small bell that stood on the glass counter top beside a copy of the *Antiques Trade Gazette*. There was no response and he waited a full minute before shaking the bell more vigorously. Still nobody appeared and looking around at all the untended antiques displayed in the shop he decided to investigate. He left his helmet on the counter and went through the open doorway that led to the storeroom.

John was amazed by the amount of space behind such a narrow shopfront. It seemed to go on forever and was stacked high with furniture from every English period. He threaded his way among a few stacks of Regency chairs calling out Mr Jackson's name until he came to a small open space, an oasis that had a large desk in its centre with a single light hanging over it.

On the desktop there were ledgers, a telephone and small objets d'art. There was also the slumped figure of the antiques dealer. Blood had flowed from a gaping wound in the back of his head to cover one half of the desktop and drip onto the bare floorboards.

John instantly knew that he was looking at a murder scene and that he had to get as far away from the place as possible. He hurried back through the storeroom and entered the shop just as Anne was closing the front door behind her.

'Why hello, John. Why are you here?' she asked mischievously. 'I didn't expect to see you back so soon,' and she gave him a teasing look.

'I remembered that I was supposed to give the snuffbox to your father and came back,' he stammered, too flustered to play along with their pre-arranged plan.

'You couldn't find him in the storeroom? He's generally there at this time of the day doing the receipts for yesterday. By the way, I like your new-look face. If it wasn't for your eyes I wouldn't have recognised you.' She held her hand out. 'Give that to me and I'll go and get him for you.' She took the snuffbox and started to go towards the storeroom door.

'No, no you can't!' John cried out in alarm as he hurried to intercept her. 'There's been a terrible accident.'

'To my father?' Anne gasped and wrenched her arm free from his grasp. 'What has happened?' She rushed through the door and dashed between the piles of furniture unerringly to reach what she had for many years referred to as her father's temporary office. There she shrieked in horror at the sight of her dead father before John's hand could stifle her. She spun around, trying to tear his hand from her mouth and fixed him with wide-open eyes.

'Did you do that to my father?' she managed to say after biting down hard, forcing the offending hand to be snatched from her face.

'Good God, no!' John shouted back.

'Then who did? You're here and there's nobody else around and you're trying to stop me from screaming. Maybe you stole that snuffbox from the showroom and you're using it now as an excuse. Are you going to kill me now?' She took a couple of paces back. 'Eliminate all witnesses, isn't that what murderers have to do?' Anne's words were coming so fast that they blurred into each other, making it difficult for John to understand everything she was saying.

'Stop it, Anne!' John shouted. 'I could never harm you.' He shook her by the shoulders and as he did so he noticed that the jade figurine wasn't on the blotter. 'I'm telling you I didn't do this to your father. Someone else did but I don't know who or why unless it had something to do with the piece of jade I delivered last time I was here.'

'You're a stranger. I can't just take your word that some petty thief did this for that small piece of jade unless you're the thief and you've got the jade in your pocket. I must call the police immediately,' she said as she looked again at her father's body and tears began to stream from her eyes. 'They'll get you to tell the truth.'

'I am telling the truth and I cannot be involved with any police.'

'That's because you're guilty!'

'No, because I'm guilty of something else,' John confessed.

'Then you will have to confess that to the police as well.' She cautiously made her way towards the phone but the splatter of blood across the Bakelite instrument made her shudder and she turned and began walking slowly back to the shop, her head turned to watch John who was following close behind. They went into the showroom and Anne went to stand nervously beside the telephone on the counter.

'I'm sorry, Anne, but if you pick that up now I will have to leave you before they arrive.

'A sure sign of guilt!' Anne snapped for she was now emboldened by the large windows and the apparent nearness of the pedestrians who were passing the shopfront. Her shaking hand hovered over the instrument.

'No, it's simply a sign that I don't want to be arrested for a really bad speeding offence on the motorway,' he half lied. 'Look, I promise to come back later and talk about this awful tragedy and try to work out who may have had a motive to do this to Mr Jackson—your father.'

John retrieved his helmet from the counter and walked slowly towards the door with his eyes on Anne who had picked up the receiver and placed a finger in the dial. 'I swear on my parents' lives, Anne, that

I did not do this terrible thing. If you tell the police that I was here then there is a good chance that I will lose my bike and most probably my job.'

The distraught young woman stared hard at his pale face, trying to believe him but then a shiver ran through her body when she recalled her father's bloodied head and she began dialling. John nodded sympathetically and left to make his way back to the bike. As he crossed the road he spotted the fluttering white piece of paper taped to the tiny windscreen and cursed beneath his breath for it was a parking ticket.

11

WILLIAM TYLER WAS STILL SLEEPING on the settee with the residue of three lines of cocaine clearly visible on the coffee table when John arrived back at the house. He went straight into the kitchen and shortly after he had made himself a coffee Alan arrived, slamming the door behind him.

'Where the hell did you get to this afternoon?' he snarled at John. 'I've been trying to find you for hours.'

'I forgot to deliver the snuffbox you gave me and went back to Mr Jackson's shop,' John snapped back as he thumped the coffee mug onto the table spilling some of its contents onto the oilcloth. 'And guess what I found there?'

'I don't care what you found. I had a job for you and it's now been given to someone else. That cost me a lot of money.'

'Damn your money. Jackson is dead!'

'What?'

'I said your antiques dealer, Jackson, has been murdered and I happened to arrive on the scene to discover his body. It was as though I had been set up to take the blame so, what do you know about it?'

'Nothing. Are you quite sure you didn't kill him yourself? You've done that sort of thing before y'know.'

John felt his cheeks burn as Alan sniggered and he felt a strong need to hit his smug-looking face. 'Why would I want to do that?' he said softly.

'Maybe you came on to his daughter and he objected,' Alan muttered before his voice rose. 'You killed him and I no longer have a bloody good cash customer!'

'Is that all you care about? The father of that poor girl has been bludgeoned to death and your number one worry is that you've lost one of your fences to off-load the spoils of your petty thieving?'

'Not so petty mate. Last year I made fifty grand clear profit on the items I sold to a number of dealers like Jackson.'

'Don't you have any sympathy for Anne Jackson?' John asked as he studied Alan's impassive face. 'Is it only money you care about?'

'If anyone is going to care it's going to be William Tyler.' Alan gave a small laugh. 'Billy's the one who had hoped to marry the bird and inherit the business when the old man finally kicked the bucket—which he's now done sooner than was expected.'

There was the explosive sound of a sneeze from the other room and the subject of Alan's detached observation opened the door and stumbled into the kitchen. 'What the hell is going on?' he mumbled, rubbing his eyes.

'None of your damned business! Go back to sleep,' Alan snapped peevishly. 'I'm talking to John about something that has nothing to do with you.'

'All right, don't lose your hair. Did you bring the stuff for me?'

'No!'

John moved around to stand beside the pristine gas cooker. 'Actually, what we were talking about does affect you, Bill. I understand you were hoping to marry Anne Jackson, right?'

'What's it to you?' Bill asked and his eyes narrowed with suspicion.

'Her father was killed today and I think you should go to Brighton and offer Anne your sympathy and support in her time of grieving.'

'Oh Christ!' Bill exclaimed sitting down and reaching for the cigarette pack lying on the table. 'That's fucked my cushy life by the sea.'

'Is that all you can say? Aren't you going to see Anne?' John looked on as the bleary-eyed man tried to light a cigarette with shaking hands and a box containing damp matches.

'There's no point. It was the old man that really interested me. He was keen on me marrying his daughter and she would do anything to keep her old man happy. Now he's dead she could refuse any offer I make and I have a strong feeling she will. Ergo, no marriage no business, so why should I bother with the bitch. Right?'

John hit him hard and although his knuckles felt an excruciating pain he also felt a strong feeling of satisfaction. Bill was rammed back against the chair and was unconscious by the time he slumped sideways and toppled onto the kitchen floor.

'That was a little unnecessary, mate,' Alan said with an amused expression.

'Totally necessary and stop calling me mate.' John stared hard at Alan with his hands still tightly clenched as he fought to control the rising desire to end his bondage to the tall man by killing him. 'We haven't been mates since the day you forced me to take Louise's life in Long Wood.'

'That was years ago. Surely you've got over that by now, Tucker?'

'Tucker died with poor Louise. I'm Davies now. Thanks to you.'

There was a groan and John looked down at the stirring man. He nudged his leg with a foot. 'I suggest you get me somewhere else to stay because if I'm close to this piece of selfish shit for much longer I'll be tempted to flush it away. Do you understand what I'm saying, Alan?'

Alan nodded and his amused expression grew into a smile. 'You can stay at my other place for a few days until we can find you a flat of your own.'

'Christ, how many properties do you make use of?'

Alan ignored the question and wrote an address on a piece of paper which he handed to John. 'I will be there after seven tonight. Park the bike in the garage which I'll leave open and don't forget to close the door so that it can't be seen.'

'Have I been driving a hot machine all this time?' John asked with suspicion creeping into his voice.

'It's not stolen but it was registered under someone else's name and to be extra careful I had a number of different plates made, none of which are associated with myself or the different addresses I use; that's why I insisted that the lock-up is padlocked after use.'

John took the keys from his pocket. 'Can you get me another bike? This one's been well and truly compromised.'

'How?'

'It was given a parking ticket in Brighton at the same time as I was discovering Anne's father.'

'That's not a problem,' Alan said, airily waving a hand. 'The plates were fakes. Just remove them and dump them in the nearest canal. You'll find spares in an old suitcase in the lock-up. Don't forget to bring that case with you to the new address.'

Bill was struggling to sit up and held his head with both hands while doing so. He groaned loudly and then looked up as John's shadow fell upon him.

'Don't say a word or I'll hit you again,' John said with a threatening clenched fist. 'Not a word, do you hear?' Bill nodded his head and then winced from the pain in his jaw.

'And don't go anywhere near the girl in Brighton or I'll be coming after you. Understand?' The scowling man on the floor nodded again.

It was late afternoon when Detective Inspector Angstrom entered The Lanes and after a brisk walk ducked under the police tapes strung around the entrance to the antiques shop. The local police had called upon the Hastings division to help cover the murder as their numbers had been depleted by the security details for the Conservative Party's annual conference.

Angstrom showed her warrant card and made her way through the showroom and into the storeroom. A detective constable from her own department was perched on a rickety cane chair while questioning a tearful young woman sitting in an Edwardian club chair with her back to the office desk. A medical examiner was studying the deceased while four other officers in white coveralls were scouring the floor and surrounding area for any other forensic evidence.

Angstrom approached the seated girl while studying her body language and facial expressions until she was satisfied that the girl was in a genuine state of shock.

'Miss Jackson?' Angstrom asked gently. The detective constable jumped up to offer the seat to his superior. She briefly glanced at the broken weave of the old cane seat, shook her head and knelt beside Anne. 'Tell me in your own words what happened,' she asked as she took one of the girl's hands and held it between her own.

Anne fell under the calm, soothing spell cast by the detective and slowly began to relate the events, stumbling briefly when she described finding her dead father, and crying profusely when she gave a description of the young man who had insisted that he wasn't the culprit but had then run away when she began dialling for the police.

'You will definitely be able to recognise this man if you saw him again?'

'Yes, this time I spent a long time looking at his face.' Anne blushed on realising what she had said. 'I mean, I thought it might be helpful to the police, to you,' she added hurriedly to cover her embarrassment.

'You had seen him before?'

'Yes, but that was when he had a very bushy beard.'

'When was that?'

'He delivered a piece of jade to my father earlier this morning.'

'Very good, Miss Jackson. We will ask you to give a full description to the police artist later when you're feeling a little better but until then, can you remember anything else that was unusual about the man?'

'Yes, apart from the upper part his face was very pale because he had just removed the beard and he had a number of tiny cuts on his face that could only have been caused by a razor. He must have been employed as a company courier although he didn't seem to have any branding on his clothing. He carried a crash helmet with a full tinted visor so he must have come by motorbike.' Anne then described the shape and colour of the helmet. 'He also gave me this snuffbox which he said he had been told to deliver to my father.'

Anne held up the silver snuffbox and Angstrom slipped on a latex glove before taking the item. She studied it carefully before sealing it in a clear evidence bag. 'I will have to take this; it may have fingerprints other than your own on it. It will be returned to you at a later date.'

Anne nodded and then looked up at the inspector with lines of puzzlement on her forehead. 'I don't know why but I got the impression that he was a very nice person. His eyes were very gentle and he tried to comfort me until I said I had to call the police,' she said and then her voice cracked with emotion. 'He wasn't the type you'd think could do this sort of thing.'

'You'd be surprised how pleasant-looking some of the nastiest villains can be, Miss Jackson,' Angstrom said with a cynical curl of the lip as she released the young woman's hand and stood up. 'Thank you for all your help and you have my sincere condolences on your loss. I will contact you if I have any further questions.'

Anne smiled briefly and then seemed to sink back into a more desolate state of mind. The detective inspector signalled to a WPC standing close by and then asked Anne if she would like the woman constable to stay with her until she felt she could stand being alone and Anne gratefully accepted the offer.

Outside in The Lanes Angstrom briefed the sergeant to ensure that nobody else entered the premises until after forensics had given the all-clear. She then walked quickly back to her car and drove along the coast to make her report in Hastings.

On arrival she sent the snuffbox for fingerprint analysis and then went directly to the superintendent's office. Wesley Cramer was in the process of finishing a pot of plain yoghurt and still had a smear on his upper lip. Angstrom couldn't take her eyes off it until Cramer realised what she was staring at and used his tongue to make it disappear.

'So what illegal shenanigans did you find in Brighton apart from a bunch of Tory ministers getting a little tipsy and fiddling their conference expenses?' he asked as he opened a brown manila file and perused the contents without once raising his eyes to welcome his favourite, secretly admired, detective inspector.

'It looks like a robbery that went wrong. The owner of the antiques shop may have interrupted a burglar on the premises and was fatally hit on the head. A blunt instrument was used. The nature of this weapon still has to be identified by forensics. Miss Jackson, the daughter, was in a state of shock when I got there but will be quite capable of giving a very accurate description of the assailant.'

'Excellent. An open-and-shut case, would you say, Angstrom?'

'Quite so, sir, but for one thing. Miss Jackson was very adamant when she said that the man wasn't capable of committing the crime. In her opinion the man didn't exactly fit the mould of a murderer.'

'I wonder how many young women think the same until they have hands closing around their neck and they feel themselves suffocating,' Cramer said as he closed the file. 'I have a pretty tight budget allocated to this case. Is there anything else?'

'Yes, sir, there is a silver snuffbox that may have the man's fingerprints on it. I've sent it to the lab and hopefully we can match any prints found with those of one of the villains on file.'

'That may save us a lot of time, Angstrom, well done.' Cramer smiled at his attractive colleague who was wearing a fetching blouse in duck-egg blue. 'It could cut the overall expenditure, too.'

'There's some checking I have to do, sir,' she said and Cramer benignly waved her from his office. Back in her own office she found a message from the detective constable who had stayed behind in Jackson's shop. It referred to a motorcycle that had been illegally parked on the esplanade at approximately the same time the murder took place. Angstrom made a note of the number and passed it on to traffic to locate the owner. She had a quick coffee and a cream-filled pastry, that she knew she would regret later, when an answer came back.

'I'm sorry, Inspector,' the voice in Swansea said. 'There is no longer any such number in the register. In fact, it's recorded as a Norton Dominator, a total write-off in a road accident twelve years ago.'

Angstrom hung up with disappointment written all over her face until Harry Anson from the records department suddenly appeared at her desk with a single sheet of paper in his hand. He pointed at the thick bundle of brown manila files that stood on the corner of her desk; 'I think your answer lies in there, Inspector,' he said with a grin as he placed the sheet of paper on her blotting paper.

'What's this, Harry?' she asked as curiosity began to lift her out of the depression she had sunk into. She took the single sheet of paper showing the results of the fingerprint check and gasped, 'My God, he's back.'

'And he's in *my* stack of files that happens to be standing on *your* desk and not tucked away in the security of *my* filing cabinets,' Anson said as he lightly reproached the inspector.

'Sorry, Harry, but Super wanted me to go through them all again with regard to the original deaths. Now it seems I have another to add to the same files which makes them all active again.'

'Therefore I'll leave them with you, Inspector,' Anson said with a broad smile as he put the evidence records book on the desk for her to initial before cheerfully leaving her office with a jaunty air.

'I don't know why you're so happy, Harry, we've now got to put together two separate case files and treat them as one. That's a lot more work on our plate,' Angstrom called after him miserably as she stared at the stack of files.

'Your plate, Inspector—*your* plate,' Harry chortled happily and quickly disappeared down the corridor.

Angstrom took the first file off the top and before leafing through the sheets of yellowing paper she called her assistant and briefed him to check the duty roster for Sergeant Alan Williams's movements over the last month. Anticipating a long evening she ordered a pizza and black coffee and began reading the files before her.

It was at ten o'clock precisely that she spotted a startling forensic error. A short length of reinforcing rod had been discovered beside the body of the girl buried in Long Wood and although blood and tissue samples were taken and matched to those of the murdered girl it hadn't been tested for fingerprints. The hairs on the back of Angstrom's neck rose as she realised the enormity of this oversight. She quickly checked with Anson in records and managed to locate the bar in a sealed evidence box and had it sent for immediate analysis. She kept her fingers crossed that the prints hadn't degenerated beyond recovery.

Down the corridor Superintendent Cramer was studying Angstrom's report on the Jackson murder and was pondering the daughter's description of the mysterious young man when the inspector returned, her face flushed with excitement.

'We have an incredible match in fingerprints,' she said hurriedly. 'The prints found on the snuffbox match those on the iron bar.'

'What iron bar?' Cramer said, patting the air with his hands for her to slow down and take it easy.

'I discovered that the prints on the piece of reinforcing rod buried with the girl in Long Wood sixteen years ago match those found on the Brighton snuffbox. The man who killed Jackson is the same man who smashed the skull of Louise Walton.'

'If my memory serves me right that was John Tucker, the teenager who appeared to have completely disappeared off the face of the earth.'

'That's right, sir.'

Cramer tapped his teeth with the tip of his ballpoint pen. 'The motorcycle he was riding cannot be traced by its registration because that was a fake however, isn't there something else we can work on to track it down?'

'We have witness statements that seem to agree on one thing at least. The bike ticketed on the esplanade was a big bike, a jet black Norton Commando with a silver lightning flash on the fuel tank.'

'Get a check on all motorcycle dealers in south London for a bike of that description. Make the search include the suburbs of London, Kent and Sussex right down to the coast,' Cramer said as he scribbled hastily on his blotter. 'Then cancel Anne Jackson's appointment with the police artist and dig out some photographs of Tucker from the files and get the artist to age them sixteen years with and without a full beard. We'll circulate those and see if we can't flush our bird out of hiding.'

Angstrom hurried back to her office to initiate the search for the mystery bike and a motorcyclist called John Tucker.

John Davies had covered the fifty miles to the new address in the county of Surrey at a moderate speed, attracting no attention to himself apart from a little admiration from other bikers he encountered on the way.

He followed the directions Alan had scrawled down and pulled up outside a respectable-looking semi-detached house on a street quite close to the river Thames. He rode up the drive and into the open garage where he cut the engine and put the bike up on the stand. A connecting door opened and Alan stepped into the garage and immediately went to the up-and-over door to pull it down.

'Do that the moment you pull in next time,' he said as John removed his helmet and gloves. He then went back into the house with John close behind. 'This will be your new base until you get something of your own so I expect you to maintain the tightest security. The place in Catford was rented under a false name so it cannot be traced back to me but this one has been purchased and I don't want it screwed up by any silly mistakes on your part—do you understand?' John nodded slowly as he unzipped and then tossed his leather jacket onto a kitchen chair.

'Good. Now we'll go to see one of my suppliers who will give you exact instructions on the delivery of a certain package.' Pouring himself a whisky he continued, 'You must do what he says or take the consequences.'

'Does this concern drugs?' John asked as he watched Alan's face closely. 'Are there no more antiques from your thieving friends?'

'Don't get funny with me, John,' Alan replied in a low, threatening manner. 'What the package contains is none of your damned business.'

'I just do as I'm told or else, is that it?'

'Right, you know what will happen. Certain witness statements and your address will be posted to the Hastings police. That should see you living the rest of your life in a ten by eight cell as somebody's bitch.'

'In for a penny in for a pound—I could kill you to prevent that from happening,' John murmured.

'That's something I don't think you're capable of doing. However, I've left an envelope in a bent solicitor's safekeeping that will automatically be sent to you-know-who if you did take my life,' Alan smirked. 'Then you'll be charged with my killing as well—you'd be running up quite a score, John.' Alan finished his drink and crooked his finger. 'Let's go. We have to meet the man at five o'clock which gives us twenty minutes.'

The two men left the house and climbed into a ten-year-old BMW that had started to corrode on the sills. Alan drove swiftly through the town and entered the exclusive wooded district known as St George's Hills. They bypassed mansion after mansion until Alan turned abruptly to stop before large ornate gates that were firmly shut. As they waited a large man in a dark suit appeared from out of the trees and he indicated that they should stay in the car. He kept his right hand beneath his jacket and it was obvious to them both that he was armed.

'Is that legal?' John asked, nodding towards the guard who was approaching them with extreme caution.

'Burglary and kidnapping is not unknown in this district and no doubt this bodyguard has a licence to carry a weapon to defend his employer,' Alan said as he wound the window down to speak to the man.

Ignoring Alan whom he obviously knew the guard bent at the waist to study John carefully. 'Who's the extra weight?' he asked gruffly with a strong Birmingham accent. His hand remained under his jacket.

'Don't be so nervous, Jimmy, it's my new courier,' Alan replied casually.

'So he replaces Ted, does he?' the man asked as he stepped back a pace and stood upright.

'As you know, mate, Ted wanted a change of scenery,' Alan said enigmatically. The guard nodded and gave Alan a knowing look that didn't go unnoticed by John. The man waved the car through the gates that had slowly opened during their brief discourse.

As the car accelerated along the winding road that was lined on both sides by bright red azaleas John turned to Alan. 'Were you referring to the Ted we knew in the old days?'

Alan didn't say anything for a few seconds and then without a change in his expression he answered. 'No, our Ted was killed years ago in a motoring accident. The guy I have been using recently decided to use his ill-gotten gains and emigrate to Australia for a better life under the sun.'

John kept staring at Alan's profile but could detect no sign that the man was lying and he slumped back into his seat and watched a magnificent Arts and Crafts house materialise amidst the tall cypress trees surrounding it.

Alan braked to a standstill by a side door with a clatter of gravel striking the underside of the car. He got out and immediately rang the doorbell. John followed him as the door opened and a clone of the guard who met them at the gate appeared. He too had his right hand tucked into his jacket in what appeared to be a state of permanent readiness.

'Hi, Alan, come in. Signor Bellini is expecting you,' he said, his eyes suspiciously focused on John. His voice was also strongly accented but John could tell that it was more Eastern European.

'He's with me. The new guy, okay?'

The guard nodded and then beckoned John to follow him as he and Alan walked round the outside of the grand house to the back terrace. The expensive paving stretched the full width of the house and on the far side there was a large twelve-seat oak table at which a big man was sitting. A jacket was draped over the back of the chair beside him and he was clipping the end of a Monte Cristo cigar. He said nothing as the guard bent to whisper in his ear. He looked up and held John's gaze with emotionless black eyes, not dissimilar to those of a circling tiger shark.

'A new rider, Alan. The last one was dealt with in a satisfactory manner?' the grey-haired man rasped, his throat obviously damaged by many years of smoking.

'He did as he was told, Signor, and emigrated to a warmer place far, far away,' Alan replied smugly.

'Good, he was not to be trusted. Can this one be trusted?'

'Fully, Signor. I have him and he will do as he is told or forfeit his freedom. Or possibly his life.'

'That is very good, Alan, but remember, you both forfeit everything if you ever fail me.' Bellini's dark eyes glistened yet never seemed to blink.

'Understood, Signor,' Alan said while John remained silent as he looked at the palatial surroundings. His keen eyes noticed the security cameras and movement detectors within the room nearest to them. The guard was also watching John, noting his interest and when their eyes met he shook his head imperceptibly. 'Don't even think about it' seemed to be what he was thinking and John turned to cast his eyes casually over the garden. Once more he could see, amidst the beauty of the trees and plants, evidence of security measures that would make entry onto the property a fool's errand.

'Now you know where to go, John.'

John suddenly became aware that Alan was talking to him and he turned to face the tall man with raised eyebrows.

'Oh, for God's sake, weren't you listening?' Alan asked.

John shrugged indifferently.

'This new man doesn't seem to take this job seriously,' Bellini said and Alan looked nervously at the calm exterior of the drug trafficker. He knew that the man had the power of life or death over them both.

'He's good, Signor Bellini. He can ride a bike like a priest after a sinner and there isn't a cop in the country who can catch him,' Alan said hastily. 'I'll brief him thoroughly after we've left and call you when the delivery has been made.'

'My colleague will let me know whether the delivery has been made or not and it had better arrive safely and on time.'

Alan nodded vigorously and tugged at John's sleeve as he turned and walked away from the table followed by the impassive guard whose hand seemed to be permanently attached to the concealed weapon.

Leaving the lush greenery of the exclusive suburb and driving back through the town Alan instructed John to go straightaway to the canal lock gates in Weybridge to meet the go-between. The man was on a boat called *Gull's Delight* and he would give John instructions regarding the pick-up and delivery.

'Why couldn't Bellini give me the instructions?'

'He never gets personally involved with the handling of any sensitive merchandise. Signor Bellini likes to distance himself from all such risk-taking matters.'

'And what will you be doing while I'm visiting sailor boy?' John demanded.

'I'll be returning to London to perform my solemn duty as a guardian of the law.' Alan laughed and John was immediately sickened by the man's duplicitous nature. He leapt from the car as soon as it stopped outside the house and hurried to open the garage door. Alan was still talking but John didn't bother listening as he strapped on his helmet and the old backpack that he had kept since he first left home and mounted the bike. The engine started, cutting the possibility of any further conversation with the bent copper and John rode away without a single backward glance at his blackmailer.

The early evening air on his exposed face helped to cool his anger and the familiar vibration between his thighs reawakened his old sense of adventure. He flipped the helmet's tinted faceplate down as he cruised down the main street, basking in the admiring looks from a group of young women who were waiting at the bus stop.

Crossing the canal bridge he turned down a small road leading to the main lock gates. He slowed to a walking pace as he left the tarmac road and idled along the dirt towpath until he spotted the name *Gull's Delight* painted in white capital letters across the dark-blue stern of a small cabin cruiser.

As John dismounted a dark-haired youth with a severe case of acne emerged from below deck. He looked at the motorcyclist inquisitively until John mouthed the word 'Bellini' and then the lad waved him aboard. The flimsy gangplank sagged under his weight and John held his breath until he had finally stepped aboard.

The family cruiser rocked slightly as he followed the youngster down a short flight of steps and into the saloon. This was cluttered with dirty washing, empty bottles, beer cans and crumpled pizza packaging. The smell of old socks and sweat was overpowering and John wrinkled his nose in disgust.

The go-between couldn't have been much older than 18. He flung himself onto the heavily stained divan and looked John up and down with curiosity. 'How fast can she go?' he slurred, jerking a thumb towards the bank.

'Fast enough,' John replied impatiently. 'C'mon, what are my instructions, where am I to go?'

'In a hurry are we?' the youth sneered. 'Look, my name's Terry, what's yours?'

'None of your bloody business and yes, I'm in a hurry because Mr Bellini's in a hurry,' John said in a threatening tone and Terry stood up quickly and reached into an overhead locker where he extracted a plain manila envelope. He tossed it onto the fold-down dining table that was between them and John picked it up.

'Aren't you going to read it then?'

'When I'm well away from this pigsty, boy.' With that stinging remark John stood up and went back on deck where he took a deep gulp of the cool, crisp night air before crossing the sagging gangplank with care. He sat astride the Commando and ripped the top off the envelope to extract a single sheet of white paper that gave directions to an all-night café that was located by the ferry terminal in Dover harbour. He had to be there at midnight precisely. John crumpled the brown envelope and tossed it into the canal before folding and tucking the directions into the side pocket of his jacket.

Terry emerged on deck and stood in the pale light that came from the instrument binnacle. He watched John start the powerful engine with covetous eyes that continued to follow the motorcyclist as he rode away on the towpath and disappeared into the night.

John estimated that he had 120 miles to cover in three hours of darkness if he was going to make it to the rendezvous by midnight. He wound the engine up and laid himself upon the tank and let the superbly engineered machine have its head.

The town clock was showing twenty minutes to twelve when John eased up to cruise through Dover. He approached the new Hoverport cautiously, his eyes open for any signs of unusual police activity but the whole area was quite deserted. He kept going until he was a quarter-mile from the walk-on walk-off port exit and soon spotted the all-night café.

He stopped outside a typical dockworkers' café that was open all hours, offering basic comfort food at very basic prices. It was his rendezvous point yet he had no idea what the person he was meeting looked like.

Removing his helmet and gloves he entered the smoky environment and ordered an americano. After paying he sat at an unoccupied table in the corner furthest from the door. The coffee was in a surprisingly stylish mug and as he took the first gulp he nearly blistered his tongue. With watering eyes he looked around the room to inspect all the customers. Everyone appeared to be a shift worker from the ferry terminal, either ending or just about to begin their shift and the constant babble of conversation was loud and deafening.

At midnight precisely a large man in a dark blue donkey jacket and woollen cap crossed the room and put his cup of tea on John's table and sat opposite. He placed a carrier bag covered with Duty Free advertisements on the floor beneath the table.

'Anyone sitting here, chum?' he growled in an affable manner. John shook his head and remained alert to any signs that the man was his contact or a possible threat.

'Bloody awful night, ain't it?' the man said in a North Country accent. Without waiting for an answer he picked up the steaming cup and after pouring a little tea into the saucer he began slurping noisily.

'Awful,' John agreed. 'Not a good night for meeting strangers on the dock or in dark alleys.'

'Unless you're there to take delivery of a very nice present,' the docker replied. Like a professional tea-taster, he took another noisy slurp from the saucer and closed his eyes appreciatively. 'It'd be worth going down a dark alley then, wouldn't you agree?'

'It would have to be a very nice gift to bother going out in this cold weather,' John muttered.

'I can tell you it's a bloody mind-boggling experience, this one.'

John felt the bag being slid forward against his leg and glancing under the table he glimpsed a large denim-clad leg slowly withdrawing. The man put his cup down and without uttering another word he left the café. John opened the bag and found a large stuffed toy. It was a panda bear that still had a price tag attached to its ear. He picked the bag up and walked casually to the door.

Suddenly a sharp voice shouted 'Oi!' and John spun round with a guilty expression on his face. It was the café owner who was holding up John's crash helmet that he had left on the empty seat. John hurried back to take the helmet from the smiling man and with a muttered 'thanks' quickly left the café.

Without even bothering to discover what terrible secret the panda held within its soft innocent exterior John stuffed the carrier bag into his backpack, zipped it up and started the Commando for the long journey back to the *Gull's Delight*.

12

JENNIFER ANGSTROM WAS IN HER OFFICE when her assistant said he had a motorcycle dealer on the line who had recognised the description of the bike.

'Detective Inspector Angstrom, how can I help you?' she asked.

'Jacob Ingram, owner of Bull's-eye Bikes. I believe the Norton described by your other officer was sold by me last year to one of your boys,' a gruff yet friendly voice said.

'Can you give me the name, Mr Ingram?'

Angstrom scribbled the name and address into her notebook and after thanking the dealer she hung up and hurried to Cramer's office. She had recognised the name and a tremor of excitement ran through her as she knocked on her superior's door. After the familiar 'come' she entered, her elation clearly showing on her face.

'You've got something, Jennifer?'

'Alan Williams, sir! Or, I should say, Sergeant Alan Williams. I believe he's the buyer of the black Norton. I've just had a dealer on the phone confirming that Williams paid cash for a bike of the same description last August. I don't believe in coincidences, sir, and I think we should question this sergeant as soon as possible.'

Cramer nodded slowly. 'So do I, Jennifer. Bring him in,' Cramer instructed as he went back to reading the case report he was holding in his hand. Angstrom hurried out and instructed her assistant, Detective Constable Phillips, to apprehend Sergeant Williams of the Metropolitan Traffic Police and notify her when he was ready for questioning.

Three hours later Angstrom received the call that Sergeant Williams was in interview room No. 2 and she rang Cramer's extension to inform him that their suspect was ready for questioning.

When Angstrom entered the room the tall man was lounging casually in a steel chair that was bolted to the concrete floor. Phillips was leaning against the wall with his eyes unwaveringly fixed upon the sergeant.

Angstrom immediately noticed that Alan was in civilian clothing. 'Off duty today, Sergeant?' she asked sitting down opposite him and placing a closed file on the table.

'Yes, Inspector,' Alan replied as he quickly assessed the feminine qualities of the woman facing him.

'What do you use for transport when you're off duty?'

'I was using my own motorcycle until that was stolen four months ago,' Alan replied. 'Since then I've been getting about in my car, a beat-up BMW, while waiting for the insurance company to cough up the money for a replacement bike. Why do you ask?'

'The bike stolen was a Norton Commando?' Alan nodded and Angstrom continued: 'Black with a silver lightning flash on the tank?'

Another nod with the suggestion of a smile alerted Angstrom to the possibility that the policeman wasn't telling the whole truth. She sat and studied the man for a few seconds, noticing that he remained unperturbed by her penetrating gaze.

'Do you remember your old friend called John Tucker?' Angstrom said suddenly and saw a flicker of recognition in Alan's eyes.

'That was a long time ago. I haven't seen him for over sixteen years or more,' he muttered.

'Therefore you should find it a rather weird coincidence that he was recently seen riding your stolen bike in Brighton.'

'Very weird indeed.' Alan felt a slight chill when Angstrom associated his bike with John.

'When did you last see Tucker, Sergeant?'

'I told you, Inspector, it was about sixteen years ago.' Alan sat upright and crossed his arms and Angstrom instantly read the defensive body language and knew that the sergeant was lying. However, she also knew that she had nothing to prove he wasn't telling the truth.

'Very well, Sergeant, you may now return to duty. Thank you for your time.' Angstrom stood up, gathered up her file and left the interview room. As Phillips continued to stare at him Alan looked at Angstrom's departing back with a slightly puzzled expression. The inspector hadn't probed any further and it worried him that she had been so nonchalant in her dismissal of him. Alan rose to his feet and quickly left the room and the police station to get to the nearest public telephone box.

Signor Bellini picked up the phone that was standing on a Victorian onyx hallstand and listened. His small eyes narrowed and he grunted after each piece of news.

'You are telling me he has been compromised as a courier on his very first job?' he asked after Alan had finally stopped talking. 'He is carrying a kilo of my finest heroin and you tell me that he's a big risk to my operation?' He listened and then nodded his head a couple of times. 'I will make sure that he cannot harm the organisation. Start looking for a replacement immediately.' The rotund man placed a finger on the cradle to end the call and then lifted it and began dialling the number of a red telephone kiosk standing on the towpath directly opposite the *Gull's Delight* mooring.

Terry had just snorted two lines and was feeling rather euphoric when the faint sound of the telephone penetrated his consciousness. He had first tried the drug during a gap year when travelling to La Paz in Bolivia. It was in *Route 36,* the most celebrated bar in South America, that he began snorting the finest cocaine at 150 Bolivianos a gram. Since then the habit had taken control of his life and now he depended solely on Signor Bellini for his supply.

The phone persisted in ringing and he hurried up onto the deck and crossed the gangplank with long strides that caused the board to bounce dangerously.

'Terry speaking, who's calling?' he asked. He physically straightened up when he heard Bellini's booming voice and he listened intently to what his boss had to say. At one point his face blanched but soon returned to normal when Bellini mentioned the bonus and 'lines' he would receive as a reward for carrying out his orders.

'Yes, sir, you can rely on me,' Terry said when Bellini had finished talking and he would have said more but his employer had already slammed down the phone. Terry returned to the boat to await John's arrival with his precious consignment.

At three in the morning the familiar sound of the heavy bike could be heard approaching. John slowly rode up to the end of the gangplank and stopped with his head turning rapidly to check the towpath in both directions.

Terry appeared on deck. 'Is everything okay?' he asked in a soft voice. 'Did you get the package?'

'I have it, mate. Now what do I do with it?' John replied in an equally low voice. An owl hooted nearby, startling both men into searching the surrounding darkness for any signs of a threat.

'You give it to me, that's what you do,' Terry said stepping onto the gangplank with one hand outstretched and the other tucked out of sight behind his back.

'Why can't I take it direct to Bellini?'

'Because that's my job and I'd get into trouble if I let you deliver it,' Terry said with an edge of impatience in his voice. 'So hand it over now!'

John went to the end of the gangplank and had placed one foot onto the narrow beam when Terry produced the automatic pistol from behind his back and pointed it at John. He had been given the order to eliminate the courier and his determination showed in his eyes.

John placed his second foot on the gangplank and then jumped forward to land in the centre, making the soft plank spring violently. Terry pulled the trigger whilst trying to maintain his balance and the bullet tugged harmlessly at the sleeve of John's leather jacket.

John used the upward momentum of the gangplank to spring forward and he collided with Terry knocking him back onto the cruiser. The young man tripped and fell heavily; his head struck a steel cleat on the deck and he lay perfectly still, the gun still clutched in his hand.

John knelt beside the unconscious youth and freed the weapon that he weighed in his hand while he thought rapidly. He could tell that Terry was an addict and knew he was under Bellini's control and a wave of compassion swept through him. Instead of using the weapon on Terry he threw it over the side and into the sluggishly flowing current.

John placed his hand on the young man's chest and felt a slight yet regular movement and with a relieved sigh he stood up. He re-crossed the gangplank and ran to the red kiosk to place a 999 call for an ambulance. After wiping the receiver with his handkerchief John then returned to the bike and rapidly rode off into the night. With a growing feeling that he had been double-crossed John made sure he only used minor roads and lanes to make his way to Brighton.

The onset of dawn had lightened the sky, casting a silvery sheen over the calm sea when he rode along the deserted esplanade and into the town. John kept his speed down and the engine hardly ticking over to avoid being noticed. He chose a safe place to park the bike before walking to The Lanes via back streets that were still damp from an earlier shower.

The antiques shop was still in darkness but he could see the warm glow of a light through the net curtains of an upstairs room indicating that someone was an early riser. John tapped lightly on the door and waited. After three more attempts a single light went on in the showroom and through the distorting bottle glass John could just about make out the approaching figure of Anne Jackson wrapped in a dark blue dressing gown. She was tapping her wrist impatiently, indicating the time and that she was closed when she suddenly recognised John and stopped short of the locked door.

'What do you want?' she mouthed.

'I need to talk to you,' John said, not knowing if she could hear him through the glass. She apparently did understand because after hesitating for a few moments she stepped up to the door and unbolted it.

'I did not kill your father!' John's first words gushed out uncontrollably when the door swung open. 'Please believe me, Anne,' he pleaded.

'I do.'

'I swear that when I found him he had already been killed and that the jade carp was missing. It was a terrible shock to me . . .' John stopped when her quiet reply finally registered.

'You do?'

'Yes, John. I believed you the first time you told me and I still do. I know nothing about you and yet I sense that you couldn't do anything as terrible as that.' She waved him inside and then relocked the door before leading the way up the narrow staircase to a long corridor and a cosy sitting room. John could see by the dying embers that the fire had been lit the previous night and the warmth still radiating from the cast-iron fireback was more than welcome after the long cold ride.

'Are you being looked after? I mean with regard to your father,' John asked in a soft voice.

'I will follow my dad's last wishes and donate his body to medical science—it's what he wanted.'

'And being here alone, doesn't that worry you?'

'Not at all and you're very lucky. I told the policewoman who was staying with me last night that I was feeling better and that she could leave me which means you can stay here with me.' Anne poured large measures of whisky into two glasses that stood on a Georgian drinks trolley and handed one to John. He accepted it with a particularly grateful look. The young woman sat down on the damask chaise longue and tucked her feet up beneath the dressing gown before indicating that he should sit in the leather chair facing her.

'Just tell me everything that happened, from the beginning,' she asked in a quiet voice as she took a sip.

John gulped at the 12-year-old malt while looking at her face over the rim of his glass. Her complexion glowed warmly beneath the light of the small crystal chandelier and as she lowered her glass her full lips glistened with drink. John felt he could trust the young woman and he leant forward to tell her everything.

John started with the tragedy at Hastings and then, skipping what had happened to Louise, he related the events that led to his employment at the fish market. As he went on to tell her of his reliance on Jane and the subsequent birth of a son Anne seemed to be taken aback but she recovered quickly. John was unable to stop talking and he told her how Alan had reappeared in his life and threatened him with the stolen police statements to blackmail him into transporting small antiques that had been pilfered from country houses.

It was at this point that Anne interrupted. 'Was my father involved in this activity?' she asked anxiously, looking around at the collection of antiques on the shelves that covered two walls.

'Your father was unaware that the items he bought from Alan and Bill were stolen. He simply believed that he was getting a very good deal as all the items came with excellent provenance, even though they were falsified.'

'Then why was my father killed if not because of something to do with the stolen antiques?' Anne demanded to know as a few tears rolled down her cheek. John wanted to rush across and comfort her in his arms but sensed that this would upset her more and he managed to restrain himself and remain seated. 'That's something I plan to find out, Anne. If only to clear my own name of his murder.'

'But you don't have a real name to clear, John,' Anne observed quietly, as she wiped the tears away.

'It's Tucker, John Tucker and I'll start using it again when I'm able to shake free of Alan's hold over me. In many ways I too died the night of the accident. It's time I reclaimed my life again.'

'How will you be able to do that?' Anne put her empty glass down and stood up. 'Unless you go to the police?'

'That I have yet to work out,' John said dismally as she walked towards him. 'I cannot go to the police and still be able to clear my name while under arrest, which means I have to find somewhere safe to live while I can think of a plan.'

'As I said earlier, you can stay here. It's the last place the police or that Signor Bellini would look,' Anne said impulsively as she gazed down at him with a look he was unable to understand. 'I have a spare room and I will go out and buy all the necessary spare clothing that you'll need for however long you need to stay.'

John was lost for words and just stared at her gratefully until Anne broke the silence by leaning forward and kissing him on the forehead. 'I know you are an honest man and I will help you to prove it,' she whispered in his ear as he stood up and she indicated that he should follow her. She led him out of the sitting room and to a door at the end of the corridor.

'This should be comfortable enough and if you want any breakfast it'll be on the table in fifteen minutes.' Anne turned and walked back towards the sitting room.

'Please don't call me John Tucker, Anne, for now I'm John Davies,' he called after her. 'At least until I can sort my life out.' She nodded without looking round and closed the door behind her.

John entered a bedroom that seemed as though it had been furnished for use in a Sherlock Holmes television production. His gaze took in the chintzy curtains, ornate pelmets, small four-poster bed and magnificent mahogany washstand; as he sat down on the bed he sank deep into the soft goose-feather quilting.

John shrugged off the backpack and pulled out the panda bear. It felt a lot heavier than the average soft toy and he guessed that it contained a kilogram or more of the drugs that Signor Bellini would want returned.

He lay back and began thinking about how he could use the drugs as leverage to gain total freedom from Alan's hold over him. As his mind became confused with random ideas his eyelids slowly drooped until he fell into an exhausted sleep.

It was midday and bright sunlight was filtering through the gaps in the chintz curtains when a light tapping on the door woke John. He was momentarily confused until he heard Anne's familiar voice asking if he was asleep.

'No, come in,' he responded and Anne entered carrying a large Victorian silver tray laden with a full English breakfast and a cafetiére of freshly brewed coffee for two.

'I thought you might be hungry after your little nap,' she said. Placing the tray on the quilt she carefully sat down on the bed so as not to upset the spread.

The aroma rising from the crispy bacon and Blue Mountain coffee had John licking his lips. 'Thank you, Anne. I have to admit I haven't eaten properly for over twenty-four hours.'

Anne picked up one of the plates and passed it to him with a set of cutlery wrapped in a paper napkin. He immediately put the plate on his lap and set to with gusto while Anne picked at her plate more slowly.

After fifteen silent minutes the tray had been cleared of all food and the couple sat looking at each other while they sipped from their cups, appreciating the richness of the coffee.

'What's your plan?' Anne asked finally. 'I am assuming that you haven't been sleeping all the time and that you've thought of your first line of action.'

'My first move is to park the bike as far away from here as possible so that Alan and his "friends" don't jump to conclusions regarding my whereabouts. I couldn't bear it if I put you in harm's way. Secondly, I'll wipe the bike clean of all fingerprints so that the police cannot link it to myself.'

'And then?'

'And then I'll telephone Alan to arrange a little trade. The statements he stole from the Hastings police for the consignment of drugs I picked up in Dover.'

'That will be the most dangerous part of your plan,' Anne said quietly, her normally smooth brow wrinkling with concern.

'I'll be careful,' John said reassuringly. 'My only worry will be if Alan is stupid enough to tell Bellini of my call because that man has already decided to kill me and he may see this as an opportunity to be a little more successful than young Terry was.'

Anne shifted the tray and moved closer in order to reach out and run her hand down his stubbled cheek. 'You will be careful, won't you?' she said with a slight catch in her throat. 'I wouldn't want anything to happen to you, John.'

'You have given me every reason to make sure nothing prevents me from coming back to you,' he murmured. 'Now you will have to leave so that I can get undressed and have a shower. I feel awful and I'm sure I don't smell too good either.'

Anne laughed lightly and stood up. 'Modesty becomes you, sir,' she said with a laugh. 'I'll put some of my father's clothes on the bed for when you've finished in the bathroom,' she said with a slight catch in her voice. Picking up the tray she left the bedroom, her light footfall fading as she descended the stairs.

An hour later John parked the Norton Commando in one of the back streets of Dover and surreptitiously wiped it all over with a wad of tissues. The location had been deliberately chosen because he knew that the police would eventually trace the bike. This information would then lead to Alan.

John was hoping that the location would confuse Alan and Bellini for it had been left standing only twenty yards from the café rendezvous. He was praying that the subterfuge would distance them from the antiques shop in Brighton. He reluctantly tossed his crash helmet and gauntlets into a rubbish skip that had been placed near the café.

Walking briskly to Dover railway station John caught the first available train to London and arrived at Charing Cross station just as both hands on the concourse clock moved onto the twelve. He immediately changed to the underground tube train to travel on to Jane's house.

As he walked down the familiar street he spotted his son playing football with the same three lads. His heart lurched at the sight of Timothy.

'Hello, Tim,' he called and the boy turned in surprise and then, recognising his father, came running along the street with a happy grin lighting up his grubby face.

John stepped to one side as he grabbed him by the arms and swung him up and onto his shoulders. 'Miss me?' he asked as the boy wriggled about until he was comfortably seated and able to take fistfuls of his father's hair to aid his balance.

'Lots-an-lots, Dad, where've-ya-been?' he gabbled excitedly and John winced as the little hands tugged enthusiastically on his hair.

'All over the country, son, and I can only stay for a little while. Daddy has a special job to do and when that's finished we can be together forever. Okay?' John climbed the steps to the front door which was wide open. 'Is your mother at home?'

'Think so. Got a friend with her that's why I was told to go out and play.'

'A friend, Tim? Does Mummy have a lot of friends?' John asked quietly as he stepped into the gloomy hallway.

'Oh, yeah! Lots of them and they're all different friends. She always takes them upstairs and when she does I have to leave the house,' Timothy explained in a sad little voice that chilled John's blood.

'Is she with a friend now?'

'Yeah.'

'Okay, thanks Tim. Now can you go to the corner shop and get me a pint of milk?' He lifted the boy off his shoulders and lowered him gently to the floor. 'You could also get some jelly babies for yourself, okay?' He gave his son a handful of change and the sparkle returning to the boy's eyes lightened his heart and he grinned back. Timothy turned and ran from the house giving a little yelp of excitement.

John looked up the stairway with a grim expression clouding his handsome features. He climbed slowly and called out Jane's name to warn her that he was coming. When he reached the landing the bedroom door was jerked open and a bald-headed man wearing a dark pinstripe suit hurried out while zipping up his trousers. He gave John a nervous glance as he sidled past and hurried down the stairs without looking back.

John entered the bedroom that glowed dimly from the crimson light of two bedside lamps. Jane was sprawled carelessly across the rumpled sheets of the bed wearing little more than silk stockings. 'Still entertaining lodgers, Jane?'

'They don't have to be lodgers to help pay the rent, John,' she replied with a sneer. 'And without your income I have to get it from whomever I can.'

'What happened to Frank Saunders in the fish market?' he asked. 'Don't you still work for him?'

'Not since you upped and pissed off, mate. Now I model for male acquaintances.'

'Do you have to do it in front of my son?'

'I always send him out to play when I have friends visiting.'

'What about the lodgers Reginald, Robert and Harold? With what they pay you, don't you have enough to live on without prostituting yourself?'

Jane sat up and hid herself from John's withering gaze by wrapping the bed sheet around her shoulders. 'No, it's not enough. I need a few luxuries too,' she snapped and she stood up and went behind the Chinese folding screen that she now used to tease her clients while undressing.

John sat on the end of the bed as she got dressed. 'You could earn a little bonus by doing something for me,' he said softly.

'You want to have sex with me?' she laughed. 'In your dreams, you bastard.'

'Timothy will be back soon so keep it down,' John snapped. 'What I want has nothing to do with desiring your body. I want you to phone someone and give them a very precise message.'

'How much?'

'You'll get a hundred pounds for ten minutes' work.'

'When do you want me to do it?' Her eyes widened with greed.

John took a piece of paper from his hip pocket and handed it to Jane who had emerged from behind the screen wearing a dull floral dress. She took the paper and read it, holding it up to the light with one hand as she fastened the last buttons on the dress with the other.

'The number to call is at the bottom and I want you to say what is written there, word for word at precisely ten o'clock tonight. Do not say anything else and, at the risk of your life, do not tell them who you are. Before giving the message you must make sure you are talking to the man named at the top of the paper. He's a crooked cop who wouldn't think twice about doing you very serious harm if you got in his way,' John said clearly enunciating each word to make sure she understood the danger involved.

Jane began reading silently from the paper, her lips forming each word and as her puzzlement increased she read it again aloud. 'I am calling on behalf of John Davies who has told me to tell you that he has the consignment you want and will exchange it for the witness statements you are holding. He will meet you in Charing Cross station on platform six at half past eleven tonight and you must come alone.' Jane looked up at John. 'Why can't you call him and make your own appointments?' she demanded sniffily.

'Because I want you to call from a phone in the station and to make sure he can hear one or more train announcements in the background.'

'And where will you be?'

'I'll be a long way away doing something else at the time,' John said and he took the woman by the arm and held her tightly. 'You do understand what I am asking you to do? It's imperative that you don't fail me.'

'And my money?' Jane asked with an avaricious glint in her eyes.

'On the success of the call I will return and give you the cash.'

'What about something on account?'

John fished out his wallet and slipped out twenty pounds. 'You'll have to be satisfied with this. You'll get the rest when I return.'

He turned and swiftly left the bedroom followed more slowly by Jane who was busy tucking the money into the top of her dress. John descended the stairs to be met at the bottom by Timothy who held out a plastic carton. John took the milk with a smile of thanks and then had to accept one of the sticky jelly babies that his son pressed into his other hand.

'Thanks, Tim, it's delicious,' he exclaimed as he bent down and scooped his squealing son up to place him back on his shoulders. John turned to catch Jane scowling at him and he gave her a mock smile. 'You should have a jelly baby as well, Mummy,' John said and took the one being passed down to him. He held it out to Jane who turned her back on them and walked into the kitchen. John shrugged and walked out of the house with his son giggling and gripping his forehead with one hand while triumphantly holding his sweet bag aloft with the other. The boys had returned to the street and when John lowered Timothy he ran off to join them, giving one backward wave to his father.

John watched as the boy offered the bag of sweets to his friends and was rewarded by being passed the football which he clumsily kicked back. The older kids shrugged as the ball shot away down the street but

Timothy immediately volunteered to retrieve it. He watched his son running after the ball before giving a deep sigh and forcing himself to leave the street. He was now on a dangerous mission and timing was of prime importance.

13

THE DISCOVERY OF THE NORTON BIKE in Dover caused a ripple of excitement in Hastings police station but this quickly died away when the forensic report showed it had been cleaned of all fingerprints.

'The last time this bike was spotted it was in Hastings and now it's in Dover. Why?' Cramer murmured as Angstrom finished reading the report to him. 'What attracted him to Dover?'

'It's a port, sir,' Angstrom replied. 'He may have been there to collect something that was coming from the continent.'

'Possibly, but why abandon the bike after wiping it clean? Was it left to lure us away from something else?' Cramer leant back and stared at the ceiling as he drew on his cigarette and exhaled, shrouding his head in a blue haze. 'He may have taken the ferry to escape to France.'

'Mmmmm. I would suggest that the rider wiped it down because he knew we already had a record of his fingerprints and on that point I agree. It was left there to make us believe that he wasn't somewhere else where he could be found easily. That would mean he is still in the country.'

'That's a little double-Dutch, Jennifer, but I think I know what you mean.' Cramer drew deeply again and Angstrom had a brief moment of concern for his health as a dense cloud was puffed out from between his lips. She had recently read a report strongly associating smoking with lung cancer and had warned her father of the danger.

'If you're right, sir, then that somewhere else is a place we have investigated before. That's where the young man could be now but where would that be?'

Cramer muttered to himself as he stared into the blackness outside his office window.

'That would most probably be his real home or possibly back at the antiques shop in Hastings,' Angstrom said excitedly.

'Surely the girl would tell us if he tried to return to the shop?' Cramer said.

'I believe Miss Jackson thinks Tucker is incapable of killing and therefore may be foolish enough to try and help him evade capture.'

'Check them both and let me know if there had been any sightings of John Tucker or the motorcycle prior to its discovery. Also check Sergeant Williams's movements because we cannot rule out the possibility that he may still have another bike hidden away to use for his own illegal purposes.'

Angstrom hadn't considered this and secretly admired her superior's quick thinking. 'That's a distinct possibility, sir. For some reason, call it women's intuition, I've never trusted that man and your theory matches his profile perfectly.'

'We deal with facts, Jennifer. We can't tell Crown Prosecution that we only have the power of a DI's intuition to convict nasty felons,' Cramer said in a serious tone and then laughed at Angstrom's crestfallen look. 'Get checking, Jennifer, and see if you can back up your presumptions with hard evidence.'

It was then that a little hard evidence appeared at the office door in the guise of Constable Phillips. 'Sorry to interrupt, Inspector, but a set of motorcycle number plates were found in Dover. They were in a trash can near to the abandoned bike and the traffic department have identified them as belonging to a BSA and not a Norton Commando and that the registered owner of that bike was one Mr Edward Barker.'

'Good God, that's the man who was killed with his wife the other day. He must have been involved somehow with either John Tucker or Sergeant Williams,' Angstrom exclaimed.

'And that "somehow" is what we need to solve,' Cramer said. 'This could be a vital breakthrough in the case so I'll speak to Sergeant Williams again and you must get the team really moving in the morning. They must check whether the BSA is still in existence and also go over the wrecked car again. Let's now see if we can at last get some positive evidence.'

Angstrom smiled and nodded. 'Right away, sir.' The inspector hurried from the office and returned to her desk where she issued orders to interview John Tucker's parents and search the Barker's garage once more. She planned to visit Anne Jackson in Hastings the following day and investigate whether John Tucker had returned to hide from the police in the antiques shop.

Cramer sat for a while meditating before picking up the phone and dialling. A phone rang in a London police station and he was connected to an extension.

'Is that Sergeant Williams?' Cramer asked.

'It is. Who is this, please?'

'Superintendent Cramer of the Hastings police. We met recently and discussed the theft of your motorcycle.'

There was a long silence before the sergeant said anything. 'Yes, Superintendent, can I help you further?'

'Not at all, I just have the good news that your motorcycle has been recovered and seems to be none the worse for wear.'

Once more there was a moment of static hiss and then Alan spoke hesitantly. 'That's good news. Where did you find it, Superintendent?'

'In Dover outside a café and very close to the continental ferry terminal. However, we strongly believe the thief may still be in England. You can collect it from the Hastings police vehicle pound whenever you like as our forensic department have now completed their investigation,' Cramer said and waited for a reaction.

'Was anything found?' Alan asked tentatively. 'Were there any fingerprints or blood samples on the bike?'

'That information still remains classified Sergeant, as well you should know,' Cramer replied in his sternest tone. 'Come and pick it up when you're able.' He paused and then went on: 'Incidentally, the thief was a man called Edward Barker and he had been using the bike as his own along with number plates that belonged to a BSA he had owned a few years ago . . . I believe you knew the man.' Without waiting for an answer Cramer rang off with the distinct satisfied feeling that he had truly rattled the sergeant.

In London Alan sat holding the dead receiver while breaking out in a cold sweat. His mind raced through all possible reasons why the bike should have been left near the drug collection point. His other concern was why the superintendent had been so secretive about the forensic report to the point of abruptly ending the call with the brief reference to Ted and the 'borrowed' plates. He checked his wristwatch, an expensive Rolex that had been given to him by Constantine Karras in Manchester and noted that it was seven o'clock and that his shift was finished. He tidied up the paperwork on his desk and taking his jacket from the back of his chair he left the station to begin his long commute back to the house in Surrey. He longed to use the powerful police bike but regulations didn't permit an officer to use it when off duty.

The clock in the Norman tower showed nine thirty precisely when Alan passed by the church in his battered BMW and parked it in his street. Six months earlier he had extorted the vehicle from a petty thief he had caught red-handed and then conveniently 'let off' with a caution and the loss of his only form of transport.

The train out of Waterloo station had kept good time but Alan was late arriving home because he had spent a lot of time in a restaurant that was close to the station car park. Alan always did his best thinking when eating and yet, after two hours, he still couldn't see a way of preventing his fraudulent life from being caught in the net cast by Superintendent Cramer.

Arriving at his home Alan tried to settle down to watch television but the sudden loud ringing of the telephone broke his concentration. 'Is that Sergeant Alan Williams?' a woman's voice inquired.

'Yes, who are you?'

'I am calling on behalf of John Davies who has told me to tell you that he has the consignment you want and will exchange it for . . . ' Jane continued in a monosyllabic tone to the end the script she had been given.

'You're Jane, aren't you?' Alan asked abruptly.

'How do you know that?' exclaimed the startled woman.

Alan hung up and stood staring at the instrument for a moment. Without pausing to switch the television off he strode from the house with gritted teeth. It seemed that John was trying to call the shots, something which Alan, who always liked to be in control, simply couldn't abide. He resolved to teach the 'cheeky bastard' not to play games with a police sergeant.

Jane had instantly gone white with shock when she heard her name and she stood trembling in the phone kiosk for a few minutes until loud rapping on the window drew her attention to the queue that had formed outside. She opened the door and staggered out and thrust her way through the crowd to leave the station.

Timothy had been left alone with strict instructions to stay in bed and to admit nobody into the house. However, Jane knew how inquisitive the little boy was and if anyone knocked on the door this late at night she couldn't trust him not to open it.

Jane ran down the escalator with her skirt flapping about her knees, thrusting people out of her way, until she arrived on the platform. There she waited impatiently for the next underground train, rocking from side to side like a caged polar bear as she peered anxiously into the black maw of the tunnel until a single headlight appeared.

He knew that he shouldn't have gone downstairs to watch grown-up television but just like his father he couldn't prevent his curious nature getting the better of him. Like all youngsters he grew tired very quickly in the evening and by ten o'clock the flickering screen and sounds of a creaking door and a woman's scream when attacked by zombies failed to disturb Timothy who had fallen into a deep sleep on the settee. However, the insistent sharp knocking on the front door eventually roused him.

He sat up rubbing his eyes and listened until he heard the knock again. The boy crept barefoot down the hallway in his pyjamas and stopped before the half-glazed front door. Two dark shapes could be seen through the frosted glass, backlit by the street lighting on the pavement. His bit his bottom lip when he saw one of the shapes distort as an arm was raised to knock again—this time with more persistent force.

'Are you there, lad?' a muffled voice inquired. 'We've come about your mother. She's been hurt badly and she is asking for you. We're here to take you to the hospital.' There was a long silence as Timothy digested this information before he rushed forward to unlock the door. It swung open and a thin, rat-faced man stepped inside and grabbed the boy's arm. Another man wearing a large overcoat entered and closed the door behind him. Before Timothy could cry out in alarm a handkerchief soaked in chloroform was clamped over his nose and mouth and held in place until a loud buzzing began inside his head.

Darkness crept in from all sides and Timothy collapsed in the stranger's arms. The second man removed his raincoat and between them they bundled the pathetically small figure within the gabardine material and carried him out to the waiting car with its engine running.

Jane arrived a few minutes later and hurried up the steps. The open front door told its own story and she immediately knew that something wasn't right. She ran into the house and abruptly stopped when she heard voices coming from the living room. Cautiously approaching the door she peered round the jamb and saw that the television was on and Timothy's favourite blanket had been tossed onto the floor.

She turned and leapt up the stairs. 'Tim! Tim! Where are you?' she shouted, running into his room. The bed sheets had been pushed aside but his favourite bear was missing. With a sick feeling Jane went down to the hall and approached the small table where the telephone stood. A single sheet of paper had been tucked under the receiver: *Do not call the police. The boy dies if you do. We will contact you with instructions. Do not tell John! The boy dies if you do!* Every letter was in a different typeface, cut from newspapers and magazines and crudely pasted on to the sheet.

Jane returned to the living room, her eyes brimming with tears, just as the credits began rolling for the late night movie she had first heard when she entered the house. This is all John's fault, Jane thought and in a fit of anger she picked up the heavy glass ashtray from the coffee table and threw it at the television. The screen imploded and there was a bright flash of light before a thin column of acrid smoke began rising from the wreckage. Throwing herself down onto the settee she covered her face with her hands and began sobbing.

Jane was still crying when the phone rang. She quickly rushed out of the room to answer it, expecting to hear John's voice but instead she heard the voice of a complete stranger.

'Good girl, Jane, you didn't call the police,' the gruff voice said condescendingly and Jane's grip tightened on the instrument until her knuckles whitened. 'Now this is what I want you to do. As soon as John gets in contact you'll tell him to call a number I'll give you or your son will meet with an unfortunate accident.'

'Please, don't harm Timothy,' Jane begged.

'Don't fret, Jane,' the voice said soothingly. 'Nothing will happen to the boy if John does as he is told. Have you got pen and paper?'

'Yes,' Jane muttered anxiously and began scribbling the number furiously.

'Make sure he calls us or else . . .' The phone went dead and Jane slowly replaced the handset in the cradle.

John had waited until he had seen Alan leave his house and drive off in his battered BMW before he risked stepping out of a dark footpath and walking down the dimly lit street. He passed the house twice, studying the windows carefully for any signs of life before turning down the alley that ran between it and the neighbour's house. This led to a service road that ran behind all the back gardens and John turned left and crept slowly in the dark until he judged that he had reached the gate that opened onto Alan's property.

The latch had been recently oiled and lifted easily without a sound. Inch by inch he pushed the tall gate open and stepped into the backyard. Faint moonlight enabled him to follow the footpath between the piles of household rubbish and building debris. Getting closer to the house he studied each window in turn and saw that only one on the ground floor showed a chink of light through the closed curtains.

The faint rustling of unseen creatures scampering to get out of his way made him shiver and he was glad to reach the rear door. Taking care not to touch the piles of litter John moved to the window and peered into the kitchen. The room appeared to be empty.

He tested the handle on the back door but it had been locked and he removed his jacket, wound it around his elbow and jabbed it into the pane of glass nearest to the lock. A sharp paralysing pain shot up his arm as his funny bone shattered the glass. After carefully unwrapping the coat he reached through the hole and turned the lock. The door swung inward on relatively quiet hinges but as the light had been left on John didn't take any chances. He paused and listened for any signs that his intrusion had been detected but heard nothing except a muted television in the next room.

It took John a full ninety minutes to complete a thorough search of the house from attic to basement. In a room that appeared to be used as an office he scrutinized every scrap of paper in the three-drawer filing cabinet to see if it was a damning witness statement.

In desperation he lifted the mattresses in the bedrooms and under the last one he discovered a small notebook containing a list of names, dates and sums of money that had either been received or paid. He tucked it into his jacket pocket and continued searching for the statements.

John had checked the train timetable before setting out and was fully aware that the last train out of Waterloo was at ten minutes to midnight. The luminous dial of his wristwatch showed that he only had twenty minutes before Alan arrived back at his house.

Those minutes ticked by relentlessly. John went back into the kitchen empty handed and slipped out into the night just as Alan was bringing his car to a standstill outside the front door. John could hear the sound of the idling engine as he strode to the back gate. When the engine fell silent he started running on the service road until he had put sufficient distance between himself and the house before slowing down to a casual walking pace.

Jane opened the door before John could insert his key and struck him in the chest with a closed fist. 'You bastard!' she cried. 'They've taken Timothy thanks to you and your bloody games.' She hit the shocked man again and again until he grabbed her wrists and pushed her back into the hallway. He kicked the door shut with his foot while keeping a firm grip on her wrists. She tried to lean forward and bite him but he easily kept her away from him with his arms outstretched.

'What the hell are you talking about?' he demanded.

'Timothy was kidnapped when I was making your stupid telephone call,' she sobbed helplessly. 'I came back and he was gone and then they called. 'They said you were to wait for further instructions.'

'Oh Christ, you gave him your name?'

'I didn't. He already knew it and told me so before hanging up. I tried to get back as fast as possible but when I got here they had already taken him.'

'Okay, calm down,' John said as he released the hysterical woman and went into the kitchen to make himself a strong coffee. Jane had followed him in and she sat down at the table unable to stop herself from trembling.

'Maybe we need something stronger,' John said taking a half-empty bottle of whisky and two tumblers from a cupboard. He poured two large measures and slid one across to Jane. 'So all we can do now is wait for their call and see what they want,' he murmured.

'You know what they want,' Jane snapped. 'It's exactly what you took from them.'

'No doubt, but I have a feeling they'll want something else, too.'

'What could that be?'

'Me. They will want me to be their courier, their lackey for the last time before they release Timothy,' John mused as he stared into the bottom of his glass. 'And I cannot do anything about it.' He gulped down the last remnants of his drink.

The phone rang in the hallway.

Anne Jackson greeted Detective Inspector Angstrom when she arrived at the antiques shop with a certain amount of suspicion. Although the policewoman had called in advance to make an appointment the young woman felt sure that the police knew something that she didn't.

'Good morning, Miss Jackson, I trust you are feeling a little better today,' Angstrom said on her arrival and was invited to use one of the stylish dining-room chairs that were arranged around a walnut art deco table. 'I would like to ask you a few simple questions regarding the man you found in the storeroom with your father.'

Anne folded her hands in her lap and looked into Angstrom's eyes without blinking. 'How can I help you?' she inquired coolly.

'Has he been back?' Angstrom asked abruptly.

'No, no. I haven't seen him since that awful time.' The hint of a stutter revealed that the young woman had lied and Angstrom stared hard into her eyes, all sympathy for the loss of her father dispensed with.

'You are aware that this man, John Tucker, is wanted for questioning with regard to two murders that took place sixteen years ago as well as the killing of your father?'

Anne kept silent and simply nodded.

'He told you about the two murders in 1964?'

Anne shook her head and then nodded before realising her mistake. Angstrom leant forward and stared hard at her face that had started to colour. 'You do realise there are stiff penalties for wasting police time?'

'Yes, yes. I thought you were talking about my father not the girl,' Anne said with a nervous hesitation in her voice.

'How did you know a girl was murdered?'

'You just told me.'

'I said two murders, I didn't say a girl was killed. C'mon Anne, tell me the truth,' Angstrom said softly. She moved to sit beside Anne. 'Has he been back to the shop and told you about what happened in 1964?'

Anne bent her head for a moment before answering. 'Yes, he did come back and he explained that he was being blackmailed by an old friend into doing things he could never have considered himself capable of before. He swore that he didn't kill the girl in Hastings and that it was an accident. It seems she had tripped and fallen against a pier support,' she added quickly. 'I don't know anything about a second girl and that's the truth.'

'The second girl was bludgeoned to death with a steel bar and buried in a wood,' Angstrom said softly as she studied the young woman and came to the conclusion that she knew nothing of that incident. 'We need to question him about his possible involvement in that murder, too.'

Anne's mind whirled chaotically when she realised that John hadn't told her everything when he had supposedly been pouring his heart out.

'When was he here?' Angstrom snapped. 'Will he be coming back soon?' Anne recoiled as though she had been struck in the face. 'You must tell me or be charged as an accessory after the fact,' Angstrom bluffed.

'Recently, he came yesterday,' Anne said tearfully. 'I don't think he'll ever be coming back.'

'What did he want?' Angstrom said in a more tender tone of voice as she realised the young woman had fallen for the man.

'He came just to tell me he had nothing to do with my father's death and to tell me how someone he knew a long time ago betrayed their friendship.' Anne hid her face in her hands as she began to weep openly.

Angstrom rose, stood behind her and placed a comforting hand on her shoulder. 'Don't upset yourself, Anne,' she murmured. 'He's not worth it.' She gave the young woman a gentle squeeze before leaving the storeroom. John Tucker will return, she thought as she walked back to the car. Angstrom used the radio and asked to be patched through to Superintendent Cramer.

'I get the feeling that Anne Jackson has fallen for our suspect in a big way,' she said as soon as Cramer answered the call. 'However, by telling her about the second girl's murder I may have shattered her belief in John Tucker,' she added and then listened carefully to what her superior had to say. After the call Angstrom contacted the local police station and passed on Cramer's instructions for a surveillance team to watch the antiques shop around the clock.

When the telephone began ringing stridently John was slumped on the settee staring at the broken television set. He had been listening half-heartedly to West Ham United winning the FA Cup on the radio and he sprang up and raced into the hallway. He reached the phone before Jane had got halfway down the stairs.

'Yes, who is it?' he demanded brusquely.

'You know who it is, John,' a very familiar voice answered. 'And you know why I'm calling.'

'For Christ's sake, Alan, don't harm the child,' John shouted and he twisted away from Jane who was trying to snatch the receiver from his hand. 'It's the consignment, right?'

'Naturally! I also want a certain item that you took from my bedroom,' Alan snapped, revealing his pent-up anger.

'The notebook? Okay, you'll get it back!' John said through gritted teeth as he tried to suppress any fear of what the thugs may do to Timothy.

'Six o'clock tomorrow morning at the same telephone kiosk that bitch Jane phoned me from. Where was it exactly—and no tricks!'

John gave him the station and the line went dead. He slowly lowered the receiver and replaced it on the cradle.

'What did he say?' Jane screamed as she grabbed at his jacket and spun him around to face her and for the first time in years he acknowledged to himself that she did care deeply about Timothy, despite all her faults.

'He told me where to take the package,' John said and walked back into the living room just as the football commentator began to commiserate with the Arsenal manager on his team's loss by one goal. He switched the radio off to silence the roaring crowd as Jane hurried into the room after him. 'When and where do you have to go? Will Timothy be there?' she asked impatiently.

'I'll not tell you where I'm going because you'll insist on being there too and I don't know if the exchange will take place then or later. Does that answer your questions?'

Jane gave a small cry of dismay and fled into the kitchen to find the bottle of gin she always kept in the flour bin.

John forced himself to ignore Jane's distress and went upstairs to retrieve the black notebook from under a rug that lay beside the bed. He put it into the backpack along with the strange package. He checked his wallet for cash before hurrying from the house without saying goodbye to Jane who had already finished her second glass of neat spirit and was wallowing in tearful self-pity.

The newsagent's doorbell tinkled a friendly greeting and John went straight to the counter where he asked the genial owner for an envelope, a cheap ballpoint pen and access to the photocopier that stood behind the counter. After promising to count the number of sheets he would use John proceeded to copy every page in Alan's black book. When he had finished he placed them all in the manila envelope while the shop owner looked on with great curiosity.

'How much?' John asked and he paid the total in cash and left the shop. Further down the street he went into the small post office to buy stamps.

John chose to stay as far away from Jane as possible for the night and after a brisk walk in light rain he booked a single room in a modest-looking hotel before going out again to look for a cheap place to eat.

As he chewed on the flavourless meat patty that had been smeared with a large dollop of doubtful tomato relish John thought carefully about his next move. With the kidnap of his little son he had been pushed too far and he could no longer surrender to Alan's coercion. He knew he had to do something drastic to break the deadlock and he threw his knife and fork down and stormed out of the café as anger and fear sent cold shivers through his body.

In the hotel room John took the manila envelope and after sealing it he used his left hand to write an address in capital letters. He hurried down the wide stairs and went to the miniature postbox that stood on the reception desk in the lobby.

He forced the thick envelope into the slot with satisfaction—in two days' time an unexpected gift would reach the police superintendent who sixteen years ago was still a detective inspector when he was pilloried by the rabid press.

After recovering his son he would end Alan's criminal career and the hold he had over him even though it meant that Alan would immediately put damning evidence into police hands to incarcerate him for the rest of his life.

14

THE TWO HEAVYWEIGHTS stood in the shadows on the far side of the station concourse with Timothy squeezed between them. Each of the burly men had a tight grip on a thin shoulder so that the petrified lad couldn't move a muscle and they waited with eyes constantly searching.

Alan nodded briefly to them as he strode past and across the lightly crowded concourse towards the row of bright red telephone kiosks. He had spotted John waiting at a bookstall, apparently leafing through a magazine that he was holding upside down. Alan passed him and went to stand next to the kiosk and John put the journal back in the rack and walked over to join him.

'You brought it?' Alan asked unnecessarily as he looked at the backpack. 'And the book as well?'

John swung the backpack off his back and thrust it violently into Alan's hands. 'They're both there, check for yourself.'

The big man unzipped the bag and removed the little notebook which he slipped into a breast pocket. He then took a small penknife and jabbed it into the package still within the backpack and withdrew it with minute particles of white powder on the small blade. He touched the blade with the tip of his tongue and nodded in satisfaction.

'Good, you kept your word and I'll keep mine.' Alan raised a hand and the two men released their grips on Timothy. John identified one of the men as being Bill Tyler and his hands curled into hammer-like fists.

Not having seen his father and not knowing where to go the little boy panicked and ran away from the men as fast as he could. He weaved between the Sunday-morning travellers before darting out of the railway station and onto the Strand.

John started to run after him but Alan held onto his sleeve. 'One last thing, John,' he stated vehemently. 'You will call me tomorrow for instructions on your next run to the docks. If you don't do this little thing my men will take your boy again. They will then teach you the same lesson they taught Ted. You'll never again refuse to do as I say. Do you understand?'

John went white. 'My friend was *your* courier?'

'Of course. He was a reasonably good man on a bike.'

'And you had him killed?' he whispered.

'Unfortunately Bellini was very dissatisfied with his performance although I have to add that Ted's wife was purely collateral damage. Bellini's men were a little too thorough in their work,' Alan laughed. John looked for any signs of remorse in his eyes but could see nothing but a flinty coldness.

John nodded. 'I understand, Alan. Now I'll tell you that you'd better warn Bellini to watch his back.' He wrenched his sleeve from Alan's grasp and ran from the station. I'll kill Alan and Bellini for sure, he thought as he scanned the busy forecourt.

He was unable to see Timothy anywhere and grabbing the arm of a man hurrying to catch his train he gasped, 'Have you seen a small boy in a white T-shirt and blue shorts running out of the station?' The middle-aged man shook his head, pulled himself free and hurried away.

A police constable was walking nearby but John turned away and headed for the main road. Reaching the pavement he saw the tiny figure dodging between the pedestrians as he headed towards Aldwych. John began running after him and managed to catch up with his son outside the Savoy hotel.

'It's me Timothy. Stop!' he cried. At first the boy hesitated but then turned. Recognising his father he ran back towards him to be gathered up in thankful arms and hugged tightly.

'Thank God, Tim,' he whispered, 'you're safe now and I'll never let anybody take you away again and I'm going to take you to a place where you'll be very safe.' John had suddenly thought of a place where the boy could be best protected and looked after.

Tremors shook the small body. 'Don't let me go, Daddy,' he cried.

'I won't let go, Tim!'

John knew that when he called Alan in the morning to tell him he'd never work for him again Alan would let loose his two thugs to exact some form of retribution. Jane's house would be the first place they would search and she would soon tell them his whereabouts if he was foolish enough to let her know.

Keeping his eyes peeled for any sign of Alan and his men he re-entered the station carrying Timothy on his arm and bought tickets. Seeing that he had three minutes to spare he went directly through the ticket barrier and boarded the waiting train. Timothy sat quietly while his father constantly checked the platform and every passenger boarding until the whistle sounded and he felt the train jolt and begin to creep out of the station.

'Where are we going, Daddy?' Timothy asked when John settled back into his seat. 'Aren't we going home to Mummy?'

'Not today, son,' John said. 'The nasty men might go there tomorrow to look for us but we'll be a long, long way away where they can never find us.'

The little boy physically relaxed and lolled against the warmth of his father, his eyelids slowly drooping as tiredness began to take its toll. John put a protective arm around him as he gazed out of the window at the rows of suburban houses, all looking the same, all flashing by in a blur. Soon the monotony of suburbia was replaced by green pasture and John felt himself relaxing and he gave way to his body's demands and slept.

After reading Angstrom's latest report on her meeting with Anne Jackson, Cramer called her to his office.

'I think it's about time we brought Sergeant Williams in for serious questioning about his movements sixteen years ago and his current relationship with John Tucker. I have a feeling we have a really dirty cop on our hands and you know how I feel about that.'

'After Anne's story I think we can only put together a tenuous case for drug trafficking, sir, and as far as 1964 is concerned we have nothing that definitely ties him to the death of Louise. However, John's confession to Anne that Williams was with him when Doris died beneath the pier could provide us with the charge of failure to report a fatal accident.'

'Coroner's report said that her head was struck twice, which makes it murder, Jennifer, not just an accident.' Cramer looked up from the stack of files and frowned thoughtfully. 'I think we can also explore the possibility that Williams had something to do with Jackson's death. Let's see what happens during the interview—let's pull him in now.'

Angstrom returned to her office and immediately instructed Constable Phillips to put out a bulletin to detain Sergeant Alan Williams and have him brought to Hastings for questioning. Roughly one hour later when Angstrom was thinking about lunch in the canteen Phillips returned to the detective inspector's office.

'He can't be found, ma'am,' he said disconsolately. 'He appears to have completely vanished after collecting his bike, the Norton Commando, from the police pound. According to the duty officer he was still wearing his uniform when he signed for it.'

'Have you put out a description on the bike?'

'Already done, ma'am and so far there's not a trace. He must have hidden it in the same place as himself,' Phillips said as he placed the timed bulletins in the inspector's in-tray.

'Have you tried his home address?'

'Yes, ma'am, but police records show that the address he gave is a Chinese take-away that keeps mail for customers who want an anonymous address.' Angstrom nodded and the constable hurried away to sample the chicken curry he had spotted on the canteen menu.

Cramer had his briefcase open on his desk and was halfway through an egg-and-cress sandwich when Angstrom tapped on the door and gave him the news. 'He knows we're on to him which will now make him a very dangerous man.'

'It could be dangerous for John Tucker too,' Angstrom added. 'His testimony will place Williams under the pier with him. However, Anne Jackson can't be relied upon to testify as her statement would be regarded as hearsay and therefore it wouldn't be admissible.'

'And we can do nothing to protect Tucker as we only have a vague idea of what he looks like, with or without a beard, or where he could be.' Cramer munched thoughtfully and Angstrom heard her stomach react in sympathy.

'I could try to follow-up on Edward Barker's movements on the days leading up to his murder,' Angstrom murmured hopelessly.

'Do it, Jennifer. It may be the only chance we have of getting a tangible lead on what Williams has been up to.'

Angstrom nodded and left the room while Cramer selected a radish from his sandwich box and savoured the hot, peppery sting on his tongue as his mind turned over all the information they had gathered so far.

The train pulled into Brighton station and came to a standstill with the screech of composite brake shoes filling the terminus. The final jolt woke John and he opened his eyes to see the amused faces of departing passengers as they looked down at the father who was sprawled across the bench seat with a little boy sleeping in the crook of his arm.

'C'mon son, time to get up,' John urged and Timothy stirred and sat up with a big yawn.

'Where are we, Dad?' he asked sleepily as he peered out of the window at the people hurrying past.

'We're at the seaside,' John replied as he tried to bring his arm back to life. 'Would you like some sticky candyfloss?'

The small boy was suddenly very awake and his eyes sparkled at the thought of such a naughty treat so early in the morning. 'Yes, please, Dad!' he exclaimed and leapt up driving the air from John's lungs as he thrust himself upward.

They left the station and were immediately forced to lean into a strong wind as they made their way towards the shop that boasted a man-sized ice cream cone standing outside on the pavement. John bought a large cloud of the sugary confection and Timothy soon coated his face in it.

John held his son's other hand tightly as they walked through Brighton and turned to enter The Lanes. Despite it being Sunday the antiques shop was open in an attempt to catch the weekend visitors and John could see Anne holding a ceramic vase while she talked with an elderly woman. He paused and waited until the woman had left, possibly to look for a holiday souvenir elsewhere, before leading Timothy into the shop.

Anne registered complete shock when she saw John and was unaware of the small child until he moved round from behind his father. 'What on earth are you doing here?' she stuttered as he walked past her and headed for the storeroom to be out of sight of the street.

'This is Timothy, my son,' John said and the boy stepped up to Anne and held his hand out in a very formal manner.

'This is Anne, Timothy.'

Anne bent slightly at the waist to take the tiny hand and looking into the bright blue eyes she could see his father mirrored there. 'He looks just like you, John, but you still haven't answered my question,' she said softly as she released the sticky hand and straightened up.

'Timothy was kidnapped by Alan and I only got him back by delivering up certain items.'

'They was nasty men. They made me go to sleep with horrible smelly stuff,' Timothy boldly interjected.

Anne looked down in horror to catch the flicker of fear crossing the boy's face as he recalled the memory of his imprisonment and instantly knelt in front of him to put her arms around him. 'Oh, you poor boy,' she murmured as she hugged him tightly.

'I need to ask you a big favour, Anne,' John said. 'Can I leave him here with you until I sort out all my troubles?'

'What about his mother?'

'She'll be the first person Alan will question. I can't leave him with her.'

'How long will you be?' Anne asked as she held the boy at arms length and smiled warmly to reassure him that he was safe. Timothy grinned back and threw his arms about her neck.

'He seems to like you, Anne,' John said, pleased that his son had taken to the young woman.

'How long?' she asked as she picked Timothy up.

'I'm going to tell Alan that I won't be blackmailed any more and as a result he'll want to shut me up. The witness statements he stole years ago won't be much of a threat to me now because I think the police will have found the Norton and know that he is somehow involved.'

Timothy wriggled down from Anne's arms and grabbed his father's hand. 'So, Timothy is his only leverage and as he has used it once successfully he'll want to try again. I have to stop him first.'

'What do you mean stop him?' Anne asked in a concerned voice. 'You don't plan to do anything violent?'

'No!' John exclaimed with a brief glance down at his son to draw her attention to his presence. Anne nodded apologetically.

'I have already put my plan into operation and I expect Alan to be arrested sometime tomorrow. I can then come and collect Timothy,' John went on.

'Very good, then I will gladly look after Timothy for you.' She held her arms out and the boy went to her.

John felt immense relief as he looked down at his son. 'Now you must be a good boy and do everything that Anne tells you to,' he said softly and Timothy nodded his head solemnly. 'I will be back in a couple of days and then we'll go and see your mother again, okay?' After another nod John smiled at Anne. 'I'd appreciate it if you could give Tim a proper meal. Candyfloss is not so good at this time of the day.'

'Nor is it at any time. It's bad for a growing boy's teeth,' Anne said with a stern expression.

'I don't think you'll find him any trouble. I have to go now and try to find some form of transport that's not as risky as trains and buses.'

'You're going to steal somebody's car?' Anne said softly so that the boy couldn't hear.

'Well . . . '

Anne crooked her finger and walked towards the back of the storeroom. 'I think I have just the thing for you,' she said and gave him the hint of a secretive smile. Father and son followed the young woman until she came to a neglected corner of the long room. Unwanted heavy furniture that once graced Victorian drawing rooms had been randomly piled up to gather thick layers of dust. Amongst these pieces of furniture was a mysterious shape covered over with a dark green tarpaulin.

'This was my father's,' Anne said, grabbing a corner. 'It was his pride and joy when he was young.' She flicked the cover back sending clouds of fine dust into the air.

'Good lord,' John cried out excitedly. 'It's a Vincent, a 1950 Black Shadow. If I'm not mistaken it must be one of the very last ever made.' His eyes caressed the powerful black bike as a lover might his mistress. The black enamel crankcase and the all-black engine, capable of powering the bike up to 125 mph, made his pulse race.

'Daddy stopped riding it when my mother died but has always kept it taxed and insured. Why, I do not know, but you are welcome to use it if it helps you to resolve things more speedily.'

'Speedily it can.' John stepped up close to Anne and gave her a big hug. 'This could be the miracle I've been looking for. Thank you very much, Anne. Now is there a way of getting it outside without having to go through the front door?'

'Of course there is, silly,' Anne said as she pointed to a large sliding door behind a stack of chairs. 'We always use it for loading and unloading large pieces of furniture and . . .' she was interrupted by the sound of a bell that came from the front of the shop ' . . . it leads out onto a service road that takes you down to the seafront.' She hurried through the maze of furniture to answer the customer's call.

John bent down to be at the same level as his son. 'Right, Timothy. I want you to stay with Anne and I'll come back for you soon. Okay?' The boy nodded and John cleared the chairs away from the exit and slid the big door open.

'Hey you! Stop!' a voice shouted and John looked back to see blue uniforms through the gaps in the furniture stacks. He swung a leg over the saddle and thankfully saw that the key had been left in the ignition. He reached down and rapidly primed the carburettor before kicking down and twisting the throttle. The magnificent machine instantly burst into life with a deafening sound that ran through the large room like thunder. Tim backed away with his eyes wide in wonder and John released the clutch. The Vincent responded like a wild beast spotting an open cage door and he was thrust back with arms rigid as the bike burst from the storeroom into a light drizzling rain.

As the two constables ran past the surprised boy and through the open doorway they caught a brief glimpse of a hunched figure in black who appeared to be as one with the black motorcycle as it disappeared from sight round the corner.

The policemen turned with disappointment on their faces. One used his portable radio to speak to a superior officer while the other approached Anne. Timothy ran and clutched at her cotton dress as though seeking some comfort from the nearness of the lady who was so nice to his daddy.

'Who was that, Miss Jackson,' the constable demanded as he looked down at the frightened boy. 'We had a report that John Tucker was seen entering these premises.'

Anne knew the futility of lying. 'Yes it was him, officer, and as I was instructed, I shall now telephone Inspector Angstrom and notify her of Mr Tucker's visit.' Anne took the policewoman's business card from her pocket and held it up for the constable to read.

'Did he steal that motorcycle from you?' one of the officers asked suspiciously and Anne knew she was in danger of being accused of harbouring a wanted man.

'No, I said that he could use it provided it was returned in the future.'

'Whose boy is this?' the other constable demanded placing a hand on Timothy's shoulder.

The boy shrunk away from his touch and Anne knelt down to hug him reassuringly. 'He belongs to Samuel, my cousin, and he's called Timothy. He will be staying with me for a few days,' she said with a straight face and was pleased to see that her lie had satisfied the constable. Both officers began walking back through the storeroom, one talking excitedly on his radio, as Anne slid the door shut and locked it. She took Timothy's hand and they slowly walked after them.

'If he comes again, let us know immediately or you'll be in a lot of trouble,' one of the officers said as they disappeared into the shop. Anne watched them exit into The Lanes. She then went to the little refrigerator and poured a glass of milk that she gave to Timothy before opening a small Sheraton roll-top desk and taking out the chocolate biscuits she guiltily kept in one of the drawers. The little boy immediately began to slurp the milk thirstily and took one of the biscuits. Before biting into it he gave Anne a shy 'thank you' and she ruffled his hair affectionately.

Even after riding a mile along the seafront John still kept the Vincent below the speed limit to avoid drawing attention to himself. He was looking for a telephone kiosk for he had decided to let Alan know immediately that he'd have to find another courier.

The fat would soon hit the fire and John was determined to make sure that none splashed his way.

Detective Inspector Angstrom took the call from Anne that confirmed John Tucker had returned to the antiques shop for a few minutes. She had already been informed that he had been seen in the proximity of the shop and had dispatched the two constables to conduct a search of the immediate area. Learning that the man was now in possession of the victim's motorcycle was not good news and she instructed Phillips to issue the registration number and description to all motorway patrols.

The distinctive motorcycle was spotted twice within the next five hours. Once pulling away from a telephone kiosk on the Marine Drive, a mile from Brighton and then on the road to Sevenoaks. In both cases the police cars were left standing by the expert handling of the powerful Vincent.

'He's heading back to London to possibly confront Sergeant Williams if the story Anne Jackson told us is true,' Cramer hypothesised. 'This could get very nasty for Tucker so alert the Metropolitan police to keep a lookout for both the Vincent and the Norton—and to apprehend both riders,' he added and Angstrom dialled Phillips to pass on the instruction.

'The constable commented on a child being present when they entered the antiques shop,' Cramer said. As far as I know the woman is unmarried so do we know who the child belongs to?'

'She said that it was her cousin's and that she was looking after it for a little while,' Angstrom said before sitting up straight. 'Or, the little boy could be Tucker's and he had taken him to Brighton for safe-keeping.'

'That, I believe, is the more logical conclusion which means he'll be back to collect his son after he's met up with Williams. Make sure the 24-hour surveillance is still maintained on the antiques shop.'

As John's journey took him close to Westerham he felt a wave of nostalgia followed by a pang of guilt about the way he had deserted his parents. He knew he would be taking a big risk if he went home but the longing to see his mother overcame the fear of being caught and he meandered along the lanes until he entered the village of Biggin Hill. He had a brief image of Bill Tyler's sneering face as he passed the end of the unadopted road and then he accelerated past the airfield gates and raced towards Bromley and his home.

As the Black Shadow approached Hawthorn Avenue John slowed to a snail's pace, checking each road for any police presence until he turned into the avenue itself and found it clear of any vehicles. He stopped outside his home and for a moment he had second thoughts about going to the door. A curtain twitched across the road and that decided the course of action for him. He dismounted and made a show of unstrapping two large pizza boxes he had bought in the village. He swaggered up the pathway as though making a delivery and rang the bell.

The wait for a response went on and on and he was on the point of putting the boxes on the doormat and leaving when he heard footsteps in the hallway and the sound of the door being unlocked. John stepped up close to the door to shield the reaction of his mother from any nosy neighbours who may be watching. However, it was John who was shocked as it was his father who opened door. Confronted by the large colourful pizza boxes Douglas was confused. It was only as he raised his gaze to the face of the caller that recognition flickered in his eyes.

'Can I come in, Dad?' John whispered nervously and a tight grip on his forearm and a tug answered his question. He stepped into the hallway and his father closed the door behind him quickly. John dropped the boxes as Douglas wrapped his arms around his son and began sobbing.

'You're alive, son! You're alive!' he cried as he looked up into the matured face. 'We thought you had died years ago. Where have you been? What have you been doing?' The rapid questions left the old man breathless and he pulled John towards the stairs. 'Your mother always believed you were close to us,' Douglas said sadly. 'She had a feeling that you were innocent of all the crimes the newspapers accused you of and so did I but the way people, even our neighbours, spoke of you affected her health.'

'What do you mean?' John said fearfully.

'She just went downhill and is now confined to bed. I was able to get early retirement to look after her—that's why I'm at home.'

John glanced sideways at his father and realized that it wasn't just himself who was older, his father had also aged considerably. Lines now criss-crossed his face where once it was smooth and the jowls were more pronounced. A full head of white hair now replaced the touches of grey in his father's sideburns that had always seemed so distinguished.

They entered his parents' bedroom and John was immediately alarmed to see how pale and drawn his mother's face was. He strode across the room and took the thin hand that rested on the coverlet.

'Gloria, darling, look who's come to visit us,' Douglas said softly as he sat down in the cane chair and took his wife's other hand.

Gloria opened her eyes to look at her husband and then slowly turned her head on the pillow to gaze at the stranger who had leant towards her. Gloria's eyes widened and her dry lips gradually curved into a smile of joy.

'John, you came home!' she croaked and he felt her hand turn within his own to grasp him tightly.

'Yes, Mum, I've come home for a little while,' John said trying to hold back the tears. He bent his head and kissed his mother on the cheek. 'I'm so sorry, Mum,' he mumbled. 'I never meant to hurt you the way I did.' He sat back and looked up at his father. 'I panicked, Dad. I didn't know what to do and I took the coward's way out—I ran and I've been running for seventeen years but now I want to stop.'

'You can, son,' his father said quietly. 'You've taken the first step by coming back to life for your mother and I. Now you must go to the police and make sure you stop running forever.'

'Not yet, Dad, I still have a couple of things to do before I can call a halt.'

'How long can you stay, John?' Gloria said as she struggled to sit up while still gripping her son's hand. It was as though she was afraid he would disappear if she released it.

'The neighbours will grow suspicious if the pizza deliveryman stays too long. I may have overstayed my visit now and they could be putting two and two together and calling the police.'

'Okay, son, if you have to go, go but make sure you see your mother again very soon.' His father's unconditional understanding became the last straw and salty tears blurred John's vision and ran down his cheeks.

'I love you, John, we both do and you must never forget it,' Gloria said as she reached up to gather one of her son's tears on her fingertip. 'Today, you have given me great joy and the strength to go on. Come back soon and I promise to make you your favourite apple-and-rhubarb pie.'

John reluctantly withdrew his hand from his mother's and kissed her before standing up. 'I'll be back soon, Mum. You can be sure of that.'

Gloria smiled and blew him a kiss as he left the room followed by his father.

'Thank you for coming home, son,' Douglas said as they descended the stairs. 'I've never seen her so well as the last few minutes; your "resurrection" has done wonders for your mother.'

'I'll be back as soon as I've done what I have to do, Dad—you can be sure of that. Then we'll all go picnicking in the woods and pick mushrooms like we used to.'

Mr Tucker turned his head away so that John wouldn't see the tears in his eyes. 'Make it soon, John,' he whispered as he opened the door.

The memory of Dafydd's last words *hwyl fawr am nawr* returned and John suddenly hugged his surprised father before the door was fully open. He then slipped out and arrogantly sauntered down the path, adopting the mannerisms of a delivery boy who'd just received a big tip. The door had closed behind him immediately but John knew that his father would be watching through the net curtain until he had ridden from sight.

The Black Shadow came to life and John continued his journey to London.

15

ALAN SLAMMED THE PHONE DOWN, stared at it for a moment and then picked up the whole instrument and threw it across the room. To lose control of John had been a blow but to be told by the fugitive that a copy of his black book was on its way to the Hastings police had destroyed his plan to use John as a scapegoat when he saw Bellini.

He had to find John before the police beat him to it and he rushed upstairs and packed a suitcase after checking his last bank statement. He knew he would have to withdraw all his savings before the police discovered his latest address, froze his bank account and made it impossible for him to use his credit cards. Seething with anger he went out into the night to ride the police bike as fast as possible to the house in the East End of London. He stopped briefly to use a phone box close to his destination and quickly dialled an unlisted number. Bellini answered.

'Something's come up and the police have got information from a snitch that I was involved in an incident seventeen years ago. I have to hide out in a safe house for a while until things cool down,' Alan told the drug trafficker.

'I'm sorry to hear this, my friend, for it means you have let me down. I think it's now imperative for you to disappear completely. I will send someone to collect my property and he will take you to a place where the police would never think to look,' Bellini said in a flat monotone.

Alan knew by the slow, cold tone of voice that Bellini didn't want him to hide from the police but that a more permanent solution was being organised as they spoke. Underworld gossip had intimated that

Bellini paid a local pig farmer to dispose of any threats to the safe running of his business. He dropped the phone, leaving it hanging by the lead and rushed from the phone box to continue his journey.

Alan assumed that Bellini didn't know of Jane's house and apart from John and himself only William Tyler and Romano Petrov, the other man who helped kidnap Timothy, knew of its existence. Neither of the men had direct contact with Bellini.

Alan turned into the run-down street of terraced houses and slowly approached Jane's house, stopping a hundred yards short so that the Kawasaki's engine wouldn't alert the woman and her son. It was just after midnight. Alan walked the remaining distance and after looking around at the empty street he quietly climbed the steps to the front door. The doorbell echoed down the hallway and he could hear stumbling footsteps approaching the door. The sound of the lock disengaging was his cue and Alan rammed his shoulder against the peeling paintwork and felt the door burst open. Jane was flung back onto the faded carpet runner and he stepped inside and closed the door behind him before she could make sense of what had happened. The big man reached down, grasped the front of her dress in one hand and pulled her up onto her feet. Before she could scream he slapped her face twice and dragged her down the hall and into the kitchen.

'Make any noise and you'll get more than a little slap,' he snarled as she clasped both hands to her rapidly colouring cheeks. 'Sit down,' he instructed and thumped her in the chest with a closed fist making her fall back into one of the dining chairs. She opened her mouth wide as he held his fist in front of her face.

'Don't say a word until I tell you to,' he said menacingly and Jane slumped back in the chair and looked up at the strange man in fear. 'Where is Timothy, is he upstairs?' he asked as he helped himself to a glass of water.

'No, he's not here.'

'Where is the little brat?'

'I . . . I . . . don't know,' the scared woman stuttered.

Without any warning Alan slapped her face again. 'Don't lie to me, woman.'

'He . . . he took our boy away. John called me and said that he had taken Tim somewhere safe,' Jane said and she cringed in the chair, fully expecting to be struck again.

'And where would that be?' Alan asked.

'I don't know. He said he had got Tim back from the men who had taken him and that he would be going away for a while.' She raised a defensive arm. 'That's all I know! I swear!' Jane's eyes were wide with fear as she watched Alan walking across to the sink. He stood there for a moment as he surveyed the dirty dishes and cutlery stacked high in the bowl.

'Is there anything you haven't told me?' Alan said softly and his lowered voice made Jane even more frightened.

'I know nothing. I can't help you. Please, don't hurt me,' her voice rose and then cracked as she watched him take the cast-iron skillet from the stove and then swiftly cross the room to her.

'But you could tell the police that I kidnapped your son, as well as little tales he told you in the bedroom during the time he was working for me.'

'Nooooo!' she managed to scream before he swung the frying pan in a vicious arc that ended against her temple. In the last moments before she died Jane looked down in horror at the blood that was streaming down her face and soaking the front of her dress. She then sank into blackness and slid onto the grubby linoleum floor.

Alan took a damp dishcloth from the table and wiped the handle of the skillet and replaced it on the cooker. He left the woman sitting on the kitchen floor with head bowed, gazing with unseeing eyes at the crimson stain on her chest, and hurried down the hallway. The door made little noise as he carefully cracked it open to check the street outside. The single streetlight revealed an empty road and he wiped the door handle with a tissue before closing the door and walking down the steps.

Alan lowered the visor of his helmet in case there were nosy curtain-twitchers and walked to his bike. The machine started at the first kick and he slowly pulled away and headed for the only place he thought John would choose to hide from him. He mentally crossed his fingers that John's parents would be willing to let their fugitive son stay with them. If they had given him up to the police he would be denied the pleasure of finding John and shutting his mouth permanently.

John kept the Vincent at a steady 55 miles per hour on the London road and then reduced his speed when he filtered onto the minor roads that led to the drug dealer's house. Alan had sounded furious when John had spoken to him on the phone and told him that all deals were off. He had no idea that his call had prompted Alan to pursue a personal vendetta against him that would lead to even greater tragedies.

The Vincent purred along the leafy roads and John kept the bike moving when he identified the wrought-iron gates that opened onto the long drive to Bellini's house. He had little time to admire the Lutyens-designed residence for he had caught sight of two dark-suited men loitering in the drive and knew that one of them was called Jimmy. Two hundred yards further on round a slight bend in the road he pulled over while he studied a little iron gate set in the high perimeter wall that gave access to the extensive grounds lying beyond.

After estimating the open space he would have to cross and noticing the two large Rottweilers prowling around the house he toed the bike into gear and accelerated away. His first priority was to acquire some form of weapon, which he knew he couldn't do legally. John suddenly changed direction and made for the canal where the *Gull's Delight* was moored. If the young cocaine addict called Terry could point the business end of a gun at him then he most probably had access to other weapons.

John parked on the road and crossed the grass verge to the towpath. He soon spotted the cruiser that was still moored where he had last seen it. He sat on one of the steel benches that were placed along the canal bank at regular intervals and settled down to a long wait for sunset and the concealing cloak of darkness.

In the gathering gloom John watched the coots as they finished diving for their last meal of the day before paddling across the canal to their camouflaged nests on the far bank. Lights were now starting to appear in the craft that were scattered along the canal and when a single porthole suddenly glowed yellow in the narrow boat John knew that Terry was aboard.

He waited another hour and when it was dark he began making his way towards the *Gull's Delight*, his eyes fixed upon the forward hatch cover and the cockpit companionway. Suddenly the door opened and light flooded onto the deck. Terry emerged carrying a steel bucket with a length of rope attached to the handle. The youth tipped the contents over the side and John could see that it was ordinary kitchen waste. Terry had waited until he was sure that nobody could see him before discarding his rubbish directly into the river. The young man leant over the side and dropped the bucket into the water and raised it up to rinse the inside, repeating the process a couple of times.

While Terry was fully occupied John crept across the sagging plank and jumped onto the deck behind the man. Terry spun around, his mouth wide open in surprise as a clenched fist struck him hard in the solar plexus. He doubled up gasping for air as John grabbed him by his collar and pulled him down the companionway and into the saloon. He slammed the door shut and turned to lean over the doubled-up figure that was still gasping for air.

'Where do you keep your gun?' he asked grabbing a hank of hair and pulling the youth's head back.

'I don't have . . .' he got no further for the same fist struck him in exactly the same spot. All air was expelled and the pain caused him to vomit before he could breathe again. He fell to the deck and rolled onto his side.

'Do I have to ask you again?' John said grimly.

Terry extended a wavering arm and pointed towards a locker above John's head. He reached up to open the locker while keeping one eye on the retching addict and found a small packet of white powder and what he had come for—an automatic pistol and two spare magazines.

John removed the gun, a Russian Tokarev, and the magazines which each held eight rounds. The make of the weapon meant nothing to him and he slipped it and the spare magazines into his jacket pocket. He took the packet of cocaine and tore the plastic, spilling the powder over Terry and the deck. Searching his pockets he found the ignition key to the boat and dropped it into his own shirt pocket.

'Leave the boat and give it all up, lad,' he advised. 'It'll only kill you in the end and if it doesn't Bellini will.' With that final comment he climbed back onto the deck and left the boat.

John started the bike and rode towards the river and Alan's place. He knew that the incriminating letter he had posted wouldn't be received by the police until the first post on the following day and he wanted to see if he could locate Alan to exact his revenge for Ted's murder and his own destroyed life before the police caught up with him. All thoughts of Timothy and how his actions might affect his son's life were buried beneath his desire for revenge.

The rain had started falling again by the time he turned into Alan's street and he approached the house as quietly as the Vincent would permit. He stopped and studied the black windows, looking for any sign of his adversary before switching the engine off. John pulled the bike up onto its stand and went to the rear of the house. The fence gate was still open as was the rear door. He paused, his suspicion aroused, before slowly entering the kitchen on the balls of his feet.

Not fully knowing whether he could ever use it for anything other than a threat he took the gun from his jacket pocket and crept into the hall but the house was completely empty. The open drawers and wardrobe in the bedroom indicated that Alan had fled the premises and was now hiding somewhere else. Bellini immediately sprang to mind but John guessed that the drug baron wouldn't want anything to do with a corrupt copper who, like himself, was now being hunted by the police.

As John left the bedroom he heard a slight noise from downstairs. A shuffling sound as though someone else was trying to move about noiselessly. He moved to the top of the stairs and saw a man in a dark suit who was holding a long-barrelled weapon in front of him. As the man turned towards the first step of the staircase John backed away quietly and squatted behind a side table in the passage. He heard the stairs creak as the man climbed and then there was a brief silence as he stopped at the top before turning and walking slowly towards where John was hiding.

The large man was only inches away and still moving when he became aware of the figure crouching on his left. He swung around to bring his right hand holding the silenced automatic to bear and John leapt up, ramming the man into the balustrade with his shoulder. The gunman's waist hit the top rail and he toppled over and fell down into the hallway, sounding like a wet sack of sand as he struck the floor. John leant over and could just make out the dark shape that lay motionless on the faded linoleum. Without any effort to keep quiet John hurried down the stairs and bent over the crumpled form. He breathed a sigh when he saw that it wasn't Alan but one of the men he had seen at Signor Bellini's house. John checked the big man for any sign of a pulse and was relieved to find that he hadn't killed him. He picked up the heavy automatic and after unscrewing the silencer he slipped both into his pocket and hurried from the house. The Vincent was still standing where he had left it and it seemed obvious that the machine had alerted the gunman and consequently lured him into Alan's house. Why send a man with a gun to this particular house—does Bellini want to silence Alan? he thought as he started the bike and pulled away.

Superintendent Cramer was browsing through his morning mail when Angstrom entered his office carrying a large manila envelope. She placed it on his desk.

'It was so thick that I had the bomb squad X-ray it before passing it on to you, sir,' she said. 'Can't be too careful these days.'

'Thank you, Jennifer,' Cramer said with a smile as he picked the packet up and slit the top with a paperknife; 'that was very considerate.'

'I also had it checked for fingerprints and we found a match.'

'Well, don't keep me in suspense!'

'It belonged to John Tucker.' There was a long silence as Cramer studied the envelope from all angles as though handling a rare piece of art before carefully tipping a stack of photocopies out onto his desk blotter. Cramer slipped on a pair of forensic rubber gloves and picked the top one up by the edges to read it.

'We'll need to check this for fingerprints as well,' he murmured as he perused the columns of figures with the detective inspector looking over his shoulder.

'Looks like a record of payments,' she said and Cramer nodded as he took the single piece of blue-lined paper that had dropped out from between the pages and unfolded it.

'This is very interesting,' he muttered as he read the brief hand-written message. 'It's from our runaway ton-up, John Tucker, and he says that these are the transactions between Sergeant Williams and someone called Bellini.'

'We still haven't located Williams,' Angstrom complained. 'It's as though he's vanished off the face of the earth.'

'Run a check on the name Bellini across all departments and let's see if that helps us throw a little more light on the case. While you're at it send this to the lab for further fingerprint checking,' Cramer instructed as he carefully slid the pile of photocopied sheets and the scrap of writing paper back into the envelope. The detective hurried from the office leaving Cramer in deep thought as he absent-mindedly stirred his cold coffee with a ballpoint pen.

Later that afternoon the fingerprint results came through, proving that John Tucker had also handled the photocopies; realizing that John had now betrayed Alan Williams, Cramer asked for the manhunt to be extended nationwide and given more priority. This proved to be partly successful when a report that a Norton matching the description was seen in the East End. A further report by a patrol car that a similar bike had been spotted on the road heading south focused attention on the cross-channel ports.

'Williams could be trying to hide on the continent although his plates and our description of him would soon have him picked up by Interpol,' Angstrom said. 'Or he may be hunting Tucker. I think Tucker's the one who may have all the answers, but he's been a veritable phantom since the day he vanished from his home all those years ago.'

Cramer slammed his palms down on the desk and sat bolt upright. 'That's it, Jennifer,' he cried. 'Williams is going to Tucker's home. He thinks he's gone to lie low at his parents' house.' Cramer stood up and grabbed his jacket from off the back of his chair. 'C'mon lass, we've got to alert the local force and get down there ourselves before Williams can hurt the Tuckers.'

Angstrom trotted after her boss with clacking heels and after they had driven away from the Hastings police station at high speed she spoke to Dispatch to enlist more localised help. Fifty minutes later they pulled into Hawthorn Avenue where Tucker was born. Two patrol cars were already parked outside the house with their rooftop light-bars flashing.

Angstrom knocked on the door that was opened by a police constable who, after checking her warrant card, stood to one side to permit them both to enter the house.

They found an extremely pale-faced elderly couple sitting in the living room with two constables and a sergeant standing behind them.

The woman appeared to be rather frail as though she had been bed-ridden for a lengthy period and had just got up. Cramer flashed his warrant card and waved for them all to leave the room. Cramer sat down in the armchair facing the couple and smiled widely to put their minds at ease.

'I sincerely apologise for this very inconvenient intrusion into your home but we have reason to believe that you may be in some form of danger,' he said in as gentle a voice as he could manage.

Angstrom crossed the room and sat in the other chair. Slightly reassured by the inspector's sympathetic face the couple visibly unwound and leant back into the soft hand-embroidered cushions.

'Alan Williams who is sought by us for questioning was last seen heading south, maybe in this direction. It is our understanding that he wants to speak to your son—'

Mrs Tucker gasped and clasping a hand to her throat sat upright on the edge of her seat. 'Alan is chasing my John?'

'Yes, we believe your son is in the country and has been living under a different name for the last seventeen years.' This did not seem to surprise the parents and Cramer noticed their lack of any response.

'But why would Alan want to chase John? They've been the closest of friends since school.' Mrs Tucker's voice quavered as she spoke and her husband took her hand and squeezed it to calm the newfound fear growing in his wife's mind.

'Your son has information that could incriminate Alan, possibly involve him in the death of the two young girls who were murdered seventeen years ago. He may want to prevent John from telling us what he knows about that night.'

'How can he prevent him?' Douglas Tucker stopped as the obvious answer to his question sprang to mind. 'My God, they were the best of mates, surely Alan wouldn't . . . ' He left the rest unsaid and put an arm round his wife's shoulder.

'He may if we let him but we won't,' Cramer said. 'I promise that no harm will come to your son.'

Angstrom looked towards her boss with a slight frown on her face. 'Has John contacted you at all in the last few days?' she asked, hoping to distract the couple from the impossible promise Cramer had made them.

Both parents remained silent and the father gave the slightest suggestion of a shrug. Angstrom made a mental note of this, believing that it was confirmation that John had spoken to one of them recently.

'You're not protecting John by remaining silent, Mr Tucker. It would make our jobs a lot easier if we could provide proper protection for your son by having him in custody,' Angstrom said.

'Right now it's the only safe place for him,' Cramer added. As he continued with gentle probing questions Angstrom took a telephone call that had been routed through to the Tucker's landline. At an opportune moment she drew Cramer to one side and told him that the check on

Bellini had shown that he was suspected of being the main supplier of hard drugs for the south of England. Cramer nodded slowly and he made a mental note to visit Signor Bellini.

While the chief inspector calmly questioned Gloria and Douglas Tucker for more personal details of their son a Norton Commando slowly came to a stop at the end of the street. The probationary constable sitting in one of the cars vaguely noticed the motorcycle in his rear-view mirror but thought nothing of it as he was totally preoccupied with the heavily retouched centrefold playmate of the month.

Alan had seen the red and blue flashing lights the moment he stopped at the end of the avenue and immediately kicked the bike back into second gear and accelerated away. It was obvious to him that John wasn't at home and therefore had to be hiding from him elsewhere. But where? He twisted the throttle and raced in the direction of London.

The two officers finished the interview with a promise to contact the parents should any more news about John become available. As they left the house Douglas Tucker stood in the bay window with a secret smile crinkling the corners of his mouth. His son was alive and, even better, the police now thought him to be innocent.

'Where on earth could Alan be,' John thought as he left Alan's house at sunset to ride through the illuminated streets of Weybridge until the obvious answer struck him forcibly. Alan would be on his way to London to look for him at Jane's house. Suddenly John felt very cold despite the snug leather jacket and gauntlets he was wearing and he opened up the throttle and took the most direct route to the terraced house in the East End.

A lone patrol car was cruising on the bypass when John unknowingly flashed past like an avenging spirit. The challenge was immediately taken up and the Ford was soon in hot pursuit of the Vincent. Roof lights flashed and a blood-chilling siren scream chased after John as he weaved through the evening traffic at a frustratingly low speed. Soon he spotted more flashing lights up ahead and knew that the chase car had radioed ahead for assistance.

John made a sharp right-hand turn across the oncoming traffic and accelerated down a side street. The patrol car tried to follow but was frustrated by the constant stream of oncoming cars and had to be content with giving the last location of the Vincent to central control.

In spite of the valuable time it would take, John left the highway leading to the city and made a wide detour to the south.

With unerring skill he used all the back streets he was familiar with and eventually reached Clapham Common without seeing any signs of police vehicles. He remained south of the River Thames until he could use the Blackwall Tunnel.

John approached the maze of tiny identical streets that surrounded Jane's house more carefully with the heavy engine merely mumbling to itself and he braked by the front steps at one in the morning.

He removed his helmet and looked up at the house. Like those on either side it was in complete darkness. The dark window-panes contrasted with the light-red brick exterior that was softly illuminated by the full moon. A stray cat approached him cautiously and then more boldly pressed her arching back against his leg. Its purr was not dissimilar to a two-stroke engine and seemed to echo down the narrow street. He bent briefly and scratched it behind the ears before hurriedly climbing the steps to the front door.

To John's surprise the door was slightly ajar, the inky gap between the edge of the door and the frame a sinister invitation to enter the house. Using his gloved fingertips he silently pushed against the door to make it swing open on its rarely oiled hinges. In John's mind the very light screech seemed loud enough to awaken the whole street but all the windows remained dark and the only movement was the stray cat climbing the steps towards him.

John noticed the broken safety chain and crept along the hallway to the rear of the house before taking a small torch from his pocket and lighting his way into the kitchen. He almost fell when he stumbled over a dark shape on the floor. John flicked the thin beam downwards and gasped when it revealed Jane in a position of prayer. Her blue dress was stained red in the light of his torch and John knew that it was too late to do anything for the woman who had been a major factor in his life for the last six years.

You may not always have been a very nice woman, he thought, but you deserved a lot better than this. John bent over to study her face and recoiled at the sight of her open, unseeing eyes. He found a soft cloth in the scullery and gently covered her face.

'Poor Jane,' he murmured and backed away until he had reached the hall. As he left the house and pulled the door shut he thought he saw the faintest movement of a curtain across the street but as the window remained in darkness he put it down to his spooked imagination. John accelerated away without noticing the same curtain being pulled back and a white face pressing against the glass. The face was straining to see who had visited Jane at such a late hour.

John rode through the night trying to decide on the best course of action until he made up his mind to return to Brighton and go to the one place where he could sleep for a while without fear of discovery. The roads were devoid of any traffic apart from the occasional truck making its way to Dover and he was able to maintain a steady pace all the way to the coast. He made a large detour to include Dover, thereby misleading any possible sightings of the Vincent and its intended destination. He was also counting on the coastal roads having fewer police patrols at night than the major highways on the more direct route.

Unfortunately John was very much mistaken. Two constables in a patrol car had been investigating a silent alarm triggered in a small industrial unit and they became suspicious of the lone motorcyclist speeding through the medieval Cinque Port of Rye at three o'clock in the morning.

One jotted down the registration and type of bike in his official notebook. This was slipped into a breast pocket for checking at the police station later. The two constables then went on to investigate the suspected burglary.

16

ANGSTROM STOPPED AT THE WROUGHT-IRON GATES and indicated to the dark-suited man to open them. He shook his head and waved a dismissive hand for her to drive away.

'Show him your credentials, Jennifer,' Cramer murmured patiently as he continued reading the file on Bellini that had been dispatched from London with a number of priority stickers emblazoned across the cover. Angstrom climbed out of the car and watched as the man slipped a hand inside his jacket. 'I trust that isn't a weapon you have in there, sir,' she said politely as she held up her warrant card. 'I'm Detective Inspector Angstrom and I would advise you to open these gates immediately or face a charge of obstructing police officers in the course of their duties.'

The man removed his hand from his jacket and shrugged indifferently before sliding the bolts back and pulling both gates wide open. Angstrom got back behind the wheel and drove towards the distant house.

'We'll check with his boss as to whether he has a permit for the weapon,' Cramer murmured as he closed the file and tucked it back into his briefcase. Angstrom braked outside the front door just as it opened and a clone of the first guard emerged.

'Looks like the gatekeeper let them know we're coming,' she muttered, eyeing the big man who had a dark bruise down the side of his face. She got out followed by Cramer who eyed the man closely.

'That must hurt a bit,' Angstrom said as she pointed at the man's face.

'Walked into a door, I imagine,' Cramer added with a touch of sarcasm in his voice. The man remained expressionless and simply waved them up the steps and into the large hall where an older man was waiting.

Angstrom quickly took in the drug dealer's appearance. The crisp white suit was tailor-made with a matching waistcoat that was stretched to its limit over a rather corpulent stomach. The open collar of the large-sized silk shirt failed to hide the rolls of neck fat and his jowls juddered as he advanced with a pudgy hand outstretched.

'Buongiorno, Signorina,' he beamed and a gold cap winked briefly at the detective inspector. 'Ah, Signor,' he said turning to Cramer after reluctantly releasing Angstrom's hand from his clammy handshake. 'How can I help you?'

Angstrom surreptitiously dried her hand on her dark pleated skirt and pointed at what appeared to be a door to the living room. 'May we take a little of your time, sir, and ask you a few questions?' she asked politely.

The man released Cramer's hand and shrugged. 'I have all the time you may need, please come this way.' He walked into the large expensively furnished room and indicated one of the club chairs to Angstrom. Both officers noted that they had been shadowed into the room by the large man who had greeted them at the door.

After Cramer and Angstrom were seated Bellini slowly sank into the settee opposite and waved a small hand as though to indicate that the questioning may proceed.

'Do you know a man called Alan Williams?' Angstrom asked and Bellini's head spun round for he had expected Cramer to lead with the questioning.

'No, I cannot say that I do, errr . . . ?'

'Detective Inspector Angstrom,' Jennifer answered for him. 'You haven't met such a man recently?'

'I believe I said that I do not know the man,' Bellini said irritably.

'Then could you explain why you have been paying the man considerable sums of money over the last three years?' Cramer murmured, his eyes narrowing as he studied the man carefully.

'I don't know what you mean, Superintendent, you must have another Bellini in mind.'

Cramer audibly snapped open the catches and removed a stack of paper from his briefcase. 'This lists over one hundred payments that have specific dates which indicate you clearly had dealings with the police sergeant.'

'Sergeant?'

'I'm sure a man as well connected as yourself was well aware that Alan Williams was a police sergeant in the traffic division. Maybe that was the prime reason you selected him in the first place,' Cramer said as he replaced the papers and closed his case.

'What was he selling for you?' Angstrom snapped. 'Drugs, medical supplies. What?'

Bellini eyed both officers and swept a lock of hair from his forehead before answering in a low voice. 'It is obvious that you have no evidence apart from that mysterious notebook that I had any dealings with this man you call Williams. And exactly what dealings are not made clear on the pages you have there. My lawyer would soon demolish any link between me and the man mentioned in those silly figures you are holding up as being so important,' Bellini crowed. 'It's all circumstantial drivel and no more than that.'

Cramer raised his chin and Angstrom rose to her feet to be followed by her boss. 'Thank you for your time, Mr Bellini. We will be in touch with more questions once we have apprehended Mr Williams.' Without waiting for the Italian to rise Cramer strode from the room with Angstrom on his heels and they left the house with the bodyguard hurrying to keep up.

Once inside the car Angstrom punched her knees in frustration. 'He is up to his neck in dirty drug business with Williams but how Tucker is involved escapes me.'

'The fact that both Williams, Tucker and even Edwards were once ton-ups doesn't escape me and I'm beginning to understand why they were recruited by Bellini.'

Angstrom looked askance at her superior. 'And what would that be, sir?'

'They are expert motorcyclists who would be able to flit about the country without any hold-ups from heavy traffic or police cars. Remember the report about the rider who out-ran three units on the Birmingham stretch of the M1?' Cramer said as he watched the narrow hedge-lined country road unfold in front of them. 'That could have been one of Bellini's couriers moving very small, lightweight items of very high value around the country. Hence the large sums of money recorded in this.' He tapped the briefcase containing the sheaf of photocopies.

'Drugs?'

'What else?'

Angstrom drove with the blue lights flashing to get them back to Hastings as soon as possible. 'We have to apprehend those two as quickly as we can as I have a feeling that Bellini will not continue to be so generous the next time he or one of his Armani-tailored thugs meet up with Williams,' Cramer said.

'You believe he'd kill him, sir?'

'I know he'll kill him and undoubtedly he'll take out Tucker too. They're the only ones who could testify against him in a court of law now that Edwards and his wife have been murdered and if those men disappear so will our case against him.'

'It all hangs on us catching one or the other.'

'Or both, Jennifer, or both,' Cramer said thoughtfully.

It was on arriving at his office that the superintendent learnt of the woman's murder in East London. A curious neighbour had gone to see why Jane had not taken in her milk when she found the door ajar and discovered her body.

Door-to-door questioning uncovered one neighbour who had seen a tall man leave a big motorcycle at the end of the street and visit the house at midnight; another woman, who claimed to have been suffering from insomnia, noticed another man come and go on a motorcycle at one in the morning. Being rather suspicious by nature she had noted down the registration and police records showed the vehicle belonged to an antiques dealer in Brighton. The report had been forwarded to both Hastings and Brighton on the off-chance that the rider might return that way. Cramer read and re-read the report until Angstrom came in and interrupted his train of thought.

'Do you think it was John on both occasions?' she asked putting a yard of telex paper on his desk. 'Or two different riders. This, by the way, gives details on the murdered woman. It appears she used to be a bookkeeper for a fishmonger in Billingsgate market and our investigation there showed that many porters remember her helping unlicensed porters get jobs with different market traders and that she gave them lodgings at her house. They didn't particularly like her because she foul-mouthed everyone and in their eyes, by getting jobs for unlicensed men, she was virtually taking the bread from the mouths of the licensed pusher-uppers.'

'Pusher-uppers?'

'Fish porters, sir,' Angstrom explained.

'Are any still in residence?'

'No, and that's the strange thing. All the men she rented rooms to and had helped to get work have disappeared.'

'Send pictures of Tucker and Williams to the Catford police. Ask them to show these to the two neighbours to confirm that it was Williams and Tucker that they saw that evening and to check if Tucker was the man living at that address. If it was them they are to circulate the head shots in the area to see if we can dig up any more witnesses,' Cramer said as he started to read the telex report.

'Already done, sir.'

Cramer looked up and then nodded without smiling as though he expected no less from the detective inspector.

'How was she killed, sir?'

'Skull crushed by a heavy frying pan which was wiped clean of any fingerprints.'

'Couldn't have been premeditated, sir, as that sounds like a weapon used in a fit of rage,' Angstrom said thoughtfully.

'Or one used to make us believe that it was a crime of passion.'

'That would then point the finger at Tucker, sir!'

Alan came to the conclusion that he needed a place where he could do a little thinking without the risk of being seen by either the police or Bellini's men. There was only one place he could risk going to that both the police and the Signor knew nothing about. He threaded his way amongst the back streets until he was able to turn onto the A21 leading south. Then with the throttle at only half-twist he cruised on to Bromley and then to Biggin Hill and William Tyler.

Alan's teeth rattled as he turned onto the rough surface of the unadopted road. He approached the house in darkness and promptly turned into the driveway and switched the engine off; the only sounds were the ticking of the cooling engine and the muted call of a solitary barn owl. He caught a brief flicker of white as the bird silently swooped between the houses.

He cautiously approached the wooden gate that gave access to the rear garden. He pushed it wide open and then fetched his bike which he wheeled onto the rear patio that extended the full width of the house. He returned to relatch the gate and satisfied that the Norton couldn't be seen from the road he went to the back door and tried the handle. As expected it was locked.

Alan tried to peer through the glass panes but was unable to see anything until there was a sudden blaze of blinding light and he found himself staring down the barrels of a twelve-gauge shotgun. The two black holes were a mere three inches from his face but prevented from coming any closer by the doubled-glazed window.

He tried looking beyond the weapon and vaguely saw William Tyler's grim face above the dazzling torch. Tyler suddenly beamed broadly, his tiny close-set eyes almost closed with amusement at the expression on Alan's face. The Mossberg 500 pump shotgun was lowered and after putting the torch on a side table Tyler reached out and unlocked the door. Alan pushed it open and advanced on the man with clenched fists by his side, his face reflecting his rage.

'Christ, Bill!' he shouted. 'You bloody well scared the shit out of me.'

'Sorry about that, Alan, but you rightly deserved it,' Tyler replied, the grin still fixed on his face as he stood the shotgun against the wall. 'After all, you were the one creeping around the house in the middle of the night. What else did you expect, a fanfare of trumpets?'

Alan locked the door behind him and turned, his face less aggressive. 'Look, I need a place to stay for a while. Somewhere to conduct operations from until things cool down a little.' He followed Tyler into the kitchen.

'I saw your ugly mug on the telly tonight. They're calling you a rogue cop. Little do they know how roguish you are,' Tyler said as he switched on the electric kettle and began spooning instant coffee into two Elizabeth II coronation mugs.

'What did the report say?'

'Not much.' Tyler went to the fridge and took out a half-bottle of milk. 'Just a picture of you in full uniform and that the police want to question you regarding the brutal slaughter of some woman in London,' he added in a tone of voice that caused Alan some concern. 'Ah, yes! And that you were last seen riding a Norton Commando motorcycle. They even gave the registration number.' Tyler turned to face Alan. 'I hope you've tucked that well out of sight because I don't want to be accused of harbouring a fugitive.'

The kettle began to boil and Alan pulled out a chair from the table. 'It's in your back garden.' He sat down. 'What else?'

'Mmm . . . they did say that there was a reward for any information that led to your apprehension.' Tyler poured the hot water and his face was momentarily disguised by the clouds of steam.

'You wouldn't be thinking of turning me in, would you Bill?' Alan's flat tone of voice sounded like a warning bell deep in Tyler's mind.

'Good Lord, Alan, what do you think I am, some kind of rotten snitch or something?'

Alan took the mug that had been passed across the table and after spooning in sugar and stirring rapidly he carefully sipped the hot liquid. 'If I thought you were capable of doing that to me, Bill, I'd have your heart on toast for breakfast,' he murmured as he scrutinised the man over the rim of the mug. Tyler picked up his mug and turned away to stare out of the window into the night, his face a shade paler than his normal pallid complexion.

'Which room, Bill?'

'What?' Tyler turned back to face Alan.

'Bedroom, which bedroom shall I use?'

'The guest room, second door from the top of the stairs. It's got an en-suite so you won't have to go far if you're caught short in the middle of the night.'

Alan stood up to drain the last drops in his mug and then taking the shotgun leaning against the wall he strode past Tyler. 'Just removing the temptation, mate,' he said with a forbidding smile that never reached his eyes and he left the room and a very uneasy Tyler.

Alan slept fitfully with the gun under the sheet beside him and he didn't fully awake until a knock at the door made him jerk upright, his hand clutching the barrel of the Mossberg. The heavy curtains had blocked out the morning sun and he blearily looked across to the alarm clock on the bedside table and saw that it was ten o'clock. After sliding the shotgun out of sight beneath the bed he called out.

'Come in, Bill!' Alan sat up as the door opened.

Tyler entered and casually crossed the room to sit in the leather armchair that stood by the window. 'Your bike is quite visible to people next door. Like us they can see from their upper windows into the garden including mine. You'll have to cover it with a tarpaulin. I've got one in the shed.'

'You can do that while I'm getting cleaned up and dressed,' Alan ordered as he swung the sheet to one side and stood up. The pyjama bottoms he had borrowed from Tyler were too large and gathered at the waist where he had tied the cord to keep them up. Tyler left the room with a scowl on his face as Alan went into the en-suite bathroom thinking about the man's expression and what it may have meant.

Thirty minutes later Alan descended the stairs to find Tyler by the hallstand with the phone in his hand. He could hear the low repetitious buzzing of the ring tone and knew that no number had yet been reached.

'I thought I said no calls, William,' Alan said with the shotgun cradled in his arm.

'I was just about to call my sister to tell her I can't make the christening,' Tyler said as he replaced the receiver in the cradle with his eyes fixed on the Mossberg.

'Christening?'

'My nephew's christening at St Luke's today,' Tyler said in an unconvincing voice. 'I need to let her know that I can't make it.'

'Leave it till later,' Alan said and walked into the kitchen. He looked out of the window and saw that the Norton had been draped with a dark green tarpaulin which barely disguised the shape of the motorcycle.

'How long do you plan to stay?'

'Until the hunt has been called off.' Alan opened the cupboards one by one until he found the packets of cereal and selected an all-bran with sultanas. 'You have plenty of milk?'

'Milkman comes tomorrow but I have enough to last until then.'

'Do you have to speak to him or anybody else?'

'No. He just leaves the milk on the doorstep.'

'Have you got any bread for toast?'

'Yes, plenty.' Tyler opened the bread bin and removed a fresh loaf.

'Excellent,' Alan said as Tyler turned to place it on the kitchen table. Alan slipped the bread knife from a rack and plunged it into the man's back.

'You lied, Bill,' he hissed in Tyler's ear as the stricken man began collapsing. 'There was no christening. You were going to call the police and then claim the bloody reward, you bastard.'

Tyler shook his head and then shrieked as Alan shouted 'liar' and twisted the knife twice before wrenching it free. The blood spurted freely and Tyler felt himself getting cold rapidly as he lost all feeling in his limbs and sank to the floor.

'If you ever thought you could possibly double-cross me you had another thought coming my friend,' Alan whispered as he jerked Tyler's head back and spat in his face. He carefully wiped the blade clean on a heavily stained tea towel before taking the fresh cottage loaf and cutting two generous slices to put in the toaster.

One thing less to worry about when I'm sleeping tonight, he thought as he stepped over the body and took the butter and a jar of marmalade from the refrigerator. As he dropped the slices of bread into the toaster he noticed a small piece of gilt-edged pasteboard lying on the draining board. He picked it up and read the invitation for Tyler to attend his nephew's christening in St Luke's church at ten o'clock that morning.

Alan dropped the card with an apathetic shrug of his shoulders and it fluttered down onto the corpse.

'You should have been more convincing, mate.'

John rode along the sleeping seafront with great care even though it appeared quiet and lifeless without the colourful promenade lights. The familiar screeching of seagulls wouldn't start until the first light of dawn streaked the sky. He thought it best to park the bike in one of the back streets near the Royal Pavilion where it would stand less chance of being noticed. The long walk to the antiques shop would also avoid making a reverberating racket if he took the Vincent down the very narrow streets leading to The Lanes.

His eyes flicked from side to side, constantly keeping a lookout for any suspicious vehicles parked in the shadows. The first pattering of drops on his helmet made him look up briefly as gathering storm clouds began drawing a thick, dark blanket over the slumbering town.

He walked as lightly as possible, quickly threading his way through the streets until he entered the The Lanes. The antiques shop was in total darkness apart from the tiny red light of a motion sensor that was flashing high up on the showroom wall. After tapping on the glass door he looked round quickly for it seemed loud enough to waken every resident within fifty yards. He waited while he studied all the windows that stared down at him like accusing eyes. A few more seconds passed before he tapped once more, wincing with each sound his knuckles made on the glass.

A light flickered at the back of the shop and a shadowy figure descended the stairs and entered the showroom. John tapped again and when Anne's face appeared at the glass he grinned and indicated that he wanted to come in. After a brief rattling of bolts the door was swung half open and John slipped in hurriedly and closed it behind him.

'Why have you come?' Anne asked anxiously as she rubbed her eyes with one hand while holding her dressing gown together with the other. 'Timothy's perfectly okay and is fast asleep.'

John followed the young woman across the showroom and up the stairs to the small sitting room where he slumped wearily onto the settee. 'I'm sorry, Anne, but I'm dead beat and this is the only place that's safe enough to get a bit of sleep.'

Pulling her dressing gown tight around her Anne sat down to face him as he slipped his leather jacket off. She was about to question him further when she saw his eyelids begin to droop. As John's head slowly fell back against the padded armrest she gently lifted his legs onto the settee and then took the paisley patchwork throw from the armchair she had been sitting in and covered the restlessly sleeping man. She watched him for ten more minutes, observing the deep lines of worry across his brow that smoothed away while he slept, before returning to her own bedoom. On the way Anne briefly looked into the spare room to check that Timothy hadn't been disturbed. He was still sound asleep with a thumb in his mouth.

Six hours later Anne awoke to the soft buzz of her alarm clock and after cleaning her teeth and splashing a little cold water on her face she slipped on the old dressing gown and went to the small kitchenette. She could smell the irresistible aroma of frying bacon and sausages and as though she had been magnetised she was drawn into the brightly lit room where John was busily juggling a fryingpan, saucepan and toaster.

'Perfect timing, Anne,' he said breezily as he removed three plates from the warmer and began heaping them with a traditional English breakfast. 'Do you want some fried bread as well?' he asked as he put the plates on the kitchen table. Anne was overwhelmed and could only shake her head as she sat down.

'Absolutely right, it'll only go straight to your hips,' John smiled as he walked to the door and shouted 'Tim!' He placed a bottle of tomato sauce in the centre of the table as the drubbing of small feet sounded in the passage. 'Can't have too many calories. Not if you want to keep that lovely figure of yours.'

Anne's cheeks coloured a little and she was thankful for the distraction when the small boy burst into the kitchen like a small tornado and threw himself onto one of the seats.

'Wow, Mrs Jackson,' he said grabbing the sauce bottle and almost emptying its contents over the sausages and baked beans. 'This looks fab.' He then looked up briefly to acknowledge his father with a broad grin. 'Hello, Dad, when did you arrive?' Without waiting for an answer or an invitation he began wolfing the food down as though he hadn't eaten for a week.

'It was your father who made breakfast today so you should thank him, not me,' Anne said as she looked into John's eyes.

'Hello, son. How have you been, okay?'

'Great. Mrs Jackson is really cool and I love Brighton,' he managed to say through a mouthful of egg and bacon while giving Anne a shy smile. 'We went to the pier yesterday and had loads of fun. I put dozens of pennies in those funny machines that try to pick up toys and boxes of sweets but didn't grab a thing.'

'You must call me Anne, Timothy. I'm not married so I'm not a Mrs yet,' Anne said as a smile creased the corners of her eyes. It was the type of smile John had never seen on Jane's face and Llinos was a vague memory with Anne sitting so close to him.

'Okay, Mrs Jackson, I'll call you Anne.'

John chuckled and put his finger to his lips to remind the boy not to talk while his mouth was full and then joined Anne in the serious pursuit of breaking their fast.

When the dishes had been cleared and the tea poured John sat back in his chair and studied his surroundings. The kitchen walls were lined with shelves crammed with decorative and commemorative plates, figurines and odd pieces of porcelain from Worcester, Chelsea and Crown Derby.

'Must be worth quite a sum,' he murmured as he turned his head to admire the pieces above the gas range.

'They were my father's pride and joy. It's his secret collection that the customers never get to see and or are ever likely to see.'

John could hear how the words caught in her throat while she gazed at the beautifully decorated pieces. 'I don't think I could ever part with them. They are as much a part of my father as the Vincent you are riding is now a part of you.'

John sat up and leant forward with his elbows on the table. 'I know how much you miss him, Anne,' he said softly. 'And I promise I will do what I can to bring his killer to justice.'

'Was it the same man who made me go to sleep and locked me up?' Timothy asked innocently. 'Did he hurt Mr Jackson, Dad?'

'I don't know who did it son but I will soon find out.'

'Then you'll kill him for me, won't you?' The boy made a pretence of fencing and then stabbing with his knife. A dribble of egg yolk fell on the white linen cloth and John frowned at the boy's clumsiness.

'No, your father is going to help the police catch that nasty man and put him in jail for a very long time,' Anne said as she pointedly looked at John with an expression that seemed to warn him not to encourage his son or do as he had requested.

'Anne's right, son,' he said taking the knife from the boy and laying it down on the plate before dabbing at the egg-yolk stain with a paper serviette. 'It's wrong to kill and all wrongdoers must be punished by the law courts only.'

Guilt had given his voice a harsh edge and Timothy looked at his father with unease. John didn't notice his son's distress for he was recalling a wood where he once scrabbled in damp leaf mould to make a grave. If anyone needs punishment it's myself, he thought.

John's mind returned to the present and he saw his son looking crestfallen and close to tears. John took his hand and continued in a much gentler tone. 'Do you remember what you were taught at Sunday School, Tim?'

The boy nodded and recited: 'You must not kill.'

'You're quite right. Now I must go and see if I can help the policemen to catch the man who hurt you. You must be very good and listen to Anne while I am away. You will, won't you?'

Timothy looked up and beamed proudly. 'Yep.'

John ruffled his son's hair in a loving gesture before looking at Anne. 'I'll try not to be too long. Is there another way out apart from the large door in the storeroom?'

'Yes, on the right-hand side of the showroom, towards the rear, you'll find a small side door that opens into a very narrow alleyway. This connects with another that runs along behind the shops next to this one and eventually takes you to a fairly quiet street leading down to the seafront.'

Anne also stood up from the table and walked round it to stand before John. 'You will be careful, won't you?' she said firmly. 'That motorcycle is a valuable antique.'

John nodded with a cool expression and was about to turn when Anne stepped up close to him and enclosed him within her arms. Her mouth was close to his ear when she whispered, 'Please, do be careful. You're very valuable too.'

She kissed his neck lightly before drawing away and returning to her chair. He looked down and saw tears in her eyes. Timothy was grinning inanely at him and he pretended to give the boy a punch on the chin.

'I'll be back before you know I'm gone,' he said with a smile that failed to smooth the worry lines on his forehead. Anne suddenly longed to see his face as it had been when he was sleeping.

He left the kitchen and went down to the showroom with his eyes fixed on the large plate-glass window for anything out of the ordinary in the street beyond.

The bolts were well-oiled and the small door in the storeroom swung open soundlessly. He stepped out into the morning chill and into an alley no wider than his shoulders and he was forced to turn sideways and walk crab-like until he reached the other alley mentioned by Anne. This went behind the unidentifiable back yards of jewellers, booksellers, haberdashers and photographers.

It was still very early and the street was empty when he emerged from the alley and headed for the seafront and the turning that would take him back to the parked Vincent. He was about to pass a public house called The Fiddler's Elbow when he spotted a uniformed police constable at the end of the street. John was standing a mere twenty yards from his bike which fortunately had bikes parked on both sides. These had masked his bike sufficiently but John didn't take any chances. He walked towards the small row of bikes and threw his leg over a red Triumph standing next to the Vincent. Pretending to put a key in the ignition he then put on his helmet and buckled it under his chin while watching the policeman out of the corner of his eyes. The man had briefly glanced at John and noted the particular bike he was sitting on with some interest before casually turning away. Even at seventy feet John could hear the burst of static as the radio was switched on followed by unintelligible speech—the policeman communicating that he had identified John Tucker.

John instinctively knew he had been recognised and he leant across and inserted the Vincent key into the ignition before hopping off the Triumph and jumping onto the black beast and kicking downward at the same time. The cold engine misfired and on the second kick burst into life with a snarl that in the morning air filled the street and beyond.

The young constable turned in surprise and seeing John astride the Vincent began running towards him while shouting into his radio. He had only covered thirty feet before the powerful machine was unleashed and John accelerated away in the wrong direction down the one-way street.

A rubbish truck that was doing its early morning pick-up suddenly turned into the street, effectively blocking the whole width of the street and preventing any chance of escape. The constable drew his baton and with renewed optimism he sprinted towards the cornered man. He was closing in with an exultant cry of success when John turned the bike and began racing back towards him. The constable hesitated, came to a stop and then foolishly stood his ground in the middle of the street with baton raised. John swerved and mounted the pavement to race past the startled man, his teeth bared in a triumphant grin.

The Vincent thundered on to leave the pavement and accelerate along the street before vanishing from sight round the first corner.

The constable let loose a stream of invective before becoming aware of the disapproving audience that had been rudely awakened and were leaning out of the upper windows that surrounded him.

17

CRAMER READ THE TELEX that had been given to him by Angstrom and pulled a face as it undeniably confirmed that witnesses had seen both John Tucker and Alan Williams at the home of Jane Carstairs on the night of her murder. Angstrom had followed up on the report and her addendum showed that John Tucker had been working in Billingsgate fish market for a number of years and that he had fathered a son who was registered as Timothy Davies with the father's name given as John Davies.

The superintendent snapped his fingers. 'That's it, Jennifer,' he exclaimed. 'The small boy you saw in the antiques shop has to be Tucker's son, Timothy.'

Angstrom took the proffered telex and running her finger down located the description of the boy given by one of Jane Carstairs' neighbours. 'It matches, sir,' she confirmed. 'Blonde hair, blue eyes, height, everything. He must have left his son with Anne Jackson for safekeeping after the murder of the boy's mother.'

'Whether he's the one who killed her is still open to conjecture but my money is on him. Go back to Brighton and question Miss Jackson about this and if it proves to be young Timothy Davies, real name Tucker, then make sure you find out where the father has gone and what he's planning to do next.'

Angstrom nodded, closed her briefcase and hurried from the office to go to the antiques shop yet again. She wondered why Tucker would secrete his son in Brighton if he was the one who had killed Jane Carstairs.

The clock on the dashboard showed ten o'clock when a black motorcyclist roared round a sharp bend in East Dean and hurtled towards and then past Angstrom, forcing her to swerve over to the extreme left.

'Idiot!' she yelled as she glanced in her mirror to see the rapidly receding bike disappear round the bend. As she went into the next bend it occurred to her that she had just been passed by their fugitive and she hurriedly reached for the radio mike.

'Inspector Angstrom requesting roadblocks on the Eastbourne road to apprehend a black Vincent motorcycle being ridden by the man wanted for questioning.' After giving more details and asking that these also be passed on to Superintendent Cramer she proceeded on to Brighton to question Anne Jackson; she knew it was futile to chase the speeding ton-up.

Ninety seconds later Cramer received the message and after studying the large wallchart showing all the roads on the south coast he exclaimed, 'He's heading towards Hastings, towards me,' and his eyebrows rose in surprise. He immediately issued orders to Traffic Control and the well-oiled machinery of interception went into action. Patrol cars were stationed strategically at all the major intersections leading into and out of the Hastings area and foot patrols were instructed to watch out for the Vincent and report its position the moment it was spotted.

Cramer went along the corridor to the communications room where he wandered from terminal to terminal listening to each of the incoming reports. None proved to be fruitful until a constable on foot patrol near Hastings pier spotted the motorcycle. It happened to draw the policeman's attention by the way it was dangerously weaving through the morning traffic that thronged the coastal road. Orders were immediately issued to all mobile units and every road east of Hastings became the focus of intense scrutiny.

Sergeant Watkins had been a serving officer for twenty-two years and was looking forward to his early retirement when the instruction to form a roadblock on the road leading to the historic town of Rye came through on his radio. He nodded to Thompson, a probationary constable, who immediately reached forward to activate the light-bar and siren as the sergeant turned the car broadside to the on-coming vehicles. This effectively blocked the lane coming from Hastings. The traffic was soon backed-up for a quarter of a mile and both Thompson and Watkins left the patrol car to direct the traffic one vehicle at a time from each direction on the remaining lane. Cars going to Hastings were slowed by the young constable while the sergeant studied each vehicle that was coming from Brighton before permitting it to weave round the police car.

They had been doing this for ten minutes when above the constant murmuring of idling car engines they could hear a distant whining sound like that of an angry wasp. It grew in volume until it became a loud howl as the Vincent drew closer. The policemen looked at each other and then the young constable hastily halted his lane of traffic and ran back to the patrol car to report the possible approach of the suspect.

As Thompson was making contact with Traffic Control John approached like a heat-seeking missile, leaning slightly left and right as he centre-lined towards the roadblock without any reduction of speed. Sergeant Watkins stepped into the centre of the clear lane and adopting the official if foolhardy stance he held up his hand.

At 75 miles per hour the Vincent was beyond stopping and John leant to the right at the last split second to hurtle past the burly sergeant with only a hair's breadth between them. Watkins froze as the apparent black angel swooped down upon him.

Thompson later reported that the sergeant's trousers had been touched by the motorcycle's fairing as it passed through the roadblock and then faded away, its blood-freezing howl diminishing to a mere whisper.

He's left Hastings and passed through Rye and seems to be in a big hurry to get somewhere, Cramer thought when told what had transpired. 'Where the hell is he going and why?' he asked no one in particular.

John knew precisely where he wanted to go which was why he had left the main road and begun to cut inland and travel northward. His innate pigeon-like instincts sent him in the direction of Biggin Hill where he knew Alan's partner kept a safe house.

While John cruised unnoticed down winding, tree-lined lanes beneath a canopy of dark green Inspector Angstrom was entering the antiques shop. She shook the small brass bell standing amongst small wood carvings of bears and wolves on the glass-topped counter.

Footsteps could be heard crossing the floorboards above her head and then descending the stairs. Open sandals and delicate ankles first appeared followed by a floral cotton skirt and the welcoming smile on Anne's face. This suddenly froze when she saw who was waiting by the counter and Angstrom could see the young woman's guilt plainly written on her face.

'Good morning, Inspector.' Anne's greeting was laced with false bonhomie and Angstrom grinned.

'I think you know what I'm going to ask, Anne,' she said as she made a fuss of taking the notebook and pen from her breast pocket. 'Have you seen John Tucker recently?'

'No . . . well . . . not recently.'

The hesitant reply alerted Angstrom and she asked the same question again only this time more slowly and accompanied by an accusing expression.

'You think I'm lying?' Anne stuttered.

'No, I think you are being obtuse.'

'Look, I'm not stupid. You asked if I've seen John recently and I said no because you never made it clear what you meant by recently,' Anne said crossly to cover her agitation, her face suffused with colour.

'Within the last twenty-four hours,' Angstrom said quietly. 'Does that clarify the word?'

'Yes . . . yes I have seen him. He came last night, stayed and left an hour ago.'

'And you didn't notify the police that he was here?'

'Of course not, he's innocent of all those things they've been saying about him on the television. He didn't kill any girls and I know he is totally incapable of doing such horrible things.' Anne had picked up one of the carved bears and her knuckles had whitened while gripping it.

'When he left did he say where he was going?'

'No. All he said was that he was going to bring the killer of my father to justice,' Anne whispered as she looked down at the bear remembering the fondness her father had for Bavarian craftsmanship.

'Is the little boy his son?' Angstrom said in a quiet voice, realising the anguish the woman was still suffering. 'Is his name Timothy?'

'Yes, John asked me to look after him until he returned.'

'So he will be coming back?'

'Only after he has caught my father's murderer.' Anne put the bear down gently and looked up at Angstrom. 'Take it from me, Inspector, he is a good man.' Then Anne unexpectedly added, 'Would you like to meet Tim and have a cup of tea?'

Angstrom was surprised by the sudden offer but quickly recovered to accept. 'Please call me Jennifer,' she said as she followed Anne up the stairs to the sitting room. Timothy was waiting on the landing and quickly took Anne's hand for the sense of security it gave him.

'He will be able to stay with me, won't he?' Anne asked in a low voice so that the boy couldn't overhear. 'I think he'll feel a lot safer with me looking after him.'

'I cannot give you a definite answer to that but I'm sure Tim can stay until we've apprehended John. Then he'll be cared for by Child Services until the results of the court case have been determined,' Angstrom said without too much conviction in her voice.

Tim had flung himself onto the settee and was happily crunching his way through a fistful of ginger biscuits as the two women murmured to each other while waiting for the kettle to boil.

Ninety minutes after leaving Brighton John was filtering out of a minuscule lane and onto the main road leading into Biggin Hill. Checking in both directions for any police vehicles he accelerated up the long incline until he was entering the village. He turned down the rough road and parked the bike outside the detached house which was set back from the road.

He removed his helmet and carefully surveyed the front garden. Japanese laurels rising to head height and crowded together almost obscured the house. He ignored the front door and walked on the lawn to avoid crunching the gravel as he headed towards the side gate. Peering over the top he saw the shrouded shape of a motorcycle standing on the lawn and immediately knew that he had found Alan.

The latch lifted silently and he quickly slipped through and closed the gate behind him before walking round the house and onto the ornate brick patio. Large French windows stood wide open and the ends of orange sun-filter curtains had been sucked outside and were blowing capriciously in the light wind.

John cautiously moved toward the open doors and dropped to his knees to peer under a billowing curtain and into the large living area.

Compared to the bright sunlight outside the interior of the house was gloomy but he could see that it was unoccupied. He silently slipped inside and quickly crossed the carpet to the only door that stood open and led to the kitchen.

'Should have been more convincing, mate.'

John froze when he heard the muttered words coming from the kitchen and he held his breath as he waited for the voice to speak again. He quietly felt in his pockets and remembered that he had hidden both firearms in the antiques shop.

Nothing more was said and all he heard was the distinctive sound of steel-tipped boots crossing the kitchen. John knew from experience that they were the kind of boots worn by motorcyclists. The clicking sound suddenly stopped as the person stepped onto the thick carpet in the hallway. Looking over his shoulder John spotted Alan's crash helmet and gloves that had been carelessly discarded on an armchair close by the door leading into the hallway. As the handle turned and the door began to open John swiftly stepped into the kitchen and out of sight.

He listened behind the door as Alan gathered up his possessions and went out through the French windows. There was a brief silence and then he heard the sounds of cursing as the tarpaulin snagged on the motorcycle before finally being dragged off and thrown down in the garden.

It would only be a matter of minutes before Alan would spot John's own bike parked in the road. He quickly hurried across the kitchen to reach the front door before his quarry could open the side gate. In his haste he tripped over a shadowy form in the gloomy kitchen and fell to the floor to be confronted by William Tyler's terror-filled, lifeless eyes. John pushed himself away and his hands slid in the red pools of stickiness surrounding the body. In his panic his hand banged against something hard and his fingers instinctively closed round the handle of the murder weapon. In horror he tossed the knife to one side, rose to his feet and rushed from the house with only one strange thought lodged in his mind . . .

'I knew he wouldn't make it to 33.'

Alan was still trying to control the spring-loaded gate while attempting the awkward task of pushing his bike through the gap when John got to the Vincent. He knew he couldn't start the bike with Alan so close and decided on camouflage instead. With his pulse pounding in his ears he manhandled the bike up onto the sidewalk; thankful that there was no fence he gathered speed and pushed the bike deep into the dense shrubbery. The laurels closed around him and the Vincent hiding him from any casual eyes just as Alan began wheeling his bike down the drive. He paused within ten feet of John, mounted the Commando, buckled his helmet and kick-started the bike to ride out into the road. The fading sound of his engine triggered an audible sigh of relief from deep within a mass of purple blooms.

Leaving the bike John hurried back inside and went into the kitchen to wash his hands in the sink. While wiping his jacket with a damp tea towel he kept his eyes averted from the body on the floor; by doing so he was unaware that he had left his own bloody fingerprints on the linoleum floor and the weapon.

John retrieved his crash helmet from where he had dropped it behind the kitchen door and hurried through the living room to leave the house. As he crossed the room he recognised an object standing on the mantelpiece. It was a delicate carving of fish in green and white jade and an electric bolt went through John. He was now sure that it was either Tyler or Alan who had killed Anne's father.

John wondered what the motive could have been—Tyler was a weak and greedy man and the death of Anne's father would be of no benefit to him. In fact, it would have been to the contrary for he had wanted to marry his daughter. On the other hand it may have been Alan who was simply tidying up all the loose ends that could be used against him should he be brought to trial. Alan took the piece of jade not for its value or that it may be traced back to him but simply because it could be taken.

By cold-bloodedly killing Tyler Alan had shown that he hadn't lost his taste for killing. As John closed the front door firmly his desire to bring Alan to justice burned even brighter.

The Vincent started on the first kick once it was out of the shrubbery and John rode away without noticing the elderly woman standing in her doorway. She had watched the stranger come out of 'nice' Mr Tyler's house with deep suspicion in her eyes.

A note on Tyler's desk calendar reminded Alan that another shipment was due to be collected that day and he decided to pay a visit to Dover. His first task was to find the man who would be handling the shipment and confiscate it for he knew that Bellini would think twice about killing any man who had possession of his heroin. Believing Tyler's house to be a safe hideaway Alan planned to return there that evening with the shipment and then to call Signor Bellini in the morning with a proposition he could hardly refuse: the shipment of heroin and John Tucker's head for a false passport and safe passage to Bogotá.

Alan was an old hand at dodging police patrols and like John he kept to the minor country lanes to reach Dover. At midday he pulled into a country public house and discreetly parked the bike out of sight of the road. He ate a leisurely ploughman's lunch of crusty white bread with two types of cheese and pickles and no alcohol in order to satisfy his hunger and keep his riding skills sharply honed. He checked the time and continued his journey at two o'clock to arrive in the outer suburbs of the channel port an hour later.

Alan left the Commando in a gloomy alley before going to the nearest cinema. It was the matinée showing of a film called *Smokey and the Bandit II* and the cinema only had a scattering of elderly pensioners of whom some were dozing rather than watching the fast action. The story washed over Alan who was fully occupied planning his next move to manipulate Signor Bellini. He knew that he had to adopt a new identity and get to a country that had no extradition treaty with Britain. Such a move required a lot of money and Alan was banking on what he had to offer to meet his needs.

The 'Bandit' was once more being chased by 'Sheriff Burford T Justice' when Alan stood up and left the cinema. With a strong sense of purpose he strode back to the bike and rode down to the marina that was closest to the passenger ferry terminal. He went to the normally pre-arranged café to start searching for the dock worker whose job it was to meet passengers carrying the right kind of hand luggage.

At seven Alan spotted the familiar heavy-set man in a donkey jacket walking towards the café and he quickly purchased a broadsheet newspaper from the display rack and another coffee. He returned to his seat by the window and opened the paper seconds before the man entered and sat down at a table. Alan had only picked up three deliveries from the dock worker but he was taking no chances on him being recognised.

The man lingered over his coffee and Alan was beginning to worry about the waitress who kept looking hopefully at his empty cup when the door opened and Terry entered. Alan recognised him immediately even though his youthful face still had a large purple-and-yellow bruise from the time when John had knocked him down on the boat.

Alan raised his paper a little higher as Terry sat opposite the man and began talking animatedly. The man nodded, looked at his watch and Alan saw his lips form the word 'midnight' before he hurried from the café. Terry ordered a drink from the miserable-looking waitress and lingered another thirty minutes.

The waitress looked at Alan expectantly and he nodded knowing he would have to force another weak, flavourless coffee over his tortured tastebuds while he waited for Terry to leave the marina. It was clear to him that the two men had planned a meeting and Alan wanted to make sure that he was present; he had a good idea that it would be here at the dockers' café, same as the last five shipments.

He still had four hours to kill. He moved the bike to a small side street that was only a stone's throw from the rendezvous and walked back into town, keeping his eyes open for Terry whom he knew would also be whiling away the time until he could take delivery. Alan re-entered the same cinema and took a back seat so that he could survey the other patrons when the lights went up. Burt Reynolds had now been superseded by John Travolta who was playing an urban cowboy but once again Alan wasn't interested in the action on the big screen and kept on scanning the dozens of heads in front of him.

Four rows in front and slightly to the right Alan recognised the familiar teased up 'big' hairstyle of the teenager. Flickering light from the screen occasionally brightened his profile making identification positive and Alan sank down into his seat and turned up the collar of his leather jacket. He realised he had been given an opportunity to make the meeting with the dock worker a lot easier. Alan checked his left leather boot to ensure he still had his knife sheathed inside and then he walked down the aisle to the row where Terry was seated. He had already noticed that the seat next to the youth was vacant and he sidled in with his back slightly turned towards him and sat down.

Terry looked askance at the person sitting beside him and froze when he recognised Alan. Alan held a finger up to his lips and pointed towards the screen. Distracted by the unexpected gesture the teenager looked up at the spectacle of 'Bud' dancing with 'Sissy' and failed to see the long blade that would soon enter his rib cage and pierce his heart. Terry's mouth gaped in shock and then his eyes glazed as he lost consciousness and died. Alan kept his gloved hand on the knife to hold the youth upright and only when he felt sure the corpse would not fall forward did he let go and stand up.

He left the cinema with his collar turned up and his eyes averted and walked quickly for twenty minutes before choosing a restaurant for his evening meal.

Eleven o'clock had just chimed and the sound of police sirens was coming from the direction of the cinema when Alan adjourned to the dock workers' café to await the man in the donkey jacket. The throng of men in their working clothes buzzed with conversation and laughter when Alan opened the door and spotted his target. He raised a hand when the man looked his way and smiled at the man's puzzlement.

'It's okay,' Alan said holding out his hand in greeting. 'Terry's dad died suddenly and he had to rush home. Signor Bellini asked me to stand in for him. Did you bring it?'

The man ignored the hand and proceeded to unfasten the toggles of his donkey jacket to be more comfortable in the steamy café. He put the case he had been carrying under the table between his legs and glanced down as if to say, 'What the hell do you call this then?' before nodding.

'I'm sorry to eat and run but I have to get back to Signor Bellini as soon as possible.' Alan reached under the table, took the case, stood up and walked away leaving the dock worker looking more puzzled than when he had first seen Alan approaching him.

Alan had walked a few paces when he heard the man call after him. 'Hey, I think I'd better first call Signor Bellini before you take that case.'

With the case still gripped tight in his fist Alan turned with a tight smile on his face and watched the man approaching. 'You're right, let's find a telephone.' He walked on, turning his head from side to side in a pretence of looking for a red telephone box while he slipped his free hand inside his jacket and extracted the automatic pistol. Alan quickly turned into a quiet street and began running, luring the burly docker to chase after him.

'Hey, stop! I'll beat your bloody head to a pulp if you don't,' the docker called out as he gained on the motorcyclist who was deliberately running awkwardly in his heavy boots.

They had reached a corner where the street light had been shattered by a young vandal when Alan suddenly stopped, spun around and pointed the gun at his pursuer with an extended arm.

The docker's eyes opened wide in terror and he tried to stop himself and duck at the same time but it was impossible to avoid the heavy 9-mm bullet that 'whumped' through the donkey jacket and into his chest. The loud explosion that followed was muffled as though his ears had been blocked. Then the second bullet ended all sensation and he slumped onto the hard pavement. Alan turned and began running until he had put three streets between himself and his victim before slowing to a casual walk.

After walking along the opposite side of the street twice to check if the Commando was being watched he returned to the bike and was soon cruising slowly out of the channel port and heading back to William Tyler's place with Signor Bellini's briefcase. It contained heroin with a street value of £4 million.

18

JOHN RODE THROUGH THE WOODED DISTRICT of St George's Hills and slowly approached the large Bellini mansion for no other reason than to clear his mind while thinking of a way to avoid being captured and spending the rest of his natural life in prison. The germ of an idea glowed deep in the recesses of his mind and then flared; he decided that he had to trap Alan into confessing his role within the drugs network and also his part in the murders. John stopped and made an awkward U-turn with the locked-down handlebars before retracing his journey on the narrow road back to the nearby town of Weybridge.

There was a small electronic shop just off the high street and he parked in the street that ran beside the narrow-fronted business. The bell attached to the door jamb jangled as he entered and John wove his way between stacked displays of televisions and hi-fi audio equipment to the counter.

'How can I help you, sir?' a reedy voice asked and a shiny pate rose from behind the latest 21-inch colour set. 'I'll be with you in a few seconds. I just have to—' There was a soft click and the screen lit up, dazzling John with a brilliant alpine snowscape. He was instantly deafened by the cries of a thousand spectators as tiny Lowry-like figures hurtled down impossibly vertical slopes.

'Sorry about that!' the saleman shouted as he reached for the remote to bring the sound down. 'What can I do for you,' he added when the sound had dropped to a bearable level.

John grinned at the man's discomfiture. 'I would like a tiny recording device. Something the size of a cigarette case that can be easily concealed in a pocket.'

'Aha,' the salesman replied with a soft, knowing voice and a tap on the side of his nose. 'You want to—'

'What I want is none of your business,' John interrupted. 'What have you got?'

The little man pursed his lips and turned to study the shelving behind him. After shuffling boxes in and out of the racks with dazzling speed he paused and carefully placed a small white box on the glass. 'This is the finest magnetic tape player with an inbuilt microphone and a choice of playing times of fifteen, thirty and ninety minutes depending on which cassette you purchase. It's ideal for dictation or—'

'I'll take it,' John snapped. 'And make it the ninety-minute tape.'

The salesman nodded and rang up a price and John reacted with a silent 'ouch'. He grudgingly took out his wallet and counted out the requisite number of notes. The salesman put the purchases in a small carrier and John snatched the bag and strode to the door.

'Thank you, sir. *Do* call again,' the salesman called without too much enthusiasm and raised two fingers as his only customer of the day hurried out followed by the irritating sound of the bell.

Unmindful of the man's crude gesture John trotted back to the Vincent. He paused, reflecting on his own bad manners and considered returning to apologise. He glanced at his watch and saw that he had lost enough time and mounted the bike to ride back to the quiet tree-lined avenues of St George's Hills. He planned to await Alan's return to Bellini's place to receive new orders, not realising that Alan was also persona non grata as far as the Italian was concerned.

John found a small track nearby that went into the wood and followed it for twenty yards before stopping out of sight of the road. He unpacked the recorder and inserted the new cassette which he then tested with a forced whisper. It was loud and clear on playback and John crossed his fingers that it would work when he most needed it to. He gathered up some bracken to camouflage the bike and then made a crude bed not too far from the machine.

Inspector Angstrom returned to Hastings at midday and gave a detailed account of her conversation with Anne.

Cramer nodded. 'So she doesn't have a clue as to where he has gone and yet I've just received a report from the Biggin Hill police that a man fitting his description was seen leaving a house there.'

'She made no mention of Biggin Hill, only that he was going to bring her father's murderer to justice.'

'Which it seems he may have done. A man was found stabbed to death in the same house Tucker was seen leaving. Apart from a witness to his presence a fingerprint report confirms that it was Tucker who had handled the knife that killed Mr William Tyler. It appears, Inspector, that the man we've been wanting to protect from Williams doesn't need our help after all. Now we have to issue a warning that Tucker is highly dangerous and should be approached with extreme caution.'

'Somehow I cannot believe he is capable of murder, sir,' Angstrom said, her face still shocked by the news. 'It may be that he is hot on the heels of Williams and arrived just after the murder took place.'

'You could also be grasping at straws, Jennifer.' Cramer stood up and walked round his desk. 'How can you explain the fingerprints on the weapon and in the blood on the floor?' Angstrom shrugged with a bewildered look on her face.

'However, before we face the unlikely possibility that Alan may have been the killer let's try harder to catch them both first.'

Angstrom followed her boss out of the office and into Central Control where five civilians and the same number of officers were manning the phones and busily using large Underwood typewriters around a long table. Clerks ran hither and thither collecting the foolscap sheets as they were dropped into in-trays. Messages were also being displayed on a master screen in front of the control officer who checked the priority of each before murmuring into his throat mike to dispatch patrol cars.

The manhunt had been given far higher priority by all regions since the murder in Biggin Hill and similar control rooms across the country were following the same procedure in checking every possible sighting of the two bikes. Across the southern half of England hundreds of innocent motorcyclists were being stopped and their identities checked before being released.

Cramer briefly spoke to the control officer who confirmed that there had been no positive sightings of the two motorbikes apart from three possibilities in the area around Weybridge. Additional patrols had been sent into the town and surrounding districts.

A severe pain in a calf muscle awoke John and clenching his teeth he rolled around in the damp bracken until he was able to partially sit up to alleviate the agony. The cold night air had chilled him to the bone and his clothes, saturated with dew, had only made things worse.

The sun had yet to rise in the leaden sky and in the gloomy light he limped through the thigh-high ferns that glistened with cobwebs to his camouflaged bike. The bottle of water in one of the saddlebags was half full and he thankfully gulped a couple of times to relieve the extreme dryness of his throat while wishing he had a toothbrush.

The sausage roll he had saved had hardened within the cellophane wrapper but after crumbling it into small pieces and washing it down with a little more water he was able to stem the shooting hunger pains in his stomach to some degree.

John wiped his jacket and the bike seat with the oily rag he found in the other saddlebag and gently raised the stand. Listening carefully for any other unusual sounds he slowly pushed the bike through the wood until he was able to peer between the sycamore trees and the shrubbery at the entrance gates to Bellini's country house. He left the bike amongst the greenery and crept closer so that he could clearly observe who might be coming and going. There was the chink of one small pebble striking another and John watched as a dark-suited guard appeared from the gloom of the bushes buttoning up his flies. The guard strolled up to the ornate gates, peered between the wrought-iron bars and then turned to lean his back against them. It was obvious that he had been on watch all night and despite it being a midsummer month he was now feeling the morning chill for he occasionally had to stamp and beat his arms against his sides to keep warm.

John crouched down and patiently waited for what he believed would be a new chapter or the last chapter in his life.

It had just gone midnight when Alan cautiously approached Tyler's house. Alerted by the flashing lights and a number of vehicles in the potholed road he kept on riding and turned down what was aptly named Jail Lane and kept going towards the next village called Downe. The police presence had made it clear to him that his safe house had now been compromised and he guessed that it must have been John's fault. He now had nowhere to spend the rest of the night and it would be dangerous to continue riding as he would be the focus of attention for any patrolling police car.

Alan slowed and stopped outside Downe House, the historic home of Darwin, and sat thinking out his next move. The churring of a nightjar and a frog's harmonising chirrup were the only sounds that disturbed the monotonous silence of the woodland around him. He decided not to wait until morning but to call Bellini immediately and he rode slowly to the bright red telephone box in the small town square. As soon as the heavy door was opened and the light went on Alan punched the bulb with a leather-covered fist to break it. The box was plunged into darkness and he inserted the coins, dialled the memorised number and then waited as he listened to the *burrupp, burrupp*, until after the tenth ring the call was answered.

'Who the hell is this?' a voice shouted angrily. Recognising Jimmy's voice Alan pushed button A.

'I want to speak to Signor Bellini NOW!' Alan barked into the mouthpiece.

'Do you know what bloody time it is? You can't speak to the boss because right now he's sleeping and he hates to be disturbed.'

'Whisper £4 million into his shell-like and see if that wakes him enough to take this call.'

There was a moment of silence before Jimmy replied, 'Okay, just wait.' Alan could hear dwindling footsteps on the marble floor of the cavernous hallway and finally just the static of the instrument in his hand. Three minutes elapsed and he had to insert more coins before a hoarse voice spoke.

'What the fuck do you want and what's this about £4 million?' Bellini said. 'If that's you, Sergeant Williams, be prepared to meet your Maker. The word's out and everyone's talking about the five grand I'm willing to pay for your head.'

'Then you'd better recall your words and swallow them because I have a nice little package that I think belongs to you. I will return it along with John Tucker's head if you can give me a little something in return,' Alan said calmly.

'And if the hit is still on?'

'Then I'll be soaking your package in petrol and watching it burn. It must be an exciting life experience to see so much money going up in flames. Think about it, Bellini.'

'So what do you want in return?'

'A passport in a new name, a ticket to Bogotá and fifty thousand American dollars in used notes—it's nothing compared to what you'll make on the resale of your package.' There was a very long silence and once more Alan had to feed the telephone before the drug trafficker agreed to the terms.

'Very well, Bellini, send Jimmy and only him down to the main gate at eight o'clock this morning and I'll hand him the name and photograph to be used in the passport. Do not try to trick me as I will not have the package on me and if something happens to me you'll never be able to find it.'

'I hear you, Sergeant,' Bellini snarled and hung up.

Alan listened to the burring line for a few seconds before he also hung up and left the kiosk. He rode out of Downe until he spotted a suitably thick hedgerow. Concealing the bike behind it he lay down in the long grass and pulled his leather jacket over his head as protection from the dew. He needed sleep to clear his head before he dared venture onto the roads again.

At six-thirty Alan awoke and after running on the spot for five minutes to increase his circulation he began his long cat-and-mouse journey to Bellini's house. Three times a police patrol attempted to apprehend him and each time he evaded their pitiful chases on the winding country roads. As he reached St George's Hills Jimmy was already waiting at the gate and Alan pulled up beside him.

'Hi, Jimmy,' Alan greeted him. 'Don't try anything otherwise the delivery will be lost in transit, okay?'

Jimmy simply nodded and took the folded piece of paper that Alan thrust between the bars. It was accompanied by two passport-size photographs on the back of which was scrawled the name Henry Jenkins.

'To be ready tomorrow, right?' Alan said firmly.

Jimmy just glared at him and Alan accelerated away into the dawning day completely unaware of the extra pair of eyes that followed him.

Alan had awoken that morning with a sharp rock sticking in his rump and the wild idea that John had most probably taken his son to the one person left whom he could trust. Alan knew that he had already eliminated the mother, Jane, which left John's parents whom the police had already checked out and finally there was only one other he could think of—Anne Jackson. Alan clearly recalled how John had reacted to Tyler's comments regarding Jackson's death and he knew it had to be the daughter.

He pointed his bike south and began riding towards Brighton yet again.

John sucked in his breath when Alan drew up at the gates and he patiently waited until Alan had gone and Jimmy had plodded back up the drive before he pushed the Vincent out onto the road and followed in pursuit with no plan in his head other than to stop Alan and somehow extract a confession.

The Vincent howled like a wounded forest beast as John leant into each twist and turn without unwinding the throttle. The sound he was leaving behind spread out through the wooded hills, rattling the windows of the luxury mansions and awaking the good and the sinful alike.

Soon John was able to catch short glimpses of the Commando ahead of him and he wound the throttle in an attempt to catch up. Just as he was leaning at a forty-five-degree angle, with the footrest trailing a shower of sparks behind, a farm tractor pulled out into the narrow lane. John was unable to stop and he threw the bike over on its side while lying back. Man and bike separated and both slid beneath the hayrick that was being towed behind the tractor until they were nearly united again in a drainage ditch. John had travelled the thirty yards distance on his back and was fortunately protected by the thick leather clothing while the Vincent had spun on its side with the engine screaming and the rear wheel still racing.

Seeing the bike disappear beneath his rig the farmhand immediately stopped and jumped down from the tractor to see if he could give assistance to the fallen rider. He found John sitting in six inches of green slime-covered water and offered a hand.

'Are you all right, lad?' he asked in a heavy Sussex drawl. John nodded and took the hand thankfully and let the man pull him up the bank.

'Can't say the same for your lovely bike, though,' the farmhand said in a philosophical tone of voice. 'Looks right beat up, it does.'

John walked along the bank to where the bike lay half in and half out of the water in the ditch. The engine had long since stalled and steam rose in fine tendrils from the hot exhaust.

'Can you give me a hand to get it up?' John asked and the man eagerly agreed after explaining that he first had to move his tractor before anyone else came round the blind corner. It took the farmer the longest five minutes in John's life as the distance between him and Alan increased with each passing second. During this time he inspected himself and found that apart from a painful friction burn on his left arm and a bruised buttock he was in reasonable condition.

It was another ten minutes before the puffing and wheezing men were able to haul the heavy motorcycle up onto the road and put it upright on the stand. While John studied every inch of the bike the farmer constantly apologised for having caused the accident and John politely counter-apologised for holding the man up from his work.

He eventually decided that the hardy Vincent had suffered no major damage and that the small dents in the silencer and the scrapes in the paintwork could be easily repaired. He threw a damp, smelly leg over the seat and kicked down. The bike backfired a number of times before John heard the familiar throaty roar of the engine. With a cheery wave to the astounded farmhand he toed into gear and accelerated away.

Thirty minutes later John had to admit to himself that he had lost Alan and he pulled into a lay-by to think about his next move. Why was Alan going this way, he thought and then jerked upright.

'He knows about Tim and Anne,' he said aloud, horrified. The discomfort in his left arm was forgotten and soon he was speeding towards the A24. This was the only highway that went directly to the south coast and he knew he had to take a chance on being spotted by the police for it was the only way to beat Alan Williams to the antiques shop.

It was early morning and the traffic was sparse with only a scattering of families getting an early start for the best spot on the beach. John let the Vincent have its head and memories came flooding back of the exhilaration he had felt when he and his friends raced until the magic ton was reached. He also recalled the sensation of young girls' arms gripping him around the waist as they screamed excitedly whenever he leant his old Dominator at an impossible angle on each bend in the road.

The familiar sound of a police siren cut through his reverie and he glanced back to see their red and blue lights flashing close behind. John grinned grimly and tugged the scarf up and over the bottom half of his face before opening the throttle even wider. The needle crept up and the Vincent hurtled past and between vehicles that were lightly buffeted by his passing. The patrol car was soon left struggling to catch up with the bike that was now touching ninety-five miles per hour.

John knew it wouldn't be long before a radioed message fed a chase car onto the two-lane highway in front of him. His eyes flicked up to read every signboard he flashed past until he saw a sign indicating a turn-off that would screen him from the chase car as it passed the same turn-off and raced fruitlessly on after the phantom motorcyclist.

He slowed down until he reached the next fast stretch of road and then began his last fifteen-mile dash to Brighton with his heart pounding and thinking 'I must get there first' over and over again.

As he entered the outer suburbs of the town he became increasingly watchful for any Norton motorcyclists wearing black leathers. He passed a couple of constables walking the beat but they appeared to take very little interest in him and he continued until he was only a stone's throw from The Lanes.

John parked the bike and ran through the empty streets until he reached the small open square where he stopped suddenly. A Norton Commando was on its stand outside the antiques shop. Alan had arrived first.

With dread in his heart John approached the shop and looked through the glass into the showroom. He was unable to see anyone and he quickly dodged to one side and walked to the narrow alleyway that led to the side door at the rear of the storeroom.

The door was ajar and it was clear that the lock had been forced. He pushed it open as slowly as possible to avoid making any noise and slipped inside. He waited for his eyes to become adjusted to the darkness before threading his way through the mountains of antique furniture.

John had almost covered half the distance to the showroom when the lights suddenly came on to flood the big storeroom with harsh white light.

'So nice of you to join me at the seaside, John,' a familiar voice said from inside the showroom. 'You've saved me the trouble of trying to find you. Mr Bellini would like to have a word with you as you've caused him a lot of grief and he doesn't take too kindly to that.'

John didn't reply and stealthily moved back the way he had come but the side door had been wedged shut by something heavy outside.

'Sorry John. I took the precaution of making sure you left this place one way only.' The voice was close and turning around he saw Alan step from behind a Georgian bookcase. He had a large 9-mm automatic pistol in his hand and it was pointing at John's midriff. 'You never could outrun me on a bike, John. You'll just have to admit that I'm a better rider than you could ever hope to be.'

John glanced around him looking for some avenue of escape. 'What have you done to my son?' he said as his mouth began to feel dry from the tension. 'You'd better not have—'

'Or what, John?' Alan interrupted. 'What can you do about it? Nothing, that's what, but you needn't worry, I have your little brat and his surrogate mother locked in the bathroom upstairs. I knew you would guess where I was going which is why I set this little trap.'

John had been edging towards a Louis XVI chest of drawers while Alan was gloating and he suddenly leapt behind and along a winding route between stacked pedestal desks, arts-and-crafts wardrobes and Chinese cabinets.

Alan had raised the pistol and fired when John moved but the bullet harmlessly splintered its way into the drawers. He ran to where John had disappeared from view and seeing the fleeing figure move behind a Victorian dressing table he fired again. The bullet shattered the expensive glass mirror and the air was filled with the staccato sounds of falling shards. Alan retraced his steps and ran to the showroom doorway where he stopped, blocking the only exit, and waited for John's next move.

'You are a fool, John. Why didn't you go to the police sixteen years ago and tell them what had happened in Hastings?' Alan jeered. 'It would have saved you from being on the run for the best part of your life.'

'You know I couldn't because of what had happened in Long Wood,' John shouted back and was rewarded by the report of the gun and the crash of fine burr walnut being struck by a heavy-calibre bullet quite close to him. John slowly moved to reach the carved oak coffer he had investigated when he last visited the storeroom.

'That's where you've been a fool John. You didn't kill the girl in Long Wood, I did.'

'But you said she was dead and told me to bury her,' John said, his mind in a whirl.

'That's true, mate, but I lied. You hadn't hit her hard enough to kill her, you only rendered her unconscious. Louise died later when you put her in the hole I made you dig.' There was a sudden burst of callous laughter. 'Don't you understand? You buried her alive, moron. I knew it but you didn't.'

There was a long silence during which John crouched down and stifled an angry scream by pushing a fist into his mouth.

'And Doris?' he groaned out loud.

'The same, mate. It was a pure accident that she fell and hit her head but it was me hitting her head against the pier leg again when you weren't looking that did for her. Well, we couldn't have her blabbing about my attempted rape, could we?'

'My god, Alan, you're a bloody animal.' John edged along behind an Edwardian bureau that stood beside the coffer. 'Did you kill Jane as well?'

'Of course. She could identify me later as the kidnapper and I couldn't have that, could I?'

The drawer was a tight fit and it rasped as John pulled it open.

'What are you doing, John? You know you can't hide and you certainly can't escape so you'd better come out and I'll take you to Signor Bellini who's been dying to see you since you interfered with his neat drugs operation. Why couldn't you do as you were told and play ball like a good little boy?'

'Bellini's after you as well, isn't he Alan?'

'Not when I return his last shipment of heroin along with you,' Alan said and then he laughed. It was a harsh sound unlike the laughter of the man John had known as a teenager. There was no goodness left in Alan and John feared he had no soul either. The pleasant memories of two young boys flying kites on the heath and sliding on frozen ponds were gone forever.

'It wasn't me who killed William Tyler,' John called out as he took the two pistols he had secreted in the coffer. After dropping one magazine into his trouser pocket he removed the magazine from the Tokarev. It was full. He quietly slid it back into place, pulled back the slide and slipped off the safety catch. He put the heavier pistol and its silencer back into the drawer and slid it, inch by inch, until it was closed.

'Bill had become a liability as had Terry,' Alan said as his eyes flicked around the crowded storeroom in an effort to catch any movement.

'Terry! You murdered Terry, too? He was just a kid, a teenager,' John shouted angrily as he gripped the weapon and aimed carefully at the neon tube nearest to him.

'He was a stupid kid! A druggie! Just one of many outside the all-night chemist in Piccadilly Circus.'

John fired and the heavy report of the gun coincided with the explosive disintegration of the light and a section of the storeroom fell into deep shadow. He fired again and the back half of the large area was reduced to darkness.

'So you've got a gun from somewhere,' Alan laughed and shot in the general direction of the brief flash of light from John's weapon. 'I guess I'll have to go and get your bloody boy and teach you a lesson like I did his mother.'

As fast as he could John began dodging amongst the furniture, moving towards the showroom with a new sense of urgency. A brief shadowy movement in the doorway caused him to pause and proceed with more caution. He looked up and then shot out the last tube, plunging the whole storeroom into deep shadow. Only the doorway leading to the showroom showed any light.

He waited with fear gnawing away in his mind until he could stand it no longer and he trotted towards the patch of light. He stepped through and a number of brilliant lights switched on, their white beams shocking him into immobility.

'Drop the weapon!' a voice shouted. 'Drop the weapon and raise your hands.'

John let the gun slide between his fingers and it fell to the floor as he squinted and tried to see who was beyond the powerful glare that had forced him to half close his eyes.

'Get down on the floor!' the same voice commanded forcefully.

'My son, he's upstairs with my son,' John cried out and turned to look up the stairs. Another light lanced towards him from the same direction and he averted his eyes, totally blinded. 'My son!' he cried again.

'Get down on the floor and put your hands behind your back.'

John fell to his knees with tears of frustration running down his cheeks and then fell forward. He put his hands behind him.

Heavy boots ran towards him and the gun was kicked away beyond his reach before another boot struck his ribs and a searing pain ran through his chest.

'Enough of that,' a more commanding voice said. It was a woman's voice and John racked his memory to place it as plastic hand-ties bound his wrists together. Arms then looped under his armpits and he was yanked painfully onto his feet to face an attractive woman in her late thirties. Her hazel eyes were intently studying him as though he were some rare virus in a petri dish.

'Check upstairs, Sergeant,' she commanded and an officer holding a Webley pushed past John and climbed the stairs two at a time. 'You are John Tucker?' she asked and he nodded, still staring up the stairs as though expecting the worst news. 'Then you're just the man I want to have a long talk with.'

Angstrom began walking towards the front door and John resisted the urging of the two men flanking him. 'My son and Anne, are they all right? I must know before you take me,' John pleaded.

The detective inspector turned and held a hand up to the two men while she looked at John with a softening expression. They all waited until the sergeant appeared at the top of the stairs carrying Timothy in his arms. Anne was following close behind and she pushed past the officer and hurried down to where John stood.

'Thank God you are unhurt. I heard all the shooting and thought the man had killed you,' she said. 'He returned and tried to open the bathroom door but with brave Tim's help we managed to jam the door. Then it all went silent for a few minutes before we heard shouting downstairs.' She tried to put her arms around John but the sergeant took her arm and gently tugged her away.

Timothy wriggled free when he saw his father and the sergeant was unable to prevent the boy from flinging his arms around his father's waist in a hug that seemed to go on forever.

'A man tried to take us away,' he burst out. 'But me and Anne beat him, didn't we, Anne?'

'We sure did. And it's Anne and I.'

'That's what I said, we both did it together.'

John couldn't help smiling and was still grinning when the two officers led him from the shop. The first thing he noticed was that the Norton motorcycle had disappeared. 'Did you impound the bike that was here?' he asked the inspector.

'We've taken no bikes, why do you ask?'

'It must have been taken by Alan just before you arrived. Possibly after he found he couldn't get to Anne and my son. He wouldn't have hesitated to shoot and probably thought it prudent to try some other time.'

'Try what, Mr Tucker?' Angstrom asked as he was bundled into the back of the patrol car. She knew what Williams was planning but she wanted to hear it from John's lips.

'To kill me of course.'

Angstrom went round the car and climbed into the passenger seat. 'Why would he risk such a thing with a man who is such a dangerous killer?'

'I'm no killer,' John said adamantly.

'How can I believe that. The girl beneath Hastings pier and the girl in Long Wood, not to mention the woman you were living with in London and a certain Mr Tyler in Biggin Hill—You're quite the little mass murderer aren't you?' Angstrom had never liked being the 'bad' cop when it came to interviewing suspects and John's anguished expression touched her. He fell silent and looked sadly through the glass at his little boy who was waving goodbye.

The patrol car sped away to take John to a police cell in Hastings. Anne briefly lifted her hand in a sad gesture of goodbye before kneeling on the pavement to cuddle and comfort Timothy.

The car hurried along the coastal road with blue lights flashing as John stared out at the brightening day. Shrieking gulls were now elegantly riding the thermals and keen yachtsmen were heading out to sea pulling on the sheets to catch as much of the breeze as possible.

At the police station the plastic restraints were removed and John was asked to empty his pockets. The heavy pistol and silencer plus the spare magazine had already been taken at the antiques shop to which Angstrom had briefly said, 'We'll have to talk later about this little lot.'

Keys to the Vincent, loose change, wallet and his belt were carefully listed by the custody sergeant. The microcassette recorder was then removed from John's shirt pocket.

'What's this?' the sergeant asked, holding the object up like an auctioneer presenting an unidentifiable lot.

'That's a confession that the inspector might like to hear,' John said. Angstrom stepped forward and took the recorder that was still showing a flashing red light. The tiny disc of tape was rotating slowly and could be seen through the clear plastic covering. The inspector pushed the STOP button.

'A confession?' she asked as she led John to the interview room.

'Rewind and switch on and you will hear the voice of a truly contemptible person who I once thought was my closest friend. At least I pray the cassette was able to record under cotton and leather clothing,' John said with a grimace as he was shown where to sit.

Angstrom sat opposite and placed the recorder on the steel table between them just as Superintendent Cramer entered the room. She pushed the RECORD button on the transcript machine.

'Superintendent Cramer is now joining D.I. Angstrom in the interview room with Mr John Tucker,' he said in a loud voice as he pulled up a chair and sat next to Angstrom. 'I am told you have a confession on tape, Mr Tucker,' he continued in a lower and much warmer tone. 'Is it your confession or somebody else's?'

'You'll find it belongs to Sergeant Alan Williams who has wasted sixteen years of my life and has been forcing me to do things that no normal person would ever consider doing.'

'Sergeant Williams has been putting you under extreme duress?'

'Play the tape and make up your own minds,' John said quietly.

Cramer nodded and Angstrom reached to push the REWIND button. When the miniature reel of tape stopped with a click Angstrom pressed PLAY and sat back in her chair.

'So nice of you to join me at the seaside, John . . .'

The voice had been muted by the layers of clothing but it could be clearly identified as the sergeant's voice. The muffled reports of Alan's gun made all three jump slightly and then as the conversation between Alan and his intended victim continued the two officers glanced at each other with looks of understanding as everything became crystal clear to them.

'Drop the weapon! Drop the weapon and raise your hands . . .'

The police command stirred Angstrom back to reality and she reached and switched the cassette recorder off.

'You honestly believed that you had killed Doris and then you let Williams hold that over you for sixteen years?' she asked, shaking her head in disbelief. 'If you'd come to us in the first place forensics would have proved you innocent and saved all the grief you've endured.'

John nodded and bowed his head. 'I know that now,' he whispered. 'But in 1964 it was a completely different story. Then I was young enough to believe that I would definitely hang by the neck and be buried in some unconsecrated grave in a prison. It would have killed my mother. Then he let me believe that I had killed Louise and encouraged me to bury her.'

'It's so sadistic. To bury a young girl alive is too horrible to contemplate. How could anyone do such a thing?' Angstrom interrupted.

'We now have a positive link between the two murders in Dover and Sergeant Williams,' Cramer said as he slid a file in front of Angstrom. It contained details of the murders in Dover of both Terry and an unidentified dock worker.

'How did you know I was at the antiques shop?' John asked.

'A constable on the beat, not knowing who you were, still made a note of you riding into town and not long after that your bike was identified by a traffic officer. We guessed that you were visiting the shop and that the child there was most probably the attraction as he was your own son.'

'Thank God you turned up when you did.'

'We'll need a full statement from you, Tucker,' Cramer said. 'And then we will decide what to charge you with. It could be anything from failure to report a death, illegal handling of stolen property, trafficking drugs or simply exceeding the speed limit on Her Majesty's highways.'

'But we'll not be charging you with murder, John, possibly manslaughter at the most,' Angstrom added softly as she placed a pad of paper and a pen in front of him. 'Just start at the beginning and put as much detail into your statement as you can. This will help us to nail Bellini and his network here and on the continent.'

John nodded, picked up the pen and began writing.

19

IT WAS LATE AFTERNOON when Angstrom entered Cramer's office and placed the signed statement before her boss. 'I think this is a pretty good day's work, sir,' she said with a touch of pride in her voice.

'Not until we've got Sergeant Williams under lock and key and the total drug operation netted, Jennifer,' Cramer replied as he idly flicked through the statement. 'However, this is a bloody good start.'

'What do we do with Tucker now. The cells?'

'No, I think we know where we can pick him up if we need to. However, I have had a word with the DPP and Tucker's clever use of a tape recorder may prove to be his "get out of jail free" card. We may not need to spend time hunting for him again as he'll now be willing to help us, as much for his own sake and that of his son. He has also effectively saved the force a great deal of tax payers' money. The crown prosecutor thought that he had suffered enough duress to last him a lifetime and he will try to lighten any charges brought against him.'

'So, I can take him back to Brighton and his son.'

Cramer nodded and Angstrom broke into a broad smile that greatly enhanced her attractiveness to Cramer and he instinctively smiled back. Angstrom blushed and to his disappointment she quickly left his office to give the good news to John and have him officially signed out by the custody sergeant.

John thanked Angstrom and accepted her lift back to Brighton and his son with great alacrity. The evening traffic was beginning to build and the thirty-five-mile journey went slowly as John explained how he had managed to survive for so long without any official identity papers. Angstrom listened in fascination to his story and only interrupted occasionally to clarify odd points.

It was the magic hour of the day when twilight was still lingering without any shadows being cast. The police car drove into The Lanes and slowly cruised into the square to stop outside the shop. No lights were switched on.

'We still have to apprehend Williams so take care and keep the doors locked,' Angstrom advised as John got out of the car. 'Constables will be making routine checks at the shop but if there is any hint of trouble call my number.' She passed him her card that was printed with both her office and mobile phone numbers.

John thanked her and the driver and then went to the shop entrance where he knocked on the glass. As the patrol car slowly drove away the lights came on in the showroom and he saw Anne running down the stairs with a look of joy on her face. 'Why did they let you go?' she cried breathlessly the moment the door was open.

'Aha! You wanted them to keep me locked up forever,' John replied with mock seriousness.

'No, silly!' She threw herself into his arms and he immediately felt as though he had really arrived at a place he could call home. 'What I meant was, what convinced them of your innocence?'

'It was a tape recording of Alan when he was here trying to kill me,' John said as he watched a small figure bound down the stairs with loud whoops of happiness. He closed the door behind him and then gathered Timothy up in his arms and hugged him before kissing the top of his curly head. 'I could do with a really nice cup of tea, Anne. The stuff they offer in police stations can never be called drinkable by anyone who has a single taste bud in his mouth.'

John climbed the stairs and went into the living room with Timothy while Anne turned off the showroom lights and then put on the kettle. Outside in the gathering dusk a strolling figure paused at the shop and then walked on, his boots resounding on the paving. Melding with the shadows another figure watched the constable pass by and then he retreated back to where he had left his Commando.

John awoke after the first sleep without nightmares in sixteen years. Something heavy was pressing upon his broad chest and it took him a moment to recall the events of the previous evening. As pleasant memories of their love-making surfaced he turned his head and saw

Anne's face only inches from his own. Her eyes were closed, her long lashes curling up as they rested on high cheeks that were rosy from the warmth of sleep. It was the weight of her arm that had woken him and it rose and fell gently with each breath he took. He ran a finger down from her forehead to her cheek and along her jawline while he studied every detail. Anne stirred, opened her green eyes and immediately smiled when she saw John looking at her. 'Did you sleep well?' John asked softly.

'Deliciously well,' she replied and she yawned and stretched like a cat, her arms high above her head. As she was still naked beneath the sheet the movement exposed her firm breasts to the cool air of the morning. She put her arm around him and pulled him close until their warm bodies were moulded together and her lips avidly began to seek his own . . .

'Good morning, Dad,' a child's cheery voice said. The couple jerked apart as though stung by bees and John pulled the sheet up to their necks. 'Good morning, Anne,' Timothy added as he jumped up onto the bed in his pyjamas and threw himself down between them.

John sat up, taking care not to pull the sheet down and reveal Anne's lack of nightclothes and he ruffled the small boy's hair. 'Where did this little froglet spring from so early in the morning?' he asked as Tim rolled over to sit astride his father's stomach.

'It's not early, Dad,' he protested, bouncing up and down and winding his father. 'It's very late and I'm hungry.'

With some difficulty John took the wristwatch off the side table and was instantly wide awake. 'Good grief, it's nine o'clock!' he exclaimed and he lifted the active boy and put him down beside the bed. 'You go and brush your teeth and get dressed and we'll meet you in the kitchen.'

'Race you!' the boy cried excitedly.

'Right. First one there gets jelly beans for afters.'

The boy gave a loud 'whoop' and ran from the bedroom and John rolled over with an increasing desire to make love to Anne again.

Anne sprang out of bed with a laugh. 'No time for that now,' she said walking towards the en-suite bathroom. 'There's a race to be won.'

John watched her beautiful body as she lithely moved across the room. Her narrow back flared into the perfect swell of her bottom crowning the elegant tapering of her long legs. Now fully aroused by the sight he leapt up and ran to join her in the shower.

Thirty minutes later the couple finally joined the boy who had been impatiently kicking the chair legs with each swing of his feet while working his way through a packet of chocolate biscuits. They both apologised profusely for taking so long to brush their teeth and then hurriedly began cooking the long-awaited breakfast.

Fifty miles north-west as the crow flies Alan was riding up the driveway to Bellini's house, scattering gravel in his haste. Two heavy-set men who had their hands permanently tucked inside their double-breasted jackets met him at the front door. One of these was Jimmy Partridge.

Alan swung the briefcase round from where it had been hanging on his back and followed Jimmy into the house and along the hallway to the library. Signor Bellini was sitting before the cold inglenook fireplace and drawing deeply on a Romeo y Julieta cigar. A dense and very expensive blue cloud had gathered above his head while he had been waiting for the sergeant. On the low coffee table before him lay a thin blue book. It was a much-coveted British passport.

'You have brought my shipment, yes?' he grunted without looking up.

Alan lifted the strap over his head, placed the briefcase on the table and snapped the catches. He raised the lid to show the eight large glassine bags of pure high-grade heroin packed inside. He bent to reach for the passport and a black malacca cane whipped down to crack on the walnut top beside the passport. He jerked his hand away.

'And the head. Where's my head, Sergeant?'

'I encountered a little difficulty with its removal and it will take a little longer than I expected,' Alan said beneath his breath.

'Then you don't get paid.' The cane touched the blue cover and then pressed down to slide it away from Alan. Bellini reached forward, picked it up and slipped it into the side pocket of his smoking jacket. 'The head! Get it!' he screamed and struck the table again with the heavy cane.

Alan felt his elbow being gripped by Jimmy who then led him out of the room and back to the front door. 'I'd do it soon if I were you, mate,' he said. 'Mr Bellini doesn't like to be kept waiting.'

Ignoring the sardonic waves of the two guards Alan left Bellini's estate and rode south. As the machine vibrated between his thighs he was thinking of a way to avoid being apprehended by the police. He needed to have John alone for a few minutes. He stopped in a small wood to change the number plates on the bike with a set he had tucked in his jacket and then swapped the same leather jacket for a blue windcheater. He discarded the jacket and old plates in a thicket along with his helmet and goggles and slipped on a pair of aviator sunglasses to keep the insects out of his eyes.

It took another forty minutes of riding below the speed limits to reach Shoreham-by-Sea which was only four miles from The Lanes. Alan stopped at a petrol station and filled the tank with his back turned to the closed-circuit television camera to avoid identification.

Reaching Brighton pier he put the Commando amongst a dozen other bikes that were parked there and chose a café from which he could covertly watch the antiques shop. After eight coffees and some rather strange looks from the staff he had accurately timed the constable on his beat and had calculated that each check was on the hour precisely. Alan watched the police officer turn the corner and looked at his watch; it was now five past eleven and he had a window of fifty-five minutes to carry out the task set by Bellini. The waitress watched him with suspicion and went to dial a number the moment he left the café.

Alan went to the side door and found that it was securely locked. Steel bars had also been installed to ensure it remained permanently sealed. He shrugged and returned to stand outside the shop and peer into the window. The closed sign was still hanging on the door and he could detect no movement inside the showroom. I'll have to wait till he leaves, he thought as he went back to the café. Noticing the expression on the waitress's face through the window he guessed that she had suspected something and abruptly turned away and returned to the seafront. There he began the search for the very distinctive Vincent and eventually found it down a small road opposite the pier. Alan hurried back to his own bike which he then parked close to John's for a quick getaway.

The amount of coffee he had consumed was beginning to play merry hell with his stomach and Alan went into a scruffy-looking sandwich bar from where he could keep a watch on the ranked motorcycles while using their toilet facilities and satisfying his hunger.

Angstrom had received a message from Central that reported the sighting of Alan Williams in close proximity to the antiques shop. She rushed back to the station and into Cramer's office, interrupting his meeting with the chief superintendent.

'Sorry, sir, but Williams is in Brighton and has been seen stalking the Jackson shop,' she managed to say before being waved into a seat and into silence by the chief who was distinctly irritated.

'Is this the man we've been trying to catch for a week, no, let's face it, two weeks?' he said with sarcasm dripping from his thick lips. 'Yes, sir,' Cramer said. 'We've been seeking him along with John Tucker whom we have subsequently caught and interviewed.'

'At least he's been charged then?'

'No. He was found to be innocent of all the crimes laid at his door and it would appear that Williams is the principal perpetrator.'

'Whom you still have to catch?'

Angstrom stood up. 'Can I go now, sir? Every minute is valuable if we are to even consider the idea of catching the man.'

The senior officer looked around at the woman, his eyes narrowing at the junior officer's own form of sarcasm and waved her back into her seat. Cramer contradicted this angry gesture with one of his own that ordered her to go and to go fast. She left before the chief superintendent could countermand Cramer's order and collected Constable Phillips from her office before hurrying down to the motor pool in the basement.

Phillips was an advanced driver and with lights flashing and the occasional burst of siren he smoothly negotiated the midday traffic as though it didn't exist. Traffic lights clicked favourably for them and the highly tuned car made excellent time on the familiar route to arrive in The Lanes before the office and shop-workers' rush to lunch in Brighton began in earnest.

While the constable hurried into the antiques shop to check that all was okay Angstrom walked into the café mentioned in the report and the waitress very quickly identified Alan's headshot from a dozen others. Angstrom hurried across the small square and sighed with relief when she found Phillips talking to John.

'Have you seen him recently, sir?' she heard the constable ask.

'Not today if that's what you mean.'

'He was spotted outside the shop shortly after ten this morning,' Angstrom interjected. 'He is obviously targeting you for a reason. Do you know what that might be?'

'I don't believe Alan was aware that I had recorded his voice in the storeroom so it can't be for revenge. However, I have been the big blowfly in Bellini's ointment and he's difinitely not a man to cross.'

Angstrom thought for a moment. 'This can only mean that Bellini has made Alan your assassin. He wants you killed, your blood in exchange for all the aggravation you've given him and Alan has accepted this contract because he wants something from Bellini. Something very important that he cannot get or find for himself.'

'Who wants to kill John?' Anne asked in a frightened voice as she slowly descended the stairs.

'Don't panic, Anne,' John said and he put an arm around her shoulders. 'It's Alan. He has been seen near here but the police have got things covered. He cannot possibly get into the shop.'

While Angstrom had been talking to John the constable had stepped to one side and was using his portable radio to convey the latest information to Central Control.

'Excuse me, Inspector,' he interrupted. 'Central have now put two more cars in the area, one an armed response unit, and three more constables have been allocated to patrol The Lanes.'

'Good work, Phillips,' Angstrom said before turning back to Anne. 'Don't worry, Miss Jackson. We'll soon have him in custody and you'll get back to normal living again.'

'I don't think anything can ever be normal again, Inspector,' Anne said softly and turned her grief-stricken face away to bury it in John's shoulder.

'Please Anne, try to put on a brave face if only for Timothy's sake,' he said softly as he rubbed his palm up and down her back. Anne looked up and Alan kissed her lightly on the forehead, making her smile and visibly relax.

'It would seem that you two have found something that makes you more than mere acquaintances?'

'Nice things can occasionally emerge from disasters, Inspector,' Anne said with a slightly embarrassed yet infectious laugh that had John, Angstrom and even constable Phillips joining in.

'That's really good to hear,' Angstrom said as she walked back to the front door. 'You can also rest easy with all the extra patrols about the shop and try not to fear for we'll soon have Williams in custody.'

She raised a hand in farewell and Phillips followed. The police car pulled away and John suddenly felt naked and extremely vulnerable. He locked the door, involuntarily shivered and put an arm around Anne's waist as they began walking back upstairs to Tim who was attempting to catch one of the tropical guppies with a tea strainer.

All of a sudden John stopped and waved Anne on ahead. 'I won't be long, Anne, there's something I have to do in the storeroom before coming up for that cup of tea you promised me.'

John knew that nothing was finished yet because Ted and his wife, and Jane, the mother of his son, deserved proper justice and he felt compelled to do it himself. It had all begun with an accident beneath a pier that had ended in murder. John vaguely felt responsible for Alan's deeds which made it his duty to stop him before he killed again. Moreover, Bellini's men, under his orders, had slaughtered Ted, his old school friend and a fellow ton-up, and therefore they all had to pay the price for their deeds.

He hurried down, two steps at a time and entered the storeroom. Making his way to the rear he located the oak coffer and opened the drawer to remove the large pistol and the silencer. On close inspection he saw that it was a Beretta and the box magazine was fully loaded with twelve rounds of 9-mm parabellum bullets. He removed his sweater and wound it round the weapon and returned to the shop.

'Just going to get something from the bike, Anne. I won't be long. Make sure you lock the door after me,' he shouted up the stairs and hurriedly exited the shop before Anne could come down and question him.

John trotted through the maze of streets followed by an obvious plain-clothes policeman until he reached the Vincent. Using his ignition key he unlocked the small saddlebag and casually dumped the sweater inside as though it was simply a precaution against cooler weather.

He then mounted the bike completely unaware of the sharp eyes inside the sandwich bar that followed every move he made. The constable who had been following John was using his mobile radio for he had also spotted Alan who was baring his teeth in the humourless grin of a hunter.

John threaded his way down to the seafront where he picked up speed to lose any police tail as he left Brighton. He passed one patrol car going the other way but the officers hadn't received any instructions from Central yet.

John passed the magnificent Royal Pavilion and stayed with the main road until he had left the urban district of Brighton before taking a westerly direction on numerous back lanes. He rode slowly as he didn't want to arrive in St George's Hills until after the sun had set.

20

SIGNOR BELLINI DREW HARD ON HIS CIGAR and rang the tiny silver bell to summon his evening drink. Jimmy entered carrying a silver tray on which stood a brandy glass and a bottle of Hine Homage cognac. He placed it on the desk.

'Did you find out where our Sergeant Williams went after leaving us this morning?' Bellini asked as he watched the bottle being tipped and the fine golden stream flow down the side of the balloon glass.

'Yes, Signor,' Jimmy replied. Putting the glass before his boss he continued, 'Anton trailed him to Brighton and a small antiques shop. It would seem that there was some kind of fight inside because the police were called which prevented Anton from getting close.'

'Does the shop have some significance?' Bellini sipped appreciatively before drawing on his cigar again and letting the smoke trickle from between his fleshy lips.

'I think that this is where Williams used to off-load some of his smaller antiques and also where John Tucker was hiding. I saw him talking to the police outside and I had the distinct impression that he had some sort of relationship with the woman who lives above the shop.'

'Excellent, Jimmy.' Bellini glanced at his Rolex before speaking again. 'It is now ten o'clock and I want you and Anton to return to the shop before midnight. You will then eliminate Mr Tucker without leaving any witnesses and then find the sergeant and kill him too.'

'Yes, sir,' Jimmy said quietly with eyes glittering at the prospect of a hunt that would end in a kill. 'I'll get Anton and leave immediately.' He strode from the room with an eager spring in his step.

Bellini sipped once more to savour the fiery spirit passing over his palate and then opened the file that lay before him. It listed the next twelve months' deliveries and his first priority was to find trustworthy replacements who could meet the continental ferries on time and transport the product to the hidden storage centre moored on the river. This had been Terry's task but his disappearance after being sent to Dover was a mystery and Bellini had a suspicion that the sergeant was responsible.

As he ran a finger down the dates the French windows, left slightly ajar in the summer heat, were flung wide open and John Tucker ran in with the Beretta aimed at Bellini's head.

'Don't move or make a sound, Signor,' John warned. He walked round the desk to confront the drug trafficker as the weapon, made even more menacing by the long silencer, was pressed against Bellini's forehead. 'Did you order the killing of my friend Edward Barker?' John snapped.

Bellini felt his palms grow damp and the silencer was jabbed hard making him jerk back. He swallowed and then with forced calmness found he was still capable of speech. 'He used to work for me, yes. He was a good motorcyclist and therefore he did the same work as you were doing for Williams.'

'That was not the question. I'll ask you again. Did you kill him?' The silencer was moved from the forehead and pressed against his left eye.

'I believe your friend . . . ' Bellini fell back and the heavy silk drapes behind him were splattered with blood and brain tissue as a bullet from nowhere entered the right eye. It had removed the back of the Italian's skull and John froze, unable to move, as he looked down in horror at the mess that was once a man's head.

'Don't move, John,' a familiar voice said unnecessarily for John was incapable of any sudden movement. He turned his head slowly and watched Alan cross the room from where he had been hiding in the adjoining library. He also had a silenced weapon in his grip and now it was pointing at John's chest.

'This was inevitable,' he smirked as he poked the dead man's leg with his toe. 'He had a contract out on me which meant Jimmy and the Ukrainian would have caught up with me sooner or later. They're good and I don't rate your chances or those of Anne Jackson and Timothy.' John took a step towards Alan who raised the gun and pointed at his head. 'I wouldn't do that. Why don't you give me the gun.'

'What do you mean Anne and Timothy have no chance?' John asked as panic-induced vomit rose in his gullet.

'Bellini's last instruction to his men was to kill you and eliminate all witnesses. They're on their way now, that's why I found it so easy to get into this house. Very soon the police will catch up with you for all those murders.'

'Not me, Alan,' John said, his mind thinking about the danger that his son and Anne were in.

'What do you mean?'

'I recorded your pretty little speech in the antiques storeroom and now the police know the truth and are doing all they can to find you.'

'Damn you, John! I thought there was a chance that I could forgive you for your lack of loyalty to me but now I will just have to kill you.'

John looked around for some means of escape.

'The gun, John. Give it to me now or I'll shoot you in some rather painful places. I won't kill you until you've really learnt what the word agony means.'

John extended his hand and as soon as Alan stepped closer John whipped the long silencer of Alan's gun to one side and slammed his own into Alan's face. A low *phutttt* was the only sound as Alan's finger involuntarily squeezed the trigger while stumbling backwards. The missile hit a porcelain vase standing on the baby grand piano and 600-year-old fragments flew through the air, one grazing John's cheek and drawing blood.

While Alan was falling down John had dodged to one side and now he sprang through the French windows and into the darkness of the garden. Dodging from one shrub to the next he crossed the wide lawn and entered the small copse of trees just as cedar bark mysteriously exploded beside his head. Alan had obviously recovered and was chasing after him through the garden.

John ran as fast as he could in the dark without risking injury and was soon confronted by the high brick wall that surrounded the property. He kept running while tucking the gun into his belt and at the last moment leapt as high as he could to grasp the metal railing that ran along the top of the wall. His body impacted with the bricks driving air from his lungs and he had to hang for a second to recover his breath before swinging his legs up and onto the top. Brick dust puffed into the air as bullets, sounding like wasps, began hitting the wall close to his body.

John knew it was only a matter of time before Alan was close enough to get one accurate shot off and he rolled over the single rail and dropped down the other side of the wall. Once more he was left breathless as the impact with the hard earth drove all air from his body. Stumbling to his feet he began running through the undergrowth that ran beside the wall until he saw the dark outline of the Vincent parked behind the dense buckthorn trees.

'You can't outrun me, John,' a muffled voice shouted from beyond the perimeter wall. 'You know I'm the better rider.'

John took the automatic and put it inside his jacket before zipping it up. He then kick-started the bike and as soon as the engine was running he released the clutch and accelerated down the unlit road. As he raced past the main gates he glimpsed a distant headlight and knew it was Alan's bike at the top of the drive. When he was a teenager John had always been content to take second place but for the first time in his life he knew that it was of paramount importance for him to beat Alan on the road.

He had sufficient fuel for a fast run to Brighton and he toed through the gears and felt the power of the machine responding to his touch. John raced through the suburbs defying anybody to get in his way as he jumped the red traffic lights and centre-lined, with headlight on full beam, forcing oncoming vehicles to move over as far as they could.

John had turned onto the main road south and was touching ninety miles per hour when he glanced back to see a single headlight half a mile behind and travelling fast in the outside lane. John felt his palms grow sweaty as he wound the throttle more and flattened himself on the fuel tank. The needle steadily crept round until he was doing over 100 mph and still accelerating. At 115 he dared to use a precious split second of concentration to take a look behind and was relieved to see that the Commando's headlight was now further behind. John didn't relent and maintained his speed despite the protest of horns when he went by too close and caused the lighter vehicles to be buffeted.

Replaying the route in his mind he decided to use the same road to reach the coast and then to use the seafront road. A large pantechnicon loomed ahead and as he positioned himself he saw a similar vehicle overtaking and heading towards him. Without winding the throttle down he placed the front wheel on the white line and as he held his nerve he also held his speed. Bass-sounding airhorns and an intense buffet of air blasted him from both sides as all three were aligned across the road in the tenth of a second it took John to pass through the gap and then he was screaming away into the night.

As he rode into the built-up outer suburbs of Worthing he was forced to slow down and frustration began to build as the time-consuming manoeuvring through late-evening traffic threatened to erode the commanding lead he had built.

Passing the entrance to the golf club he saw a road sign for the upper-Brighton road and immediately swung off and headed parallel to the coast. There was still no sign of Alan and he physically slumped on the bike with relief. Twice he was held up for precious seconds by serious roadworks before he finally approached Brighton pier.

Without any concern for secrecy he rode into the The Lanes and braked hard outside the antiques shop. It was all in darkness and John hammered on the door hoping that all was well. It was a quarter to twelve and lights were beginning to go on across the road in response to the noise he was making. Suddenly a light went on in the shop and he could see Anne coming down the stairs. She was tying the dressing gown cord around her waist and her tousled hair showed that she had been sleeping. John indicated that she should hurry and as she pulled back the last bolt he pushed his way in and slammed it shut behind him. John pushed all of the bolts home and taking the bewildered woman by the arm he quickly led her back up the stairs.

'What's happened, where did you get to?' Anne mumbled sleepily.

'I'll tell you as soon as we're safely upstairs.'

As they began to climb there was a renewed banging on the door and John's hand slipped inside his jacket to grip the butt of the automatic. He spun round and his tense shoulders slumped on recognising a young constable standing outside.

John let the policeman in and then relocked the door before answering the constable's question. 'Everything's fine, officer,' he said. 'I've just witnessed a murder, been shot at, chased on the road and I expect the murderer to come here any minute to try and kill me, Anne and my son.'

Constable Phillips nodded and immediately activated the radio that sat high on his shoulder.

'Constable Phillips at Jackson's Antiques. Requesting immediate armed back-up.' He pushed a button and all three heard the hissing and crackle as Central Control acknowledged his request a split-second before the radio disintegrated and the 9-mm bullet struck the constable's collarbone. John caught the falling man and frantically waved at Anne to keep her head down and to follow him before dragging the shocked, semi-conscious officer across the showroom and behind a George III mahogany linen press. Another bullet shattered the main shop window and furrowed the side of the heavy piece of furniture.

'That's a few hundred pounds off the £3,000 it was worth,' Anne managed to joke as her shoulders shuddered with fear. 'Since I've met you, John, you've cost me a great deal of money.'

John nodded solemnly as he explored the officer's shoulder that was bleeding copiously but luckily no real damage had been done. He tore the man's shirt and made pads that he pressed tight against the entrance wound and the more destructive exit, making the constable wince.

Anne had watched John working for a few seconds before the constable's urgent need overcame her terror and she quickly moved closer to help John stem the bleeding by holding the pads in place.

'Who did the shooting?' she whispered.

'It's either Alan who had been hot on my heels, or two gunmen who worked for a drug trafficker.'

'Worked?'

'Alan shot their employer dead not so long ago but only after Bellini, that was his name, had ordered his men to kill me, Alan and any other witnesses,' John explained as he put his hand inside his jacket and carefully peered round the linen press. Nothing moved outside in the dark and John released the automatic and withdrew his hand.

'What have you got there, John?' Anne asked when she noticed his hand under his jacket.

'Something for an emergency . . . should it arise.'

'If it's a gun, John, I would prefer it if you'd dispose of it as soon as possible.'

John nodded. 'Of course, Anne, but not right now. I may have a use for it. Okay?' He crossed to the counter where the phone stood. The plate-glass window gave a sharp *tuk* sound a microsecond before the bullet shattered the small cuckoo clock on the wall behind John. As splinters of glass fell he used the counter as a shield and sank down out of sight from the window. John unzipped a breast pocket and took Inspector Angstrom's card out. He dialled the number and after twenty rings he tried the second number which was answered immediately.

'Detective Inspector Angstrom, how can I help you?' The woman's voice sounded bright and alert as though she had been up when he called.

'We're having a little trouble at the shop,' John said as he stared out through the glass into the blackness beyond.

'I've heard and I'm already on the way with six armed officers. Where's Constable Phillips?'

'That's what I'm calling about, Inpector. Your man has been shot and needs an ambulance fast.'

'Life threatening?'

John could hear real concern in Angstrom's tone and he hurriedly tried to reassure her. 'No, thank God. The bullet appears to have missed any vital organs and Anne is successfully stemming the flow of blood.'

'Thank you, John, we're just entering The Lanes so we'll be with you in sixty seconds. One of our men is a trained paramedic so he'll be able to look after Constable Phillips until the ambulance arrives.'

The line was broken and John turned to Anne with a grim expression. 'I don't know who fired the shots through the window but I do know we have three men who want me dead. I cannot afford to have them coming here and putting you at risk and therefore I must return to Bellini's place and confront them there.'

'That's madness, John. Let the police handle it,' Anne pleaded. 'They are far better at dealing with these kinds of men than you could ever be.'

'But I know what Bellini's men look like, Anne, they don't,' John said without realising that both Angstrom and Cramer had seen the gunmen on their visit to the mansion. He put his hand inside his jacket to move the weapon to a more comfortable position. 'I'll leave Alan for the police to catch. Just tell the inspector when she arrives that he is most probably still close by and if she puts a police net around Brighton she may have him.'

John walked quickly to the door and peered out into the night. There were no more shots and before Anne could restrain him he started to leave. 'I'll see you tomorrow,' he whispered and slipped out into the night. The Vincent was still warm and started first time. He left the square a mere few seconds before the armed response cars approached from a different direction and screeched to a halt outside the shop. Officers piled out of the two vehicles and some took defensive positions outside while others rushed into the showroom. Inspector Angstrom followed, wearing a bulky bulletproof vest and immediately took charge.

While the paramedic tended to the wounded officer Anne explained to Angstrom what had taken place and that John had left to chase the two gunmen back to St George's Hills.

Angstrom hurried outside to use the car radio and Anne went upstairs to check on Timothy. She quietly crept into his bedroom and switched on the teddy-bear night light she had bought for him the day before. Pulling back the blanket she found only two pillows. Timothy had disappeared.

She screamed and ran to the window that was now wide open. The flat roof of the storeroom was only two feet below the sill and it was obviously the route the boy's abductor had taken.

An armed officer appeared beside her with his Webley at the ready, a questioning look on his face.

'John's son, the child has gone, Timothy's been taken!' Anne exclaimed and the officer leapt through the window and ran the length of the flat roof looking over the side and into the alley. He looked all around before turning to face the distraught young woman: 'Nobody here.' The boy was gone.

Jimmy put his foot down and the V12 Jaguar responded with a low growl that both men could feel. Anton stared out at the cats' eyes that briefly caught the headlight beams before disappearing beneath the bonnet as his partner moved from one lane to the other.

'Well, the sergeant led us to the right place but we were lucky we weren't spotted by those patrolling constables. I've never seen a little shop so heavily guarded,' Jimmy said morosely. 'There was no way we could get close to Tucker without giving ourselves away. At least that's what we're going to tell Bellini.'

'They seemed to be more interested in where the shooting was coming from,' Jimmy said as he swerved to avoid an oncoming car with flashing headlights.

'Do you think Williams hit the bastard?'

'I bloody hope so,' Jimmy muttered. 'Cos that will mean we only have one to dispose of and that's Williams himself.'

The Jaguar purred through the moonless countryside and the dark amorphous mass rushing past occasionally became single trees and shrubs when the headlight beams swept round corners. The two men had slipped into a thoughtful silence and the rest of the journey was almost completed before Anton spoke.

'Will Signor Bellini give us time to sleep or will he insist that we stand guard until Williams returns with Tucker's head?'

'Being the bastard he is he'll keep us waiting,' Jimmy snarled as he swung the car to enter the open gates and accelerate up the drive to the big house that was still showing a blaze of light in all the windows. The two men got out and entered the hall.

'You go and get something for us to eat from the kitchen and I'll see Bellini,' Jimmy ordered and Anton shrugged non-committally and slouched down the hall. Jimmy made a rude gesture behind his partner's back and then opened the door leading to the study. He walked in prepared to make his apology and then stopped dead.

'Christ, what happened here,' he whispered as he surveyed the carnage on the other side of the desk. Bellini was in his chair, exactly where Alan had left him and although the blood was still wet on the curtains it had already begun to darken. Jimmy approached and looked closely to make sure that the man was dead but the bloody mess where his eye had been was evidence enough. He scoured the scene and the slight movement of the drapes alerted him that the French windows were wide open.

This is the work of Williams, he thought as he removed the piece of paper that was still clutched in his late employer's cold hand. He read the dates and the code letters for the destinations and realised he was holding a fortune in his hands. Jimmy knew about Terry's cruiser on the river and had followed him once to discover the second boat, a long narrow boat where the drugs were stored before being distributed around the country. He folded the paper and slipped it into his pocket just as Anton entered the room carrying a tray heaped with cold meat, bread and Bellini's favourite wine.

'I couldn't find you in the sitting room so I thought I'd look here. How about a little ploughman's lun—' He stopped short and looked at Jimmy with suspicion clouding his face.

'It wasn't me, mate. He was like this when we arrived, trust me,' Jimmy said with a shrug and spread his hands.

'Williams?' Anton asked after putting the tray down on the desk and studying the corpse with professional interest. 'It would take a good marksman to put a bullet there.'

'Not if his gun barrel was only inches away,' Jimmy said. 'Look at the red marks around the other eye. It appears as if a barrel was pressed against it. He couldn't miss at that range,' Jimmy added in a bored tone as he selected a slice of cheddar cheese and tore a piece from the French stick.

'I agree but there's no gunshot residue around the eye that was shot. Explain that if you can.'

Anton filled two glasses from a dust-covered bottle of Nuits-Saint-Georges Premier Cru. The intense cherry-kernel aroma lured the two men into taking a few sips while their minds were racing, evaluating their personal standing and how they could capitalise on the Italian's death.

'Does he keep much cash in the house?' Anton tentatively raised the first thought that had occurred to both men.

'I'll check.' Jimmy went to the far side of the study and grasped the heavy frame that held a Rubens reproduction. There was a click as it swung away from the wall to reveal the Burton Biosec 6000 wall safe. 'I've seen him use this keypad so many times I memorised the sequence and can do it blindfold but I'll need his finger for the scanner.'

'No problem,' Anton said as he went round the desk and slid a vicious long blade from the sheath strapped to his arm. He grasped the dead man's right hand and with one stroke removed the forefinger. He carried the grisly object over to Jimmy who pressed the tip on the biometric pad. There was a series of clicks within the safe and the door clicked open an inch.

'Good,' Jimmy declared as he swung the door wide open: the safe was packed with neat bundles of mint-condition banknotes.

'Shit, is that for real?' Anton shouted, his eyes popping as his Ukrainian accent became more pronounced. 'There must be a fortune in there.'

And that's nothing compared to what's in that, Jimmy thought as he glanced at the briefcase standing in the well of the desk by Bellini's legs. Two or three million in heroin if I'm not mistaken.

Anton was too absorbed in retrieving neat bundles of £10,000 each to take any notice of Jimmy and what he was staring at so greedily.

'Look at this, Jimmy,' he exclaimed excitedly. 'Fifty bundles equal half a million!' He turned in ecstasy to face Jimmy with a bundle in each hand—and stared straight into the muzzle of a Glock 38 that was pointing at his head. He dropped one of the bundles and reached inside his jacket. The bundle hadn't reached the carpet before a heavy bullet shattered the gilt frame of a painting hanging by his head. Anton froze instantly.

'Sorry, me old mate,' Jimmy said. 'Now we haven't got a boss this has to be the parting of the ways. To keep things fair you can keep that money and I'll take the drugs in the briefcase.' Anton visibly relaxed when he realised that he wasn't going to be killed. 'However, it's on condition that you leave the country immediately. If I see you again after you leave this house I'll put a bullet in your head.' Jimmy waited for the Ukrainian's response as he thought about the unimaginable amount of money he could get for the drugs in the case and those stored in the narrow boat. It made the bundles in Anton's arms look like a pittance.

'You have a deal, Jimmy,' Anton croaked, his eyes still fixed on the automatic.

'Good, then go back to the Ukraine or wherever you want but don't remain in England for more than twenty-four hours.'

Anton looked away from Jimmy, his eyes frantically searching until he spotted Bellini's sports bag standing by the French windows.

'Can I use that for the money?' he asked pointing at the bag. Jimmy glanced across the room and nodded.

Anton hurried to the window and turned the bag upside down. Two tennis rackets and an assortment of crisp white sports clothing were unceremoniously dumped on the floor. Anton rushed back to the safe and began to empty the contents into the bag.

'Get going, Anton,' Jimmy said. 'And don't forget what I said about seeing you again.' He reached into the knee-hole to take the heroin-packed briefcase before leaving the house in much higher spirits than when he arrived.

Jimmy stood in the porch whistling tunelessly as he watched Anton drive away in his Mercedes before getting into the Jaguar and pulling away from the house. He was on his way to the canal and the vast fortune that would last him a hundred lifetimes. As he drove between the gates and turned right he was unaware of a motorcycle that was slowly approaching from the left with its lights doused.

As the Jaguar accelerated down the road John could make out the silhouette of one man through the rear window. He made a quick decision to follow the car and return later to deal with the other bodyguard.

Fifteen minutes later John realised they were heading towards the stretch of canal where Terry's boat was moored and he reached into his jacket to reassuringly touch the weapon he had put there. It was now four o'clock and John sensed that very soon he would be easier to spot. He was running three hundred yards behind the Jaguar and was confident that the driver would be unable to pick out a black-jacketed rider on an all-black bike against the backdrop of dark trees that lined both sides of the road for a little longer.

The Jaguar took a road that ran alongside the towpath and although John expected it to slow down and stop by the *Gull's Delight* he was surprised when the car kept going. He followed for another two miles before the car finally came to a standstill opposite a dark green narrow boat.

John stopped and quickly switched off the engine before the driver opened his door. The bike's distinctive sound would be audible in the heavy silence hanging over the canal. The man left the car carrying a briefcase and after quick glances in both directions he strode over the narrow gangplank and onto the boat. For a brief moment John caught sight of the man's face and he recognised Jimmy Partridge, one of Bellini's heavies.

John pushed the bike into the trees and then crept closer to see what Jimmy was doing. As he drew within twenty yards of the narrow boat he heard a door lock snap and the roof panel grate as it was pushed open. The harsh screech of unpolished wood on wood resonated over the water, disturbing small frogs that plopped into the slow-moving current.

Jimmy tripped a switch in the main saloon and suddenly golden shafts of light lit up the towpath. John withdrew a few paces and crouched down. He could now see the burly shape of Jimmy walking the length of the boat and disappearing into a room up front. After a long pause he re-appeared and when he extinguished the lights John quickly darted back into the trees. Once more there was the teeth-setting noise as the hatch was forced shut.

Jimmy got back into the Jaguar minus his briefcase and left.

John boarded the narrow boat and stepping onto the deck he saw in the dim light the two little doors with the sliding hatch above that gave access to the saloon. He opened the hatch and cautiously went down the half dozen steps until he was standing in the dark saloon. He fumbled on the wall until he found a switch and the long room was immediately flooded with battery-powered light.

The seats lining both sides of the saloon were upholstered with a heavy chintz material that had golden braid and tassles like a film set in an old Agatha Christie film. A small wood-burning stove with a black flue stood midway in the saloon; it was icy cold to his touch.

The plush pile of the dark red carpet sank beneath his boots as he walked to the door at the far end. Three bolts were holding it shut and John slowly slid them back. As the last one became free two things happened at the same time. First, the lights flickered, faded and went out, presumably as the battery went flat and second, he was suddenly knocked back by the door being forcibly thrown open. John stumbled, tripped on the carpet and almost broke his coccyx as he sat down with a heavy thump. A small shadowy figure had hurtled into him in the dark and was now trying to scramble over his body and John found himself grappling with a minitornado that he soon understood was a young child.

'Whoa!' he cried. 'I'm not going to hurt you.'

At the sound of his voice the figure instantly stopped struggling. 'Dad? Is that you, Dad?'

With a feeling of disbelief John put his arms around the boy and hugged him tight. 'What on earth are you doing here, Tim?' he whispered into the top of his head.

'A man came into my bedroom and took me and then he made me sit on the back of his motorbike. He tied me to it and said that if I tried to jump off or didn't hold his jacket tight enough and I fell off the bike would drag me on the road until I had no face.'

John hugged the boy who was near to tears. 'Golly, you're a brave little fellow. Anne will be so proud of you.'

'Really? Are you proud of me, Dad?'

'Yeah, of course I am.'

'Before you opened the door there was another man who was surprised to see me. He hit me and locked me in again.' John hugged his son again and 'shushed' reassuringly.

'You're okay now, son, so let's see what else we can find on this bad boat.' John reluctantly put his son down and searched in the dark for the oil lantern he had seen earlier in the glass-fronted cabinet. He lit the lamp with one of the matches that had been left beside it and as he replaced the shade the soft glow grew and spread until they could both see one another.

Despite the streaks of moisture on his cheeks Timothy was giving his father a broad smile that revealed the endearing gap where two milk teeth had once proudly stood. John swallowed the lump that had risen in his throat and squeezed the boy's shoulder before going into the forward cabin. The cabin walls curved into the prow of the vessel and was filled by a large double bed on which lay a rumpled multicoloured spread. Timothy had clearly been using it to keep warm. John began opening all the high lockers on both sides of the hull and discovered that each one was crammed with glassine packages the size of a house brick. He knew what they were and with a grim expression he knelt on the floor and looked beneath the bed—the briefcase had been hastily pushed there by Jimmy. He undid the catches and wasn't surprised to discover more packets of drugs. John searched further and uncovered another, more battered briefcase that was packed with brand-new £50 banknotes. There were also two forged passports, both made out to strange names but with the same photograph of Terry. This must be money he'd stolen from Bellini so that he could start a new life somewhere, he thought sadly.

Something I've got to do now, John said to himself. He snapped the case shut and went into the saloon.

'We must get out of here and get you to a place that is safe, Tim,' he said decisively as he rejoined his son. 'I want you to take this heavy case and carry it up on deck while I do a little more work down here. Okay?'

Timothy nodded enthusiastically and grabbing the case by the handle he tried to swing it up onto his shoulder and nearly fell over. John held the briefcase until he was steady on his feet again and safely walking down the saloon before taking the oil lamp from the shelf and searching the floor. Near the steps he found what he was looking for: a hatch that led down to the engine room at the rear of the boat. He lifted it and was instantly overwhelmed by the thick oily stench of a much-used marine diesel engine and bilge water.

John climbed down and studied the small compartment by the lamp's limited light until he spotted a tin can standing beside the 42 hp BMC engine. Cleaning spirit or lamp oil if I'm not mistaken, he thought as he unscrewed the cap and sniffed the contents, recoiling from the pungent smell with a grimace before giving a satisfied smile.

John returned to the front cabin where he began emptying all the lockers onto the double bed. The drug bricks mounted up until he had a tidy pile of 150 kilograms of pure heroin which would have a street value of many millions. Finally, he reverently placed the two passports onto the pile of drugs as though on a funeral pyre and began pouring the lamp oil over everything. He backed towards the door and then out into the saloon while still pouring the highly flammable fluid and when the can ran out halfway down the boat he struck a match and dropped it onto the trail of liquid.

The flames immediately began racing away from John towards the front cabin and he quickly turned and leapt up the steps just as there was a loud 'whumph' and the whole front of the boat burst into flames. John relieved his over-excited son of his awkward burden while the little boy stood staring at the inferno. Taking his tiny hand in his own he led him safely ashore to the half-hidden Vincent.

'Do I get to ride with you, Dad?' Tim said eagerly as he watched his father mount the motorcycle and place the case on the fuel tank in front of him.

'Absolutely, son. This will be your first ride with me,' John said with a broad smile as he reached down to grab his son's arm and help him clamber up behind him. 'Now make sure you hold on tight. Put your arms around my waist and grip your hands in front of me.'

John felt a warm glow of pride as the little arms held on to him. He barely glanced at the narrow boat when the front windows began to shatter from the extreme heat and he kicked the bike into life and accelerated out of the undergrowth and back onto the tarred road.

'I'm going to take you back to Anne and notify the police so that they will look after you until I return,' John shouted over his shoulder as he accelerated and headed south. He felt the small boy's head nod where it was pressed securely against his back.

Approaching Brighton he began studying every vehicle, moving and stationary, for signs of the police. He became even more cautious when he passed the museum and art gallery and kept his speed down to ensure he didn't attract any attention. He finally stopped and parked near English's Oyster Bar and the two walked hand in hand to the rear entrance of the antiques shop.

The door was still locked fast and putting a finger to his lips he encouraged his son to walk close behind him. John decided to take a chance and they crept silently along the narrow alley until they reached the lane at the front of the shop.

John could see no officers and when he reached the door he sighed with relief when he found it unlocked. They quickly entered the showroom and John flipped the sign hanging on the door to read CLOSED and shot the three bolts. With Tim grinning from ear to ear they made their way to the stairs. Just as they began climbing Anne appeared at the top and gave a joyful cry of surprise when she recognised them.

'Tim, Tim!' she cried. 'Thank God you're safe.' She rushed down and picked the boy up in her arms and held him tight.

'Surprise!' he shouted into her ear.

Almost deafened by his happy cry she still managed a broad smile. 'It certainly is a surprise, a really big surprise.' Anne turned to look at John accusingly. 'Did you take him, John?'

'No, I found him where Alan had stashed him. Although for what reason I can only guess.'

'Revenge?'

'A distinct possibility. Although I think it was a form of leverage to make me go with him to Bellini. Did you notify the police?'

'I did that as soon as I saw he was missing and they're still hunting for him.'

'Then I want you to call Inspector Angstrom and let her know that Tim is home but don't say anything about me or . . . this,' John said and put the briefcase on the top step.

Anne's heart skipped a beat when she heard John say that Tim was at 'home' for that could only mean one thing, he planned to stay.

'What is it?' she asked picking the case up to test the weight.

'Cash,' John said quietly. 'Drug money that I've liberated.'

'You can't keep it, you'll have to hand it over to the police.'

'Why?' he asked with one eyebrow raised. 'After the last sixteen years I think I've deserved some if not all of it.'

'It's money made off the back of misery. Thousands of addicts who have had no say in how they live or die have contributed towards that briefcase of money, John. You cannot possibly think of keeping it for yourself.'

Anne's heartfelt argument touched John and with a pang of guilt he nodded slowly. 'You're right, Anne, however, I object strongly to handing it over to government officials who will most likely squander it on weapons for a nonsensical war in a country that most people cannot even pronounce.'

'Then what can we do with it?'

'I'll become a generous unnamed benefactor who wishes to donate a few million to Narcotics Anonymous. At least we know that it's an organisation that will do a lot of good with it. What do you think?'

Anne smiled broadly and led the way into the kitchen. 'Would you like some tea or perhaps something a little stronger?' she asked as she put Tim down. Taking the kettle from the stove she began filling it at the tap.

'Lemonade, please,' Tim said heading towards the refrigerator.

'It's milk for you, my boy, and then it's straight to bed.'

'No tea for me, thanks,' John answered as he turned to leave the room. 'I have a couple of jobs I need to finish before I let the police finally catch up with me and subject me to another round of time-wasting questions.'

Anne slammed the kettle down, startling the boy. 'If you're planning to chase after Alan Williams and those dangerous drug peddlers, don't!' she said heatedly. 'You'll get yourself killed and where would that leave Tim and I? In the proverbial hot soup, that's where.'

Tim looked up on hearing the angry tone in Anne's voice and John glanced back to see the anguish in the young woman's eyes.

'I have to do it, Anne. I have to redeem and free myself. I just wish you could understand what I mean.' John stumbled from the room and then sprang down the stairs, two steps at a time, to run out of the shop and into light rain.

The road he chose led back to Bellini's house.

21

MIDNIGHT HAD COME AND GONE when Superintendent Cramer rose from behind his desk, stretched his body and wandered out into the corridor to see who else was working the graveyard shift.

Inspector Angstrom was in the briefing room talking to a small group of special task officers who were listening intently to every word she said.

Angstrom turned to the board behind her on which were pinned pictures of Alan, John, Bellini and two other men whom Cramer vaguely recognised. 'First of all,' she said pointing at Alan's picture with a laser, 'this man, Sergeant Alan Williams, is now known to be the killer of a number of people. A tape recording made by this suspect, John Tucker,' and she moved the red dot across the board to John's photograph, 'releases him from all suspicion. However, he is pursuing Williams and the general consensus of opinion is that he wishes to take some form of revenge for the death of his close childhood friend Edward Barker who died with his wife in an automobile accident contrived by Williams.'

'Remind me, Inspector, who are those two men?' Cramer asked, startling Jennifer with his presence at such an early hour. He was pointing to the two surveillance pictures, one of a man in dark glasses getting into a car and the other of someone standing by a set of large ornamental iron gates.

'That's Jimmy Partridge, sir. He's also known as "Shotgun" for obvious reasons and he's Bellini's so-called chauffeur. The other is Anton Voloshin, a Ukrainian who arrived in the UK as a supposed political refugee and now acts as one of Bellini's enforcers. The man has a liking for the good life as long as his benefactor, Signor Silvio Bellini, pays for it all.'

Cramer grunted as he studied the board. 'Please go on.'

Angstrom smiled and turned back to the squad of men. 'Our prime tasks are to bring in Bellini and his men for further questioning and then to ensure we hunt down and terminate Williams before he does Tucker and his young son any harm.'

'Terminate, Inspector?' Cramer said with raised eyebrows and a sardonic smile. 'Now what do you mean by that? Nothing at all like the American CIA use of the word I trust.'

'I'll have an armed-response team ready, sir, but we'll only use them if it becomes vitally important to do so,' Angstrom said matching his smile. 'This man could be a danger to the general public when we corner him and I would rather exercise the extreme option than allow him to harm any innocent members of the public.'

'Nobody in this room heard Inspector Angstrom say that, is it understood?' A unanimous nod of heads and a few wide grins assured him of their support and Cramer turned to Angstrom. 'Very well, continue.'

Angstrom finished the briefing with instructions to approach all the suspects listed with extreme caution. Apart from one man in plain clothes the officers filed from the room already exchanging ideas, planning and coordinating their search patterns.

'Bellini and his men?' Cramer asked.

'I will be going to his place immediately with a narcotics division team led by Inspector Goodman,' Angstrom replied indicating the casually dressed stranger and Cramer looked the man up and down before nodding his approval.

'I shall join you on this visit using my own car,' he said and returned to his office to collect his jacket. Inspector Goodman looked at Angstrom with a quizzical expression.

'He's an old-school hands-on superintendent,' she explained with the hint of an apology in her voice. 'And the best,' she added proudly as they left the room to join the team waiting downstairs. Cramer met them at the lift and they travelled down in silence, all lost in their own thoughts about the welcome they may receive at the St George's Hills address.

The black van moved swiftly, followed by Cramer's car and as the sun began to show above the horizon they entered the exclusive, manicured suburb mainly populated by Russian oligarchs, drug lords and an eclectic mix of multibillionaires and members of parliament.

They swept through open gates that the team recognised from the photograph in the briefing room and skid to a halt in a shower of fine gravel.

The large oak door stood wide open as though Bellini had been expecting them and the team filed in swiftly with Inspector Goodman holding the warrant above his head as a clear challenge to any residents who should appear.

'Inspector,' a voice shouted and both Angstrom and Goodman turned and hurried into the oak-panelled room that appeared to be a study. One of the officers was standing beside the chair in which slumped the late Bellini. He was unnecessarily pointing at the dead man's head.

Angstrom briefly looked but then pointed across the room at the open safe. 'Looks like a falling out of thieves,' she muttered to nobody in particular. 'I wonder where Anton Voloshin and Jimmy have got to.'

'I think you're right, Jennifer,' Cramer said. 'This could be the work of Williams.'

'Or "Shotgun" Partridge, sir,' Angstrom replied as she strode across to study Bellini close up. 'Mind you, Partridge loves his sawn-off and this looks like the work of a handgun.'

'What about John Tucker?' the drugs-squad leader added. 'This could be his way of getting to Williams and committing his final act of revenge.'

'It's not Tucker and I'll put my pension on that,' Cramer said as he strode to stand beside Angstrom who was peering into the safe. 'It doesn't match the man's psychological profile.'

There were some loose papers, a small necklace case and what appeared to be a little white dust on the velvet shelf at the back. He reached out to touch it with the tip of his forefinger and then dabbed it on his tongue. Cramer jerked his head back to study his finger. 'Heroin,' he exclaimed with a distasteful expression on his face. 'One hundred per cent pure, too.'

'It's a bit late to collect it as prosecution evidence but it's nice to know that one of the big importers of that shit has been eliminated,' Goodman said cheerfully as he too tested the residue on his tongue.

'Get the crime-scene boys to come and sort this mess out and let's see if we can now find Voloshin, Jimmy and Williams,' Cramer said briskly as he turned on his heel and left the room with Angstrom closely following.

Goodman gave instructions to his men to guard the crime scene until the technical investigators arrived and went out of the house to catch up with Cramer. 'I think my task has come to an end here so I will now try to locate where the drugs have been hidden. They must be somewhere in the house or on the grounds,' he said as Angstrom slipped into the back of the car after Cramer had taken the seat beside the driver.

'I have my doubts that you will find it stashed here, Goodman,' Cramer said. 'Bellini wouldn't have been foolish enough to remain that close to the drugs for any longer than he needed to. He would have chosen a facility that wasn't too close or too far away either.'

Goodman nodded. 'I agree but I still have to go through the motions for *my* bosses.'

Cramer gave a knowing smile and touched his driver on the shoulder to get going. Angstrom gave a perfunctory wave to the harassed inspector who half raised his hand in response as he stood and watched the car accelerate down the drive.

They drove past a dark Jaguar parked down an access road leading into the woods. The driver frowned and continued to wait until he saw a Police Technical Unit van drive through the gates. Now knowing better than to return to ransack Bellini's house for more jewellery and antiques he pulled out from under the trees and drove slowly in the opposite direction.

Jimmy knew most of Bellini's contacts in Britain and decided he would have to be satisfied with the fortune he could get for what was hidden on the narrow boat. He decided to pick up the cash he knew Terry had siphoned off for himself and take some drug samples to a buyer up north to begin establishing his own credibility and drug network. Jimmy changed direction and drove to the canal. He was approaching the boat when a bright red glow slowly grew in the sky ahead. He slowed the car and after the next bend in the road he was confronted by a manned roadblock. Beyond the hastily erected barrier an officer was waving a torch as two fire tender crews battled a fierce fire that appeared to be floating on the canal water. The killer abruptly felt icy-cold and the hairs on the back of his neck stood up when he realised that it was the narrow boat and that millions of pounds' worth of white powder was going up in the dense pall of smoke that rose above the flames.

'This is Williams' doing,' he thought aloud and was startled by the sudden appearance of a police officer at his side window. Jimmy powered the glass down.

'Sorry, sir, but you'll have to turn around and make a detour. This is a highly dangerous fire and I'm sure you'll understand why we have had to close the road. My apology for any inconvenience,' the young constable explained and Jimmy nodded.

'Perfectly all right, Constable.' Jimmy closed the window and still shaking from the shock of what he was witnessing he made an awkward three-point turn in the road and drove away. As he went round the bend he was passed by a fast-moving car going in the opposite direction. In its brief moment of passing Jimmy saw the driver and felt that he knew her.

The early-morning commuters had yet to crowd the highway which made the two police officers' trip from Bellini's to Hastings as swift as their outward journey. As soon as they arrived at police headquarters they began checking messages in their respective offices. Cramer flicked through his e-mails most of which comprised his superior's demands for instant results in the hunt for Sergeant Williams.

Angstrom found a telex in her in-tray that made her sit upright as she read about a narrow-boat fire that was taking place on a canal near St George's Hills. It had been forwarded by the liaison officer in the local police station who had been notified of her interest in any unusual happenings in Signor Bellini's neighbourhood.

Two appliances had been called out but they were unable to contain the conflagration that was threatening to sink the narrow boat in the shallow canal. The firemen hoped that this would be the case for it would help them extinguish the flames and enable them to get back to the station for a hearty breakfast.

Damn, she thought, now I'll have to go back again. She took her coat from where she had tossed it and after instructing the desk sergeant to let Cramer know she left the building.

Angstrom was approaching the scene of the fire when a fast-moving Jaguar passed her and she instantly recognised the driver as being 'Shotgun' Partridge.

In seconds Angstrom was talking to Central Control and giving a vague description of the car and colour. Pungent smoke was lingering over the water as she came to a halt and went to survey the ruined narrow boat that had literally sunk as she was approaching. The dense pall of smoke was still rising to be dispersed by the light wind.

Fire tender crews were beginning to roll up their hoses and the constable left in charge of traffic walked over to Angstrom ready to remonstrate with a member of the public who had dared violate his cordon of blue tape.

'What time was the alarm first given?' she asked the youngster as she held up her warrant card.

The constable visibly stiffened and pulled his shoulders back as if on parade. 'Four in the morning, Inspector. It was the old couple living in that blue and grey houseboat on the bend in the river.' He pointed to a mishmash that was unquestionably home-made. 'They said it was the breaking glass that woke them and when they looked out the old gentleman thought he saw a motorcycle ride away.'

'Motorcycle?' Angstrom raised an eyebrow. 'Was he able to give a description of the rider or the make of the bike?'

'Too far away I'm afraid but he did notice something very unusual: there was a small child holding on to the rider and he appeared to be wearing pyjamas.'

'The motorcyclist was wearing pyjamas?'

'No, Inspector, the child was. Silly old duffer must have been half-asleep and imagined it, I expect.'

'Or, he was a very observant old duffer, Constable,' Angstrom said thoughtfully and walked away slowly towards the wreck with the puzzled policeman staring after her. Tendrils of smoke were still coiling up into the still air. The sight of the heavily charred bed in the forward cabin some forty feet from the engine compartment sowed the seed of suspicion that the fire was not accidental. She hurried back to the car and put in a call to Superintendent Cramer.

'Any news on the Jaguar, sir?' she asked as soon as the connection was made. 'I'm sure it was "Shotgun" Partridge.'

'Nothing yet, Jennifer. An all-points bulletin has been issued but the car seems to have vanished completely.'

'Have there been any messages regarding the missing Tucker boy, sir?'

'Yes, good news on that front, Jennifer. The desk sergeant took a call from Miss Jackson only twenty minutes ago. She said that the boy had been brought back to her by the father who has left Brighton again but she doesn't know where he's gone.'

'I know what he's been up to, Superintendent,' Angstrom said. 'He came to a narrow boat moored in Weybridge where he rescued his son and set fire to the vessel. I'm standing beside what's left of it now. I have a feeling it was the place where Bellini stored all his drug supplies and that's why Tucker destroyed it. I will be requesting a forensic team to check on whether any drugs were present.'

'When it's just you and I, Jennifer, please call me by my first name. I am aware that everyone prefers to use WC behind my back but I would be honoured if you would call me Wesley, okay?'

'I don't know if I can be so familiar, sir,' Angstrom stuttered, glad that her boss couldn't see the bright colour rising above her collar.

'Be assured, Jennifer, you can.' Before she could say anything more he continued. 'So you think Tucker killed Bellini in order to extract information on the whereabouts of his boy whom they had taken in the first place?'

'No, Wes . . . sir, I believe that Williams killed Bellini and when he was unable to open the safe he left. Partridge then arrived on the scene with Voloshin and they opened the safe and shared what money they found.'

'You think Voloshin had the safe combination.'

'Yes I do.'

'And Williams?'

'I think he was the original kidnapper of little Timothy and for a totally different reason than money. He may have wanted to put Tucker back under his control where he had kept him for so many years.'

'You're still convinced that Williams is an extreme control freak as well as a psychopath?'

'I do. I believe the clinical term for his condition is Obsessive Compulsive Personality Disorder and that Williams is prepared to commit murder if he cannot maintain control, sir,' Angstrom said fervently.

'Wesley.'

'Wesley, sir,' she murmured and then hurriedly broke the connection before the constable approaching the car could see her blushing.

'Any further instructions for me, Inspector?' he asked and Angstrom pointed at the road both ways and told him to keep the curious motorists and pedestrians well away from the remains of the narrow boat.

'Apart from the investigation by the fire brigade I have ordered a thorough forensic check and the results will be copied to me. The fire chief has been informed so, Constable, make sure nobody goes within one hundred feet of the crime scene. Is that understood?'

The policeman snapped to attention. 'Yes, ma'am, nobody.' He was still standing rigidly to attention as Angstrom drove to Bellini's house.

Alan rode past the single police constable guarding the blackened hulk on the canal, his nose crinkled in disgust at the mixed odour of smouldering timbers, burnt engine oil and bilge water. He barely glanced at it to avoid being considered too interested but because his behaviour was so unlike others who were slowing down to get a good look Alan immediately drew the attention of the young constable.

The policeman was aware of the frantic manhunt being conducted across the south of England and he studied the rider who was very tall, well-built and not dissimilar to the description that had already been put out in the morning briefing. He tried to identify the bike as it headed for the curve in the road and was able to note the registration number before it vanished and he thumbed the switch on his shoulder radio.

Alan rode on and headed for Bellini's where he hoped to recover the new passport he had seen on the desk. He planned to get rid of the two bodyguards, Partridge and Voloshin, for they would undoubtedly have the briefcase that he had returned earlier and the contents would see him safely settled in Colombia.

As he approached the gateway he saw the roadblock created by two patrol cars and he braked to a standstill. A car following tooted angrily at his sudden stop and swerved around him alerting the officers who had been dozily looking the other way. They turned and saw the approaching car and as they prepared to check the vehicle one of the officers noticed the stationary motorbike beyond. Pointing at Alan he said something to the other officer who ran to his car and grabbed the radio microphone. Alan knew he had been recognised. He toed the Norton into gear and rapidly U-turned and accelerated away, confused and uncertain what to do next. It was obvious to him that the police had found Bellini and would be tearing the house apart for any evidence of drug trafficking. They would most probably find his new passport and guess that he wanted to leave the country. Alan thumped the fuel tank with the heel of his hand and swore loudly and profusely. On impulse he decided to take a chance and board a ferry; first he had to steal an appropriate passport that matched his height and basic features.

Keeping his eyes fixed on the road ahead Jimmy Partridge withdrew a folded piece of paper from his top pocket and held it up. He had taken it from Bellini's lifeless fingers and a quick glance ascertained that the next pick-up was scheduled for the following day. Knowing that his Jaguar would be top of the watch list for every patrol car in the south he decided to ditch it for a less obvious form of transport.

Jimmy saw a sign for a local railway station and he followed the road to turn into the commuters' car park. His eyes lit up when he saw the large selection of vehicles that had been parked for the day by city workers. He took the ticket that was spat from the machine and the striped barrier lifted. Cruising to the far end of the car park he reversed into one of the remaining bays and left the Jaguar with its doors locked.

A small, dark green Volswagen Polo eventually became his choice and he professionally unlocked it and worked beneath the dash until the engine burst into life.

After a quick rummage in the glove compartment he found a pair of sunglasses and the season ticket that opened the barrier. Soon he was cruising on the main road aware that he was relatively safe until early evening when the owner would be looking for his car.

John had also spotted the police presence at Bellini's gates and hid his bike in the bushes alongside the road. This thick cover lined the estate wall he had previously been forced to clear in order to escape but this time he sought to confront Alan and end his hold over him forever. Or at least die in the attempt.

He pushed through the shrubs until he was faced by the old red-brick wall. Removing his gauntlets he prepared to climb the seven-foot-high barrier.

'I wouldn't try to do that, John,' a woman's voice said conversationally.

John spun around, his hand automatically slipping into his leather jacket and came face to face with Inspector Angstrom. His bewilderment made her smile as she continued, 'I saw you pushing the Vincent off the street when I was talking to the officers at the main gate and followed you,' she said. 'What did you hope to achieve, John?'

'Alan is in there somewhere, I'm sure,' John said, his hand still within his jacket. 'I have to find him to end it all.'

'He propably was here because Bellini had forged a new passport for him which had a Colombian visa. We found it in the house and it obviously means Alan intends to leave the country and disappear forever.'

'And I must stop him!'

'Not that way,' Angstrom said nodding her head at his hidden hand. 'That would only end your life—with a life sentence in jail.'

'Even that would be a form of paradise: no longer to have the spectre of Alan constantly looking over my shoulder and threatening my parents as well as Timothy and Anne.'

'Leave the protection of the ones you love to us, John; as far as scaling this wall is concerned we have the house and the whole estate covered and we'd only apprehend you before you got twenty paces. Please let us be the ones who put him where he can never control your life again.'

Angstrom started walking towards John with her hand outstretched for the weapon. 'Give it to me, John. If we don't find him here we've got all the air and sea ports sealed as tight as a drum.'

John whipped the Beretta from beneath his clothing and held it at arm's length with the muzzle only a foot from Angstrom's face. 'I'm sorry, Inspector, but I must do it my way,' John said as he waved the end of the silencer menacingly in her face. 'Please don't make me use this.'

Angstrom lowered her extended hand and watched sadly as the nervous man sidled past her and hurried back to where he had left the Vincent. The sound of the engine starting and the bike pulling away made Angstrom run through the shrubs and stood helplessly by the side of the road as John raced away.

The Vincent flowed over the road surface like a newly sharpened skate on virgin ice and John abandoned the idea of using minor roads and headed for the main highway. He had a feeling that Alan would be going to Dover very soon if it was his plan to leave England. Time was of the essence and he took the precaution of checking the fuel tank. The needle was flicking into the red zone and he stopped at the first service station. As though in sympathy with the machine he too felt a sudden need to refuel his body but he dared not waste time eating; as soon as the tank was filled he quickly paid and continued his race eastward.

The miles clicked by and only once was he chased by a patrol car but it was unable to match his speed as he constantly increased the pace to exceed the hundred mark and rapidly went from one county to the next. He was soon racing down the A2 and approaching the outer suburbs of Dover where he hoped to find his freedom at last.

22

Alan had left the Commando in the car park and booked a room in the hotel. This was a mere three hundred yards from the ferry terminal which he hoped would make his task easier. The receptionist raised an eyebrow at his lack of luggage but as it was a quiet time of year he gave Alan the key to a double room on the first floor.

After checking the room which was adequate for his means with clean, crisp sheets and a soft mattress, he returned to the ground floor and wandered into the bar to join the sprinkling of guests, all of whom appeared to be holidaymakers.

'How can I help you,' the attractive barmaid asked the moment he perched himself on a high bar stool. She had had yet another fight with her partner and was sizing up the handsome man as a distinct possibility to ease her loneliness when the shift ended.

'A large black coffee and some buttered toast,' Alan replied and he in turn studied the woman as she turned away and deliberately bent over with straight legs to reach cups on a lower shelf.

'I can recommend the Manuka . . . honey,' she said as she stood upright.

'Nice and sweet, is it?' Alan said rising to the bait.

'It spreads easily and is very smooth and tasty on the tongue.' She gave Alan a wink as she placed a table mat on the bar top. As she put the sugar bowl and milk jug on it she had to lean forward, exposing her ample cleavage, and she looked at Alan with a clear invitation in her blue eyes.

He placed the preposterous, clunky room tag on the bar so that the room number was face up. 'Maybe I can have a different spread at suppertime?' he asked, leaning forward to leer over the bar counter at her legs.

The barmaid laughed coarsely. 'Legs eleven, eleven o'clock would give you bingo, sir,' she said as she poured his coffee. She turned away, tossing her peroxided hair coquettishly before leaving to prepare the toast in the small kitchen behind the bar. Alan waited until she had gone and then spun round on the stool to study the other guests.

It was obvious why the barmaid had chosen him for a little fun as there was only the typical motley collection of middle-aged tourists. Most were Europeans just beginning their holiday and the remainder were nationals leaving for the continent in the morning.

Alan ignored those who sounded European for it was unlikely they would be holding British passports. The rest he sorted by age until his gaze settled on a group of six football fans travelling to France for an international match. One was clearly the trip organiser and his corpulent 50-year-old figure was stretching a No. 6 football shirt. Three were in their late twenties and the remaining two were both about Alan's age. One had a moustache which was ideal if his passport photograph showed the same. This would give Alan the perfect reverse disguise as he could explain to any immigration official that he had decided to shave it off to please his French girlfriend.

Although it was only late afternoon the football fans had already started drinking as evidenced by the many empty bottles of beer that were cluttering their table.

The barmaid returned with two slices of hot toast on a plate and two large pats of butter. She placed a small pot of honey by his hand with a murmured promise that it would be 'very sweet on the tongue' before moving along the bar to serve another customer.

While he ate his toast Alan watched the group of fans in the large mirror behind the bar. It was clearly their intention to get drunk to celebrate the start of their break from work. As he savoured the delicious honey he began thinking of the right moment to make his move.

He had finished his third cup of coffee and the toast when the older man weaved his way towards the rest-room. Alan recognised this as his chance and he walked across to the table just as one of the younger fans stood up, staggered and had to be fortuitously held upright by Alan's firm grip on his elbow.

'Steady on, friend,' Alan said. 'You nearly came a cropper there.'

'Thanks mate,' the twenty-something slurred and he sat down again. 'Thought I wanted a pee too but now I don't,' he added, pronouncing each word carefully and as clearly as eight pints of bitter in the course of two hours would permit.

'Why don't you join us and have a beer,' one of the other men said enthusiastically. 'Who do you support?'

Alan had already made a point of identifying the embroidered emblems and the shirt colours. 'Same as yourself, Arsenal,' he said as he sat down next to the big man with the moustache. He accepted the proffered beer and took a long drink straight from the neck of the bottle.

The group cheered and then began chanting their own version of the club hymn. Alan joined in, his eyes noting the bags beside the chairs and under the table. He clinked his bottle against the big man's and started to sing even louder.

'Have you got a fag, mate?' Alan asked.

'The man bent down and rummaged in an open sports bag for a while before victoriously withdrawing a cigarette packet and holding it aloft. After Alan had lit up he deliberately coughed and bent forward as the fan pummelled his back enthusiastically. While leaning forward Alan fumbled in the unzipped side pocket of the sports bag and felt the distinctive shape of a passport. Swiftly extracting it he thrust it into his sock and pulled the trouser leg back down to conceal the odd shape.

Alan sat upright and arrested the thumping hand on his back with a broad smile. 'Thanks a lot, mate, something went down the wrong way.'

'Haven't learnt to smoke properly yet?'

'Something like that.' The whole group thought this remarkably funny and burst into raucous laughter.

'Look, I have to leave you guys now.' Alan stood up and put the half-empty bottle down which was instantly snatched up by one of the younger fans. 'I'm booked on the last ferry to Calais. Thanks a lot for the beer and good luck at the game.' His words were greeted with a further rendition of the club's battle hymn at maximum volume and Alan walked to the lift bank with a slight smile curling the corners of his cruel mouth.

Keeping out of sight of that particular group of fans until they had left for their ferry in the morning was now Alan's prime objective and in his room he rang room service to order his evening meal. He was prepared to remain there until it was safe to emerge and then take the first ferry.

He flicked through the passport and grunted with satisfaction: the age and height of the bearer approximated his own. The photograph could undoubtedly stand a perfunctory examination and if queried he could only hope that his excuse for the removal of the moustache would see him through immigration. He memorised the personal details before putting the passport in the side pocket of his leather jacket.

The meal of pork sausages, mash potatoes and onion gravy helped to relieve his extreme hunger that hadn't been assuaged by the toast earlier and he lay back on the bed and allowed himself to slowly sink into a light sleep.

The abrupt sound of the door buzzer woke him and he realised that he had slept longer than intended. He went to the door and looked through the peephole to see the distorted image of a young woman with carmine red lips and long blonde hair waiting outside.

As soon as the door opened she slipped in to avoid being seen by other members of the hotel staff. 'I'm not supposed to socialise with guests,' she whispered as she brushed past Alan and went into the room. She threw herself into the chair that had Alan's jacket hanging on the back and pulled off her shoes. 'My name's Cynthia and my feet are killing me. I've been on them for twelve hours straight.' Alan made a sympathetic face and opened the minibar. 'Drink?' he asked.

'Mine's brandy,' Cynthia said as she leant back to emphasise the fullness of her breasts beneath the white cotton blouse while she ran her fingers through her long hair.

Alan emptied a small bottle of cognac into a glass and handed it to her. He then pulled the ring-pull on a cola and took a long swallow.

'Are you on the wagon or something?' she asked, eyeing the can with suspicion as he sat on the edge of the bed.

'I like to keep a clear mind when I'm on the job,' he said with a sly smile and Cynthia smiled and made a show of crossing her long shapely legs. The 'hiss' of rubbing nylon stirred Alan's libido and he looked at the woman with lust clearly written on his face.

'I like a man who knows what he wants and goes for it,' Cynthia said as she stood up and walked to the bed to sit beside him. Alan took the unfinished drink from her hand and put it on the bedside table along with his can.

'And I like a woman who knows how to spread her honey on toast,' he growled as he put an arm around her waist and pressed his lips against hers. She responded by parting her full lips, admitting his darting tongue.

Their lovemaking was fast and furious and ended in an explosive and rather noisy conclusion that had the headboard rattling against the bedroom wall. They both fell asleep within seconds of each other with only one thin sheet covering their sweat-coated bodies.

Alan suddenly woke up at four o'clock with all his senses fully alert. He realised that the woman wasn't beside him and he turned his head slowly until he could see Cynthia bent over his jacket. Her nakedness was alternating between red and blue as it reflected the neon message hanging outside the window. Alan watched as she rifled through his wallet, extracting not all but just a couple of bank notes so as not to arouse suspicion. Cynthia then held up the purloined passport to catch the flicking light and he saw a slight frown appear on her face.

'Have you taken enough for your services?' Alan said softly and the woman jerked upright with shock.

'I haven't taken anything,' Cynthia said.

'Oh?'

'Just enough to cover my taxi fare home. I was also a little curious as to who you were.' In her embarrassment at being caught she stumbled over her words.

'And did you?' Alan said, his voice still menacingly soft.

'I discovered that you're a thief,' Cynthia blurted out.

'How did you arrive at that conclusion?'

'This!' Cythia held the passport up in a gesture of mock bravado. 'It was reported lost by an Arsenal fan just before I came off duty last night but it looks like you stole it from him.'

Alan casually flipped the sheet away from him and swung his legs round to sit on the edge of the bed, his eyes never moving from Cynthia who was nervously stuffing his wallet and the passport back into his jacket.

'I won't tell anybody,' she stuttered. 'You must have a very good reason for taking it and as you were a damned good lover my lips will remain sealed.'

'Uh-huh, of that you can be sure, Cynthia,' Alan said as he stood up and moved towards the woman. She backed away with alarm in her eyes until her buttocks pressed against the cold door leading to the en-suite bathroom. It opened slightly and she turned, dashed in and began closing the door but Alan was faster. His bare shoulder hit the wood panel and the door burst inward throwing Cynthia off balance. She staggered and toppled backwards, striking her head on the ceramic sink before landing on the tiled floor. Alan jumped astride her, pinning her upper arms with his knees and grasping her throat in a deathly grip. The woman's long legs thrashed but she failed to dislodge the weight of the tall man who had now begun to squeeze her neck mercilessly.

It didn't take long before she was dead but Alan remained gripping her throat while he listened carefully for any sounds coming from the corridor outside his room. Satisfied that nobody had heard the brief tumult he took his hands away and began manoeuvring Cynthia in order to lift her into the bath.

Recalling her active performance the previous night Alan was surprised at her weight but finally he had her tidily laid out in the bath and covered with spare bath towels.

He returned to the main room and made a point of hanging the DO NOT DISTURB tag on the door handle. He then had a quick shower to remove the previous night's dried sweat before lying down on the bed and attempting to recapture the sleep he had lost.

The sun had just set when John arrived at the docks in Dover. He began searching every back street close to the ferry passenger terminal for the Commando before giving up and beginning to check the hotel car parks. At the fourth hotel which was closest to the terminal he found what he was looking for. The shape of the fairing and the short, slightly drooping handlebars were an instant give-away. John quickly rode to the far side of the carpark where he left the Vincent hidden behind a Volswagen camper van.

The hotel reception had just received an influx of passengers from the recently docked ferry from Calais and John was able to make his way through to the bar without attracting any attention.

The bar adjoined the main dining room and both were busy when John took a seat. A buxom barmaid with long blonde hair and a big welcoming smile approached him.

'What can I get you, sir?' she asked and John asked politely for a pint of lager. 'You're lucky, sir, this part of the bar is about to close and

I'll be off duty in a few minutes,' she said as she pulled on the pump well aware what the arm action did for her upper torso.

'Long day?' John asked as he put the right money on the bar and took the proferred glass that was streaming with condensation. She nodded but he didn't notice because his attention had been caught by the sight of full-grown men crawling around on their hands and knees, studying the carpet. 'What on earth are those fellows up to. Are they drunk or on drugs?'

'Almost drunk but not on drugs. It appears one of them has lost his passport and is insisting that he had it when he left home,' the woman said as another barmaid walked behind the bar. 'I couldn't really care less and Maggie's here so I'm off.' She was clearly disappointed at John's lack of interest in her and she left to keep her appointment in room No. 76.

John watched the men slowly give up and drunkenly make their way to their rooms to sleep off the effects of the drink before they caught their early-morning crossing, minus one of their mates, and started all over again at the bar. He finished his own lager and slowly strolled to the reception desk while carefully keeping an eye open for Alan.

'Excuse me, I was expecting to meet a friend in the bar who may be a guest in the hotel,' John said when the tired-looking junior manager approached him. 'Could you tell me if you have a Mr Alan Williams staying here.'

'It is against hotel policy to give the names of our guests, sir,' the man replied with a tight unctuous smile.

'It's not his room number I want, just confirmation that he is a guest here,' John said with an equally ingratiating expression. The manager sighed, relented and turned to the registry where he ran his finger down the list of bookings for the day.

'No, I'm sorry, sir. We don't appear to have a Mr Williams staying here.'

'Thank you,' John murmured and hurried to where he had last seen Alan's bike and breathed a sigh of relief when it was still parked in the same bay. Knowing that Alan was undoubtedly staying under a false name John walked to his bike and sat on the saddle thinking about his next move. He had a feeling that Alan was planning on boarding a ferry the following day and therefore wouldn't be needing the Commando any more. Lying in wait for him in the car park would therefore be a waste of time.

John decided to return to the ferry terminal before the first sailing in the morning and wait to see which way Alan would go. It would then be a simple matter of waiting until the ideal opportunity arose in which to confront the man.

The red Polo pulled up to park outside the familiar café and Jimmy Partridge went in to see if he could recognise any of the regular couriers that Bellini employed in the docks. The usual donkey-jacketed man wasn't there but he vaguely knew a thin rat-faced man who was sitting in the corner nursing a milky mug of coffee. An empty plate with dried egg yolk and a smear of congealed bacon grease was indication that the man had stopped in for an evening meal and Jimmy ordered a cup of tea at the counter before strolling the length of the café and sitting opposite the man.

'Cigarette?' Jimmy asked, offering his pack of Senior Service to rat-face who looked up suddenly with dark suspicious eyes.

Jimmy shrugged when his offer wasn't taken up and shook one out for himself. 'Bellini sent me,' he added and then flicked the Zippo lighter and drew deeply on the cigarette before he puffed a cloud of smoke into the face of the morose man. 'I'm to pick up the next delivery tomorrrow and every one after that. Just spread the word to all the guys so that they know that "Shotgun" is now the man, okay?'

'What happened to Dandy, who done for 'im?' the man hissed with anger flickering in his eyes.

'Dandy?'

'He was the mule topped in one of the alleys near 'ere.'

Jimmy thought quickly for a story that would satisfy the suspicious docker. 'A rival gang tried to muscle in on our little arrangement but don't worry, they've been dealt with and can't trouble us again.'

The man stared back into Jimmy's cold eyes for a long time before he slowly nodded and put his mug down. He slid out from the bench seat and stood up. 'I'll be here at nine tomorrow morning. Have the money waiting.'

Jimmy nodded and then watched the man as he shuffled out of the café and disappeared into the street that had been darkened by vandals using catapults on the street lighting. He returned to sipping his tea and tried to work out how he could raise the fee of £500 that the couriers demanded for each delivery. After a few thoughtful minutes he returned the empty cup to the counter and asked if there were any good gambling clubs in the neighbourhood.

The café owner looked at Jimmy as though he were mad or an undercover copper. 'There's no gambling 'ere, guv,' he muttered as he dried a glass with a tea towel that had seen much cleaner days.

'Is there nowhere a chap can find a little action?' Jimmy asked sliding a tenner over the counter top. The round, puffy features revealed the owner's greed and the note disappeared as fast as it had appeared.

'You could try the basement flat at No. 10,' he whispered before turning away to place the streaked glass on the shelf. Jimmy nodded his thanks and slowly walked the length of the dark street until he saw No. 10, followed by an angled arrow roughly daubed in white paint that clearly showed the way down rusty cast-iron steps to the basement flat.

There were no signs of life and the window was dark. Jimmy knew this could be achieved by heavy blackout curtains to prevent any peeping tom or prowling policeman from seeing what was going on within.

He opened the rusty gate at the top with the minimum of squeaks and slowly went down, step by step, until he came to a rather solid-looking door. He could see no security cameras or even a peephole in the door and quickly took a pistol from his holster and screwed on a homemade silencer that was the size of a cucumber.

He tapped on the door with the butt end of the pistol. He lowered himself to brace his back against the steel stanchion that held up the porch roof and put his empty hand on the concrete floor and waited. There were faint footsteps that grew louder and then the rattling of locks and a chain before the door swung open an inch and an eye appeared.

Jimmy unleashed both feet against the door whilst balancing himself up on one stiff arm with his back pressed hard against the stanchion. The door crashed inward, snapping the chain and throwing the man who had answered it against the hallway wall. His head took the brunt of the collision and he slumped to the carpet unconscious. Jimmy leapt over his body and ran down the hall to kick the living-room door. The moment it flew open he dropped to his knees and heavy calibre bullets meant for his chest *phutted* over his head.

In one split second Jimmy counted three men, two armed with levelled pistols, the third with a short-handled axe. The silencer coughed twice and the men who had hesitated before shooting again fell back, one with a bullet through his forehead and the other with a punctured heart. The man with the axe screamed and rushed across the room at Jimmy but he too was shot dead.

Jimmy slowly stood up and surveyed the carnage wreaked in three seconds and then his eyes fell on the stacks of notes on the coffee table. The men appeared to have been in the process of counting the money before Jimmy gatecrashed the card cheats' illicit party. He quickly took the bundles and stuffed them into every available jacket pocket until only change was left scattered across the table.

As he walked towards the front door the semi-conscious man groaned and Jimmy nonchalantly kicked him in the head. He put the silencer and pistol away before quietly leaving the apartment. As he closed the door behind him he wiped it with a handkerchief to remove any prints he may have put there and climbed the steps to pavement level.

The street was still silent and nothing stirred apart from a stray mongrel that was chewing on a bone—he growled at the man as he passed by.

The Polo started quietly and he drove to an isolated spot on the esplanade to count the money which came to £18,000. He expelled a fervent 'yes!' beneath his breath before returning it to his pockets.

Angstrom met with Cramer and after a slightly embarrassing silence —both of them recalling their last telephone conversation—her words came out in a rush as she recounted how she had intercepted John in his attempt to climb the wall of Bellini's estate.

'Jennifer,' Cramer interrupted. 'Let's put the case to one side for a moment. We've worked together now for over eighteen years and you know how I feel about you.' He glanced towards the door and Angstrom walked across to shut it and then she returned to the chair facing his desk with an air of expectancy. 'I know I'm a little older than you—'

'Fifteen years, sir,' Angstrom interrupted and immediately regretted speaking as she clenched both fists in her lap with nails digging painfully into the palms of her hands.

'It's not much when measured against the strength of my feelings for you, Jennifer. I'm not saying I love you with the passion of a hormonal young teenager but the complete sense of contentment I feel when you're around is not something I can readily ignore.'

'Please, sir . . .'

'Wesley.'

'Wesley, please understand when I say that I have similar feelings but that's all they are. They're good vibrations. I believe we are what most people would call extremely close friends who have a fondness for each other and it can be no more than that. I would take a bullet for you Wesley because I respect, honour and admire you greatly.'

'And I would take one for you because I love you, Jennifer,' the superintendent confessed and he sighed heavily and opened the folder lying on the desk in front of him. 'Let's leave it at that and see what develops.'

'That's for the best, sir,' Angstrom answered in a low voice while still studying her nails.

Cramer grimaced and quickly changed the subject by pushing a manila folder across the desk. 'You'll find that all ports have been sealed and there's been no sign of Williams trying to leave the country. Are you sure this is what he'll attempt to do?'

'Yes, Wesley, I'm positive,' Angstrom answered in her brisk business-like manner. 'I also believe that John Tucker is hot on his heels and is going to the Dover ferry terminal to try and intercept him.'

'Why does Tucker want to stop Williams? Surely he'll be glad to see the back of the man?' Wesley said as he watched Angstrom read the report of passenger traffic at all the major departure points.

'To kill him, sir,' and I would like to suggest that I travel to Dover with Phillips and try to stop him doing this foolhardy thing.'

'Is Constable Phillips back from sick leave now?'

'I'm glad to say that he's fit and well and has insisted on reporting back for duty yesterday morning.'

Cramer nodded. 'He's a good man. Take him with you and I'll be joining you too.'

'You, sir?' Angstrom said with surprise. 'Is that really necessary?'

'Both men are armed and will kill anyone getting in their way and I will be ordering a full armed-response team to be on standby to cover every eventuality.'

Angstrom looked at the superior officer with affection welling within her but he didn't look up as he began reading another report he had taken from his in-tray.

'I'm sorry I cannot reciprocate your deepest feelings for me, Wesley,' she said softly. 'I hope it will not affect our relationship which I've truly valued over the years we have worked together.'

'No, Jennifer, it won't change a thing.' He looked up to smile briefly and then back at the paper in his hand. 'Good night, Jennifer.'

Angstrom walked from Cramer's office with what felt like a leaden weight in her chest and began walking faster in order to leave the station as soon as possible. Her normal habit of playing a Whitney Houston disc on the drive home was neglected and she arrived at her apartment in total silence.

23

THE PASSENGER TERMINAL at the dock was crowded with boisterous tourists who stood on the concourse in small groups. Some simply talked loudly to be heard above the general hubbub of noise while mothers yelled from sheer habit at ill-behaved children. Only a few were aware of the men who had appeared on the balcony above them and in the terminal foyer. The armed-response team wore dark sunglasses and carried Heckler & Koch MP5 sub-machine guns slung around their necks.

One traveller who did become aware of the team was a burly man in a dark suit who, as soon as he spotted the first man in the foyer, turned on his heel and strode out of the terminal. Jimmy was very familiar with police traps and he walked quickly back to the distant hotel and the red Polo in the car park.

As he passed the first parked car the doors opened on the next vehicle and he was confronted by three police officers. Two he recognised as Cramer and Angstrom but the third was unfamiliar. It was that officer who ordered him to halt and raise his hands where they could be seen.

'Jimmy Partridge!' he cried out. 'You're under arrest in connection to the murders of—'

He got no further for Jimmy had snatched the sawn-off weapon from under his long jacket and instinctively pulled the trigger. Phillips staggered back and looked down at his chest with surprise on his face before crumpling to fall upon the tarmac.

Cramer instinctively stepped in front of Angstrom and the next discharge threw him back against the inspector and rammed her into the shielding protection of the police car.

Jimmy looked around to see three armed-response officers racing towards him with weapon butts pushed into their shoulders. He turned and ran to the stolen car. Quickly fumbling in his pocket he found the key and the engine burst into life.

The officers were still seventy yards away when he accelerated towards the exit and smashed through the black-and-white wooden barrier. Fearful about hitting innocent pedestrians the officers held their fire and watched helplessly as their target began to drive away down the esplanade.

Inside the police car Angstrom, filled with white-hot rage, leapt out to snatch a Heckler & Koch from the first officer to arrive and swung the machine-gun on the roof of the car, professionally tracking the distant dark shape showing through the rear window of the Polo. Allowing for the car's forward motion she gently squeezed the trigger and the heavy weapon recoiled lightly into her shoulder as a semi-automatic burst of ten 4.6-mm bullets, capable of penetrating the body of any unarmoured car, streamed from the barrel.

The officers paused and watched in fascination as the Polo seemed to brake suddenly and then continued moving along the road with dimishing speed until it came to a standstill.

Angstrom handed the hot weapon back to the stunned officer and the armed-response team ran towards the car with weapons still at the ready. Angstrom wearily slid down the side of the police car and cradled Cramer's head in her lap.

'I'm sorry, Wesley,' she murmured as tears began to form and sting her eyes. 'I wish I could have told you how I really felt.' She ran a hand gently down his cheek. 'I thought that confessing my love for you, a senior police officer, would be totally inappropriate. I was wrong and now you'll never know the true depth of my affection.'

Suddenly there was a groan and Phillips stirred and rolled over onto his side. Angstrom looked up in surprise and saw the young constable push himself up to sit on the tarmac clutching at his chest.

'My God, these Kevlar vests are bloody painful,' he declared.

The inspector gave a small cry of relief at the constable's lucky escape and then the sound of running boots made her turn to see the remainder of the armed-response team rushing from the terminal towards her. She lay Cramer's head down carefully and quickly wiped her cheeks before the first officer arrived. It was Inspector Goodman and his face paled when he saw the downed officer.

'This is awful,' he croaked. 'Who shot him?'

'Jimmy Partridge. He must have been here for a pick-up and spotted your men in the terminal,' Phillips said while looking at his slain boss in disbelief.

Goodman had noticed the redness in Angstrom's eyes and he took her hand and helped her to stand up while one of his men attended to the stunned Phillips. She wavered a little before she was able to control her balance and then she looked towards the Polo. The officers had reached the stationary vehicle and were circling it with weapons at the ready. Goodman's radio gave a blast of static and a tinny voice delivered a terse report.

'Driver dead, three-inch grouping through back of head. Will require fingerprint identification. One sawn-off shotgun on lap recently fired and handgun in pocket. Over.'

'Seal area and keep all sightseers, especially those with cameras, well away. Over,' Goodman instructed and then switched off. 'We'll have to get the local boys involved in cleaning up this mess.' He stopped when Angstrom winced at his choice of words for she had been looking down at the dead officer.

'Sorry, Inspector,' he mumbled and walked away to give instructions to the men who were still arriving from the terminal. They all looked at the superintendent with shock and horror on their faces until their anger began to grow, each feeling a passionate desire to seek revenge for the murder.

'You're too late, the bastard's over there,' and Goodman pointed to the distant Polo. 'Detective Inspector Angstrom took him out with a single burst.'

The men looked at Angstrom with new respect and murmured their congratulations. Angstrom nodded and after instructing Phillips to get himself checked by the team's paramedic she walked towards the seawall to gaze out over the water and watch the soaring gulls that hung on the wind. They appeared to her like lost spirits seeking the way to another more peaceful world. She silently prayed that Wesley knew the way.

Within the terminal the travellers had been completely unaware of the drama that had unfolded outside. It was in this milling crowd that a scruffy docker called Pete was waiting and as he searched the crowd for Jimmy he kept a tight hold on the supermarket bag.

Pete heard the distant gunfire above the vocal hubbub and recognised the *burrrrpp* for what it was. He hurried out into the foyer and then cautiously stepped outside to see a group of armed officers running towards the hotel car park. Without thinking he impulsively began to run in the other direction until a commanding voice told him to halt. Pete knew he couldn't outrun a high-velocity bullet. He stopped and turned around with his arms outstretched to show that he was unarmed.

The big teddy bear in the shopping bag was quite heavy and it wasn't long before his right arm began to ache as he watched the police officer approaching with his weapon raised and ready to shoot. Pete's upper arm began to ache and it began to droop.

'Keep your arms up. Keep your arms up or I will fire,' the officer commanded but Pete's puny strength was battling against three kilos of pure heroin and his arm was unwillingly brought down a little more.

'Up. Keep it up!' The officer's voice had a slight falsetto edge that revealed his panic at the suspect's failure to obey the command.

'It's too heavy. I will have to drop it,' Pete cried out and it slid from his fingers and a fortune fell with a loud thump. The officer ran forward and forced Pete to lie face down while he applied the handcuffs.

Alan had been standing in the hotel lobby when he first heard and then saw the shooting taking place outside. The massive plate glass window gave the impression that he was watching a giant movie screen as he followed the Polo's vain attempt to escape and the single machine-gun burst from the police car that ended Jimmy's chances.

'Nice shooting, Inspector,' he murmured appreciatively as he recognised the woman leaning on the roof of the police car. His hand impulsively went to the bulge beneath his leather jacket. He continued to watch as Angstrom slowly slid down with her back against the car and he smiled when he recognised the motionless man she was holding.

My poor Superintendent, he thought. Did the nasty man shoot you dead? Alan laughed out loud to the amazement of the horrified spectators standing near to him and ignoring their reaction he went to reception to complete his checkout.

Returning to the door he saw an officer wearing a black kevlar vest point to the hotel and he knew that the normal routine of taking witness statements would begin there. Alan turned and walked through the lobby and down the corridor past all the ground-floor suites until he came to the fire door at the rear.

The alarm sounded as soon as the bar locking the door was pushed down and the wide door swung open. Alan hurried through and trotted round the various outbuildings and delivery trucks until he reached the car park. A quick glance revealed that none of the police had started to sweep the car park for witnesses yet and he was soon astride the Commando and turning the key in the ignition.

The roar of the engine firing up reverberated across the car park and two officers standing by the Superintendent raised their heads. They then spotted the rider racing for the exit. After a couple of seconds a cry from Inspector Angstrom alerted them to the danger.

The officers began unslinging their weapons but before they could bring their guns up to aim Alan had already passed through the shattered exit and pulled onto the esplanade.

Alan went in the opposite direction to the stalled Polo where shoulder radios had already alerted the team members of Alan's escape.

A second motorcycle starting up and racing through the car park made the officers swivel round and take their time in lining up their weapons on the fast moving Vincent.

'Don't shoot!' Angstrom screamed out as she leapt behind the wheel and started the police car. 'It's Tucker . . . track me.'

The officers immediately understood what she had meant and they called Central Control and requested a fix on Inspector Angstrom's patrol car. The minitransponder behind the dashboard had started sending out a signal as soon as Angstrom started the engine and Central Control could now pinpoint her position and instruct support vehicles to follow her.

Goodman had run from the hotel lobby when he heard the roar of the motorcycles and after a quick debrief by one of his men he ordered the team to join him in the electronically-equipped police van where they could receive directions.

Alan glanced over his shoulder as he sped along the crowded seafront and spotted the black motorcycle 200 yards behind and keeping pace with him. He cursed beneath his breath as he recognised John and in his lack of concentration he almost wiped out a family crossing the road. Gaining the safety of the pavement the parents accompanying their two small children were still angry enough to shout obscenities at John as he too thundered past.

Angstrom knew from experience that people on holiday were often careless when it came to road safety and she forced herself to keep the speed down until she was well clear of the town and on the open road travelling east. She then put her foot down and although she was soon topping 70 mph she was unable to catch up with the two speeding motorcyclists. They were now ton-ups again and in their own environment. She started crying as she relived the last few moments she had with Wesley. His unnecessary death stoked the flames of her anger to white hot. The two men she was chasing had been the catalyst for every criminal incident that had occurred over the last few days and she was determined to end it and give the man she had secretly loved the chance to rest in peace.

The speedometer needle was jumping about on the 85 mph mark when Alan leant into a long gentle curve in the road and was able to look back. He swore when he noticed John only a hundred yards behind him and slowly gaining. Alan flattened himself and tucked his elbows in tighter to his body to reduce drag to a minimum and was satisfied when the needle crept up to pass the 95 mph mark.

Traffic was exceptionally light and slow-moving drivers who were eager to overtake made it more dangerous when they pulled out at half the speed of the ton-ups coming up behind them. Twice Alan was forced to pass between two cars jostling for position with only inches to spare. Horrified drivers didn't even have the time to react and blow their horns before both bikes were dwindling on the horizon.

Angstrom could achieve 105 mph in the supercharged patrol car but was wary of pushing the car to the limit on a narrow two-lane road. Even with blue lights flashing and the siren shrieking its warning she was frequently forced to slow down and wait until the cars pulled over.

The Commando was topping 107 mph on the straight and as John's Vincent grew ever nearer Alan decided that he had to kill his pursuer soon. Knowing that even attempting to use the gun at high speed was impossible he decided to take a slower road where he could suddenly stop, turn and be able to hit his target.

A small road sign showed that the next turning on the right would take him down to the coast and at the last minute he braked violently raising a pungent blue cloud of burning rubber from the rear tyre. He swiftly turned down the byroad and was soon racing on the ten-foot-wide track at 75 mph. A quick glance showed that John had overshot the same road and was turning back. I'll get the bastard now, Alan thought as he continued until he was forced to brake as the road turned sharp left to follow the shoreline.

Entering the byroad John twisted his throttle to send the Vincent hurtling along the surface that was more used by farm traffic than high-speed motorcycles. He had to concentrate and study the road ahead in order to avoid cracks and potholes. Alan had disappeared from sight but he spotted the brief twinkling of a red light in the distance which indicated that Alan had braked for some unknown reason.

Angstrom only became aware that the ton-ups had left the main road when she saw them a half-mile on her right and racing in the same direction as herself.

A sign flashed past and it subconsciously registered as the service road to the coastguard station. With screaming tyres she braked in time to wrench the wheel and slide across the tarmac in front of oncoming traffic and onto the dirt track that headed seaward.

The mournful horn of a semi-trailer faded behind her as she accelerated along the pitted dirt road, the car jolting and bumping on the water-damaged surface.

A quarter of a mile distant she watched as the leading bike came to an abrupt standstill and someone, probably Alan, left his bike to stand in the road with arms extended towards the oncoming motorcyclist.

My God, he's going to shoot John, Angstrom thought and she put her foot down harder, causing the super-charger to burst into life. Her shoulders were thrust back into the seat as the car leapt forward and despite the poor condition of the track it reached 90 mph.

Angstrom was attempting to reach the gunman before John Tucker and was only 400 yards distant when she realised she would lose the race for his life.

John had spotted the stationary bike at the last minute and was braking hard when suddenly there was the sound of a siren and car horn coming from the left. He threw the bike over and rolled off in the dust just as Alan fired his automatic. Although his aim had been distracted by the sounds of the approaching police car he believed he had hit his target and gave a loud laugh.

Alan turned towards the approaching car and he slowly brought the weapon up in the textbook two-handed grip he had learnt at police college. Inspector Angstrom's face was clearly recognisable as his finger slowly began to take up the slack on the trigger.

Alan heard the report of a gun in the same moment as his elbow disintegrated. He fell onto one knee with white-hot agony lancing up his arm. He turned to see John standing about fifty yards away beside his bike and aiming a weapon at his head. Alan shook his head in disbelief and stood up. His left arm hung uselessly at his side with blood dripping from his fingers to stain the crude road surface dark red.

'Damn you, John,' he shouted. Gritting his teeth in an effort to suppress the pain he threw a leg over the saddle of the Commando, toed it into gear and accelerated away with only one hand gripping the handlebars to steer and use the clutch.

He had only travelled a short distance when Angstrom pulled up and got out of the car to run to John. 'Are you okay?' she asked. 'Did he hit you?' John shook his head and pulled the Vincent upright. 'You can't go after him, John. Leave it, he won't get far before we have him.'

'I have to, Inspector,' John said as he started the bike. 'I have to finish it.' With that final explanation he shoved the pistol inside his jacket with one hand and and revved up with the other, cutting off her protestation before releasing the clutch. The Vincent raced after the Commando which was now speeding uncontrollably towards the end of the road.

Her heart racing Angstrom ran back to the car and turned to follow them as she tried to think of a plan to stop John from killing Alan or vice versa.

Suddenly the road terminated and became an expansive meadow and Angstrom was forced to drive the car onto the grassy, slightly rutted surface. She continued to chase the two riders who were now silhouetted against the sky as they raced towards the cliffs. The soft surface had slowed them both and John was finding it difficult to catch up with Alan who was also plainly struggling hard to control his bike with only one sound arm.

A deep ditch that a farmer had been digging to lay a water pipe to a horse trough on the far side of the field proved to be Alan's downfall. The front wheel went into the ditch and twisted sideways with such force that he was unable to hold the handlebars straight and he was thrown from the saddle to crash violently onto his shattered arm. His scream rolled away across the field and was lost amongst the cries of the seagulls soaring above his head.

Alan staggered to his feet and began running just as John also discovered the ditch too late. The large front wheel of the Vincent descended and then ploughed deep into the opposite clay bank bringing the bike to an immediate halt. John somersaulted over the front wheel and the air was driven from his lungs as he landed on his back. He rose, breathing heavily, and began to trot after Alan who was now nearing the cliff edge.

The police car hit the trench at speed, testing the suspension and Angstrom's head on the roof lining. It continued on for another twenty feet before suddenly stopping with a shattered front suspension.

She spotted something lying on the ground beside the abandoned Vincent. It was an automatic pistol and she leapt out and retrieved the weapon before continuing on foot.

As she drew nearer Angstrom saw that both had stopped running and were facing each other, standing side on and only thirty feet apart, like two duellists from a bygone age.

She stopped running and bent over to catch her breath before gasping, 'Alan Williams, I arrest you for the murders of Doris Trencher and Louise—'

'Stop!' Alan screamed in pain and anger as he pulled the automatic from under his jacket and pointed it at John. 'I'll kill him if you come one step closer.'

'Then I would be forced to shoot you, Alan,' Angstrom said as she turned her body slightly to reveal the Tokarev she was holding against her hip.

'You leave me no choice then,' Alan snarled as he spun to face Angstrom and aimed the pistol at her head.

'NO!' John screamed and began running towards his childhood friend as the inspector began to raise her weapon. She was too slow to prevent Alan from shooting her but fortunately, in the last split second, Alan saw John's movement in his peripheral vision and twisted to fire at the new threat instead. Alan's gun went off at the same time as Angstrom's Tokarev and Alan pirouetted on one foot as the heavy 9-mm bullet struck him in the chest and spun him round before he fell back onto the rough ground.

Still clutching the large handgun Angstrom stared at the man she had downed with shock registering on her face until a faint groan made her look towards John. He had fallen to his knees and was clutching at his bloodied side with spread fingers.

The inspector dropped the gun and ran to the wounded man. She forced him to lie back on the grass while she inspected the damage. Tearing his shirt open she found that it was a clean in-and-out wound and that the bullet appeared to have missed all vital organs. She quickly tore strips from his shirt and made pads for him to press against the bleeding wounds.

'I'll call for help,' she said and ran back to the police car to use the radio. As she sat in the car clutching the hand mike with bloody fingers she was horrified to see Alan stir and then slowly rise to his knees. With a sudden burst of static Central Control came on line. As she continued to watch Alan struggle to rise to his feet Angstrom requested an air ambulance for a shooting incident.

With a crippled arm and blood-soaked jacket Alan stared across the distance at Angstrom. He raised a hand in a mocking gesture of farewell before he turned and staggered away across the meadow. John attempted to stand up and follow him but the pain was far too much and more blood spurted from under the pads. He sank back and watched the man who used to be his best friend slowly walk away in the direction of the cliff edge.

The sound of a distant siren began to compete with the shrieking gulls and as it grew louder Angstrom looked in her rear-view mirror and saw a patrol car racing across the rough field towards her. She guessed that it was Inspector Goodman and that he had used her transponder to pinpoint her position.

The young officer left the car the moment it slithered to a halt and leaping over the ditch he ran to her open door.

'Are you okay?' he called and she nodded and pointed through the windscreen to where John was lying.

'He's been shot in the side but it's not too serious,' she said. 'An air ambulance is on the way.'

'Did you shoot Tucker?'

'Of course not, Goodman, he did,' and Angstrom pointed to the figure who was holding his chest and standing on the edge of the chalk cliff. 'He did and I shot him. I thought it was a fatal hit but somehow he has miraculously managed to walk that far.'

'I'll bring him back while you look after Tucker,' Goodman said and left to organise the three men who had also spilled out of the patrol car. The heavily armed men spread out and advanced slowly on the hunted man.

'Put your hands where I can see them,' Goodman shouted as they drew near and he could now clearly see that the man was swaying on his feet. The massive internal bleeding and excruciating pain was blurring Alan's vision and making his movements sluggish. He turned slowly to face the four men who had machine-guns raised, aimed and ready to fire.

Goodman spotted the automatic in the man's hand when he turned and immediately screamed, 'Drop the gun, drop the gun!'

Alan looked beyond the inspector to where John was being tended by Angstrom and saw his old friend's face turn towards him. A wave of agony ran through his body yet he was still able to grin goodbye as he struggled vainly to raise the hand holding the pistol.

The simultaneous two-second burst of concentrated fire from four Heckler & Koch machine-guns threw Alan back and his lifeless body began the long plunge through the air to the rocks below.

His disappearance was followed by a long silence.

Jennifer sighed and looked down at John. 'Thank you for saving my life, John,' she said softly.

'Thank you for giving me my life back.' John turned his head to stare at the spot where Alan had last been standing.

'You're very welcome, Mr Tucker.'

POSTSCRIPT

After a short spell in hospital where he was visited frequently by his parents, his son, and Anne (who was to become his wife), John was formally arrested and brought to trial.

The charge of neglecting to report what he thought was the accidental death of Doris Trencher, but was in fact Alan Williams's first act of murder, and the charge of the manslaughter of Louise Walton were laid against him.

Forensic evidence, Alan's uniquely recorded confession and a certain Detective Inspector's report ensured that John's custodial sentence was reduced to the minimum that the law allowed.